ABOUT TH

Steven Smith lives in Suffolk v
This is his third novel.

www.stevensmithauthor.com

BY STEVEN SMITH:

THE TREE OF LIFE
The Map of the Known World
The Ordeal of Fire
The Last Days

This Sacred Isle

www.stevensmithauthor.com

STEVEN SMITH

THE LAST DAYS

monster field press

First published by Lulu.com in 2012
This edition published by monster field press in 2016

Copyright © Steven Smith, 2016
All rights reserved

ISBN-13: 978-1537035963
ISBN-10: 1537035967

A CIP catalogue record for this book is available from the British Library.

Set in Garamond

For Abby and Lucy

- SYNPOSIS -

Prester John rules the Known World with an iron grip; his fanatical *Redeemers* stalk the land, crushing any resistance. Adults are branded with the Null, which removes their free will and brings them under the Redeemers' control.

Elowen Aubyn, a fourteen year old girl, lives in the Orphanage of the little town of Trecadok. Bullied and lonely, she yearns for freedom and excitement. Her life is changed by an encounter with a stranger named **Tom Hickathrift**. Hickathrift declares he is an *Adept*, a shaman of mysterious powers, and an agent of the *Illuminati*, a forbidden sect sworn to overthrow Prester John. He tells Elowen that her mother was an Adept also, and furthermore asks her to travel with him to the Illuminati's hidden Sanctuary in the northern land of Prevennis. Frightened and confused, Elowen refuses to run away but is left with no option when **Vortigern**, seeking Hickathrift's aid, arrives in Trecadok. Vortigern possesses a map, which reveals long-lost secrets that could threaten the rule of Prester John. However, he is closely pursued by Redeemers. They attack the town and murder both Vortigern and Hickathrift. Before he dies, Hickathrift entrusts Elowen with the map and begs her to seek the Sanctuary of the Illuminati.

1

Reluctantly accompanied by **Diggory Bulhorn**, the head-boy of the Orphanage, Elowen embarks on a dangerous journey, hunted relentlessly by the Redeemers. Along the way she is befriended by **Bucca Gwidden**, one of the ancient *Eldar* folk and a wolf named **Ulfur**; Bucca teaches Elowen about the *Earthsoul*, the energy that sustains all life and forms the source of an Adept's power, and she begins to learn how to control its power.

Needing to cross the sea to reach Prevennis, Elowen and her companions find passage with the smuggler **Black Francis**, himself a fugitive from the slave-trading *Sea Beggars*. Before they set sail in his ship, the *Husker Du*, they are attacked by a Redeemer; although they escape, the Redeemer badly wounds Elowen with a poisoned blade.

Meanwhile, in Prevennis, **Prince Asbjorn**, known to all as Bo, spends most of his time exploring the half-drowned lower chambers of the Hammersund Palace. The King's second son, he is all but ignored by his mother, **Queen Isabella**, and the rest of the court. Being albino, he is considered weak and inferior to his older brother and heir to the throne, **Crown Prince Haakon**. Their father, **King Olaf**, has long defied Prester John by refusing to allow his people to be branded with the Null, and by protecting the *Barbegs*, who are Eldar inhabitants of Prevennis.

But there is treachery afoot. Haakon desires the throne, so with the aid of his doting mother and **Lord Lucien**, Prester John's most deadly servant, betrays and murders King Olaf. Bo refuses to pay homage to his brother so is sentenced to death. Yet, with the aid of **Bjorgolf**, Chief of the Barbegs, Asbjorn escapes from the palace and soon encounters

Elowen and her companions. They flee through the Hlith-vid forest, and at the invitation of Bjorgolf, seek refuge at the Gladsheim, where Elowen heals from her injury.

However, this respite is short-lived. Determined to find the map Elowen carries, Lord Lucien leads his army against the Gladsheim. Bjorgolf tries to persuade the tribe to stay and defend their home but he is opposed by **Draug**, who wants to depose Bjorgolf and become chief himself. Bjorgolf persuades the tribe to follow him and a bitter and humiliated Draug chooses exile, vowing revenge.

As battle approaches, Black Francis leaves the Gladsheim, much to Elowen's disappointment. Although hopelessly outnumbered, the Barbegs have one slim chance of deliverance: on the border of the Gladsheim lies the Myrkvid, a forest trapped in a curse of a permanent winter. Elowen breaks the curse by summoning **Ekseri**, the guardian of the Mrykvid. Gathering the forest creatures about him, Ekseri marches to fight alongside the Barbegs.

Bjorgolf appoints Asbjorn to lead the defence of the Gladsheim. With only a few hundred Barbeg warriors they hold off the enemy long enough for Ekseri and his host of wild animals to join the fray. Yet they cannot turn the tide of battle and are driven back with heavy losses.

However, with defeat seemingly inevitable, Black Francis and his crew unexpectedly return and bombard the enemy with the guns of the *Husker Du*. This surprise attack gives Elowen and her companions the chance to regroup and attack anew; the enemy's strength wanes and the battle is won.

Lord Lucien comes face to face with Elowen and upon

3

learning she is the daughter of an Adept, mysteriously spares her life before fleeing the battlefield.

During the battle, Asbjorn faces Haakon in combat and slays his brother. Although fearing he lacks the ability to be a true leader, Asbjorn realises he cannot ignore the suffering of his people and vows to claim the throne and rid Prevennis of the followers of Prester John.

With the battle over and Lord Lucien gone, Elowen is free to complete her journey. Accompanied by Diggory, she sets off for the Sanctuary. En route they are attacked by Draug, who blames Elowen for his exile; Diggory fights him off, though he reluctantly spares the Barbeg's life. Finally they reach the Sanctuary, and safely pass the map into the care of the Illuminati. There, Elowen further develops her skills as an Adept, hoping to emulate her mother.

However, Elowen's hopes for peace and security are swiftly shattered. Grunewald, one of the two Masters of the Illuminati, tells of the *Four Mysteries*, which form the path to finding the Tree of Life. He has planned a quest to find the Mysteries and insists Elowen be part of it. However, she is tricked into helping **Rubens**, the other Master of the Illuminati, to seize power in the Sanctuary. He plans to use the map to find the Tree of Life, not to defeat Prester John but to gain immortality, a gift the fruit of the tree is believed to offer. His plans are soon thwarted though, as Lord Lucien, helped by the treacherous Draug, discovers the Sanctuary and attacks it. Redeemers destroy the Sanctuary but Elowen and Diggory evade capture, thanks to their friend **Lárwita**, who flies them to safety in a hot air balloon of his own making.

Although Elowen and her friends escape the Sanctuary, slave-trading bandits swiftly seize them. Held captive, they seemed doomed until the terrifying Baba Yaga sets them free. Before they can escape though, Diggory and Lárwita are taken prisoner by soldiers of the *Society for the Propagation of Pious Labour*, who had been summoned by the bandits.

Elowen flees, going with Baba Yaga to her home deep in the forest. There, Baba Yaga teaches her how to control and use the Earthsoul's power. Elowen sees a vision of Diggory and Lárwita in captivity and, despite Baba Yaga's protests, sets out to save them.

The search for her friends brings Elowen to the city of Rynokgorod. In the city, she encounters **Arigh Nasan**, an *Orok* who tries to persuade her to accompany him south to Omphalos, a gathering of the Eldar and the few remaining Illuminati. Elowen refuses, and continues to look for her friends. She eventually finds them held as slaves, but in trying to free them she is captured herself by the Watchmen, the spies of **Bishop Serapion**, the ruler of Rynokgorod and an ally of Prester John.

Bishop Serapion tortures Elowen and sentences her and her friends to death, but Arigh Nasan and his companions, who include **Krukis**, and another Orok, **Batu**, rescue them.

After escaping Rynokgorod, Elowen persuades her companions they must travel east across the steppes to the city of Erdene to find the temple of Bai Ulgan, the resting place of the first Mystery, the Mystery of Earth.

Meanwhile, Bo and Black Francis lead resistance against the rule of the Mother Church in Prevennis. After a successful ambush, Bo and his companions seize a secret parchment. They take it to **Sesheta**, an agent of the Illuminati, who translates it and tells them it is a Patriarchal Edict, which gives details of Prester John's plan to extend the Null to infants. However, before Bo can act on this knowledge, he is betrayed, and, along with Black Francis and the crew of the Husker Du, captured by the Sea Beggars.

The Sea Beggars take them to the Beauteous Isle. Bo and one of his companions, the fierce **Valbrand**, escape the Sea Beggars and flee into the heart of the island. There they meet the *Kojin*, the once rulers of the island, now subjugated by the Sea Beggars. **Princess Moriko**, the daughter of **Okaasan**, the Kojin Queen, is a captive of the Sea Beggars and Bo agrees to attempt to rescue her. Accompanied by **Prince Jeimuzu**, Moriko's brother, Bo journeys to the fortress of the **King of the Sea Beggars**. Finding passage through the terrifying Catacombs, the lost realm of the Dawn Men, the indigenous people of the island, they break into the fortress. They free Moriko but while attempting to escape, Bo is recaptured by the Sea Beggars.

The next day, Bo is taken to the amphitheatre, along with Black Francis and the crew of the *Husker Du*, to be executed. However, the Kojin, emboldened by the rescue of the Princess, attack and defeat the Sea Beggars. During the battle, the King of the Sea Beggars is slain, and the Kojin once again claim the island as their own. After the battle, Bo, Valbrand and Black Francis set sail for Omphalos, hoping to deliver news of the Patriarchal Edict. Prince Jeimuzu and a detachment of Kojin warriors travel with them. Princess Moriko asks to accompany them, but Okaasan refuses her request.

6

After an arduous journey, Elowen and her companions finally reach Erdene. Before they can go to the temple of Bai Ulgan though, they are forced to seek the permission of **Sukhbataar Khan**, the ruler of the city. This he grants, but he has betrayed them. For as Elowen and her friends come to Bai Ulgan, Lord Lucien is already there. Krukis also proves treacherous, and swears loyalty to Lord Lucien.

With her friends' lives threatened, Elowen agrees to Lord Lucien's demand to seek the Mystery of Earth on his behalf, and so enters the deadly labyrinth. However, with bravery and cunning, she passes the test and claims the Mystery. Lord Lucien seizes the Mystery and then asks Elowen to join him. When she refuses, Lord Lucien tells Elowen about her mother, stating she was actually a servant of Prester John and a feared enemy of the Oroks, named **Burilgi Maa**. He also tells her he found and murdered Baba Yaga. Shaken by these tidings, Elowen chooses to leap into the raging underground river rather than side with Lord Lucien. He believes she is dead, and thus leaves to return to the Ulsacro Palace, giving orders for Elowen's friends to be executed.

Elowen survives her fall and, with the aid of **Itugen**, the Earth Elemental, rescues her friends from the Redeemers. Yet, they do not escape tragedy, as the bitter Krukis murders Lárwita. Freed from the enemy, Arigh Nasan challenges the Khan to the ancient custom of the *Halz Tulaan*, a fight to the death. The cowardly Khan nominates his most deadly warrior, **Chinua**, to fight for him. Arigh Nasan wins the fierce struggle, but he spares Chinua's life, as he fought with chivalry and courage.

7

Deposed, the defeated Khan tries to stab Arigh Nasan, but, alerted by Elowen, Chinua kills him before he can do so. Injured in her defence of Arigh Nasan, Elowen recuperates in the Khan's palace. Finally though, she realises she must continue the quest to find the remaining Mysteries and, eventually, the Tree of Life. In a vision, Itugen shows Elowen the Ogonberg, the resting place of the Mystery of Fire. Arigh Nasan agrees to send Batu and Chinua to accompany her and Diggory. Sadly leaving the grave of the murdered Lárwita, and aware of the deadly foes stacked against her, Elowen heads west to continue her quest.

PART ONE

- CHAPTER ONE -

The Shadows Between the Trees

Snowflakes danced in mesmerising patterns. The skeletal trees shivered, and the mournful cry of a crow carried the misery of winter. Elowen swore as the snow drove horizontally into her face. Her cheeks and nose ached with the bitter cold. Keeping her head lowered, she tried to step into the footprints of those walking in front of her. Snow collected on the treads of her boots, weighing down her feet. She glanced up at the sky, feeling tiny beneath the slate-coloured veil of unbroken cloud. Winter stripped colour from the forest, leaving a landscape of white and greyish brown, enlivened only by the odd splash of green from a holly or yew, defiant against the onslaught of snow and ice. An eerie sense of stillness permeated, of life hiding, waiting beneath the frozen carpet for the distant promise of spring.

The Orok warrior Batu led their company. With a tight grip on the lead rope of Takhi, his sturdy mare, he strode ahead, his keen eyes searching, probing, ever alert for danger. Diggory shadowed Batu, attempting to keep up with him as if for protection and reassurance. Elowen went next and behind her their other Orok companion, Chinua. His lumbering footsteps thudded in the snow and he urged Ivuli, his large but reluctant horse, forward with whispered words. Chinua had little understanding of the Common Tongue, so his only method of communication with Elowen and Diggory consisted of a series of broken sentences and impatient gestures and grunts. Despite this, and her earlier fear of the Orok, Elowen had grown fond of Chinua during their long journey across the steppes and took comfort from his formidable presence.

It had taken them seven days to ride from the Orok city of Erdene to the eastern edge of the Altheart Forest, the boundary of the ancient land of Varna. Before they had left Erdene, Elowen and Batu had consulted scholars and mapmakers to pinpoint the location of the Ogonberg, the resting place of the second Mystery, the Mystery of Fire. But despite their efforts, and the clues provided by Elowen's vision, they could still only guess at the Ogonberg's position, a guess based more on traveller's tales and legends than any tangible knowledge.

Enveloped by the trees, Elowen felt the darkness, the *age* of the forest press upon her. Although foreboding and grim in the pale winter light, Elowen did not find it as terrifying a place as she had expected. The Oroks told tales of a land in permanent darkness, haunted by ghouls and demons, but Elowen had witnessed nothing so terrifying. She felt the Earthsoul, and her connection with the land sparked memories within her, flashbacks to traumatic events: the face of Lárwita as she cradled him in her arms and watched him die; her guilt as she left Baba Yaga alone; the pain as she plunged her arms into the bubbling cauldron of Bishop Ser-apion. The memories jabbed at her like physical blows.

As if to sweep away troubling thoughts, Elowen wiped her face. Tired and miserable, she walked mechanically. Blisters prickled her heels and her knees ached. Despite such discomforts, Elowen found a small degree of solace in the simple, purposeful process of moving forward. It con-trasted with the swirling confusion in her mind. She was a Messenger, just as the Saviour had been, born miraculously of an Adept mother. But her mother had betrayed her kind and served the tyrant Prester John. The Oroks had named her *Burilgi Maa* and cursed her memory. Elowen knew she too possessed tremendous power through her control of the Earthsoul. In the Sanctuary, she had learnt many of the skills of an Adept, skills honed during her stay with Baba Yaga. However, she hesitated to call herself an Adept, for although sometimes the power excited her, other times it repelled her utterly. As her mastery of the Earthsoul grew, it awoke within her other feelings, other desires she strived, consciously at least, to deny. Elowen found her dreams twisted her into the form of *Burilgi Maa*. Just as her mother had once done, she rode at the head of armies, crushed en-emies, all with a love of violence that boomed in her heart. She felt no fear, no wavering intent. Where did such dreams come from? And why, if they stood for everything she did not want to become, were they so seductive?

'It's getting colder,' said Diggory, looking back at Elowen and snapping her out of her reverie.

She increased her pace to walk alongside him. She said, 'The days are short, and spring is still far away.'

'Aye, this is colder than Prevennis,' he said, brushing snow off his shoulders. 'It's the sort of weather the Barbegs might enjoy.'

'Maybe, if they have survived,' said Elowen. 'With the Sanctuary lost, the Barbegs have few allies now. The Gladsheim is vulnerable.'

'Perhaps Asbjorn and Black Francis can help beat back the enemy in Prevennis—I wouldn't underestimate them.'

'No, but it won't be easy,' said Elowen. Black Francis and Bo were never far from her thoughts. They had parted many months earlier, when she and Diggory had left for the Sanctuary. Elowen wondered how they were, or even if they were still alive. She sometimes imagined herself having conversations with them, somewhere safe, with all traces of danger vanished. Elowen took comfort from these fantasies, and they sheltered her from the misery of her situation, but the real world always crept back in. She doubted she would ever see Black Francis or Bo again.

'I wish we were going somewhere warm,' said Diggory.

'We have to find the second Mystery before we can think about *that*,' said Elowen dabbing the cracked, sore skin around her mouth and nose.

Diggory grimaced. 'How could I forget? By God, I hope it's easier to find than the Mystery of Earth, and less dangerous.'

'I hope so too,' said Elowen. The mention of the first Mystery picked at the thin scabs of horrible memories: the labyrinth's suffocating, devouring darkness, the unbearable presence of Lord Lucien. At least Lord Lucien believed her to be dead, and so he hunted her no more.

14

Batu stopped, and signalled Elowen and the others to do likewise. The Orok looked around, turning his head slowly. As Batu pulled an arrow from his quiver, a wild boar burst from the undergrowth. A bulky male with vicious-looking tusks, it charged with head lowered at Elowen. Before she could react, Diggory leapt in front of her, putting himself directly in the boar's path. The boar slashed upright with its tusks, hacking at Diggory's legs, before disappearing back into the undergrowth.

With a wince and a groan, Diggory sat in the thick snow, holding his legs. Batu pushed Elowen out of the way and knelt to inspect the boy's wounds. He said, 'You are fortunate, my friend. Boars are ferocious when disturbed, but its tusks grazed your skin, causing a flesh wound only. However, let me apply some clean dressings to stop the wound from turning bad in this cold.'

While Chinua kept watch, Batu pulled out bandages from one of the saddlebags on his horse, and used them to dress the injured part of Diggory's leg.

'It might be a flesh wound but it damn well hurts,' said Diggory, his face screwed up.

'Your injury does you honour, as few have the courage to hurl themselves at a charging boar,' said Batu as he finished tying the bandages. He went to settle his horse's nerves.

'Why did you do it, Diggory?' said Elowen, still shaking. 'The creature was coming at me, not you.'

Diggory averted his eyes and mumbled. Only when Elowen pressed him to repeat it did he say, 'It's my duty to protect you. I promised I would. Your life is more important than mine.'

15

Elowen shook her head. 'Don't say that, it isn't true.'

'It is. I want to prove myself. I'm not an Adept or a warrior, but I'll do what I can. Besides, it was my fault Lárwita died. I want to protect you—I need to make amends.'

Tears welled up in Elowen's eyes. The loss of Lárwita remained raw. She still carried his book, into which he had poured his ideas and plans. Keeping the book somehow kept a part of him alive. She swallowed hard before she replied, 'His death wasn't your fault, Diggory. Not at all. Krukis was a murderer and Lárwita died standing up to him.'

Diggory lowered his head. 'Do you ever think about your parents?'

Knocked back by his question, Elowen said, 'I don't…know. I know nothing of my father. And the more I hear about my mother, the less I like—'

'Cornelius Cronack never told me what happened to my parents. Perhaps they died. Perhaps they didn't want me. The reason doesn't matter; I just wish I'd known them. It always feels like something's missing. Do you feel the same?'

'I…I suppose.'

He sniffed and wiped his nose. 'You know, Elowen, after all we've been through you're the closest to family I've got, the closest to family I've ever had. I don't know why you're so good to me. I don't deserve it. I bullied you in the Orphanage. I felt worthless, so I bullied you and others to feel better. You must have hated me.'

'Whatever bad things you said or did in the Orphanage, you've repaid them a hundred times over,' said Elowen.

Then she laughed and said, 'If you keep being so nice to me people might think we're sweethearts.'

Diggory screwed up his face. 'Ugh, I don't think of you that way.'

'I'm relieved to hear it,' said Elowen, giggling.

Diggory smiled. 'You are my best friend, though. I don't want to lose you, not like I lost Lárwita.'

'I don't want to lose you either, so be careful. Don't put yourself in danger on my account.'

He winked and said, 'I wish you'd said that to me after we'd just escaped from Trecadok. It would have saved me a lot of trouble.'

Elowen nodded. 'Yes, that's true. But I wouldn't have got very far without you.'

Diggory stood slowly. He winced as he placed weight on his injured leg but shrugged away Elowen's offer to support him. He said firmly, 'I can manage.'

Elowen called out to Batu, 'Is there somewhere safe we can set camp for the night?'

The Orok looked over his shoulder and gave her a rueful smile. 'I doubt there are any safe places in these lands. The *Teredonas* haunt this part of the forest.'

'*Teredonas?*' said Elowen, frowning.

'Yes, the wood-gnawers,' said Batu, scratching his moustache. 'It is the Orok name for the Khiltoi.'

'Khiltoi, I've heard of them,' said Diggory, looking worried. 'Godless savages.'

'Godless perhaps, savages for sure,' said Batu, his face as stern as an owl's. 'But if we are careful we should avoid them. I promise to find somewhere to camp by nightfall.'

17

He was as good as his word. As the sky darkened, they stopped beside an ancient, hollowed-out tree, so bloated it looked as though it had exploded from the inside. After attending to the horses, Batu kindled a small fire, and handed out strips of salty dried meat and solid lumps of dried curds—their usual fare on the journey. Once she had eaten, Elowen sipped some mare's milk. After drinking it daily since they had left Erdene, she was beginning to enjoy its bitter taste.

The food and crackling fire provided a semblance of comfort, and to lift his companions' spirits, Batu told ancient Orok tales. Some of the tales were amusing, such as the story of King Shajai and the sheep. Elowen found others frightening, like the tale of Kushi the Cursed, who was granted by the gods his wish of immortality, but as he forgot to ask for eternal youth, he aged and lived out centuries of torment as little more than a shrivelled skeleton before he was finally allowed the mercy of death. Elowen and Diggory sat enthralled as Batu spoke. Chinua smoked his pipe, a look of contentment on his face.

Batu's final tale told of how the Oroks believed the world came into being. He made broad gestures with his hands as he spoke. 'At the beginning of time, all was chaos, trapped within a giant ball of mist. Then, the spirits of the elements took shape, and they set in motion the rhythms of life.'

Elowen closed her eyes; the words of the story, the rhythmic intonation of Batu's voice, conjured images in her mind and animated shapes and colours. The Orok pulled out a pale green pendant from his pocket. He placed it in the palm of his hand and gently tapped it with his fingers as he told his tale. 'The elements divided the heavens from the earth, and formed the sun, the moon and the stars, bringing light and warmth. They gathered the water into rivers and seas, and populated them with fish. They raised mountains and levelled the plains. Plants, birds and beasts sprang into being. And last of all, they forged two figures from clay, one male and one female, and breathed life into them.'

'Why do you ignore God and the Saviour?' said Diggory. 'The Holy Book says God created the world.'

Batu smiled. 'I do not say the tale I tell you is the truth. It is however, what I believe. You are free to believe whatever you hold to be true. I value free thought and speech, for like all Oroks, I have seen too much of tyranny.'

'But with Arigh Nasan as khan, surely things will be better now for the Oroks?' said Elowen.

Batu exhaled slowly. 'Arigh Nasan is a noble soul, yet he comes to power at a perilous time.'

'Do you think he'll be able to summon an Orok army to march against Prester John?' said Elowen.

'He will try but it will not be easy. Many tribes are remote from the troubles of the west, and might see little reason to go to war. However, I trust Arigh Nasan can persuade enough of them, and that the Oroks will meet this challenge.'

'Even Prester John might be wary of an Orok army,' said Diggory.

Batu clenched the little green pendant in his fist. 'Let us hope so. Now, we must rest. We shall keep watch in turn. Elowen, you are first.'

Diggory and Chinua fell swiftly to sleep. Batu checked the

horses and then sat beside Elowen. As he arranged his blankets he said, 'Wake me if you see or hear anything unusual.'

'Don't worry, I will,' said Elowen.

The Orok laid his blankets down and whispered, 'I should have spoken of this before, but I have never found the right time. Perhaps there will never be a right time. I am referring to your mother, *Burilgi Maa*.'

Elowen's throat dried, and she feared she saw danger in the Orok's serious eyes. 'Arigh Nasan told me you knew.'

He smiled, his expression softened. 'I never blame the child for the sins of the parent, even when the parent was as dreadful as *Burilgi Maa*.'

Elowen looked down at the ground. 'I sometimes fear I inherited her weaknesses, her evil.'

Batu widened his mouth in surprise. 'If so, I am utterly fooled, for I detect no trace of her cruelty within you. Her name is hateful to me, but I think no ill towards you, Elowen. It is important to me that you understand this.'

'You are kind.'

'Not a word often used to describe me! Besides, within each of us flows the blood of less distinguished predecessors. When I was a child, my grandfather, a fierce warrior in his youth, would sit by the fire and tell me stories of butchery and murder. He revelled in his gory memories. He gleefully told me of slaughtering his foes, burning crops, razing cities to the ground. The tales repulsed me. Oroks are born warriors, but I vowed never to fight or kill for pleasure. The blood in our veins is not all we are. We have a choice. We can slavishly follow our forefathers, or we can take a path

20

of our own choosing. I trust you, Elowen. I believe in you. If it were not so, I would not have agreed to aid you on this quest. I trust this reassures you?'

'It does.'

'That is good,' he said. He leant forward and passed her the little green pendant. 'Put this in your pocket, I would sleep easier if you did so.'

Elowen frowned. The pendant was in the form of a dragon, its body arranged in a contorted position. 'Why? What is it?'

'It is made from jade, which defends against demons and spirits. The people of ancient Seres buried their kings in suits of jade, silk thread and gold, in the belief that it would protect the spirit of the deceased and preserve the body from corruption. Baseless superstitions some might say.'

Elowen looked doubtfully at the jade pendant. 'Do you believe it has such power?'

He winked at her. 'I believe in anything that might keep us safe. The odds are so stacked against us, why not seek any help, however small? Now, forgive me, my eyes burn for sleep. Wake me when two hours have passed.'

*

Elowen sat with her blanket wrapped tightly around her legs. Chinua snored deeply, while Diggory muttered and smacked his lips in his sleep. Only Batu slept in perfect silence. The horses rested while standing, heads and necks drooped. The wind slowed to a faint murmur. It snowed fitfully, exuberant flurries followed by stillness. The snow

21

reflected the moonlight and created strange shadows. At a glance, a tree resembled a giant, with gnarled, leafless branches as its claws. Eerie cries sounded from deep in the forest. Elowen knew them to be the calls of harmless nocturnal creatures, but they stilled her blood nonetheless. She remembered the little pendant Batu had given to her; she held it tightly but it did not make her feel any safer. She longed for her watch to be over.

In a whisper, she sung a hymn, the tune and words fractured memories. She was tired and her eyelids felt heavy. She yawned and rubbed her stinging eyes. The shadows moved again and moulded a face with human features but carved from wood. Elowen stared. With her heart pounding, she realised it was no trick of the moonlight. There was a face. It belonged to a tall figure, stood beside the tree closest to her, not six yards away. She screamed. Batu and Chinua leapt to their feet, already drawing their weapons. Diggory blundered around, lost in his blanket.

'What is it?' said Batu.

'Look there,' said Elowen pointing at the tree and the figure beside it, except the figure had vanished.

'I see nothing,' said Batu.

'It was there, just there,' insisted Elowen. 'It stared at me. It had a face but its skin was like bark. I think…I have seen things like them before. Back in the Witchwood, I saw Oakmen, horrible things. Bucca Gwidden saved me from them…'

'I have heard of the Wood Wights of which you speak, but I do not think you saw one of them,' said Chinua. He walked over to the tree, his sword at the ready. He looked around the tree and traced his fingers through the snow at the trunk's base. He shook his head and said something to Batu, who replied abruptly in the Orok language. Batu turned to Elowen and said, 'The forest can play tricks on the mind, especially when you are tired.'

Annoyed, Elowen rolled her eyes. 'I know what I saw. It was standing right there.'

'There are no footprints,' said Batu. 'No one was there, Elowen. Perhaps you fell asleep for a moment. There is no shame in that.'

'I wasn't asleep,' said Elowen angrily. 'I was awake and I know what I saw.'

Batu stroked his chin. 'Well, you were vigilant, I concede that. Let me keep watch for now. Get some sleep.'

Elowen wanted to protest but her desire for sleep and her fear of the forest at night overrode such thoughts. She curled up beside a startled-looking Diggory. The last thing she saw before sleep embraced her was Batu cross-legged on the ground, his sword on his lap.

*

They set off again at first light and tracked alongside a slow-moving river—patches of ice floated on its surface. The snow eased to a faint dusting but a bitter wind scythed through the forest. The horses snorted as they walked, their breath steaming in clouds above them.

The ground remained iron-hard, although Elowen spotted in the snow close to the water's edge the criss-crossed tracks of foxes, badgers and deer. Birds, driven by hunger, darted hither and thither, rare signs of movement and life. A crusty, sparkling layer of snow crowned the bushes and shrubs, and lay as a second skin upon the black branches of the trees. A few plants peeked through the drifts, like drowning men gasping for air.

The previous night's events left Elowen drowsy and grumpy. She walked with her head down, not engaging in conversation. She knew she had seen the mysterious figure and was angry and frustrated the others refused to believe her. Perhaps they thought she was losing her mind.

Batu steered them away from the river and onto a wide, rutted track. He said, 'This is the only road through the forest, built in antiquity to speed along the Imperator's legions. It should prove the swiftest way and by following it we avoid travelling through lands plagued by the Khiltoi.'

'You call this a road?' said Diggory, crunching his foot into a puddle filled with grey ice. 'I can see civilisation hasn't reached these parts yet.'

'Considering the dubious gifts supplied by civilisation, perhaps we should be grateful for that,' said Batu.

Snow-bound trees lined each side of the road. They looked sickly, with greyish, dead branches. Orange and red-stained slush spread around their trunks. A faint smell of smoke lingered in the air and a cold sensation played down Elowen's back that had nothing to do with the snow or icy wind. The strong connections with the Earthsoul she had experienced in the deepest parts of the forest, the warmth and energy that had flowed through her, were extinguished. She felt numb, her senses dulled.

As they rounded a bend in the road, there stood a Sentinel, an obelisk of Cold Iron stark against the trees, with more of them in the distance.

'Now I see why this part of the forest sickens,' said Batu.

'I cannot believe Prester John is stretching his power to places as remote as this,' said Elowen.

Batu tilted his head as he stared at the Sentinel. 'His thirst for domination is impossible to quench. In this we see—'

Chinua interrupted him by whispering urgently in the Orok language; he headed for the trees, gesturing for the others to follow. Batu's eyes widened in alarm and he said to Elowen and Diggory, 'Off the road, *now*.'

'What's happening?' said Elowen.

'Is it another boar?' said Diggory.

Batu gave no answer. Instead, he bundled Elowen, Diggory and the horses into the darkness formed by the trees. Once there, he whispered, 'Keep low. Do not move. Do not speak.'

Elowen squatted and looked through a gap in the branches of a bush. Four riders approached at great speed. They rode huge black steeds, and were dressed in white robes— Redeemers.

Elowen nearly choked in fear. Three of the Redeemers rode past, but the fourth slowed to a canter, the breath steaming out of his horse's nostrils. The Redeemer dismounted. He looked around, turning his head slowly, his face hidden by his hood. Then with short, heavy steps, he walked over to the Sentinel. He touched the smooth surface, his fingers tracing patterns on the Cold Iron. He shivered once and then froze, his eyes trained exactly on the spot where Elowen and her companions were hiding.

25

'Keep silent,' whispered Batu. 'He may sense our presence but he cannot see us here.'

Seconds passed. Still the Redeemer stared, leaning his head forward. Then he jerked, as if he were a puppet brought to life by unskilled hands. Hunched over, he walked back to this horse, mounted it and galloped away.

For the first time since the Redeemers had appeared, Elowen breathed, gulping air into her aching lungs.

'They were looking for us,' said Diggory, echoing Elowen's own thoughts.

Batu flashed a glance at Chinua before answering, 'We do not know that for certain. I had hoped this region of the Altheart would be free of their presence. It is not safe to take the road, instead we must head northwest, back into the forest.'

'But won't that take us close to the Khiltoi?' said Elowen. 'You told us that would be dangerous.'

He rubbed his forehead. 'Yes, and it may prove to be so, but less dangerous than being found by Redeemers.'

Harassed by the rising wind, they left the road and plunged back into the forest. Batu led them on a zigzagging course; as far as Elowen knew they could be going round in circles and she lost all sense of direction. She just had to trust the Orok knew where he was going. They traipsed through brambles and thickets of hazel. Oak trees, naked of leaves, stood silent watch. In the waning light, they took on a sinister aspect, their branches clawing; their creaks sounded like bitter, angry curses. Elowen was heartened to see a squirrel with its thicker, silvery grey winter coat. It stopped to stare at the intruders before scurrying up to the higher

26

branches of a tree. Mixed flocks of birds scuffed around on patches of ground bare of snow, searching for insect eggs or pupae hidden beneath the mulched leaf litter. The birds scattered as Elowen and her companions drew near.

Elowen doubted she would ever be warm again. Every joint, every bone, and the blood running through her veins, felt frozen. Despite trying not to, she thought of hot fires, warm food, soft, comfortable beds and blankets; such visions tantalised and tortured her.

Batu stopped and pointed ahead to a stretch of the forest marked by a line of fallen trees, all ripped from the soil, as though a sudden tempest had gouged out an arrow-straight path. Batu knelt down and studied some of the broken branches and trunks. He sniffed and said, 'The air carries a tang of metal. Something strange has happened here. Something I do not understand.'

Chinua wandered around the felled trunks, muttering to himself and shaking his head. The horses were skittish. Elowen sensed their unease.

'It is like some huge beast has charged through the forest,' said Diggory, tugging nervously at the edge of his mouth.

'There is no beast alive that could have done this,' said Batu. 'Come, we must find somewhere to shelter soon. Night draws in.'

Hastening away from the line of felled trees, they picked a route that sloped downwards. It led to a bowl-shaped dell fringed with ash trees and filled with stunted, fat-trunked oaks, and moss-carpeted granite rocks jutted defiantly out of the snow. A dreamy mist lingered in the dell, softening the edges.

'This is as good a place as any to camp,' said Batu.

'We're not exactly spoilt for choice,' said Diggory. 'At least we're out of that infernal wind.'

Elowen looked around. The twisted oaks resembled savage spirits, frozen in the middle of a frenzied dance, waiting for the passers-by to move on so they could continue. Carved into the knobbly, gnarled bark were primitive shapes and figures. Elowen wondered if they were the work of a bored traveller, or served a more sinister purpose.

After he had tied the horses to a tree, Batu tried to light a fire with his steel piece and flint; he cursed and swore as the moist air thwarted his efforts. With Chinua's help, he got a modest, smoky fire going, and, after Batu had cleared some patches of snow, they all sat around it. Despite the welcome warmth, Elowen was not comforted. A nagging sense of being watched troubled her. She tried to dismiss it as a figment of her imagination but she noticed how the horses kept making a snorting sound with their nostrils. She tried *Linking* with them but all she felt was their nervousness, their fear.

'Eat, Elowen,' said Chinua, breaking her thoughts. He chucked her a lump of dried curds and pointed to the fire. 'Sit closer. Keep warm.'

Diggory screwed up his face. 'I wish we had something better than these curds.'

Batu smiled. 'If you are hungry, you will eat them. Our supplies are running low. I had hoped to hunt in the forest, to find deer or some rabbits at least. But I fear it is too dangerous to go wandering through the forest alone.'

'Is this fire not a risk?' said Elowen, pointing to the steadi-

28

ly rising column of smoke. 'It's a signal to any unfriendly eyes.'

'We cannot survive a night without fire,' said Batu. 'It is too cold, even for Oroks. I remember once—'

The sound of branches snapping silenced Batu and he jumped to his feet, his bow at the ready. Chinua drew his sword from its scabbard and gripped the handle with both hands, ready to strike.

Elowen heard trees falling. Trunks thumped and branches cracked. And the sounds were getting louder.

'Something's coming,' said Diggory, his voice trembling.

Two ash trees on the edge of the dell lifted violently from the ground and toppled forwards. Through the space left by the felled trees came something beyond Elowen's darkest fears. A head made of stone, a head without limbs, without any body, like a floating statue. Its eyes appeared shut and a long prominent nose ended above pursed lips. The forehead was narrow, and the top of the head flat.

The head swooped down into the dell. Smoke issued from its nostrils and it made a grinding noise. Cracks widened in the ground and the trees to which Takhi and Ivuli were tied tumbled. The horses screamed in terror and bolted away into the forest. Batu loosened an arrow, striking the stone head between its eyes, but it bounced off harmlessly. Diggory put himself in front of Elowen and threw a stone. It struck the cheek but shattered on impact, leaving no mark on the head. The eyelids opened wider, revealing two glowing orbs of incandescent brightness. The lips parted, and the head uttered a scream.

Elowen thought the scream would crush her head; she

groaned as pressure pushed on her jaw, cheeks and neck. She saw Batu and Diggory on their knees doubled in pain, holding their ears. The head hovered close to them, its mouth now wide open, a hideous gaping black hole. Visions exploded in Elowen's mind. She saw Redeemers riding monstrous horses. They charged towards her, wreathed in flames and smoke. She heard her name called out…distant…echoing…growing louder…

'EL-O-WEN!'

The visions ceased. The voice belonged to Chinua. He stood upright, grim-faced. He pointed at the head, which slowly approached her, glaring with its brutal burning eyes.

Chinua shouted a word, a word Elowen could not understand. Only after he repeated it several times did she recognise what he was trying to say: *Earthsoul*.

She tried to block out the scream. The Earthsoul flowed through her. The golden threads weaved and danced. She willed them to surround the head, like a mass of writhing snakes. Her skin tingled, hot as though brushed with flames. Her muscles tightened and stretched. Pain shot through her body. Her enemy resisted. She had to be strong. She had to fight. The lessons of Baba Yaga came to her: *Settle your body. Feel the weight of your feet on the ground.*

Elowen focused her mind and every inch of her body; through the golden threads she gripped the head and pushed it down to the ground. It resisted like a fish snared on a hook, but its ferocity waned. In the corner of her eyes, Elowen saw Chinua lunge at the head. He thrust a dagger into its right eye. Molten metal poured from the eye-socket and hissed as it burned through the snow and mud. Batu scrambled to his feet and fired an arrow straight into the open mouth and then another into the left eye. Smoke belched from the mouth and after a doleful groan, the head settled on the ground and moved no more. Its stone skull cracked in several places, allowing foul-smelling yellow and green vapours to escape.

Released from the struggle, the strength drained from Elowen's limbs and she fell, landing on her backside. She managed to stand up but trembled uncontrollably, her body protesting at the strain of the enormous effort she had endured.

'Is it dead?' said Diggory, his legs shaky, his face as white as the snow around them.

Batu gingerly inspected the stone monstrosity, giving it careful pokes with the end of his bow. 'Yes, if it ever was alive. This is not a demon summoned from the underworld to haunt us. It is a creation of Prester John. His sorcery is black indeed.'

'Prester John *made* that thing?' said Elowen, her face screwed up in disgust.

'And others like it,' said Batu. He turned to Elowen. 'You saved us. I see why Lord Lucien fears you.'

Chinua pointed at Elowen, a rare smile lighting his face. 'You. Brave.'

She picked up his knife, the blade twisted and warped by molten metal. She passed it to Chinua and laughed. 'This is yours, I believe.'

He bowed and winked as he took the knife in his huge hands. 'No good for fight.'

'Maybe not,' said Batu. 'But it is a token of your bravery.'

Diggory rubbed his eyes. 'When it screamed I...I saw things, horrible things. It got inside my head, controlling me.'

Elowen nodded—she had experienced the same feeling.

'They are named Egregores, but I know little about them, other than they are cursed with infernal powers,' said Batu. 'We have lost the horses—a grievous blow. As tired as we all are, we should push on and get away from this place.'

'We won't be safe blundering through the forest in the dark,' said Elowen, her head still pounding and her limbs numb.

'There should be enough moonlight to aid us,' said Batu. 'We cannot stay here, Elowen.'

'You're going nowhere, *colgreach*.'

Elowen looked up in alarm. Strange warriors ringed the dell, each over seven feet tall and draped in cloaks. Some had lime-washed and spiky hair. Most alarming of all was their skin, which had the texture and colour of tree bark. Their eyes glowed like beads of amber. They carried primitive weapons, such as wooden clubs, flinthead axes and slings.

'Who are they?' Elowen heard Diggory whisper.

Batu said, 'Khiltoi.'

CHAPTER TWO

The Hidden People of the Forest

The Khiltoi jumped down into the dell. They made whistling sounds and calls, and waved their weapons in a threatening manner. Elowen looked for a gap, but there was no escape route. Diggory edged in front of her. 'If any of these savages want to hurt you, they'll have to get past me first.'

'Do not antagonise them,' said Batu.

One of the Khiltoi pushed forward. Taller than the others, his bark-skin was brownish red and a moustache framed his top lip. He wore plain, loose breeches, a linen tunic and a cloak of sheep's wool, fastened by a wooden brooch on his right shoulder. He clutched a fearsome-looking weapon: a flat wooden club with its sides embedded by obsidian blades. His movements were fluent, like a stalking cat. His limbs creaked as he stretched and tensed his muscles. Elowen recognised brutality and wildness in his eyes.

He said a few words in a language incomprehensible to Elowen, before starting to speak in the Common Tongue. 'I am Corcoran. This land belongs to my people. Who are you, *colgreachs*? Why are you here?'

'We are simple travellers,' said Batu, after giving their names. 'We stopped here for the night, hoping for shelter.'

Corcoran pointed at the fallen Egregore. 'You brought the vile *námhaid* here. Are you servants of the *Moljnir*?'

'If you mean Prester John, then no,' said Batu. 'Indeed we are very much his foes.'

'That thing *attacked* us,' said Diggory. 'We destroyed it, you should be grateful.'

The other warriors whooped and howled. Corcoran sneered and ran his fingers along the obsidian blades on his club. 'Grateful? You trespass in our lands, lighting fires in sacred places and attracting *námhaids* who defile the forest with their filth. And you expect our gratitude? You do not belong here. Your kind have only brought misery and suffering to my people.'

'We are no threat to you,' said Batu. 'We share a common foe.'

Corcoran stared at Batu. 'You speak fair words but they veil something ominous. In recent days, we've seen *drouks* riding close to the forest on their black steeds. They are like ghosts, bringers of death. Perhaps no coincidence brings you and the *drouks* together in the forest at the same time. Perhaps you're in league with them. The *Moljnir* has many spies.'

'*Spies?* That's ridiculous,' said Diggory, his cheeks flushed with anger and his voice rising. 'We have fought—'

'Keep your tongue behind your teeth,' said Corcoran. 'Or I'll rip it out.'

Sensing the situation was getting out of control, Elowen said, 'There's no need for violence. Please, let us go on our way. Truly, your people will be safer if you allow us to complete what we've set out to do.'

'I wasn't talking to you, *colgreach*,' said Corcoran. He pushed Elowen backwards. Wrong-footed and surprised, she tumbled over.

Instinctively, Diggory lunged at Corcoran, who flicked him away as easily as man would with a wayward child. Diggory sprawled onto the ground, his nose and mouth bloodied.

'How dare you touch me with your filthy rodent hands?' said the red-skinned Khiltoi, standing over Diggory and holding aloft his obsidian-bladed club.

'Corcoran, NO!'

The cries and the shouts stopped. A female Khiltoi, lithe and wiry, pushed through the crowd of warriors. She wore a woollen cloak-like garment, woven in colourful patterns of green, crimson and purple, and pinned on at the breast by a bone pin. She had long braided hair and a necklace of glass and amber beads hung around her neck. She carried a sling and a stout, knotty club carved from blackthorn wood.

She pulled Corcoran back. 'This is not our way. We don't kill in cold blood.'

Corcoran gave her an unyielding stare. 'We do if we're threatened by the *Mojnir's* henchmen.'

'We watched them destroy the *námhaid*,' she said. To Elowen's discomfort, she pointed at her. 'She used the power of the *bládh*.'

Corcoran grunted. 'Bryna, you have cast aside your wits. You think this pale sapling is a *bana-buidhseach*?'

'You saw the golden threads,' said Bryna. 'She used the

bládh to destroy the *námhaid*. Don't ignore the evidence of your own eyes. Take these *colgreachs* to the Dachaigh. There Ceannard can judge them. The codes of justice bequeathed by the ancestors demand it should be so.'

Corcoran bared his teeth. 'Justice? The old ways didn't help us during the *glac'har*. They won't help us now. They no longer hold any meaning for me.'

'That is because you are consumed by bitterness,' said Bryna. 'If we are to have any hope of surviving these harsh times, we must not forget our ancestors. If we destroy our roots we cannot grow. Bandraoi says he who does not listen to the voices of the ancestors is like a lost child.'

Corcoran spat on the ground. 'Very well, take them to the Dachaigh. Be sure to bind their hands and blindfold them.'

Bryna looked uneasy with this condition, but demurred. Elowen wondered about the relationship between the two Khiltoi. Corcoran appeared to be an important figure, a leader or chief, but Bryna also commanded respect.

The Khiltoi warriors blindfolded Elowen, Diggory and the Oroks, and tied their hands firmly, though not painfully, with cord. Elowen saw no sense in resisting. The Khiltoi were too many and too strong. She thought despairingly about their quest to seek the Mystery of Fire; she hoped the Khiltoi would eventually release them, but their intentions were not clear.

Elowen felt someone take hold of her arm, a strong but tender grip. She heard a whisper, 'Don't be afraid, I won't let you fall.'

It was Bryna, Elowen was sure of it.

Bryna said, 'I won't speak again until we reach the safety

of the Dachaigh, for we must walk in silence now night has fallen.'

Elowen heard Corcoran say to the Khiltoi warriors, 'Suithad! We march northwards. Go swiftly and silently.'

Bryna gently pulled Elowen forward and the march began. She walked as briskly as she dared; every now and then Bryna pulled her in one direction or another, or even lifted her briefly off the ground. Elowen felt like a toddler, learning to walk under a watchful parent's supervision. The Khiltoi warriors made little sound save for the soft crunching of their feet in the snow.

Already drained by her fight with the Egregore, Elowen stumbled wearily forward. Bryna detected her tiredness; without warning, she whisked Elowen up and onto her back. Even with the extra burden, Bryna did not slow. Secure in the Khiltoi's hold, Elowen drifted into a kind of half-sleep, her consciousness invaded by snippets of dreams. The Egregore's leering face. The voices of Baba Yaga and Lárwita, voices she would not hear again in the waking world.

Many hours later, Bryna softly placed Elowen back down on her feet. Bryna removed the blindfold and whispered in Elowen's ear, 'We are here. This is the Dachaigh, our home, where our ancestors settled when the world was young and the forest reached from sea to sea.'

The morning was bright and fresh, the keen sun reflecting sharply off the snowy landscape. It took Elowen a few seconds for her eyes to adjust to the light and take in her surroundings. Ahead of her, a hill rose from the forest. A series of ditches, earthwork ramparts and stockades followed the hill's contours, enclosing strips of pastureland for small herds of grazing sheep, goats, pigs and cattle, and a settlement of several dozen straw-roofed round houses. An entrance way zigzagged through the complex circuits of defensive works, interrupted at several points by wooden gates. A few wind-battered trees clung onto rocky slopes, as though they had wandered far from their companions in the forest, and now waited, stranded, lost and lonely.

As they looked upon their home, the Khiltoi warriors made joyful guttural sounds and sang songs. Elowen stared at the Dachaigh in wonder. It was a hidden place, a secret place, somewhere frozen in time. Yet she knew from bitter experience that nowhere was truly secret, or truly protected from the ruinous reach of the enemy. The Sanctuary of the Illuminati had once seemed safe from the evil of Prester John, but reality had pierced that comforting shield of invulnerability. Elowen turned away from the hill to see her friends blinking in the sunshine, their blindfolds removed. Diggory, his face bruised, gave Elowen a rueful smile. The Oroks looked pensive and whispered furtively to each other. Corcoran raised his hand and said, 'Watch the prisoners at all times. Be mindful of tricks and treachery. Follow me.'

A steep, slush-soaked track formed the entranceway into the Dachaigh. Corcoran strode forward like a conquering king. The restless wind moaned and shrieked as Elowen and her friends were marched up to the settlement, which was filled by windowless roundhouses, each with a conical thatched roof and walls fashioned from wooden posts joined by wattle-and-daub panels. As well as the roundhouses, Elowen spotted other domestic structures such as drying racks for clothes, a haystack, compost heaps, wood racks for storing timber, and a straw beehive with a covering of reed.

Aromas of smoke and cooking meat mixed with the pungent stench of dung. Mongrel dogs, panting and wet with snow, barked and scampered after cats. Khiltoi women worked ceaselessly: feeding animals, carrying buckets full of water drawn from barrels, collecting firewood, and keeping a watchful eye on the rowdy children. Meanwhile, the Khiltoi men repaired roofs, walls and stockades, or kept guard on the gates, armed with slings, bows, stone-tipped arrows and clubs.

The arrival of Elowen and her friends went far from unnoticed. The Khiltoi stopped whatever they were doing to watch. The adults looked on suspiciously. The children pointed, their excitement sparked by fear of the unknown, of the alien creatures now in their midst. Elowen guessed that the Khiltoi, for all their physical strength, were no strangers to fear. They clung on to an existence on the margins of life, out of sight of the modern world, a world that longed to devour them greedily.

Corcoran said to the warriors, 'Leave us now. Bryna and I will take the prisoners to Ceannard.'

'Who is Ceannard?' said Diggory as the warriors dispersed.

'He is the Chief of our people,' said Bryna, cutting in before Corcoran could answer more bluntly. 'He's long-lived and wise. He must judge if you are a danger to us. If he deems you are not, you might be given leave to continue your journey through the forest.'

'What if he does think we're dangerous?' said Elowen.

Bryna flashed an uncomfortable look at Corcoran, who grinned malevolently. The question remained unanswered.

Corcoran directed them to the largest structure in the settlement: a rectangular hall with a pitched thatched roof and walls made of wooden planks. Khiltoi warriors kept guard outside. They pushed open the door and bowed as Corcoran approached.

The door opened into a single long room. With the few windows all shuttered, the only light came from candles and lamps burning animal fat, and from the central fire built on a raised clay hearth, oblong in shape. Colourful woven tapestries hung from the walls, and straw and sweet-smelling herbs covered the floor. Unsettling carvings of primitive creatures decorated the roof-supporting pillars; the creatures seemed alive, as though they clung to the wood and scurried about when not being observed. A table ran the length of the hall, served by two long benches and dotted with wooden and clay utensils and storage pots.

The hall stretched to a high seat at the far end, reached by a dais of five steps. Upon the seat sat an elderly Khiltoi, tall even by the standards of his people. He wore a silk tunic and a long cloak of many colours. His face looked weathered, with patches of greyish flesh, and his mossy beard reached his stomach. Elowen guessed he was Ceannard, Chief of the tribe. Another Khiltoi stood beside the throne. Slender, she wore a green cloak and a long, embroidered tunic with a hood that left half of her face in shadows.

Corcoran and Bryna bowed in front of the dais, and assembled Elowen and her companions in a line.

40

'We found these four *colgreachs* wandering in the forest,' said Corcoran.

'What brings you to our lands?' said Ceannard, his voice hushed like the murmur of wind through thickly leaved branches. 'In these troubled times few outsiders travel through the forest except those in thrall to the *Moljnir*.'

Batu swallowed and flashed a glance at Elowen before replying. 'We seek something of enormous value, something we believe can be found in the Altheart.'

Corcoran exhaled, as though trying to vent some of his anger. He said, 'So, the *Moljnir* is now using thieves and grave robbers to carry out his dirty work. You seek to plunder treasure from our barrows, I doubt not.'

Batu shook his head. 'We have no interest in your barrows. I can tell you little of our purpose—'

'How convenient,' said Corcoran.

Batu ignored the interruption and stared straight at Ceannard. 'I can assure you everything we are trying to do is concerned only with the destruction of Prester John.'

'And yet your appearance has coincided with sightings of the *drouks* on the borders of our lands, as well as the appearance of a *námhaid*,' said Corcoran.

'A *námhaid*?' blanched Ceannard, looking genuinely unsettled. He fidgeted nervously in his seat.

Corcoran nodded. 'It ruined whole swathes of the forest.'

Ceannard shivered and looked nervously at the hooded Khiltoi beside him, acting like a child seeking his mother's reassurance. He said, 'This is ill news. And if, Corcoran, you suspect these *colgreachs* are in league with the enemy, we cannot suffer them to live.'

41

Elowen noticed Khiltoi warriors lurking in the shadows of the hall. As Ceannard spoke, they had edged closer. Elowen's mouth was dry and her heart hammered; she wilted under the hooded Khiltoi's relentless stare.

'But we destroyed the Egregore,' said Batu, looking angrily at Corcoran. 'You witnessed the fight.'

Ceannard fidgeted again and gnawed at his long fingernails. 'Corcoran, is this true?'

'Yes, it is true,' said Bryna, before Corcoran could answer.

'That was a worthy deed,' said Ceannard, looking to the hooded Khiltoi for affirmation and receiving it with a nod.

'Yet it was not achieved solely through arms,' said Bryna. She pointed at Elowen. 'She controlled the golden threads of the *bládh*. She used her power to ruin the *námhaid*. I believe her to be a *bana-buidhseach*.'

Ceannard sat back in his chair, his limbs and bones creaking. He coughed and said, 'A bold claim, young Bryna. I doubt your guess. In these withered days, surely few have such ability.'

Corcoran scoffed and shook his head. 'In the confusion of battle, Bryna mistook the weird vapours produced by the *námhaid* for the sacred threads of the *bládh*.'

'I know what I saw,' said Bryna.

'Elowen's stronger than any of you,' said Diggory, his anger erupting. 'She's fought Redeemers and survived. And she destroyed the Egregore, a foe that would have killed any of you. You're the weak, frightened ones, not her.'

Corcoran grabbed Diggory by the shoulders and pushed him down onto his knees. He drew out his obsidian-bladed club. 'I should kill you for your impudence.'

Elowen forgot all tiredness. Fear for Diggory's life caused her weary limbs to cast aside pain and suffering. The golden threads twirled around her, vibrant, incandescent. With all her thoughts focused on Corcoran, the threads flooded over the Khiltoi, ripping the club from his hand and hurling him backwards over the table, which shuddered violently under the impact.

Anger gripped Elowen. She stood over Corcoran, glaring down at his terror-stricken face. She wanted to hurt him. She wanted to *kill* him. She felt so strong, so powerful. Corcoran was a mere trifle, an insect to crush. She only had to stretch out and he would be dead...

A hand grasped Elowen's arm. Her first instinct was to attack but soothing words stopped her. 'Be calm. Do not use the power of the *bládh* to commit acts you are bound to regret when your temper cools.'

Elowen looked round. The hooded Khiltoi held her arm. In a melodious voice she went on to say, 'Child, do not kill out of anger. Step back.'

Slowly, Elowen's scrambled thoughts and emotions settled. Her racing heart calmed to a normal rhythm. Her breathing relaxed. She shook, feeling weak as the golden threads' vibrant power faded. The hooded Khiltoi placed her hand on Elowen's back. 'Peace, child. Your fury is passing.'

Corcoran clambered to his feet, cursing and snarling. He jabbed a finger at Elowen. 'She's a demon. She must die.'

Elowen glanced at her companions. Their expressions of shock and fear sickened her. They looked *afraid* of her; Diggory stared in disbelief, as though he did not recognise her. She felt ashamed. She had never known such potency, such power. Anger and hate had controlled her, giving her strength she did not know she possessed. She had become a creature of instinct, of base emotions, a savage primordial beast locked within the confines of her body. And she had *enjoyed* it. Watching Corcoran on the ground, afraid for his life, at her mercy, gave her a primal thrill, an intoxication she had never experienced before. The experience dislodged thoughts she had wanted to repress, thoughts of her mother, the one named *Burilgi Maa*. Elowen wondered if her mother had experienced the same pleasure, the same exhilaration, in aggressively wielding the power of the Earthsoul. In her mind she repeated, *I am not like her, I am not like her.*

'Bryna is right,' said the hooded Khiltoi, steering Elowen to stand once more in front of Ceannard. 'I am Bandraoi, of our people, so hear me now. This child is a *bana-buidhseach*, and one stronger than has been seen in the forest for moons uncountable.'

Elowen said, 'If by calling me a *bana-buidhseach* you mean I am an Adept…I've some control of the Earthsoul, but I did not complete my training and—'

'You have strength and skills that cannot be taught,' said Bandraoi. 'You are a *bana-buidhseach*. It cannot be doubted.'

Elowen swallowed. An Adept. She found it difficult to confront the word and the idea so bluntly. It carried echoes of her mother's terrible deeds.

Ceannard lowered his mossy eyebrows and squinted at Elowen. 'It may be so, Bandraoi, but her powers are a threat to our people.'

'She and her friends must be driven from the forest, or slain,' said Corcoran.

'You speak from fear and ignorance,' said Bandraoi, to Bryna's enthusiastic nods. 'In times gone by we welcomed the arrival of a *bana-buidhseach*, even one from outside of the forest.'

'That was different,' said Corcoran. 'That was before the *glac'har*. We've learnt to be suspicious of outsiders. Is this not so, Ceannard? In this time of danger, dare we take any chances with strangers?'

Ceannard tugged at his ear. 'This is a difficult situation to judge.'

'Then let us make it easier for you,' said Batu. 'We are not grave robbers, nor are we spies of Prester John. If you aid us, you could provide no better service to defeating Prester John and all he stands for; if you thwart us, you are as good as handing him complete victory, and dominion over all lands, including your own.'

'Bold claims these *colgreachs* make,' said Corcoran.

Ceannard clasped the arms of his chair and looked at Batu. 'Your words are vague, your aims unclear. If you wish for me to look favourably upon you, tell me your true purpose for being in the forest.'

Batu looked at Elowen. She nodded. They had to tell them. The Orok swallowed and said, 'We seek the Ogonberg, for a powerful artefact we need is hidden there. It is vital we gain this artefact before those loyal to Prester John can find it. We must find the Ogonberg. You know these lands—if you could tell us where it can be found, you would help us greatly.'

Bryna frowned and spoke quietly to Bandraoi, who shrugged and shook her head. Ceannard looked confused. 'The name of Ogonberg means nothing to me.'

'Perhaps you know it by another name,' said Elowen. She carefully described what she had seen in her vision.

When she had finished, there was a long silence before Bandraoi said, 'You said you came by this knowledge in a vision?'

'Yes,' said Elowen. 'Do you know of this place?'

Bandraoi pulled down her hood. Her brow was broad and tapered to a narrow jaw. She spoke more quietly than before. 'Yes, we know it well.'

'We have to get there,' said Elowen. 'Will you help us?'

Corcoran laughed. 'Yes, it would be just punishment.'

'What do you mean?' said Batu.

'The place you speak of is known to our people as Uffern,' said Bandraoi, wincing as she spoke, as though the words pained her. She leaned forward. 'It lurks like a ghost in our songs and dreams. Even we Khiltoi fear to go there. Tales speak of a monster, a beast that devours flesh, blood and bone. It dwells in the depths of Uffern. The Wyvern it is named. This horror serves its master, Cholos, a sorcerer of uncanny power and guards a hoard of plundered treasure.'

Elowen's heart began to beat rapidly as she listened to the terrifying description of the Wyvern. She guessed Cholos must be the fire Elemental. She glanced at Diggory, who looked back at her, his face white, his eyes wide.

'Uffern is cursed,' said Corcoran. 'Only those filthy Brisnings choose to live there.'

46

'Knowing this now, is it still your wish to go there?' said Ceannard.

Elowen turned to her companions. They had risked so much for her. She hated to lead them into yet more danger. But there was no other choice. Trying to smother the tremor in her voice, she said, 'Yes, if you would guide me there, I'll go.'

Ceannard sighed. 'Then go you shall.'

Corcoran folded his arms in front of his chest. 'She's not to be trusted.'

Ceannard held up his hands. 'I have not finished. I give the *bana-buidhseach* leave to go but it is not without conditions. Bandraoi spoke of the Wyvern's hoard. Within it is the Bolcán Stone, a possession precious to the ancestors. It is an emerald set within a cup of stone. As Chief, it should be mine, but the Brisnings stole it long ago. Get this treasure and return it to me. As a bond of your word, your companions must remain here. Bring me the Bolcán Stone, and they'll be set free. Fail to do so, and they become our slaves. Are these terms acceptable to you?'

Corcoran smirked and nodded in satisfaction. Elowen looked at her friends. Chinua stood still, his expression dour, inscrutable. Diggory looked panic-stricken. Only Batu spoke, saying, 'Elowen, this is dangerous. If you go—'

Elowen did not want to go, but it was the only way to free her friends. She said, 'I'll accept your terms, I'll go to Uffern.'

'I won't let you go alone,' said Diggory.

'Be silent, boy, or I'll cleave your maggot mouth from your swine head,' said Corcoran.

'Surely she must take one friend with her on this perilous quest?' said Bryna. 'That would be merciful and just.'

'I agree,' said Bandraoi. 'Such magnanimity pleases the ancestors.'

Ceannard rubbed his beard and then flicked his hand towards Diggory. 'The boy can go with her, as punishment for his insolence.'

Elowen said, 'I don't want him to come with me. I'll do this alone.'

'The boy goes,' said Ceannard. 'I have decided.'

'He mustn't—'

'Enough,' said Ceannard. 'You do not make demands of me. The boy goes, but you need a guide too. Bryna, as you are so concerned about the *colgreachs*, I ask you to take them to Uffern.'

For a split second, Bryna looked worried but she hid her concern. 'I would be honoured.'

*

Unbroken grey cloud barred the sun. Snow fell softly, silently, ghostly flakes drifting on the breeze. A carrion crow scavenged for dead rabbits or voles. Finding no morsels it took off, flapping laboriously. With Bryna striding ahead, Elowen and Diggory left the Dachaigh and headed north.

Diggory stomped with heavy footsteps and only lifted his eyes up from the ground to stare intensely at Elowen. Tired of his sullen mood, she said, 'What's wrong?'

'Why didn't you want me to come with you? Don't you trust me?'

48

'It's not that…I don't want to put you in any more danger.'

'And we're not already in danger? I understand the risks I'm taking. I'm not a child.'

'I know, but…'

He broke eye contact and his voice quietened. 'You can't do this all alone, Elowen.'

'I know and I'm sorry,' said Elowen. 'I wanted to do the right thing. I wanted to protect you.'

'You have enough to think about without worrying about protecting me.'

Bryna cleared her throat. 'Our pace slows, we should not dawdle.'

'How far is it to Uffern?' said Elowen, glad to change the subject.

'Barely an hour's walk from here,' said Bryna.

Risking another question, Elowen said, 'Will Batu and Chinua be safe in the Dachaigh?'

'They are safer than you are about to be,' said Bryna.

'Have you been to Uffern before?' said Diggory.

'I saw it once, long ago. I've little desire to go there again. If you step into that place willingly, you're either brave or mad. You might not come out of there alive.'

'Well, if you hadn't stuck up for us I think Corcoran would've killed us already,' said Elowen.

Bryna rolled her eyes. 'He has a hot temper. He talks ceaselessly of war. He is angry and headstrong, and I fear the day he becomes chief. Ceannard is weak and relies heavily on those around him, but at least he is wise and thoughtful. Corcoran's rash and looks only inward, he cares nothing for the outside world. Like many in the tribe, he's haunted by the *glac'har*.'

'What was the *glac'har*?' said Elowen.

'It was the darkest time in the story of our people. The *Moljnir's* followers came to the Altheart. Drouks. Námhaids. Men with fire and axes. They cut down much of the forest, and slew many of our folk without mercy. It was said the sky wept with misery.'

'But your tribe survived?' said Diggory.

'The gods and ancestors protected us. The Dachaigh remained hidden. But I believe we cannot hide for ever. We cannot defend ourselves alone, and we have no allies. For many years, the *filidh*, those you would call the Illuminati, aided us but no more. News reached us of their destruction.'

That uncomfortable memory prickled Elowen. In a cracked voice, she said, 'Have you had the summons to go to Omphalos?'

Bryna snorted. 'Yes, but Ceannard, at Corcoran's urging, ignored it. I argued we should send warriors south to aid the Illuminati and the Eldar, and I know Bandraoi agreed, but we could not persuade the Chief. He's too afraid. So, we Khiltoi stand alone, to face whatever fate awaits us.'

'Who is Bandraoi?' said Elowen. 'Is she the wife of Ceannard?'

Bryna laughed. 'Wife! No, Bandraoi is the *taghta*. She leads our prayers and rituals, and helps to heal the sick and injured. The ancestors and the gods work through her. She's wise beyond measure. And when she dies, I am expected to succeed her.'

'That sounds like a great honour,' said Elowen.

'Indeed, though I'm scarcely worthy to receive it.'

'Why do you say that?'

'I'm not as wise as Bandraoi. She tries to teach me but I struggle. The more I try to be like her, the more I fail.'

'Then don't try to be like her,' said Elowen. 'You are wise and intrepid. You'll be *taghta* in your own way. Different from Bandraoi, but not inferior.'

'You bless me with kind words. Perhaps you should be *taghta* instead of me.'

Elowen smiled wanly. 'I think I have enough to contend with already.'

The trees thinned, and Elowen beheld a hill with steep rocky sides and a flat top. Sulphurous vapours issued through cracks and fissures in the rocks, lending the air a bitter flavour. From the summit came occasional puffs of smoke and leaping streaks of flame. A path wrapped around the hill like a constricting snake.

At the foot of the hill, a few trees stood stooped, hunched and sickened, with yellowing trunks oozing sap and roots pushing up from the ground like the skeletal hands of shallow-buried corpses. Against the surrounding forest, the hill appeared incongruous, as though it had fallen from the sky, or been hewn by cunning intelligent hands rather than shaped by time and the elements. Elowen trembled. It was just as she had seen in her vision.

'This is Uffern,' said Bryna. She sat cross-legged on a dry patch of ground and gestured towards the twisting path. 'If you dare, you must go that way. I can go no further.'

Elowen hesitated and stared at the fume-choked hill. It

51

looked alive, hissing, pulsing, breathing. Fear and dread emanated from the rocks, mocking any challenge.

'By God, this hill is cursed,' said Diggory, his voice quivering. He turned to Elowen and said, 'I'm sorry for being sharp with you before. I know you were trying to protect me.'

'Don't say sorry,' said Elowen. 'And I think I'm the one that needs protecting now.'

'I'm with you,' said Diggory, placing a trembling hand on Elowen's shoulder. 'Whatever festers inside this place, we'll face it together.'

- CHAPTER THREE -

Uffern

Steep, narrow and studded with countless sharp rocks, the path ascending Uffern did not welcome visitors. The smoke and vapours left a sickly, acrid taste in Elowen's mouth, and her eyes stung and watered. She heard Diggory retch and he spat out globules of saliva and mucus. They wound round and round the hill until they reached an arched entrance flanked by columns carved into the rock; beyond, an orange and red light glowed as waves of hot air blew through. Elowen heard the sound of metal striking metal.

'I guess we have to go in here,' said Diggory as he peered inside.

'WHO DISTURBS THE MASTER'S PEACE?'

The voice shook the rocks and the ground beneath Elowen's feet. She heard footsteps and a lengthy shadow formed in front of the orange glow.

'Keep behind me,' said Diggory.

The shadow shortened and retreated. Elowen had expected a huge, monstrous being, but the figure in front of them stood scarcely four foot tall. Fierce eyes stared out from beneath a prominent hairy brow. His thick beard flowed down to his chest. His muscular torso was naked, his arms, chest and hands tattooed. He carried a fearsome war hammer in his right hand.

'I am Zwerg of the Brisnings and thou art foolish to come here. Go, before I slay thee.'

'We need to see Cholos,' said Elowen.

'Thou art bold to come to this threshold and make demands. Follow me and I shall bring thee to Cholos. Thou shalt come to regret thy impertinence.'

The entrance led into a stiflingly hot tunnel, lit only by the glow ahead. The tunnel opened up into a cavern with crude depictions of flames and salamanders painted onto the walls. A forge fire filled one end of the cavern, hurling out heat and light. The smoke escaped through a crack in the soot-blackened ceiling. A host of spears, shields and swords were heaped against a wall. An anvil and piles of hammers, rasps and files lay in front of the forge fire. Elowen noticed a grill of iron bars set in the floor.

Two more of the tattooed Brisnings worked in the cavern but a hunchbacked man who lurked half-hidden by the dancing shadows drew Elowen's attention. He stood in front of a table, picking at a plate laden with onions and garlic, and slurping from a pitcher of red wine.

'Cholos!' called Zwerg. 'Thou hast visitors.'

The hunchbacked man turned and hobbled lamely towards Elowen and Diggory. He had piercing amber-coloured eyes and his skin was black with soot. His ugly, hairy face curled into an angry sneer. The fire Elemental. In a voice that reminded Elowen of metal being dragged across stone, he said, 'You're the first female to darken my

54

doors since my wife fled, damn her memory! There is the stench of Khiltoi about you. Have you been to their foul nest?'

Seeing little reason to lie, Elowen nodded and said, 'We have been to the Dachaigh.'

Cholos picked at one of the scabs on his face. He gestured towards a pile of jewellery and precious stones. Amongst them, Elowen saw an emerald set within a stone cup, just as Ceannard had described. Cholos said, 'And I guess they mentioned the Bolcán Stone?'

'Yes,' said Elowen. 'It is a cherished heirloom of the Khiltoi, and they want it back.'

The Elemental licked his lips, his tongue pink and fleshy like a cow's. 'I'm sure they do.'

Elowen pressed him. 'And there is something else, something even more important.'

Cholos frowned. 'Oh, yes? And pray what would that be?'

Elowen tried to swallow, her throat and mouth parched. Sweat dribbled down from her forehead and stung her eyes. 'I have come for the Mystery of Fire.'

'You are an *Adept*?' said Cholos in surprise. He hawked up phlegm and spat it on the ground. 'A rarity in these days. So, you found the Mystery of Earth, I presume?'

Elowen nodded.

He snorted. 'I am not a soft touch like Itugen. Whatever your reasons for seeking the Mystery, I care not. Do not appeal to my good nature about the Tree of Life. I've been abandoned for too long in this cesspit to care about the world outside. The Mystery of Fire is *mine*.'

Elowen hesitated, not sure how to react. She wondered if

the Elemental was joking, or trying to test her commitment. She straightened herself and said with as much confidence as she could muster, 'I must have the Mystery of Fire. I'm prepared to risk *anything*.'

Cholos winked conspiratorially at the Brisnings and said to Elowen, 'Risk anything? That is rash talk, the sort of talk that might get you killed.'

'I'm not afraid,' said Elowen, not entirely truthfully.

'Not yet, perhaps,' he said. He leant down and picked up a piece of reddish volcanic rock. 'This is the Mystery of Fire, forged in the mountain's fiery bowel. Do you desire it?'

'Yes,' said Elowen eagerly.

Cholos held it out to her, only to pull it away as she reached out to take it. He laughed. 'I do not surrender my possessions so lightly. Are you prepared to risk your life for this and for the Bolcán Stone?'

Elowen wavered for a second before the memory of Batu and Chinua came to her; for their sakes if nothing else, she could not back out now. She said, 'Yes.'

'Then I am satisfied,' he said, smirking. 'Come closer.'

Elowen stepped forward, her feet clattering onto the iron bars of the grill. Diggory cried out a warning but before she could react, the ground beneath her feet fell away. She found herself sliding down a narrow, smooth-bottomed tunnel.

She dropped feet-first into a cave. It was dark, the only light produced by sparkling crystals in the rock and phosphorescent fungi growing in crevices. Scorch marks stained the cave's rough walls and menacing stalagmites rose from the floor. The heat made it hard to breathe. The cave smelt like a charnel house and the undisturbed air left Elowen with a sulphurous taste in her mouth.

She heard distant laughter and looked up. She saw the grate some thirty feet above her, through which Cholos and the Brisnings peered, laughing and jeering.

'Survive the cave and I swear I'll give you the Mystery of Fire,' said Cholos in a mock solemn tone. 'I'll let you take the Bolcán Stone as well.'

Some instinct made the hairs on the back of Elowen's neck stand up. There was a brooding presence in the cave. Fear sharpened her senses. Her eyesight adjusted to the dim light. Heaps of jewels and weapons littered the cave, and half-gnawed bones, mostly *human* bones. Elowen saw a large tooth, the size of her forearm, within the bones. It looked like a canine tooth, long and sharp-tipped.

Elowen noticed part of the ground was moving. Bending down, she saw dozens of salamanders, all writhing in white ooze. She felt sick and frightened. Shadows on the other side of the cave moved and took shape. Elowen heard breathing. Something was there, something alive. When it emerged from the shadows, it was a creature beyond Elowen's most feverish nightmares. The Wyvern.

As tall as two men, the Wyvern stretched out its huge bat-like wings and swirled its barbed tail. It had two muscular legs with taloned feet and its skin resembled armoured plates, gold and red in colour. Piercing amber-coloured eyes shone from its serpent head and it opened its mouth to reveal a host of vicious teeth, although a jagged stub of tooth jutted from where a canine should have been.

Elowen sensed the Wyvern's malice and wickedness. It

was alive, flesh and blood but in some way unnatural. The salamanders swarmed around the Wyvern, who knelt down and licked them, its long tongue spreading sticky ooze. It glared at Elowen like a hungry cat facing a cornered mouse. Without trying to, without wanting to, Elowen *Linked* with the Wyvern. It was painful, causing throbbing pressure behind her eyes.

Have you come to prove your courage by fighting me?

Elowen shook her head. 'I've not come to fight. I've no quarrel with you. I don't want to hurt you.'

The Wyvern made a curious, unsettling snorting sound. *But I want to hurt you.*

With a bellowing roar, the Wyvern lunged at Elowen. She leapt to one side, avoiding the snapping, slavering mouth. The Wyvern's tail whip-lashed, missing Elowen's head by inches and smashing the stalagmite behind her into a shower of splinters.

Breathing hard and outstretching its wings, the Wyvern scowled at Elowen. *There is nowhere to hide. Others have come here before you, great warriors. All died. I am the oldest of my kin. Long ago it was prophesied that I cannot be harmed by any weapon forged by the hands of Men.*

Elowen kept moving, dodging behind the stalagmites, trying to keep her distance from the creature, trying to buy time to think, to decide what to do. There was nowhere to run to and she clearly could not reach the grate far above her. She had no weapons, so a physical fight against the Wyvern would be hopeless.

She tried to remain calm, feeling the Earthsoul's energy flow through her body. The golden threads glowed and pul-

58

sated. The Wyvern attacked again, this time lifting from the ground, its wings flapping furiously. It dived at Elowen, mouth slavering, its hawk-like talons gleaming. She mustered all her strength, surrendering her whole body, every aspect of her being, into controlling the Earthsoul. The golden threads wrapped around the Wyvern, holding it in mid-air. It stared at Elowen, eyes burning with anger and confusion. She felt as though the struggle to control the golden threads would break her. The effort stretched her muscles, crushed her bones. The sound of rushing blood pounded in her ears, louder than any drum. She fought on, enduring the pain, and at last the Wyvern yielded and was thrown back across the cave.

The creature landed heavily, skewering its left wing on a stalagmite. It lay on its back, spitting and bellowing, trying in vain to free its wing. Elowen knelt on the wet, slimy ground. The effort of the fight had been immense, but she stood and cautiously approached the Wyvern. In the corner of her eye, she saw the dagger-sized tooth on the ground. She picked it up.

Although the Wyvern remained pinned down by its wing, Elowen kept her distance. She said, 'Do you yield?'

The creature stopped struggling and threw her a baleful glare. *You have not defeated me yet. Prepare to die.*

The Wyvern pounced at Elowen, his wing ripping from the stalagmite in a spray of blood, skin and bone. Its jaws widened to bite Elowen's legs, but she moved swifter and used the tooth as a weapon. The tip pierced the creature's skin, driving through the skull. The Wyvern exhaled once, shuddered and collapsed in a broken, lifeless heap.

Elowen looked down at the corpse: the salamanders crawled all over it, licking and nuzzling, as though trying to bring it back from the dead. Killing normally sickened and appalled her, but this time was different. Energy swelled within her. She felt strong, and proud to be strong. She had shown her skill as an Adept. She thought again of her mother. In her mind she repeated, *I am not like her, I am not like her.*

A plaintive cry carried down from above; the grate in the ceiling of the cave opened and through it dropped a rope. Understanding the purpose, Elowen took a firm grip of the rope and allowed herself to be pulled up. Rough hands yanked her back into the cavern. Diggory, his face alight with relief, tried to help her to her feet but the Brisnings dragged him away.

Cholos hauled Elowen upright, his burning eyes as fierce as those of the Wyvern. He spat in her face. 'Adept witch. You have slain that which was dearest to me!'

'The Mystery and the Bolcán Stone are mine,' said Elowen, refusing to be intimidated. 'You promised, you swore.'

Cholos snarled and pushed her away. With a bitter laugh he said, 'I swear all the time, but I never give away my possessions. You've had a wasted trip, girl. And you and your friend shall pay for the damage you've caused me.'

The Brisnings lined up in front of Elowen and Diggory, all armed with war hammers. Cholos said, 'Kill them.'

Zwerg attacked first. Diggory put himself in front of Elowen and shoulder-barged the Brisning to the ground before he could strike with his hammer. Diggory fell upon him and silenced the Brisning with a hard punch to the jaw.

As Diggory stood, nursing his hand, the other two Brisnings joined the fray, yelling battle cries as they attacked. From the pile of weapons, Diggory picked up a wooden shield and deflected their blows but he staggered backwards, shaken and unbalanced. Elowen moved to help him but she felt a sweaty, strong arm around her neck. Cholos's hot, onion-laced breath blew into her face.

'I'll enjoy killing you,' he said. Elowen felt the icy tip of a knife against her neck. 'The Mystery of Fire is mine. It will always be mine. You'll never find the Tree of Life.'

The Elemental's grip was incredibly strong. Elowen tried to resist but to no avail. The fight with the Wyvern left her too tired to rouse and control the golden threads. She glimpsed Diggory falling to the floor, holding the shield up against the Brisnings' hammer blows. They were both lost…

Cholos grunted and loosened his grip. Without hesitation, Elowen stamped on his foot and kicked him away. He ripped off a handful of fur from her coat as she fell. One of the Brisnings attacking Diggory yelled out in pain and fell backwards, clutching his forehead. Into the cavern burst Bryna, announcing her arrival with an ululating cry. She carried her sling in one hand and her wooden club in the other.

The only conscious Brisning swung his war hammer at the Khiltoi, but Bryna easily dodged the blow and then knocked him down with a single strike of her club.

'Bryna!' said Elowen. 'What are you doing here?'

'I could not sit idly by and wait for your return.'

Cholos crawled to his forge, his forehead dripping blood.

He swore and said to Bryna, 'I thought I'd warned you cursed tree-dwellers to stay away from here.'

'Your threats and warnings are empty now,' said Bryna. 'Your beast is dead.'

Diggory picked up one of the Brisning's war hammers and strode over to the prostrate Elemental. His face glowed red and he said, 'You deserve to die.'

'NO!' said Elowen. 'Not like this.'

Diggory closed his eyes and tossed the hammer away. 'But he tried to *kill* you.'

'He's right, Elowen,' said Bryna. 'Cholos has befouled the forest for too long. No good can come of allowing him to live. A cleaved head no longer plots. You must do this, Elowen. Finish the task.'

Bryna handed Elowen her club and gestured towards Cholos. Elowen remembered the feeling of power she had experienced in the Wyvern's cave. Intoxicating. Exhilarating. The thrill of possessing the power of life and death in her hands. A voice in her head called out, *Kill him. Kill him.* The golden threads formed around her, faint, thin but discernible. Any tiredness left her. She felt strong again.

She looked down at Cholos. He lay at her mercy. Sprawled on the floor, bloodied and trembling, she felt a sudden swell of pity. She handed the club back to Bryna. 'I'll take the Mystery of Fire and the Bolcán Stone, but I don't need to take his life. I'm not a murderer.'

Elowen picked up the Mystery. Despite being honeycombed with holes, it felt surprisingly heavy. It tingled in her hand. She brushed her fingers over the stone and discovered some faintly scrawled symbols on one side. Bryna peered at it and said, 'These are runes of the ancient forest language.'

'Do you understand them?' said Elowen.

'No, only Bandraoi could make sense of such things. You must take it to her.'

Meanwhile, Diggory picked up the Bolcán Stone and handed it to Bryna, who held it up admiringly. 'Never did I dream that I would see this.'

'You are all so *proud*, aren't you?' said Cholos. He heaved himself upright, wiping the blood from his forehead and nose. 'Enjoy your moment of triumph, for it shall be brief indeed. You can do nothing to stem the coming tide. The enemies you try to resist are too powerful.'

'So we should just submit to Prester John?' said Elowen.

'His victory is inevitable,' said Cholos.

'You are a traitor and a coward,' said Diggory. 'Stay here and rot.'

'Forget him,' said Elowen. 'He's not a danger to us now.'

Cholos grinned evilly, with an expression on his face that Elowen did not like. 'The end is close. I sense it. The world is changing. The Last Days are coming.'

His words sent a shiver down Elowen's spine. Cholos stood and watched as they left, his eyes like flames, his face animated by a spiteful smile.

*

A city of tents and wagons stretched across the meadow. Campfires sparkled like stars; the fitful wind twisted the smoke into spirals. Just two days earlier, the meadow had slumbered, left quiet and dormant by winter's grip but not snowbound, cosseted by the warmer winds blowing from the south. But now a furious hubbub carried from the camp: the shouted drills of musketeers and pikemen, the chinking of armourers' and blacksmiths' tools, the neighing of horses, woodworkers sawing.

Lord Lucien stood outside his wagon, positioned on a small bluff on the camp's edge. He looked away from the three figures, two Redeemers, the other short and wizened beneath rags, who inched their way towards him along the narrow path leading up from the meadow. He did not want to have to acknowledge their presence until the last. Instead, he let his gaze drift over the camp. Despite his black mood, it pleased him to see the extent and condition of the army. Two weeks earlier, the host had set out from its muster at the Ulsacro, announcing through triumphal songs and pamphlets that it was marching to confront rebels on the border with Prevennis. Yet it was a deception. A week into the journey the Grand Army rested at Iruzur. The next night, three quarters of the force, including the strongest regiments and many Redeemers, broke camp in secret and marched east. Only a small rump of the original army continued north the next day.

Lord Lucien had led his army across a carefully plotted route, avoiding all major towns and cities, for secrecy was of the utmost importance to Prester John's plan. They finally camped at Latibulum, a mere day's march from Prester John's winter residence at Inganno. There they waited for the signal to advance and spring the trap.

So far, the plan had gone smoothly and Lord Lucien knew

he had every reason to be satisfied, but a cold feeling grew in his stomach. Troubling thoughts, *doubts*, tormented him. He prayed ceaselessly to God to soothe his raging mind, but received no succour. His mind returned constantly to Elowen and he found it difficult to dwell on anything else. His desire to find her, to have one more chance of reasoning with her, gave a special urgency to finding the second Mystery. His search had proven frustrating and hitherto fruitless. He had summoned to the Ulsacro mystics, scholars and natural philosophers in the hope they would unlock the secrets of the Mystery of Earth. But beyond a vague notion that the little clay tablet denoted a location to the east, they failed to discover anything substantial. So, Lord Lucien turned to other methods: without Prester John's knowledge, he had sent out patrols of Redeemers and Egregores across the eastern lands seeking clues to aid his search. Scouts were due to return that very evening and Lord Lucien waited impatiently for news. But first he had to greet his Master. The news of the Patriarch's visit had surprised and unsettled Lord Lucien. He did not welcome it, and guilt at his disloyalty tore at his soul.

As the Patriarch approached, flanked by his Redeemer bodyguards, Lord Lucien bowed.

'Forgive my clumsy disguise, my friend,' said Prester John, throwing off the beggars' rags, to reveal his simple woollen cowl and cape. 'My visit here must remain a secret.'

Lord Lucien suppressed a gasp of shock as he looked at Prester John. Wispy strips of Cold Iron discoloured his cheeks and forehead. His yellowing eyes watered and weeping sores encrusted his lips and nose. Dry skin sagged from his bones. Lord Lucien settled himself and said, 'You must be weary after your journey from the Winter Palace at Inganno.'

'An old man is always weary,' said Prester John, smiling to reveal his grey, rotten teeth. 'I have been softened by the warmth, wine and fine food of the Ulsacro, it seems.'

'Your strength is undiminished, I am sure,' said Lord Lucien, hiding the surprise and disgust at the Patriarch's atrophy. Prester John was increasingly dependent on the Cold Iron within his flesh and bones to sustain him, and for all the gifts it conferred, the Patriarch's face showed the cost of its use. Lord Lucien cautioned his Master against excessive infusions but Prester John always swept aside such concerns. Moreover, Lord Lucien could not deny that as the Earthsoul's potency dwindled, the power derived through Cold Iron increased. In Gorefayne, the Society for the Propagation of Pious Labour drove their thousands of slaves to dig deeper and deeper mines. They toiled to produce the quantities of Cold Iron demanded by the Mother Church. Prester John, and the Brotherhood of Redemption, wove threads of pure Cold Iron into their skin, veins and bones, thriving, exulting, on the strength it supplied. Lord Lucien buried his misgivings and went on to say, 'I am deeply honoured to greet you here, but forgive me for being curious as to the purpose of your visit.'

Prester John dabbed delicately at his streaming eyes. In a tinder-dry, raspy voice he said, 'It should be little wonder. I see you in the mirror much less these days.'

Unnerved by the reply, Lord Lucien hesitated. 'My labours absorb me utterly.'

Prester John waved a hand. 'Say nothing of it, I understand completely. The Almighty demands much of all pious followers in these tumultuous times. Although it is a blessing to serve Him, our labours leave us drained.'

'It is so, My Lord.'

'But fear not, loyal friend. Our impending victory shall provide you with the rest you crave and so deserve.'

'If God wills it.'

'He does, my friend, He does,' said Prester John, folding his hands. 'God works through me. I am His instrument. I know His will, and it guides my actions. I know He appreciates your faithful service in His name. And yet, I am concerned for you.'

'Concerned, my Lord?'

'Yes, I sense you are *distracted*. This I have detected, ever since your return from the accursed Orok lands.'

Lord Lucien selected his words carefully. 'My service to you has never faltered.'

'I do not claim it is so, yet your obsession with finding the child both perplexes and troubles me. What threat does she pose?'

The mere mention of Elowen rattled Lord Lucien. 'My Lord, she is strong—'

'But you possess the Mystery of Earth,' said Prester John, pointing forcefully at Lord Lucien, his voice growing louder. 'What hope do our opponents have of finding the Tree of Life now? Save for a few scattered loyalists, we have destroyed the Illuminati, and the first Mystery, the essential step to following the path, is forever out of their reach. Even if the child is an Adept, of what consequence is it? We have slain hundreds of Adepts, all more powerful and wiser than her. You misjudge her strength. Perhaps the memory of her mother clouds your judgement?'

Lord Lucien paused, not wanting to answer the question. He said, 'If she could be persuaded to fight alongside us, as her mother once did, then she might prove a valuable ally.'

Prester John pursed his lips. 'We have no need of her. Do not waste another moment searching for this girl. One day, the Mother Church *will* discover the Tree of Life and destroy it, but until that day, our priority is to eliminate the final remnants of resistance to my rule. I want all your attention on the battle. This is my command. Do you defy me?'

Lord Lucien bowed. 'Never, my Master.'

Prester John coughed, his chest heaving. With effort, he made the sign of the blessing. 'You are my most faithful servant, Lord Lucien. Your loyalty reassures me and pleases God. I return now to Inganno and leave you to prepare for the battle to come. When next we meet, it shall be to celebrate victory. God be with you, my friend.'

Lord Lucien watched as Prester John, flanked by the Redeemers, disappeared into the night. The Patriarch's visit had been a test, an examination of his loyalty. Prester John had never been comfortable with Lord Lucien's friendship with Athena Parthenos; perhaps he foresaw a threat in the existence of Elowen, a fear of powers beyond his control.

An unseen tear, born of guilt and frustration trickled down Lord Lucien's cheek. He wanted to serve his Master and follow his instruction as keenly as he followed the word of God. But in his need, his *obsession*, to find Elowen he felt compelled to defy Prester John. It worried him that the Patriarch believed that the crushing of the Sanctuary of the Illuminati diminished the danger of the enemy finding the Tree of Life. Lord Lucien thought a risk still existed. If by some miracle Elowen or one of the Illuminati managed to find the Tree, could his Master's accomplishments and conquests be undone? He tried to push such fears to the back of his mind; the genius and strength of Prester John surely guaranteed victory. But quietly, Lord Lucien resolved to continue his search for the Tree of Life.

He heard the pounding of horses' hooves and four Redeemers emerged from over the brow of the bluff. They nimbly dismounted and bowed in front of Lord Lucien. One of them said, 'We bring news, Lord Lucien. The Egregore searching the Altheart Forest near Teorann has been destroyed.'

'*Destroyed?* How?' said Lord Lucien. This was unexpected. Lord Lucien considered the Egregores to be his Master's finest creations. Flawless machines driven by Prester John's will and control of Cold Iron.

'I witnessed the signs of a fierce struggle,' said the Redeemer, sounding reluctant to bring such tidings. 'Before the Egregore was silenced it exposed an enemy; we all felt a cry of great power. Its cry carried across the forest. We heard two words repeated within the message. The *girl*. We hastened but, being five miles west, we only reached the Egregore to find its ruin.'

'And no sign of…the girl?'

'There were many tracks, my Lord,' said the Redeemer. 'Khiltoi tracks, I believe. I ordered a small patrol of our brothers to remain in the region, searching for other clues. I trust I have not done ill.'

'No, it was a wise choice,' said Lord Lucien. Many years before, Lord Lucien had led an expedition to exterminate the Khiltoi, and despite many successes, he knew some of them had survived, like cockroaches.

'More we have discovered, Lord Lucien,' said the Redeemer. 'We questioned peasants who dwell close to the Altheart's border. They spoke of a haunted place in the forest, a fiery hilltop they named the Ogonberg. It is the dwelling place of a demon, or so they believe in their superstitious ways. We were following that lead before the Egregore's call summoned us. The peasants gave us clear directions to find this hill. Perhaps it is the place you are looking for.'

Yes, perhaps it is, thought Lord Lucien, a quiver of excitement in his stomach. He said to the Redeemer, 'We must set forth at first light. Instruct Hohenheim to accompany us, and tell him to bring his *creations*.'

As the Redeemers hurried to carry out the order, Lord Lucien knelt down and made a silent prayer to the Almighty. A prayer for strength, for the courage to follow the path he felt compelled, perhaps against reason, to follow. Haunted by the memory of Elowen's face, he needed to find her. In his dreams, he saw the flashing eyes of Athena Parthenos, whom the terrified Oroks named *Burilgi Maa*. Elowen possessed her mother's eyes. He would find no peace until she stood by his side, just as her mother had done, or until she was dead.

CHAPTER FOUR

Triumph of Hohenheim

By the time Elowen, Bryna and Diggory reached the Dachaigh, the last of the sun's rays had draped over the hill. The frigid wind bustled through the snowbound trees and blew icy blasts across the settlement. The roundhouses seemed to huddle together and puff themselves up like sparrows trying to keep warm.

A wooden gallows now stood at the foot of the hill. Two headless bodies hung upside down from thick rope. Their bloodstained robes flapped in the wind: Redeemers.

'In the name of God,' said Diggory as he stared up at the gibbet. 'What has happened here?'

Grim-faced, Bryna said, 'I know not, but I sense we'll have the answer soon enough. Hurry.'

Elowen kept thinking about Batu and Chinua. Were they still safe? She had fulfilled her part of the bargain; she hoped the Khiltoi would not fail to honour theirs.

Ignoring the guards' suspicious, withering glares, they passed through the blockades and gates. To Elowen's surprise, Bryna picked up a narrow path that turned away from the settlement and over the brow of the hill.

'Where are we going?' said Elowen.

'To the Nemeton,' said Bryna. 'It is the most sacred place in the Dachaigh. There the knowledge of our tribe is carved into the stones and trees, past and present as one. Ceannard has summoned the tribe.'

'Is it to do with the dead Redeemers?' said Elowen.

Bryna ignored the question and went on to say, 'When we get to the Nemeton, remain silent. It is where we perform our rituals and submit our offerings, and through them the Nemeton is kept strong.'

'Rituals and offerings,' said Diggory to Elowen. 'Sounds like witchcraft to me.'

Elowen rolled her eyes and whispered to Diggory, 'Mind what you say, we don't want to insult them.'

'Sorry, but this whole place gives me the creeps. I get the feeling we're walking into another trap.'

'We'll be fine,' said Elowen, trying to reassure him, although she shared his doubts. She trusted Bryna, but she was less sure about the other Khiltoi, especially Corcoran.

They descended the far side of the hill and came to a grove of silver birch trees. Thick balls of mistletoe nested in the leafless branches. There was no undergrowth beneath the trees, just a carpet of damp grass. Interspersed amongst the birches were many small wooden carvings, some of animals and birds, others showed images of gods and spirits. At the far end of the grove grew an ancient and gnarled oak tree. Moss smothered its bole and many of its roots had broken free of the earth and splayed like the knobbly fingers of a venerable hand. A ring of standing stones circled the oak tree and two torches flanked it, their flames vivid in the failing light.

Elowen had a liminal sense of standing upon the threshold of another world, the colours and shapes softer, sounds muted, as though the grove belonged to a dream and not the real world. The tribe gathered in the grove, and they faced the oak tree, their heads bowed. Bandraoi addressed them, her words embellished by elaborate hand gestures. Behind Bandraoi lurked Ceannard and Corcoran.

'What's going on?' Elowen said Bryna in a hushed voice.

'The *taghta* is invoking the spirits of the ancestors. She seeks their guidance on matters concerning the tribe. There have been many mysterious signs and portents of late, and the ancestors help us to interpret them.'

Bandraoi became aware of the arrival of Elowen and her companions. She cried out and beckoned to them. The tribe parted, forming a straight pathway to the oak tree. Bandraoi's blue-grey eyes sparkled with anticipation. 'You have returned!'

Corcoran pushed in front of the *taghta*, his face screwed up in surprise and anger. He poked a finger towards Elowen and Diggory and said, 'You're not welcome here. Your very presence is sacrilege.'

'Hold your tongue, Corcoran,' said Bandraoi.

'No, they've brought death to the forest.'

'What do you mean?' said Elowen.

Bandraoi shared an anxious look with Bryna. 'One of our patrols discovered *drouks* close to the Dachaigh. Our warriors slew two of the foul creatures, the other *drouks* fled.'

With a shiver, Elowen remembered the decapitated Redeemers hanging from the gallows.

'Three of our brave warriors were slain, poisoned by the

diseased blades of the enemy,' said Corcoran. 'We need no further proof that the minions of the *Moljnir* are closing in. These *colgreachs* bring disaster upon us all.'

Bryna pushed Elowen out of the way and held out the Bolcán Stone. 'You all know what this is.'

A ripple of excitement rushed through the crowd as they recognised the artefact.

'The ancestors be blessed,' said Ceannard reaching out to grasp the stone.

Bryna handed it to Bandraoi and glared at Corcoran. She said, 'You should thank Elowen, for it was through her bravery that the stone has been returned to us. And you repay her with baseless accusations and threats.'

'We have only your word on that,' said Corcoran. 'For all we know she could be in league with Cholos.'

Bryna gave him a look of utter contempt. 'You speak from ignorance. Elowen defeated the foul Wyvern, a task beyond any of our finest warriors. She's done as she promised. She's proven her worth.'

'Yes, it cannot be doubted she is a *bana-buidhseach*,' said Bandraoi, caressing the Bolcán Stone.

'What about Batu and Chinua?' said Elowen. 'Are they safe?'

Ceannard nodded. 'Yes, we Khiltoi never renege on our bargains. As you've returned the stone to us, the Oroks will be released unharmed.'

'But what of the other prize you sought?' said Bandraoi.

Feeling self-conscious, Elowen handed her the Mystery of Fire and said, 'Bryna believed you'd understand the runes written upon it.'

The *taghta* held it at arm's length to read the writing, squinting as she did so. 'These are old runes, not used in living memory. They are faint and I cannot be certain of their meaning, but my interpretation is that they read: *only the fiery tongues of Omphalos may read me*. The full meaning may be obscure, but to discover the secrets of this rock, your destination is clear.'

'Omphalos,' said Elowen, almost talking to herself as Bandraoi handed the Mystery back to her. 'It seems I'm fated to go there.'

'Yes, and I believe you should not go alone,' said Bandraoi. 'We Khiltoi should accompany you.'

Ceannard puffed out his cheeks and said, 'In these dangerous days, we should look to protecting our own borders. Let the *colgreachs* go free, but I see no need to venture into foreign lands and to interfere in matters that do not concern us. We are safer here.'

Bryna said, 'I am not *taghta* but it is clear to me no coincidence brought Elowen, a *bana-buidhseach* to our land. We have had the summons, as have all Eldar. We must accept.'

'And will you, *female*, lead our warriors against the enemy?' said Corcoran. 'It will take more than this sapling's conjuring tricks to defeat the *Moljnir*.'

'This sapling, as you name her, was brave enough to enter the Wyvern's cave,' said Bryna in a fiery voice. 'You cannot claim the same.'

Corcoran's hands made fists as he fought to conquer his fury.

'Bryna is right,' said Bandraoi. 'As long as the *Moljnir* endures, we'll never be safe. More *drouks* and *námhaids* will

75

come. In the face of their onslaught, we are surely doomed. We must confront this evil to have any chance of survival. Corcoran, you are our finest warrior, will you undertake to do this on behalf of your people?'

Seemingly caught between pride at Bandraoi's flattery and frustration at being manoeuvred into doing something he did not want to do, Corcoran cast his eyes down and said, 'If Ceannard wills it, I'll go.'

As though buckling beneath the responsibility, Ceannard shifted his weight from one foot to another and crossed his arms. 'I'm reluctant to leave the Dachaigh undefended.'

Bryna said, 'Corcoran could muster a hundred warriors to march to Omphalos and still leave the settlement well defended.'

'Is this so, Corcoran?' asked Ceannard, sounding as though he would be very glad if it were not true.

Corcoran's gaze moved upright as he made mental calculations. 'We would not be able to patrol the forest but it should ensure enough warriors remain for the defence of the Dachaigh, and to help with the crops if we have not returned by spring.'

Ceannard looked uncomfortable. Picking at his mossy beard he said, 'The crops? I hadn't thought of that. I fear Prester John but famine is a greater danger still. We shouldn't act rashly, perhaps it'd be wiser to wait and see what the next few days bring.'

'Time is already short,' said Bandraoi, her voice now stirring to a shout. 'As I have counselled all along, we must answer the summons. If we stand alone we are ruined. We must fight alongside those sworn to oppose the *Moljnir*.'

Many of the watching Khiltoi shouted their approval. Corcoran, despite eyeing Elowen with suspicion, finally nodded his agreement.

Ceannard swallowed. 'I approve this *expedition*, may the ancestors bestow their blessings upon it. Corcoran, muster your warriors and be ready to leave at first light.'

'I wish to go too,' said Bryna.

'That's out of the question,' said Ceannard.

'I need warriors beside me, not plant tenders,' said Corcoran.

'I've seen so little of the world,' said Bryna. 'If I am to be *taghta* one day, I need to experience more. The lands beyond the forest should not be a mystery to me.'

'Bryna should go,' said Bandraoi. 'She is young and the time has come for her to prove her worth to the tribe.'

Ceannard admitted defeat with a tired wave of his hand. 'Go, Bryna, if that is what you desire.'

'Then it is settled,' said Bandraoi, winking at Elowen. The *taghta* led the Khiltoi in a final blessing, invoking the ancestors and the numerous gods that protected the trees, plants, stones and waters of the forest.

As the ceremony finished and the gathering returned to the settlement, Bryna took Elowen and Diggory to the Chief's hall. There they found the Oroks waiting for them. Batu sprung to his feet when they entered and greeted them with a cry of relief. Even Chinua beamed happily.

'You are safe,' said Batu. 'I feared for you both. And the Mystery of Fire, you have it?'

Elowen held it up for him to see, and explained what Bandraoi had told her.

'So, we must go to Omphalos,' he said.

'Yes, and the Khiltoi are coming with us,' said Elowen. She told him about Ceannard's decision. Batu looked concerned and spoke to Chinua in the Orok language. Chinua frowned but stayed silent.

Flashing a wary glance at Bryna, Batu said, 'This is not to my liking. We need to travel in secret, not as part of a warband.'

'We Khiltoi know of paths hidden to others,' said Bryna. 'In happier days, our forefathers often travelled in the lands south of the Altheart. We'll take the path through the Petrified Forest.'

'The Petrified Forest!' said Batu. 'I should be reluctant to go that way. It is a haunted region, one Oroks have always avoided.'

'That is because you do not know it,' said Bryna. 'Our ancestors left markers in the land for us to follow. We'll be safe and it'll prove difficult for any enemies to find us there.'

'Perhaps, but I would never underestimate the Redeemers,' said Batu.

*

The Khiltoi warriors mustered at dawn. Tall, powerfully built and armed with a variety of clubs, stone-tipped spears, bows and slings, they looked formidable. Elowen saw that each warrior had washed their hair in lime and drawn it back from the forehead to the crown and the nape of the neck, leaving it thickened, like a horse's mane. But for

Elowen a nagging doubt remained. For all the courage and physical strength of the Khiltoi, compared to the enemy's guns and cannon, their weapons were primitive. In their native forest, they would be deadly in skirmishes and ambushes against any foe. In pitched battle, the outcome was less certain and far less promising.

It was snowing heavily, the sky blowing down thick puffs of flakes. Elowen nervously tapped her pocket, inside of which nestled the Mystery of Fire. Diggory waited beside her, shivering and teeth chattering. He said, 'It's freezing standing here. Why are we waiting?'

'We await Bandraoi,' said Bryna. 'The *taghta* must give the company her blessing, and as we head into the southern lands, we may be glad of it.'

'What are they like, the southern lands?' said Elowen.

'Great civilisations once spawned there, flourishing in fertile lands blessed by the sun,' said Bryna. 'But by order of the Mother Church, the *Moljnir's* hordes tore through them like a plague, slaying, burning, pillaging. There are few people there now, but the eyes of the enemy are still watchful.'

Bandraoi appeared, her cloak billowing in the wind. She carried mistletoe in one hand and made signs in front of the company. 'May the ancestors bless you and your path. Let their power surge through you. Rise bright and clear.'

She stepped aside and Corcoran lifted his obsidian-bladed club and shouted, 'Suithad! Be watchful at all times, be ready to fight. Our people depend on you. Do not fail them. Glory to our ancestors. Death to our enemies.'

Swinging the club above his head and making an ululating cry that the other warriors imitated, Corcoran strode down the path. He glared at Elowen and Diggory and said, 'I suffer your presence on this journey but I consider you little more than worthless baggage. If you slow us down or irritate me, I'll cast you aside.'

Diggory looked at Elowen. 'This is going to be fun.'

The Khiltoi set a fierce pace as they pressed south through the forest. For Elowen, days rolled into other days, they existed as jumbled collections of moments and sensations: the wind blowing waves of powdery snow around the tree trunks; her feet sinking into deep drifts; aching muscles; freezing nights sheltering in slender tents.

Within three days of leaving the Dachaigh, they reached the southern tip of the Altheart, which was marked by a broad, sparkling river. A hilly and rock-strewn land lay ahead. Sheltered by a line of alder trees, the Khiltoi warriors gathered on the riverbank. Corcoran said in solemn tones, 'This is the ford. When we cross here, we leave our land and pass into the outside world. Savour this moment, for we do not know if we shall ever return to the Altheart as mortals.'

'There's nothing like some good words of encouragement,' said Diggory to Elowen.

'It's getting late,' said Bryna, pointing west to the sinking sun. 'It would be safer to camp here tonight and ford the river in the morning.'

Elowen thought Corcoran was going to disagree with Bryna, something he did constantly, but the obvious sense of her suggestion convinced him and he concurred with a grunt.

They made camp around a central fire. The Khiltoi carried

a number of simple tents, using poles lashed together with rope and animal skins tied to them. Elowen shared a tent with Diggory, exposing her once again to his varied range of snores. She kept the Mystery of Fire in her right hand, her fingers tracing over its rough edges. Despite her tiredness, her mind kept ticking over troubling thoughts, blocking out sleep. Unsettled, she tried to engage Diggory in conversation and prodded his back to wake him.

'Do you think we can get to Omphalos without being found by the Redeemers?' she said.

Diggory groaned and fidgeted, banging his elbow into Elowen in the process. He yawned widely and said, 'We've dodged them so far. Even if they do find us, I reckon they'll have a hard time getting past these Khiltoi. Remember those two Redeemers hanging outside the Dachaigh.'

Elowen remembered their headless corpses with a shiver. 'I hope you're right. I wonder what Omphalos will be like.'

Yawning again, Diggory said, 'We'll find out when we get there, I suppose. *If* we get there.'

'I wish I knew why I have to take the Mystery of Fire there.'

'Bandraoi didn't know?'

'If she did, she certainly didn't say.'

'I wouldn't worry about it then.'

'I do worry though. I worry I'm not capable of doing what has to be done.'

'You're strong,' said Diggory, his voice fading to a sleepy whisper.

'Perhaps I've been lucky so far. What do you think?'

Diggory's snores dashed any hopes of an answer, let alone

a reassuring one. Elowen closed her eyes. She loitered on the borders of sleep, images and sounds born in dreams plastered on the waking world. Panicky shouts joined that collage of senses. Groggily, Elowen realised the shouting belonged very much to the real world. Batu pushed through the entrance of the tent. The Orok said, 'The Teredonas have seen something. Come and see.'

Followed by a dazed Diggory, Elowen crawled out of the tent, gasping at the sudden exposure to the cold wind. As she stood, she realised all the Khiltoi warriors were awake, out of their tents and pointing at the sky. Elowen's gaze followed the direction of their hands.

In a gap between the broken clouds, a reddish-white star shone as bright as the full moon.

'What is it?' said Elowen.

'A portent,' said Bryna. 'The star changed this very night.'

'You woke me up to look at a *star*?' said Diggory.

'The stars help us to divine the future,' said Bryna. 'Men can scorch the earth, poison the rivers and seas, but the stars remain forever out of reach.'

Diggory pinched the bridge of his nose and closed his eyes. 'So what does this star tell us?'

'I know not,' said Bryna. 'If only Bandraoi were here, she could read the signs of the star. Look how brightly it burns!'

Corcoran stomped through the camp, urging quiet. 'Hush this din; shouts might draw enemies to us. Return to your tents. Star or no star, you must rest ahead of the journey to come.'

'But it is a sign that doom is at hand,' said one of the warriors. 'One of these stars was seen just before the *glac'har*.'

82

'Hold your tongue unless you want to spend the rest of the night on sentry duty,' said Corcoran.

Accompanied by a hum of worried whispers, the Khiltoi returned to their tents. Only Bryna lingered, her neck craned, staring at the brilliant white star.

*

'The stars look strange tonight.'

A Redeemer pointed skyward but Lord Lucien ignored him. He stood outside his wagon, looking at the Ogonberg. The hill vented steam and vapours, and brooded with malignant energy, a place untouched by order, control and civilisation, a place abandoned to brutish, capricious spirits. His heart skipped. This had to be it: the resting place of the Mystery of Fire.

Hohenheim the Alchemist had travelled with them in his windowless wagon. Lord Lucien hated the alchemist's very presence, and his eyes flashed over the obscene images that decorated the wagon: three circles of red, white and black in the centre of the sun, with a dragon beneath, biting his own tail; a robed man stood upon conjoined lions; a large toad surrounded by leaves and droplets of blood. Hateful, heretical symbols.

Lord Lucien ordered six Redeemers to remain behind to guard the wagons and the horses; the rest followed him up the path and into the entrance of the hill. As they stepped inside the narrow tunnel, heat enveloped them, the smoky air stripped of any wholesome qualities. A revolting smell of rotting flesh wafted.

A voice, echoing and varying greatly in pitch and volume with every word, greeted them. 'Who comes now to disturb my peace?'

As Lord Lucien and the Redeemers stepped into the cavern, a hideous figure emerged from the shadows to greet them, lame and ugly, misshapen as a lump of clay in unskilled hands. Fiery-tinged eyes told of sin and wicked thoughts. 'Ah, I can guess what it is you seek. I am Cholos.'

'The Mystery of Fire,' said Lord Lucien. 'Give it to me.'

'It is no longer in my possession,' said Cholos, his face twitching as he spoke.

Anger rose within Lord Lucien, his whole body tensed for violence. 'What do you mean? Are you not its guardian?'

'I was. The Mystery has been claimed, just a few days ago.'

'Claimed? By whom?'

'A child. They called her Elowen, I believe.'

'A curse upon you if you lie,' said Lord Lucien.

'I tell no lie,' said Cholos, taking a backward step.

Lord Lucien clenched his fists. Elowen had found the Mystery. Again she had defied him; again she had escaped him. 'And the girl still lives?'

'Aye, she took the Mystery and slaughtered my beloved,' he said, pointing down to a grate, down to some darkness where Lord Lucien did not wish to look. 'She has broken my heart.'

'Was she alone?'

Cholos shook his head. 'Nay, there was a lad with her, brave-hearted and doughty despite appearances. And one of the Khiltoi savages helped her too, foul brute. My Brisning servants fled in terror, so here I am, all alone now.'

'And where was the girl going?' pressed Lord Lucien.

'Returning to the Khiltoi nest, I suppose. Where she planned to go after that, I know not. She left only this.'

The fire Elemental handed Lord Lucien a piece of fur torn from Elowen's coat. An idea formed in Lord Lucien's mind.

'I can tell you no more,' said Cholos. 'So now I guess you wish to kill me.'

'Your guess is accurate,' said Lord Lucien, drawing his sword.

The Elemental laughed. 'My physical body is weak, but I am more than this jumble of feeble bones and oily flesh. I am of the fire of the hearth, the bright morning sun.'

Cholos took a step back and turned into a sudden ball of flame, which burned for a second and then vanished.

Lord Lucien and the Redeemers stood in a stunned silence, hardly believing what their eyes witnessed.

'Should we search the caves for him?' said one of the Redeemers.

'No, he is unimportant,' said Lord Lucien, wary of the Elemental's tricks. He looked down at the piece of fur from Elowen's coat he held in his hand. 'But we must consult with Hohenheim immediately.'

Lord Lucien strode out of the cavern, the Redeemers struggling to keep up with him. His anger at having lost the second Mystery mixed with grudging admiration of Elowen's courage and audacity. She truly was her mother's daughter, blessed with all her cunning and strength. If only he could find and persuade her that their destinies were entwined, that the path her mother had taken was the right one for her too. He had to find her, and she was not yet out of his grasp.

Lord Lucien approached the alchemist's wagon. As though he had expected the visit, Hohenheim pushed open the doors and descended the three steps to the ground. He wore fur-lined robes and a red hat. His skin had a faint yellow tinge, not tanned by the sun or wind but from some other less natural cause. His eyes were unsympathetic and topped by scarcely perceptible brows. With his long fingers, he stroked the corners of his thin, unyielding mouth.

'Hohenheim, I have need of your services,' said Lord Lucien. 'I have a task that requires a man of your talents.'

The alchemist bowed. 'You are too kind, my Lord. I'm a humble wandering sage. I do the best I can.'

Lord Lucien smiled his secret smile. Of the many words he could use to describe the alchemist, humble was the least of them. Lord Lucien knew the stories told about the alchemist. Murderer, some said. *Child* murderer, most said. But he needed Hohenheim. He held up the piece of fur. 'I wish to find the girl this belonged to. She could be far from here now, and there is no trail. Could one of your *creations* find her?'

Hohenheim moistened his lips with his tongue. 'Would it be necessary for this girl to die?'

'No. I want her found but not harmed. You once boasted of a creature that could send thoughts across distance. Was this idle talk?'

The alchemist rubbed his hands together. 'He is a marvel, proof of the ingenuity of Man. You must meet him.'

Hohenheim made a guttural cry and a creature crawled

out of the wagon. Lord Lucien looked on in disgust at the wretch spewed forth by the alchemist's twisted science. It was only two feet tall, and impossibly thin and hairless.

'This is Unheimlich, my greatest triumph,' said Hohenheim like a proud parent. 'Through him I believe I've unlocked God's secrets of life. I created him under perfect astrological conditions. I filled a bag with bones, seed, skin fragments and hair from several animals and birds, and with slivers of Cold Iron. I laid him in the ground for forty days and fed the growing embryo with blood, regularly and prudently. I used incantations recorded in ancient *grimoires* to spark life within him. He has the eyesight of a hawk and the agility of a cat. His bones and muscles are not restricted like those of Men. And he sees far with his mind. He can reach you over any distance. Here, I'll demonstrate. Please, Lord Lucien, lower your head.'

Warily, Lord Lucien did as Hohenheim asked. Like a shy infant, Unheimlich sidled closer to him and his cold, clammy fingers touched the top of Lord Lucien's head—the creature made the connection. Lord Lucien felt as though his mind and body were not his. His vision swayed, and he realised he was not seeing through his eyes, but through those of the creature. For one sickening moment, Lord Lucien was looking up at himself. Disorientated by the verminous being, he shook off Unheimlich's touch.

The slightest of smiles tugged at the corners of Hohenheim's lips. 'The connection is made. Now when Unheimlich has something to report you'll see as he sees.'

Still disconcerted by the experience, Lord Lucien said, 'How will he find the girl?'

'That's the easy part. His senses are unparalleled. Even the faintest smell is enough for him. Please, give him the piece of fur.'

Lord Lucien did so. Unheimlich knelt down and cradled the fur in his little hands. He first sniffed and then licked and slobbered over it like a dog. He stood and sprinted into the forest, his limbs moving like those of some demented spider.

'He has her scent,' said Hohenheim, tapping his fingertips together and gazing proudly at the gap in the trees into which the creature had vanished. 'He'll find her, I swear it. He never tires, nor slows. He'll run under sun and moon. He needs no food, no water. And when he finds her, she'll never see him, for he is cunning and can squeeze into the smallest of places.'

'And he will tell me when he finds the girl?'

'Be sure of it. Unheimlich will come to you like a vivid daydream. You'll see through his eyes, hear through his ears. Even if she is many miles away, he will track her down. She cannot escape him.'

'And what if she discovers the creature? If he fell into the hands of the enemy he could reveal much.'

'If Unheimlich is captured, he'll know what to do.'

Lord Lucien stewed with a mixture of repulsion and excitement. He worried he was betraying his conscience. Surely God did not mean for such things as Unheimlich to exist? But he swallowed his disgust and self-loathing. Hohenheim's abomination represented the best hope for finding Elowen, and surely it was God's will that she would be found.

88

- CHAPTER FIVE -

The Old Man of the Sea

The azure sea sparkled, the sun creating innumerable diamond-like specks of light on the rippling water. Gulls skimmed over the low, gurgling waves. The sky above loomed like a mirror to the expanse of water below: clean, crisp blue.

Bo stood at the bow of the *Husker Du*, enduring the morning watch. Squinting in the bright light, his eyes stung and juddered with tiredness. The creaking ropes and stays combined with the ship's groaning timbers to sing a seductive lullaby. Bo sucked in a mouthful of salty air, trying to settle his turbulent stomach and shaky legs, still wishing his feet were on dry land. Sailing brought him no pleasure. He hated the seasickness, the tedious work, the repugnant smell of the slop buckets, the wet clothes and broken sleep. But such hardships could be tolerated. He knew that the greatest challenges still awaited him, every fibre of his being sensed it. He wanted to be bold, to prove himself. He *needed* to prove himself.

Valbrand stood beside him, humming and frequently spitting into the sea, a picture of complete boredom. Hunting the rats that scurried around the hold had become the only vent for his restlessness and aggression, and he had already killed most of those. After a deep, melodramatic sigh, Valbrand said, 'God, how long is it going to take us to get to Omphalos? I want some action.'

'You mean you want some *fighting*,' said Bo.

'Aye, fighting focuses the mind and hones the body,' said Valbrand, slapping his stomach. With his thumb, he gestured to the crossbow fastened to his back. 'I haven't fired a shot in anger for many a long day. I feel guilty at neglecting my crossbow. It's a killing machine and a work of art, just like me.'

Bo laughed. 'You do seem to have been made for battle.'

'Battle is a challenge, and without a challenge a man goes slack.'

'I would have thought you had seen enough fighting to last a lifetime.'

Valbrand whistled. 'We've been busy, that's for sure. Think of all we've seen since we left Prevennis. Ironclads. The Beauteous Isle. The Kojin. The Sea Beggars. Not to mention those accursed balebeasts. I think the last few days are the first time I've been bored travelling with you.'

'Perhaps that is a good thing.'

Valbrand snorted. 'Doesn't feel like it. God, it all makes you think though. I've seen more of the world than I ever expected. My wife and daughter never left Prevennis. There's a whole world and they never got to see it. I used to tell our little girl stories about the sea, she loved those stories, especially the frightening ones with storms and monsters. You know, I'd spurn all the gold and jewels in the world just to have her sit on my lap again.'

'You must miss them terribly,' said Bo, wanting to say the right thing and wincing as he spoke, feeling his words sounded weak.

'Aye, but what's done is done and I've no more tears to shed,' he said, clearly regretting touching upon the subject. He made fists with his hands and pounded them together.

They had left the Beauteous Isle three days earlier, sailing across the vast blue expanse of the Mednoir Sea on an easterly course towards Omphalos. Surrounded by land, only the narrow Gap of Occidentem connected the sea to the Great Ocean, resulting in limited tides. It was a world away from the choppy, swollen brown waves of the northern seas, but Bo felt far from comfortable. The sea remained alien to him, forever inhospitable.

Black Francis worked the crew hard. Their skin sunburnt and brows sweaty, they swabbed the decks with mops and overflowing buckets of seawater, or polished the planks, their efforts rewarded with shouted exhortations from the Captain to 'look alive!'. The carpenter carried out repairs, placing oakum in the seams of the planks, while lookouts in the rigging scoured the sea for any signs of danger.

The Kojin remained a detached, brooding presence onboard the ship. They proved reluctant to help the crew, dismissive of what they perceived to be their inferior seafaring skills. One of the Kojin warriors never showed his face, always keeping it hidden beneath a hood. He shadowed Jeimuzu like a faithful dog and Bo wondered at the reason for such secrecy. Perhaps the warrior wanted to conceal a disfigurement. Bo decided it best not to question the many mysteries of the Kojin. Despite keeping aloof

91

from the rest of the crew, they enjoyed the voyage, thriving on the salty tang of sea air, the rhythmic sounds of the lapping waves, the squawking of gulls, the cooling spray on their faces. A dolphin swam beside the ship, its movements like a dance; it went unnoticed by the crew but the Kojin gazed in silent awe.

'How goes the watch, lad?' said Black Francis, slapping Bo on the back.

Bo had not heard him approach and jumped. A little shakily, he said, 'We've seen nothing of alarm.'

'Ah, that's good tidings. The storm fiends are lulled, for a time at least. But don't be fooled: this sea has plenty of surprises in her watery pockets.'

'Surprises or not, I'm bored half to death,' said Valbrand. 'Is there not a duty more engaging than a witless lookout?'

Black Francis brusquely dismissed the suggestion. 'I don't want lubberly clods like you two messing up my ship with your clumsy maulers. No offence intended, of course.'

'Oh, how could we be offended?' said Valbrand. He folded his arms and mumbled under his breath.

Amused by his friend's indignation, Bo looked back at the rippling, mesmeric waves. Wooden planks floated towards the *Husker Du*, followed by bobbing barrels and coils of frayed rope. He pointed to the debris and said to Valbrand, 'Look down there.'

'It's the remains of a ship,' said Valbrand, using his hand to shield his eyes from the sun. 'A shipwreck, most likely.'

'We've not seen a single ship since we left Katakani,' said Bo. 'Don't you think that's strange?'

The Captain's face twitched, as Bo noted it often did since

his ordeal at the hands of the King of the Sea Beggars. 'I'm trying to avoid the main trade routes. That's the best way to keep clear of those cursed Ironclads.'

Valbrand pointed to the floating debris. 'Perhaps an Ironclad found that ship.'

'We don't know what happened, and there's nothing to be gained from guessing,' said Black Francis.

There was a shout from a lookout in the rigging. 'To port! Man overboard!'

The crew and the Kojin scrambled to the port side of the *Husker Du*. A man floated in the water, but as he drifted closer to the ship it was clear he was dead. Face down, his long hair spread out like seaweed, while his clothes billowed around him. His limbs bobbed in the water as though manipulated by a bored, listless puppeteer.

'He's beyond our help,' said Black Francis.

Other bodies floated by. Men. Women. Some blackened by smoke. Others burnt, or missing limbs. Bo's mouth and throat went dry and a hush fell over the crew and the Kojin.

Shrimp, the ship's coxswain approached Black Francis and said, 'Something terrible has happened here. This is the work of Prester John's servants.'

'We don't know that,' said Black Francis. 'The sea is treacherous and unforgiving. Accidents happen.'

One of the sharp-eyed Kojin yelled out and pointed to a man in the water. As Bo fixed his eyes on him, he realised the man was moving, swimming with wide arcs of his lean, wiry arms. He clasped something in his left hand.

'Well, sink me,' said Black Francis. 'One of them is alive. Throw him a rope.'

'Is that wise?' said Prince Jeimuzu. 'He might be an enemy.'

'You'd prefer to let him drown?' said Black Francis.

'His life does not lie in my hands,' said the Kojin Prince. Bo noticed how, as he often did, the hooded Kojin stood beside Jeimuzu, his head lowered, and a bow and a quiver of arrows slung over his shoulder.

'I won't needlessly abandon a soul to the sea,' said Black Francis.

After lowering a rope, the crew hauled the man on-board. He was old, with snow-white hair and wrinkly brown skin, but he looked strong and in no way tired from his exertions. He wore a long, loose-fitting tunic that he tied at his waist with a belt. In his left hand he clasped a simple wooden staff. He gave a beaming smile and spoke in a voice soothing to the ear. 'I stand in your debt, friends.'

'Who are you?' said Black Francis, after checking that the man did not wear the Null.

'You may call me Epios,' he said. He looked around. 'My, this is a curious crew. I see Men and Kojin together, seldom are they fellow travellers. There is a tale to be told here, that much is clear to me.'

Black Francis scratched his head. 'Epios? Somehow your name is familiar to me, though I cannot recall how. So, did your ship sink?'

'Oh, you mean the corpses. A tragedy to be sure, but these are tragic times. Those in thrall to Prester John swarm across the oceans.'

'Yes,' said Jeimuzu, stepping forward aggressively. 'And his spies multiply like rats.'

Epios laughed. 'You think me one of his spies?'

Jeimuzu gestured towards the water. 'How is it others died and you stand here alive and well?'

'So now you accuse me of murder?' said Epios. He held up his spindly staff. 'Perhaps you think this is a weapon?'

'Don't mock me,' said Jeimuzu. His hand moved to the hilt of his sword and he said to Black Francis, 'I do not trust this one. We Kojin have instincts Men lack and I sense he is not what he appears to be. We should throw him overboard.'

'They'll be no throwing,' said Black Francis. 'He's been shipwrecked and he's welcome to sail with us. Bo, do you agree?'

Bo looked at Epios. The old man was strange, but not threatening. And regardless of any thoughts he had about Epios, the prospect of coldly abandoning him to the sea struck Bo as callous. 'Of course, let him stay.'

'You are fools,' said Jeimuzu. 'He is dangerous. It was a mistake to bring him aboard.'

'Your words are empty,' said Epios. 'You have neither the strength nor the cunning to deal with me.'

Rising to the provocation, Jeimuzu's eyes blazed. Ignoring the protests of Black Francis and Bo, the Kojin Prince drew his sword. Epios reacted in a manner that none could have predicted: in the blink of an eye, he changed from an old man into an osprey. He climbed high above the ship and then made a spectacular dive, plunging feet first, swooping down at Jeimuzu, forcing him into a panicky stoop.

The osprey landed on deck and became an old man again. Epios picked up his staff and laughed at the shaken

Jeimuzu. 'You can see now, my friend, that you are no match for me. In these waters I can take any form I wish.'

'Well, *he* is an odd one,' said Valbrand.

The hooded Kojin notched an arrow in his bow and drew back the string. In a muffled voice, he said to Epios, 'If you harm Prince Jeimuzu I promise to slay you in whatever form you choose to take.'

Epios held up his hands and said to the Kojin, 'I have no quarrel with you. I will not harm your Prince, though his insolence would justify such a deed. But I see I am not the only one with secrets. You are hiding something too, my friend. My eyes and ears are sharp.'

The hooded Kojin hesitated and relaxed the bowstring. 'I do not know what you mean.'

'Then draw back your hood, and all shall be revealed,' said Epios. 'You know my secret, now I should know yours.'

'You have no right to make demands of my people,' said Jeimuzu, standing in front of the hooded Kojin. 'Our business is our own.'

'It is all right, Jeimuzu,' said the hooded Kojin. 'I cannot remain concealed forever.'

The Kojin warrior pulled back the hood, and Bo gasped in amazement. It was Princess Moriko, the daughter of the Kojin Queen.

'What are you doing here?' Bo said. 'The Queen forbade you to come on this journey.'

'I have as much right to be here as Jeimuzu, and he agrees,' said Moriko.

Looking awkward, Jeimuzu nodded.

'The Queen will be furious,' said Bo.

'Perhaps, but there is little she can do to me here, is there?' said Moriko.

Bo had to admit that was true.

'Besides,' continued the Princess, 'I *should* be here. I fight as well as any warrior on this ship. Why should I be left behind simply because I am female? How can we fight for freedom if we deny that privilege to half our race?'

'This is certainly a day for surprises,' said Valbrand, scratching his bald head.

Epios bowed in front of Moriko. 'Please forgive me if you deem I was intrusive. I like to speak with honesty and candour, but I intended no harm or offence.'

'And none was taken,' said Moriko magnanimously.

'It seems my arrival here has caused a stir,' said Epios with a glint of amusement in his eyes. 'Trouble drew me to these waters, and I have found more trouble than I expected.'

'So you were not in the ship wreck?' pressed Black Francis

'No, I sensed their suffering, but I arrived too late to aid those in peril. I am part of the sea; I feel its moods, its rhythms. Little happens within these waters that I do not detect.'

'*Epios*,' said Black Francis. 'Of course, I know your name. The Old Man of the Sea.'

Epios laughed. 'I'm not exactly a man, as you can see.'

'It seems as though the ancient tales are all coming back to life,' said Black Francis.

'They never died, my friend, but the horrors of these times give them fresh vigour.'

'Have you seen any Ironclads?' said Black Francis.

Epios nodded and his face darkened. 'Those abominable

monstrosities befoul the sea and the air with their smoke and oil. They hunt like predators. The people you saw in the water were passengers on a ship from Kasaba, bound for the New World, refugees who refused the Null. They were unarmed. They were fleeing, not fighting, but the Ironclad ripped them apart, sparing no-one, showing no mercy. I warn you, my friends, the Ironclads patrol these waters remorselessly. I think perhaps I could be of use to you.'

'I still say he is dangerous,' said Jeimuzu.

'I am no danger to you unless you choose to threaten the seas, or the creatures that dwell there,' said Epios. 'And despite the more hot-headed amongst you, I judge you all to be true of heart and purpose. You acted selflessly to save me. That you were mistaken in my identity does not diminish the deed, and as such I remain in your debt. Therefore, with your leave, I offer to remain with you, and aid you in whatever manner I can.'

'We don't need this conjuror's help,' said Jeimuzu.

'Perhaps not today, but in the days to come I would be less sure of that belief,' said Epios.

Black Francis sighed. 'As I see it, we're sailing into a world of trouble and it can't hurt to have another pair of hands.'

'Or wings,' said Valbrand, winking at Jeimuzu.

'I agree,' said Bo, nodding at Black Francis. 'We're in no position to turn away offers of aid.'

'Then it is settled,' said Epios, tapping the top of his staff.

Jeimuzu muttered to the other Kojin warriors and stomped across deck.

'Well, this should be *interesting*,' said Epios with a mischievous grin.

*

Bo hesitated when he reached the door of the cabin used by the Kojin. He knocked once, lightly, too lightly to be heard as no answer came. He tried again. A Kojin voice rasped in their native language and Bo guessed its meaning. He said, 'It's Prince Asbjorn.'

He heard delicate footsteps and the door swung open. Moriko stood there. She wore a short-sleeved robe, tied at her waist with a convoluted knot. Disconcertingly, Bo noticed she held a dagger in her right hand. She scrutinised Bo, her emerald-green eyes narrowed in suspicion. She said, 'Why are you here?'

'I wished to speak with you,' said Bo. He knew the rest of the Kojin warriors were on deck, brooding in sullen silence as night fell.

She stepped aside. 'Enter, if you so wish.'

Kojin armour filled much of the cabin, all richly decorated with embossed and gilded clouds, waves and dragons. A row of grimacing masks of lacquered iron made Bo uncomfortable. Perhaps as a memory of their home, the Kojin had fastened ink splash paintings to the walls; delicate, ethereal, they were like windows to another world.

Moriko sat on the floor and beckoned Bo to do likewise. 'So, you disapprove of my deception?'

'No, not at all,' said Bo. 'I was *surprised* to see you, of course.'

The Princess twirled the dagger around her webbed fingers. 'It was not my intention to deceive you. If my mother

99

had permitted it, I would gladly have travelled openly, but as you have witnessed, it is not easy to change her mind once it is made up.'

'I had observed that. A trait she passed to her daughter.'

Moriko smiled. 'I am fortunate Jeimuzu participated willingly in my plan. I owe my brother much.'

'And yet you are travelling into the utmost danger.'

'Is that not so for you and everyone else on-board this vessel?' she said. She held up her knife. 'This blade was given to me at my coming of age, as such blades are given to all Kojin females of noble birth. I was schooled in its use. If the situation demands it, I am trained to fight or stab myself rather than be captured by the enemy. And, Prince Asbjorn, I *will* fight. I refuse to be a captive again. I am not afraid to die in battle, but I refuse to feel again the shame of being a prisoner. Do you understand this?'

Bo remembered Moriko's imprisonment by the Sea Beggars, incarceration in the darkness of the oubliette. 'I understand, completely.'

She nodded, a sign of appreciation. 'The King of the Sea Beggars, the revolting *Kegare*, possessed the power of life and death over me. I cannot let any mortal control me again. I have sworn to take charge of my destiny. Even with the *Kegare* dead, and his Shikome rats routed, my people are not yet safe. I refuse to wait in the Beauteous Isle for the ravaging hordes of Prester John to consume us. I want to advance to meet them in battle.'

'If that is your wish, it is surely soon to be granted. If I speak truthfully, when it comes to war, I shall not be sorry to have you fighting with us.'

Moriko sheathed her dagger. 'Let us hope the ancestors bless our actions and provide us all with strength and wisdom in these darkest of times. We Kojin have pledged to fight to the last.'

'The victory over the King of the Sea Beggars proved the Kojins' valour. And Prince Jeimuzu will lead you with courage and nobility, I am sure.'

'Unless he slaps Epios first,' said Moriko with a short laugh. 'Jeimuzu is proud and does not tolerate mockery, even when it is done in jest.'

'Epios is certain to keep us on our toes, but I am glad he is with us, all the same.'

Moriko smiled. 'He will not be the last surprise we encounter.'

*

Epios proved an entertaining companion, soon winning over the crew with salty tales and limericks. He brightened up the tedium of long days of washing, repairing, drying and cooking. However, he refused all requests to change shape again, calling it, 'a wearisome act for an aged soul.'

Two more days had passed when a chilly fog rolled in from the mountainous lands to the north, obscuring the sky, and smothering sounds and smells. The *Husker Du* moved listlessly, becalmed in the meagre wind. Black Francis marched around the deck, cursing in frustration and glowering at the billowing fog.

Enjoying a rare period between watches, Bo and Valbrand loitered on deck. As Black Francis strode past them, he said, 'I always say that in this sea you get too much wind or not enough. We're little more than drifting at the moment.'

'Couldn't Epios turn himself into a whale and push us along?' said Valbrand with a cheeky grin.

Black Francis laughed. 'Or perhaps he could turn into the kraken and scare away the fog.'

'Ah, I don't think I'll take his form,' said Epios, who appeared behind them. 'So, Captain, you do not find this wind and fog to your liking.'

'I'm not a patient man and calm seas make sorry sailors. But I know the sea well enough to understand that you must suffer its moods.'

'A wise observation,' said Epios.

There was a distant rumble. Epios frowned.

'Sounds like a storm brewing,' said Valbrand.

'No, it is something else,' said Epios.

A flash lit up the sky for a second.

'See, there's lightning,' said Valbrand, pointing skywards to prove his point.

'It is not lightning, my friend,' said Epios.

An acrid smell filled the air: the hot metal odour of gunpowder mixed with oily smoke. Bo heard the rumble again, but this time it was clearer and louder, the sound travelling from somewhere much closer. It was not thunder; it was cannon-fire. Black Francis sprinted to the ship's bow. Once there, he pulled out his telescope and strained to see what was ahead. He turned round and gestured for the crew to be silent. He mouthed a word repeatedly, his eyes wide.

'What's he saying?' whispered Valbrand.

'Ironclad,' said Epios.

Black Francis hustled around the deck, giving orders through a series of silent signals and gesticulations. He whispered to Bo, Epios and Valbrand, 'The Ironclad is close. From the bow, I saw its shadowy outline, less than two miles away I judge. I don't think we've been spotted so I'll try to steer away from it. This fog is a blessing after all. Let us pray that it shields us.'

'Why run?' said Epios. 'This is our chance to fight.'

'That's a belch of claptrap,' said Black Francis. 'If you hadn't noticed, this is a wooden ship. We've no chance against that metal monster.'

Epios said, 'Let's slay the monster. If we destroy the Ironclad, think of the other lives we could save.'

Hearing the words of Epios, Bo felt his heart beat a little faster, and not out of fear. A tingle of excitement, a primal desire to fight.

Led by Jeimuzu, the Kojin appeared on deck. The Prince said, 'What is going on?'

Black Francis said in a hushed voice, 'There's an Ironclad close—Epios thinks we should attack it without delay.'

'Aye, I think he's lost his wits,' said Valbrand, for once unmoved by the prospect of fighting.

'Not so,' said Epios. 'We have on this ship folk of power and cunning. Black Francis, you spoke truthfully: this fog is a blessing. Surprise can overcome their greater firepower.'

The Captain was unmoved. He said, 'There's no one alive who'd be keener than me to send that Ironclad to the seabed, but I won't endanger the lives of my crew in some rash attack.'

Clearly sensing something was awry, the crew gathered

around Black Francis. When they learnt of the Ironclad, their expressions changed from puzzlement to fear.

To Bo's surprise, Epios turned to him and said, 'Your voice should be heard, my friend. What say you?'

Bo spoke unguardedly, without thinking at all, allowing passion, raw emotions, to shape the words that emerged from his mouth. 'We should fight. We'll never defeat Prester John by running and hiding.'

The ship's cook, Limpet, responded angrily, so angrily that Bo flinched. 'It is easy for you to say. It will not be your crew dying.'

Some of the crew nodded and muttered agreement. Bo disliked the ship's cook, who did the least work and the most complaining. But Bo realised many listened to and took heed of Limpet's opinions, and he wondered if the ship's cook only expressed concerns others were too afraid to mention in case they looked cowardly or disloyal.

Bo composed himself. 'We are in a war, one that cannot be won by running away.'

Black Francis scratched the back of his head as he considered Bo's words. 'I don't like this plan, but I'm not one for running. Epios, do you think this is wise?'

The Old Man of the Sea nodded. 'Yes, I know it's not without risk but if we aren't prepared to take risks, what chance have we got?'

'Taking on an Ironclad isn't just risky,' said Limpet, folding his arms. 'I'd say it's closer to suicide.'

Epios ignored the ship's cook and tried to press Black Francis. 'Even if you evade this Ironclad, is there not a chance it will find us later? And then, *they* will have surprise, and what chance would we have? Here, we hold the upper hand, for a brief moment only. Seize this chance. I doubt there will be another.'

'What would you have us do?' said Black Francis.

'The Kojin are sea folk and speedy swimmers. I shall lead them to the Ironclad. We can silence their guns in time for the *Husker Du* to attack.'

'Such an action is to our liking,' said Jeimuzu, and Moriko eagerly nodded her agreement.

'Very well, I'll do as you say,' said Black Francis. 'But if I think the ship and my crew are in danger, I'll cut and run and you'll be on your own.'

Limpet trudged off, cursing under his breath and shaking his head.

Epios bowed to Black Francis, a broad smile across his face. 'Good. Circle the Ironclad at a safe distance. Circle it once and then attack. Use plunging fire, for although the sides of the Ironclad are heavily armoured, the protection on its top deck is thin.'

'I know how to fight at sea,' said Black Francis.

'I am relieved to hear it,' said Epios.

'Just be clear of the Ironclad when we open fire,' said Black Francis. 'We won't miss and I'd hate to kill those on my own side.'

'We'll not dither, I assure you,' said Epios. He addressed Bo. 'My friend, I believe you are skilled in the arts of battle. You must join our raiding party.'

'You want me to go with you and the Kojin?' said Bo, glancing anxiously at the waves.

'Of course, I presume you can swim?'

Bo puffed out his cheeks. 'In lakes and rivers, yes, but I have never swum in the sea.'

'No matter, just think of it as a big lake. And the water is warmer, you'll soon get used to it.'

'If I am to fight I need my sword, and I can't swim while carrying that.'

'I shall take it,' said Jeimuzu. 'It is no burden to me.'

Reluctantly Bo handed his sword to the Prince. Following the example of the Kojin, Bo stripped down to his underclothes. Against their sleek, muscular bodies, he felt pale and feeble. Ever since the defeat of the King of the Sea Beggars, a defeat he had been instrumental in achieving, he felt a new pressure. He had always feared that others thought him weak, indecisive, unworthy of leadership. Now he found it disconcerting that others perceived him with respect and high expectations. Any momentary pleasure he experienced from words of praise soon dissipated to leave a hangover of guilt from what he believed to be undeserved, unearned plaudits. The façade of a leader others placed over him could easily peel away, exposing the timorous child.

Epios said to them all, 'Do not be afraid of the form I take in the water. It's for your own protection. I shall not harm you, I swear it.'

'Sounds like he's planning another surprise,' muttered Valbrand to Bo. 'You be careful, lad. I suppose I should go with you but I swim like a lead weight.'

Carrying swords, bows and arrows, the Kojin lined up on the port side of the ship and dived into the water, as sure and speedy as kingfishers. Bo clambered inelegantly down ropes. As Epios promised, the water was warm and calm.

106

He started to swim and found the motion difficult at first, inadvertently swallowing mouthfuls of brine, his legs splashing in an uncoordinated fashion. The salty water stung his eyes.

At surface level, the sea looked endless, and Bo had never felt so small, so insignificant. In their element, the Kojin swam gracefully, enjoying the water. Epios leapt from the *Husker Du* and struck the water with a huge splash. He changed shape, turning into a large shark, with a conical snout, a white underside and a grey dorsal area. Epios lifted his head above the surface, revealing rows of serrated teeth. The Kojin yelled out in terror, but despite an initial heart-bursting moment of fear, Bo managed to control himself. As he stared at the shark, Bo reminded himself it was Epios and replayed his words in his mind: *Do not be afraid of the form I take in the water.*

With a huge sweep of his shark tail, Epios veered towards the Ironclad. Keeping their distance, the Kojin followed him. Bo worked hard to keep up, his arms and legs pumping. To his surprise, Moriko swam close to him, encouraging him, urging him on.

Bo tried to keep his concentration focused on the shark's dorsal fin, letting it guide his direction. His arms and legs felt so heavy and lifeless, as though the muscles no longer worked. Out of the fog, the Ironclad's sinister lines and angles took shape. He saw a vessel with a very low freeboard, a sloped casement battery on the main deck that protected thirteen heavy guns. Three gun ports faced forward, with two after, and four positioned on each broadside. The casement reminded Bo of a turtle's shell, but the thick iron plates looked impenetrable. A squat octagonal conning tower perched on the top of the casement, also strengthened by metal plates. Two chimneys rose from the vessel like watchtowers; as the merciless machines that drove the Ironclad were silent, no smoke billowed from them. Two wooden dinghies, lifeboats Bo guessed, clung to the port side of the Ironclad like oversized barnacles.

Close to the Ironclad, a wooden ship, an old-fashioned galleon, slipped beneath the waves, soon leaving only a mast peeking out of the water like the outstretched hand of a drowning man. Corpses bobbed in the water. Debris floated. The Ironclad had claimed another victim.

Led by Epios, the Kojin and Bo swam up to the Ironclad. Bo thought guns would open fire on them but their approach went undetected. On the bow, steps ran up the sloped casement and onto the uncovered and deserted upper deck.

Epios circled the Ironclad, while Jeimuzu signalled to the other Kojin warriors and Bo to climb up onto the vessel. Bo relied on help from Moriko to clamber aboard. Dripping wet and with his legs and arms numb from exertion, he stood, trying to catch his breath. He collected his sword from Jeimuzu and gripped it with a trembling hand. The Kojin shook their weapons to dry them, before Jeimuzu sped up the steps, shadowed by the other warriors. Fortified by adrenalin, Bo followed them.

Advancing in a crouched position, Jeimuzu moved around the conning tower. Without warning, he let out an ear-piercing shout. At first Bo thought he had been hurt but then realised it was a signal. In the corner of his eye, he saw

Epios, still in the form of a huge shark, swim at full speed towards the Ironclad. He crashed against the metal-plated side with such force that a huge plume of water exploded into the air and the vessel shuddered violently.

As Bo struggled to maintain his balance, he heard shouts from inside the conning tower, a trapdoor in its roof opened, and the head of a man appeared. In an instant, Jeimuzu leapt upon the tower. Before the man could react, Jeimuzu pulled him up and out through the trapdoor, stabbed him with his sword and let his body slide down the sloped side of the conning tower.

Alarm bells rang and trapdoors whipped open across the Ironclad's gun deck, disgorging a score of armoured soldiers, all equipped with muskets. The Kojin warriors greeted the arrival of their foes with battle cries and curses. Muskets sounded and a lead ball smashed against the wooden deck only inches from Bo's feet. The soldiers hastily attempted to reload, but another battering from Epios shook the Ironclad again, making them spill their lead balls, powder and ramrods. The Kojin warriors seized their chance and charged. Unable to fire in time, the soldiers turned their muskets to use them as clubs, but such unwieldy weapons were no match for the dexterity and fighting skills of the Kojin, who cut down their opponents without mercy.

But the battle was not over. A hidden trapdoor close to Bo opened and two more soldiers climbed out. One of them fired a pistol at Bo; the shot grazed his arm, leaving a shallow but stinging flesh wound. Trying to follow up his attack, he lunged at Bo with a knife but a Kojin arrow whizzed over Bo's shoulder and struck the soldier in the throat. The second soldier attacked Bo with a halberd; Bo blocked and managed to unbalance his opponent. As the soldier wobbled, Bo landed a brutal killing blow with his sword.

With blood dripping from the blade, Bo looked down at the dead man, a familiar feeling of revulsion rising in his stomach. Yet he had no time to consider it further, for to his horror a Redeemer climbed up through the trapdoor. He held a sword in one hand and a pistol in the other; he pointed the latter at the nearest Kojin and fired. The shot struck the Kojin in the forehead and killed him instantly.

The Redeemer pulled back his hood, revealing a hairless head, streaked with protruding purple veins, and mottled, mouldy skin. His bloodshot eyes glared, unblinking. Mucus dribbled uncontrollably from his nostrils and his robes carried a putrefying stench. The Redeemer moved swiftly, swinging his blade at Bo, who just managed to parry it at face height. The Redeemer attacked repeatedly, lunging and thrusting, forcing Bo backwards, close to the deck's edge.

The Redeemer brought a whipping blow aimed at Bo's midriff. Bo blocked it but the force of the attack knocked the sword out of his hands and it clattered onto the deck and skittered out of his reach. His heels touched the edge of the deck. The Redeemer lifted his blade above his head and in a voice like the moaning winter wind, said 'Die.'

The Redeemer brought the blade down but something deflected the sword and sent it spiralling into the sea. It was Epios, now back in the form of an old man. With a howl of outrage and anger, the Redeemer attacked. Old and frail he may have appeared, but Epios showed his true strength. He punched the Redeemer in the face, causing him to stagger backwards and fall on his back. Then, to Bo's amazement, Epios grabbed the Redeemer by the ankle and tossed him overboard; he splashed into the water several yards from the Ironclad.

'With all that Cold Iron inside him he won't easily float,' said Epios. Sure enough, the Redeemer slipped beneath the waves. Epios leant down and gave Bo back his sword. 'You might need this.'

Bo thanked him. 'I thought I was dead.'

'You nearly were. There are plenty more enemies to face here, I'm sure of it.'

'Then let's not delay,' said Bo. 'We have to put the guns out of action before the *Husker Du* arrives.'

Meanwhile, Jeimuzu picked up the dead Kojin's sword. Now with a blade in each hand he said, 'If there are more Redeemers, they shall pay with their wretched lives.'

With the upper deck now secure, the Kojin warriors, Epios and Bo descended a narrow staircase into the gun deck. The heat and humidity struck them like a punch. Moisture dripped from the ceiling and the metal walls. A handful of oil lamps hung from the ceiling, spluttering and hissing, offering only a weak, fitful light. The deck stank of metal, oil, wet wood and unwashed bodies.

Smoothbore cannons peeked out of the gun ports on all sides of the vessel. Bo had never seen such powerful-looking weapons and feared the terrible damage they could cause. The crew on the gun deck shouted in alarm as they spotted the intruders. Bo saw them grasp muskets, swords and bludgeons. Although not soldiers, the crew composed

111

of many tough sailors and officers, and, driven by the Null, they fought back savagely.

Muskets boomed in the low-ceilinged gun deck, missing their targets and sending showers of splinters and metal fragments, their thick smoke adding to the gloom. The swords of the Kojin flashed. Steel clashed against steel, curses and death cries. The wooden floor became sticky with blood. Forcing himself into the maelstrom of shouts and screams and blood, Bo joined in the fighting, struggling against sailors armed with knives, clubs or cannon rammers. Instinct took over, sharpening his senses. An animal part of his being, fuelled by a primitive drive for survival, buried any rational thoughts. He slew four men during the fight, inwardly crying with self-loathing at each kill.

Suddenly, the remaining crew parted and through the gap advanced two Redeemers. Yelling a battle cry and with sword aloft, a young Kojin warrior named Sentoki, charged at the Redeemers. He swung a hard blow at one of them, the edge of his blade digging into the Redeemer's shoulder. But rather than fall, the Redeemer brought his own sword down at Sentoki, who in trying to duck the blow lost balance on the sticky floor. The second Redeemer moved with predatory speed and intent, driving his sword into the Kojin's stomach.

Howling with anger, the other Kojin warriors unleashed a hail of arrows, but urged on by the remaining crew, the Redeemers advanced. Faced with such horrors, Bo grappled with the urge to flee but he managed to hold fast. Epios stepped forward.

'What are you doing?' said Bo.

Epios did not answer, but in an instant transformed into an osprey. He swooped towards the Redeemers, evading their swords. With his talons, he ripped the Redeemers hoods, tearing into the flesh on the top of their heads. They cursed and yelled, incandescent with anger; and they were distracted. Seizing his chance, Jeimuzu charged at the Redeemers, a sword in each hand. Too late the Redeemers saw the real danger. With an acrobatic leap, Jeimuzu swung his swords and decapitated both Redeemers. Their headless bodies tottered, and then slumped to the ground. The severed heads rolled towards the crew, who backed away in their keenness to avoid them. A pause, an intake of breath followed. The two sides waited in silence, a standoff, awaiting the outbreak of fresh violence. Bo wanted an end to the fighting. He shouted to the crew, 'Put down your weapons. No more of you need to die.'

Still grasping their weapons, the sailors shook their heads. One of them replied, 'We don't surrender to heretics and demons. In the name of Prester John, we fight to the death.'

'This is to my liking,' said Jeimuzu. 'Show them no mercy. Kill them all. Avenge our dead.'

Epios landed elegantly next to Bo and returned to his normal form. He started to speak when a deep rumble echoed around the Ironclad, followed by the splash and hiss of steaming water. Wide-eyed, Epios grabbed Bo's shoulder and said, 'It is the *Husker Du*. Flee, now.'

The Ironclad shuddered as a cannonball struck the starboard side.

'Get out, get out now,' said Epios, ushering the Kojin up

the steps. 'If you linger here, you'll die. This ship is doomed.'

They bundled back up the steps and onto the upper deck. The *Husker Du* sailed close to the Ironclad and fired a broadside. Cannonballs fizzed into the water and others cracked against the metal plates shielding the casement.

'They are finding their range,' said Epios. 'Dive into the water.'

He leapt from the casement and upon touching the water changed into a dolphin. Another broadside blazed and this time a cannonball landed on the upper deck with an explosion of smoke and wooden splinters. The Kojin did not hesitate. They all jumped into the sea and swam away from the Ironclad. Seeing there was no other choice, Bo closed his eyes, and jumped. He landed in the water feet first and endured a horrible moment before he struggled back to the surface.

Jeimuzu followed Epios towards the *Husker Du* and urged the others to do likewise. As he swam, Bo looked over his shoulder and saw three more cannonballs strike the upper deck with a deafening crack. He heard anguished cries from the crew. Black oily smoke billowed from the gaping holes in the deck and the Ironclad began to list sharply to port. A groaning filled the air, the sound of stretched and overheated metal buckling and splitting. The Ironclad capsized and disappeared beneath the churning surface. A sludgy oil slick fanned out from its watery grave.

Bo watched not in relief but with a sense of horror, of sickened guilt. He saw no survivors. No lifeboats launched. He treaded water until someone nudged his leg—Epios, still in the form of a dolphin. Turning away from the sunken Ironclad, Bo pushed on to the *Husker Du*.

CHAPTER SIX

The Buried City

'You're no swimmer, lad, but you've got some guts,' said Black Francis, as he and Valbrand dragged Bo back aboard the *Husker Du*.

Exhausted, dripping wet, ears pounding, Bo sprawled out on the deck. He heard Black Francis say, 'An Ironclad sunk! This is a story I'll be telling for many a year.'

Valbrand laughed. 'And each time you tell it the Ironclad will get bigger and have more guns.'

Black Francis gave him a firm but playful punch on the arm. He leant down and helped pull Bo to his feet. 'Up you get, lad. A ship's no place for lying about.'

Bo stood but his legs remained shaky. Struggling to focus, he watched as Epios, now in the form of a fulmar, circled the *Husker Du* several times before he landed on deck and changed back to an old man. The Kojin warriors showed little sign of tiredness. Jeimuzu turned to Bo. 'You did well.'

'All played their part,' said Bo. 'I am sorry for the warriors you lost. They fought with courage and honour. It is a pity we cannot recover their bodies.'

'We shall mourn them in our fashion,' said Jeimuzu. 'The ocean is a worthy grave for any Kojin. Our people were born of the white-tipped waves and it is our destiny to return there when we are no longer part of the mortal world.'

Epios bowed to Jeimuzu and said, 'The bravery of your warriors leaves me in awe.'

Jeimuzu hesitated, but returned the bow. 'I have judged you harshly, perhaps. We are stronger working together, I deem.'

'It is so, my friend,' said Epios, with a beaming smile.

Valbrand clapped his hands together gleefully. 'We certainly gave the enemy a lesson. They might not venture out to sea so lightly now.'

'That would be a happy outcome but I fear there are many more Ironclads in these waters,' said Epios. 'We should rejoice at today's victory, but it is only one skirmish in a vast war.'

'That's a cheery thought,' said Valbrand.

'I do not wish to be gloomy, but we must not deceive ourselves,' said Epios. 'When the enemy learns about the fate of the vessel we sank, they shall double their efforts to find and destroy this ship, and kill all those on it.'

'I don't expect to be at sea for more than two days,' said Black Francis. 'When the winds are favourable, I plan to crack on and head northwards. We sail for Makávrios.'

Jeimuzu frowned. 'Makávrios is a name of ill omen.'

'I've heard many tales about that place,' said Valbrand. 'In times of crisis they sacrificed their own kind to satisfy their heathen gods' bloodlust, and musicians played pipes and drums to drown out the cries of the dying.'

Black Francis scowled. 'You've heard different stories to me, but Makávrios has a queer history by all accounts. The city was founded long ago, by giants the storytellers sang, but I am doubtful of *that*. Whatever the truth of its origins, it swiftly became rich on the trade in wool, oil and wine. But disaster came. I don't know whether they angered the gods of this region, or whether the Earth itself reacted to their presence. But legend says that a catastrophe buried Makávrios, and all those who lived there.'

'Buried?' said Bo.

'Aye, for many generations, tales circulated of a hidden hoard, of wealth beyond imagination, buried deep beneath the soil. Many listened greedily to those tales, not least of them mad King Maltolt, ruler of the nearby realm of Áplistos. He became obsessed with the idea of finding the buried city's fabulous treasure. He brought in military engineers skilled in mining techniques and tunnelling. They dug deeper and deeper tunnels, and when that failed, they excavated whole sections of the city, bringing daylight to buildings and streets buried for years. Maltolt channelled all his kingdom's resources into the excavation, throwing soldiers and prisoners into the work. He raised evil taxes. He sold the produce of harvests to pay for more men, or for alchemists and charlatans who claimed to possess powers that would enable him to find the treasure. His people starved. Famine and disease claimed many lives. Maltolt ignored the anguish of his subjects and ordered his workers to keep digging.'

'What happened to him?' said Bo.

'That, I do not know,' said Black Francis, enjoying telling the tale. 'Some say his men murdered him, perhaps in a revolt. Others tell of an even darker end, of nameless terrors unleashed, of punishments not normally endured by mortal

Men. What seems clear is that the pursuit of gold and jewels drove Maltolt insane. What fate finally befell him, I suppose we'll never know. Few dare to go there now, frightened away by the legends.'

'I don't blame them,' said Valbrand.

'I'm not frightened by travellers' tales,' said Black Francis. 'Makávrios is deserted enough not to be troubled by other ships, especially Ironclads. We should be able to anchor safely at the cove of Ekrixi, close to the river-mouth, and from there it is less than a day's march to Omphalos.'

'Your plan is wise,' said Epios.

'You intend to accompany us?' said Jeimuzu.

'Yes, with your leave, of course,' said Epios. 'If you forgive my immodesty, I believe I can be of use to you in your quest.'

Black Francis laughed. 'Aye, there's no doubting that. For all the enemy's strength and foresight, they won't be expecting to come up against someone like you.'

*

The ship's hold offered Bo comforting darkness. He felt more at ease there than in any other part of the *Husker Du*. The musty sacks of wheat, barrels of water and bundles of spider-infested wood reminded him of the Hall of Artefacts in the Hammersund Palace, his refuge during many miserable childhood days. The smell of bilge water and tar did not offend him, and he scarcely noticed the scuffling of the few rats that had survived Valbrand's purge. Bo needed solitude. He needed a place where no one else would come, and on-board the cramped *Husker Du*, the hold represented his only option.

A moonless night concealed the ship, and gave the crew a chance to celebrate the Ironclad's destruction. Bo heard the sound of flutes, hand drums and fiddles. The thumping footsteps of those dancing made the wooden panels creak and groan. Black Francis had permitted the opening of a barrel of ale; an event Bo guessed was not unconnected to the increase in noise and joviality. He did not begrudge them their celebration, for they had all risked their lives. The Kojin had declined to indulge in such revelries. Solemnly they recited blessings and prayers for their fallen comrades, lamenting their loss. They dropped offerings into the wine-dark sea.

Bo felt no sense of victory, no joy to lift his heart. He had escaped the festivities by claiming he needed to sleep, in itself no lie for the day had left him drained. But the battle's aftermath lingered with him. The killing. The sounds of dying men. Bloated corpses. All conspired to make sleep impossible. Such horrors had been his constant companion for months. He wondered if his life would ever be free of them, or if he would have to spend the rest of his days in an unceasing cycle of violence, a cycle only ended by his own death. He wanted to be a leader, he wanted to be a warrior, but he felt that with every man he killed, a part of his being, perhaps his soul, died too.

'You seek the solace of darkness, I see.'

Bo jumped as he had not seen or heard Epios enter the hold. He said shakily, 'Yes, I'm afraid it's a habit of old.'

Laying his staff across his lap, Epios sat beside Bo. 'Oh,

don't apologise for it. I too wish for a little peace and quiet. Things are getting raucous above us. Many of the crew will be nursing sore heads in the morning.'

'They are used to it. I am not fond of such merriments.'

'I guessed as much, although that is not the real reason you are down here in the dark, is it?'

Bo smiled wanly. 'I suppose not.'

'You are a strange one, if you don't mind me saying so.'

'I have been called worse things,' said Bo with a shrug.

'I see torment within you. A heavy burden you carry.'

Bo sighed, and gave voice to thoughts that had long troubled him. 'Every choice I make leads to bloodshed. Think of the men we slew on the Ironclad. Did they deserve to die? Were they not slaves too, victims caught in the web of Prester John? I fear how many more must die.'

'The evil of Prester John must be opposed.'

'I know, but is the price of opposing him not too high? Perhaps we are doing Prester John's work for him. Perhaps we are puppets every bit as much as those he controls through the Null.'

Epios frowned. 'It is not so. We might have to sacrifice much to defeat Prester John, that's true. Yet still we would be left with more goodness, more of life to savour and cherish than if Prester John ruled unchallenged across the Known World. He threatens to imprison and strangle life. To stand aside, to refuse to meet his threat, to fail to defend everything that matters, would be cowardice.'

Bo jerked as if stung. 'You think I'm a *coward*?'

Epios held up his hands and said, 'No, I don't question your bravery. I simply ask you not to give in to despair. I'm

121

a truth-speaker. Our chances of overcoming Prester John are slim, but we must try. Sometimes we are asked to do tasks that others cannot do, or refuse to do. We do not ask for such responsibilities, but they are ours to bear, whether we like it or not.'

'I am being asked to bear more than I can manage, I fear.'

'If that is so, I'd be surprised,' said Epios. With that, he patted Bo on the knee and stood. He smiled and said, 'To face doubt is natural, but don't let it consume you. Don't let it stop you becoming the man you should be.'

'The *man* I should be?' said Bo. 'I doubt I will ever feel like a man, more like a scared, witless boy locked inside a man's body, like a costume, a disguise.'

'Believe me, Bo, I think you'd struggle to find a man alive who does not feel the same. Most strive to conceal it through boasts, pride and violence. They bury their fears and in doing so prepare fertile soil for weeds of anger and hatred to grow. By acknowledging your own doubts, you'll judge much better the motivations and emotions of others.'

'I hope you are right,' said Bo.

Epios winked. 'Come now, do not brood in the dark. We all need space to think and reflect, but we should not shun the company of others. Come back on deck. Breathe in the cold sea air, gaze at the stars. Laugh at the appalling dancing of the ship's crew. They move like drunken crabs!'

Bo laughed. 'I guess that does sound better than sitting down here.'

'Of course it does. Tonight is peaceful, and in these times you should be grateful for such a gift, however short-lived.'

*

Despite constant fears of another attack, the remainder of the sea voyage passed without incident, and two days after the battle with the Ironclad, the *Husker Du* slipped into the cove of Ekrixi. Horseshoe-shaped and with a narrow entrance, it felt inviting after days upon the open sea. The tall, banded cliffs surrounding the cove displayed many different colours and the turquoise water glistened.

They careened the *Husker Du* on the beach, as Black Francis was keen to repair damage caused by dry rot. The crew remained with the ship to carry out the repairs, while Bo, Valbrand, Epios, Black Francis and the Kojin left the beach to head inland. The Kojin dressed in full armour, carrying their fearsome helmets beneath their arms. Black Francis armed himself with two pistols and a musket, weapons purloined from the Sea Beggars' stash.

'Expecting trouble?' said Valbrand.

'No, but if it comes, I want to be ready,' said Black Francis as he fastened the pistols to his belt.

From the cove, the mouth of a broad river yawned open. The murky waters ran sluggishly and grey foam clung to the banks. To the immediate north rose a line of mountains, the tallest of which was conical-shaped with a flat summit. The ragged sides of the mountain were thickly vegetated, with forest and scrub visible at high altitudes. Vaporous mists curled around the summit. Something about the sombre, brooding mountain troubled Bo, a hint of evil intent. Between the sea and the mountains stretched a plain, neatly divided by the river's wide curve. A few miles in the distance, Bo glimpsed a city. He said, 'Is that Makávrios?'

'Aye, must be,' said Black Francis. 'It's hard to imagine thousands of people lived in this land once.'

A cold wind howled across the plain, a shock after days in the warm sea of the south. Epios took the form of an osprey again, making Jeimuzu flinch with unhappy memories, and flew to scout the lands ahead.

'For all the dark tales about this place, it looks peaceful enough, if dreary and grey,' said Valbrand.

'The peace may be deceptive,' said Black Francis. 'Something about the quiet here makes me nervous.'

'You're always nervous on land,' said Valbrand.

Black Francis grunted his agreement.

Epios flew low above them and landed a few feet away. He changed back to human form.

'Did you see something to alarm you?' said Black Francis.

'The way looks clear, although there is a fell scent on the air,' said Epios, frowning and rubbing his chin. 'It troubles me and yet I cannot say why.'

'It can't smell any worse than the *Husker Du*,' said Valbrand.

Black Francis looked at him with irritation. 'It won't hurt to be vigilant.'

'The river blocks our path and is very wide,' said Epios. 'I see no ford, but there is a bridge in the deserted city ahead.'

'Is it wise to go into Makávrios?' said Bo, unnerved by the tales told by Black Francis.

'It should be safe enough,' said Epios. 'I saw no danger.'

'Then we'll go that way,' said Black Francis. 'Do you agree, Bo?'

Not seeing any alternative, Bo said, 'Yes, if we must.'

124

Makávrios lay in a broad hollow, ringed by numerous grass-topped mounds. The crumbled remnants of a defensive wall surrounded the city. A series of towers punctuated the wall, some little more than time-ravaged shells, others intact, with impressive pinnacle roofs.

Tombs crowded both sides of the straight road leading into the city. Some of the largest tombs were semi-circular structures with benches, columns and altars; others had been fashioned to look like houses, with roofs, doors and windows, and painted walls—all were decayed, their stonework disintegrating, energetic weeds bursting through cracks and holes.

The entrance to the city consisted of three archways: a wider middle arch for carts and horses, flanked by two narrower pedestrian arches. The gates had long since vanished but there remained rusted traces of hinges. Vegetation tufted from gaps and splits in the stonework.

Led by Black Francis and Epios, they walked through the deserted city. The streets were paved with blocks of stone, bordered by curbs and pedestrian walkways. Tightly packed houses lined the streets, their roofs and upper stories long since caved in. Fountains marked many of the street corners, each with spouts carved in the whimsical faces. Marble equestrian statues stood at prominent positions within the city, commemorating victorious generals of battles long forgotten.

As he walked, Bo tried to imagine what the lifeless, empty streets would have been like in the city's pomp: buzzing and bustling with life; children scampering in and out of houses and shops; the smells of cooking food. The city reminded

125

him a little of the catacombs of the Beauteous Isle, the sense of memories embedded in the ash-stained stone. Echoes of the past, faint but discernible.

'This must have been a vast city,' said Jeimuzu.

'Makávrios was the capital of this whole region,' said Black Francis. 'It is said the Mad King failed to uncover the whole city, and that whole streets remain hidden beneath the soil of this land.'

'These ruins of Men are not to my liking,' said Jeimuzu. 'This place reeks of misery and suffering. I fear what evil lurks here.'

'There's nothing here except stone, weeds and rats,' said Black Francis.

Jeimuzu looked unconvinced. 'Epios, perhaps you should fly above the city again, to keep watch.'

'I have already done so and seen no threats,' said Epios. 'But even if I wanted to do so it is impossible. The further I move from the sea, the greater the pain it is to change form. On dry land I must walk as a mortal man walks.'

'Could you turn into a bear or a wolf?' said Valbrand. 'That'd help us if we encounter any trouble.'

'The creatures of the water and salty air are my kin, not those that crawl or walk on land,' said Epios. He urged them to hurry. 'The bridge is less than a mile from here.'

They took a road that sloped downhill to the river. Villas lined the road, clearly once the dwelling places of the rich and powerful. Bo caught glimpses of symmetrically laid out formal gardens with marble basins, fountains and statuettes, all choked by weeds and ashy dust. They passed more than a dozen overturned, heavily damaged wagons. Tools spilled out from them onto the road, and Bo saw three rusting ploughshares.

'These must have been left behind by the Mad King's workers,' said Black Francis.

'If so then they left in a hurry,' said Valbrand, examining one of the carts.

'Let's keep going,' said Black Francis.

'Why rush?' said Valbrand. He pointed inside a villa and rubbed his hands together. 'Why don't we have a poke around in there, see if we can find anything valuable? There might be some easy pickings.'

'We have not come here to plunder and loot,' said Bo, trying hard not to smile at Valbrand's cheek.

'You've no sense of fun,' said Valbrand.

They reached the stone bridge that crossed the river. It was constructed from two wide arches, supported by a central pillar in the middle of the river. On the near bank of the river, a dozen huge statues kept vigil. Despite their enormous size, being thrice as large as any man, Bo found them astonishingly lifelike. Stood upon circular platforms, they portrayed creatures with hair and beards that fell down to their knees, covering their chest and stomach. They each held immense clubs.

Epios stopped and looked up at the statues. He frowned and muttered under his breath.

'What's wrong?' said Bo.

Epios winced. 'I don't know. Just a feeling…'

'Hurry up,' said Black Francis, gesturing for them to cross the bridge.

Epios wailed and pointed frantically to the far side of the

127

bridge. Bo's stomach lurched when he saw four Redeemers riding hard towards them. The bridge was wide enough for them to ride side by side, and they swept across. The Kojin scattered ahead of the rampaging horses. From their mounts, the Redeemers hacked and slashed at the Kojin.

Valbrand yelled out a throaty challenge, sprinted towards the Redeemers and, to Bo's amazement, he threw himself at the nearest rider, grabbing his leg and pulling him down from his horse. Before the Redeemer could react, four of the Kojin, and the battle-frenzied Valbrand, butchered him mercilessly.

The three remaining Redeemers charged again, but as they did so, a deafening grinding noise reverberated around the city. Birds that had perched on the ruins took to the sky. Following the source of the sound, Bo looked up at the nearest statue. As he did so, the head of the statue turned to face him. Surprise paralysed Bo as he struggled to comprehend what his eyes showed him. All the statues stepped off their platforms, colour returning to them as though rain washed away their ashen surface. They stretched their limbs, bringing life to muscles long at rest. With their clubs, the giants knocked the Redeemers from their horses, and left them stricken on the ground, bodies broken and twitching. Their horses bolted back across the river. The giants bellowed in a language Bo did not recognise, and waved their clubs above their heads.

The Kojin prepared to fire arrows at the giants but Epios cried out, 'No! Do not goad them. If you choose to fight you shall surely die.'

Bo saw Epios was right. The giants were angry, but they

128

were not evil. They shouted, threatened and postured but they did not attack and Bo guessed that they would not do so unless provoked. Slowly, deliberately, Bo sheathed his sword, making sure that the giants noticed his action.

Following his cue, the Kojin lowered their bows and the giants reacted by doing likewise with their clubs. One of the giants stepped forward and leant down, peering at Bo and his companions with eyes almost hidden by his long hair. In a thunderous voice, he said, 'Why do you come here to disturb our peace? Are you thieves and despoilers? Are you collaborators of the evil ones we slew?'

Bo stepped forward and bowed. 'If we have disturbed you, then we seek forgiveness. Your battle is not with us.'

'You speak fine words but perhaps they conceal ill intent. Those who come to this city seek only to plunder its treasure.'

'We are passing through,' said Bo, out of the corner of his eyes glancing at Valbrand. 'We have taken nothing from the city. We are not robbers.'

'That is well, for had you stolen even the smallest trinket, you would not leave this city alive.'

'If it is not impertinent to ask, who are you?' said Bo.

'By which you mean both who we are and *what* we are?' said the giant. 'We are the Gigas, or at least what remains of our tribe. I am called Paleos.'

'The Gigas?' said Epios. 'I thought you dwelt far from here, in the forests of the north.'

'This city is our home, although for many years it belonged to the seafaring Men we called the Neofermenos. When the Neofermenos first came here, refugees from a distant realm, we pitied them, for they had suffered unspeakable hardship. We built the foundations of their city. When our labours were complete, we returned north, as we should not have done. The Neofermenos remained and remembered us in their songs and prayers. We should have stayed. We might have been able to protect them.'

As Paleos finished, he lowered his head. He began to sing a lament, swiftly joined by the other Gigas. Their voices made the ground tremble. The words, although incomprehensible to Bo, conveyed a sense of misery, of regret and guilt that tore at his soul. Emotion poured from the Gigas, and Bo found himself dabbing his eyes, and casting his gaze downwards, to conceal his tears. When the lament ceased there was only silence, as though the potency of the singing silenced the wind and the birds.

Black Francis cleared his throat. 'What of the disaster that befell this city? Was it not punishment for the sins of the Neofermenos?'

'No,' said Paleos, his voice roared like a cannon. He gestured towards the conical mountain. 'Without warning that peak spewed forth fire, smoke and choking ash. The violence of the mountain engulfed the Neofermenos. They were victims of terrible misfortune, not of a doom of their own making. Guilt weighed down upon us, for poorly had we chosen the site of this city. In trying to help them we had only sowed the seeds of their utter destruction. We grieved deeply, and as the years passed, we Gigas dwindled, our hearts heavy with loss. Many years later, rumour reached us that the city was being disturbed by robbers filled with lust for treasure. This we could not endure, so we left our forest and unleashed our revenge. We spared those who saw the wickedness of their actions. To the treacherous, the foolhardy and the arrogant, we showed no pity.'

Bo looked at Black Francis, remembering the story about the Mad King and his followers. He understood now what fate had befallen those unhappy souls.

Paleos continued. 'And from that day we have guarded the city to protect the peace of the Neofermenos, for this place is their tomb. So, what of you? What brings you to this land?'

'We travel to Omphalos,' said Bo.

Paleos gave Bo a hard stare. 'Omphalos, eh? You seek the Oracle's wisdom?'

'Not exactly,' said Bo, and he went on to explain the reason for their journey.

Paleos stroked his beard. 'A summons to Omphalos, you say? It is clear that the world has become far more dangerous than we realised.'

'Well, that's true,' said Black Francis. 'But if you have no objection to us carrying on our way—'

'Come with us,' said Bo to Paleos. The blood rushed to his cheeks, his muscles tensed. He knew he was being reckless but he also knew that somehow he was doing the right thing. The Gigas offered an opportunity he simply could not spurn.

'Have you gone *mad*?' said Black Francis, to the wide-eyed, nodded agreement of Valbrand. 'What are you saying?'

'Join us, answer the summons,' continued Bo, fixing his stare on the Gigas.

'Impossible,' said Paleos, tugging anxiously at his long

131

beard. 'We must protect the city. We owe it to the Neofermenos.'

'Your city is not safe as long as Prester John endures,' said Bo. 'You may have scared away brigands and grave-robbers, but those loyal to the Holy Empire will not be so easily daunted. The Redeemers you saw today will not be the last to come here. Others are bound to seek vengeance for the killings.'

'We are far from the reach of Prester John here,' said Paleos.

'Not far enough,' said Bo. 'He seeks dominion over every land. Do you think Prester John will respect the tombs of the Neofermenos?'

'He'll have to get past us first,' said Paleos.

'In time, he will,' said Bo. 'I do not question your strength, and your loyalty to this city does you great honour. But if you remain here, you merely delay the desecration of the tombs. Help us to defeat Prester John, help us to remove the worst threat to Makávrios.'

Paleos looked at the other Gigas and spoke to them in their rolling, strident language. As they talked, Valbrand said to Bo, 'This is a bad idea. We can't traipse around with these hulking giants.'

'We need to gather all the help we can,' said Bo. 'You saw how the Gigas dealt with those Redeemers. They saved our lives. Anyone who can fight against Prester John is valuable.'

'I hope they don't turn on us,' said Valbrand, eyeing the Gigas suspiciously.

Paleos cleared his throat. 'The thought of leaving the city

is painful, but I judge there is wisdom in your words, however discomforting. The wave of evil threatens us and we cannot hide from it. We shall answer the summons.'

Bo allowed himself a small smile, though the glum faces of his companions soon washed it away. Black Francis lowered his head and said, 'Well, if we're all going to Omphalos, let's go now.'

And so they crossed the bridge, Epios, Bo, Valbrand and Black Francis leading, the Kojin behind them, and with slow heavy footsteps, the Gigas at the rear. The Gigas sang morose songs as they walked, the words twisted around sorrowful rhythms.

Valbrand chuckled. 'If there has ever been a stranger band of travellers, I'd like to see it.'

'I'm glad you're amused,' said Black Francis. He made a pointed glance at Bo. 'Those Gigas are wild. This is a mistake.'

'I do not agree,' said Epios, breaking a long silence. 'We are blessed to have the companionship of the Gigas, and before the end you may have cause to give thanks for their presence.'

Bo felt grateful for the support of Epios, and prayed it would prove to be justified. He had acted instinctively, following his gut rather than thinking coolly, thinking logically. He hoped he would not regret his choice, but doubt, his constant companion, plagued him.

From Makávrios they headed north-east. Flat dusty plains soon gave way to an undulating landscape, thickly wooded in places. At the top of one rise, Black Francis pointed to a range of peaks looming to the north. 'Those must be the

Ágios Mountains. We should reach them in a day if we maintain a good pace.'

They pushed on until dark and, after an uncomfortable night camping in a small copse, set off again at the first hint of dawn. The land seemed empty, with no signs of settlements or cultivation. An untamed land. In spring, Bo guessed it must burst with flowers, providing a heady mixture of rich scents and lush vibrant colour. Now, muted by the cold hand of winter, it stood lifeless, painted in greyish brown.

By midday, they drew close to the southern foothills of the Ágios Mountains, yet a wide, fast-flowing river, too deep and swift to wade across, blocked the route ahead. Bo and his companions stood on the riverbank, watching in frustration as its frothy waters churned with fury.

'Perhaps there'll be a ford further downriver,' said Black Francis.

'If so it is likely to be some distance away,' said Epios.

'We've got no choice,' said Black Francis, picking at his beard. 'We can't cross here.'

'You can't cross, but we can,' said Paleos, resting his club on his shoulders. 'These waters are not an obstacle to us.'

'That's handy for you, but how does it help us?' said Valbrand.

'We shall carry you across.'

'Carry? I don't like the sound of that,' said Black Francis.

'I do not much like it either,' said Paleos. 'We Gigas are not pack animals. But it is the only way for us all to cross this river.'

'He's right,' said Bo.

Defeated by the lack of options, Black Francis let out a deep sigh. 'Then let's get it over with.'

After throwing their clubs across the river, each Gigas took one passenger, all except for Paleos who carried Valbrand in his huge arms, with Bo clinging around his neck.

'By the gods, I feel like an infant in my mother's arms again,' said Valbrand, squirming with embarrassment.

'Keep still or you will find yourself in the water,' said Paleos.

'He even *sounds* like my mother,' said Valbrand.

With his face squashed into thick, greasy hair, Bo felt far from secure as they crossed, his arms aching from holding on so tightly to Paleos' thick neck. The action flashed an old memory, of holding on to his father in a similar fashion—laughter, the feeling of slight fear whilst at the same time assured of his father's safe hold. The memory brought a jab of pain and he tried to push it out of his consciousness.

All of the Gigas effortlessly strode through the river. When he stepped upon the far bank, Paleos placed Valbrand down onto the ground and leant to allow Bo to jump off.

'This journey is one bizarre experience after another,' said Valbrand. He grunted a thank you of sorts to Paleos.

As the Gigas picked up their clubs, Black Francis said, 'This is the last stretch. We're close now.'

A voice thundered, 'You can go no further.'

Warriors armed with long spears and shields emerged from the trees and shrubs. To Bo they might as well have stepped out of the history books, with each warrior protected by a corset of leather, metal greaves, a round shield and a bronze helmet. They did not attack, but held back in a tight semi-circle, a barrier to Bo and his companions. Even the sight of the huge Gigas did not seem to perturb the warriors, and one of them said, 'What's the word, strangers?'

Bo looked at Black Francis who shrugged. Epios finally answered. 'The word is Omphalos.'

'Why are you here?' came the cry.

'To answer the summons,' said Bo.

The warriors lowered their spears. One of them stepped forward and removed his helmet, revealing his grim, scarred face and downturned mouth. 'Who is your leader?'

Bo realised all eyes were upon him. He swallowed, trying to moisten his dry mouth and said, 'I am.'

The warrior gave Bo a hard look. 'You look barely above a young lad. Who are you?'

'I am Prince Asbjorn of Prevennis,' said Bo, trying to deepen his voice, before going on to introduce his companions.

'Well, Prince Asbjorn, you and your followers are welcome to enter this land. Many outsiders have come since the summons was issued, but yours is truly the most unusual company I've witnessed.'

'You'll get no argument from me,' said Valbrand.

The warrior's piercing gaze quickly fell upon the Gigas. 'Do my eyes trick me or are you not the *Andrapoda*?'

Paleos tugged at his beard and harrumphed. 'Little we care for *that* name. We are the Gigas. If you choose to insult us, be assured that our fighting skills have not waned.'

'Forgive my clumsy words,' said the warrior, holding up his hands. 'These are troublesome days, and courtesy and trust are the victims of our vigilance. I am Maron, Captain of the Pertinax. We guard these borders. I apologise for the hostile reception but we have cause to be wary. We saw four Redeemers clothed in white raiment close to the river not three days ago.'

'They will not trouble you again,' said Bo. 'They have been slain.'

'You slew them?' said Maron, his eyes wide with astonishment.

'Well, the Gigas did,' said Bo, gesturing towards Paleos.

Maron bowed towards the Gigas. 'Old ones, we are grateful for your actions. You honour us by answering the summons.'

His words placated Paleos a little, and the Gigas grunted an acknowledgement.

'You have arrived just in time,' continued Maron. 'There's soon to be a council, called by the *Protos* Gnothi. More than that, I cannot say. We Pertinax are simple soldiers, and not included in the discussions of the wise.'

'Soldiers will be needed soon enough,' said Bo.

'Aye, war brews in every land,' said Maron. He put his helmet back on. 'Its bloody hand will come to us all.'

As they started towards the Ágios Mountains, Bo looked up at the gloomy peaks, feeling a surge of emotions: fear, excitement, wonder. What would the days to come bring? He had a sense of momentous motions within the world, as though the very veins of the earth moved living beings into position for one last struggle, like the pieces of a colossal game. Perhaps fate was already set; perhaps it was yet to be made. Whatever the truth, Bo knew the challenges he faced would test every drop of his resolve and strength.

CHAPTER SEVEN

The Petrified Forest

When the cold light of dawn crept over the edge of the Altheart, the bright new star still shone, unmoved by the sun's appearance. The Khiltoi looked up at it fearfully as they broke camp and prepared to leave the forest's protection. Under Corcoran's instruction, they crossed the ford, an experience Elowen found far from enjoyable. The slippery stones made it difficult to get a foothold and the icy water numbed her legs. She was relieved to stumble onto the far bank.

Scrubland stretched ahead, with low-growing shrubs and wind-bent trees scattered across gloomy hills. The wind carried a milder touch, and the peaks of the hills were mostly snow-free.

Once they had all crossed the river, Corcoran led the company south. They followed a haphazard route through the hills and Elowen wondered if Corcoran himself was lost. She expressed her concerns to Bryna who said, 'Fear not, Elowen. We Khiltoi need no maps. The landscape guides us: the hills, the stones and the sun.'

There was little sign of life, but the Khiltoi remained alert and watchful. Some scouts went ahead to observe, while others patrolled the flanks and rear of the company. Despite the Khiltoi's vigilance, Elowen felt vulnerable and exposed in the wide-open, lonely landscape.

After two more days of hard marching, distant snow-tipped peaks became visible on the horizon. Corcoran stopped and pointed to them. 'Omphalos lies within the Ágios Mountains. We should reach the foothills within three days.'

They plodded on. Bryna spent much of the time scouting ahead, but at other times she walked alongside Elowen, who out of her ceaseless curiosity mined her for knowledge.

'Have you ever been to the Petrified Forest?' she said.

'No. It is said to be rich with the *bládh*. Long ago, the gods transformed all the trees in the forest into stone. Why they did so, I know not, though once I heard that Ignis, the God of Fire robbed them of their life in a fit of anger. The thought of seeing the forest makes my heart skip. I believed it to be little more than a place of imagination, somewhere I'd never witness. Now it shall be made real to me.'

'Do your people ever travel to the lands beyond the Altheart?' said Elowen.

'Before the *glac'har* we traded in peace with many other races of Eldar, and brought countless wonders back to our lands. We learnt skills of farming, of working with wood and stone. But the darkness of the *glac'har* closed the world to us. Your coming has woken us from a deep slumber.'

'If that's true, you might not thank us when you see what you've woken up too,' said Diggory.

Bryna gave him a hard look. 'We understand the danger, and we're not afraid.'

As dawn broke the next day, they reached the Petrified Forest. An awesome, bewildering sight greeted them. Looking across a dry, scrubby plain Elowen saw thousands of fallen tree trunks, all stripped of branches and leaves. Yet she realised that these were not normal trunks, for although they showed roots, bark and growth rings, they were but reproductions in silica of trees long dead. The bark of the quartz trees was dark red-brown, and splits and chips revealed a kaleidoscope of mineral-shaded colours. Energy pulsed from the stone trees, energy that made Elowen's skin tingle and sharpened her senses. She felt connected to the land around her, feeling the soil move and vibrate beneath her feet.

'The *bládh* is strong here,' said Bryna, looking knowingly at Elowen. 'The stones of this land carry boundless power, yet I see little life.'

Although it was winter, Elowen could not imagine spring ever visiting such a place. Surely no flowers bloomed amongst the dreary hills and stone. Surely the sweet fragrance of blossom never carried on the dry wind. A few lizards scurried over and under the trees, trying to siphon some warmth from the winter sun. Birds hurried across the sky, keen to reach safer, fruitful lands.

The forest's cheerless atmosphere disturbed the Khiltoi. They spoke little and walked with their weapons at the ready, as though expecting an attack at any moment. The radiant star still loomed above them, burning through the day as well as the night.

'I hope we're soon out of this ghastly place,' said Diggory.

'It is hard going,' said Batu, the Orok looking more tired

than Elowen could ever remember. 'I greatly miss our steeds, Takhi and Ivuli, though I doubt this journey would be to any horse's liking. Even our famed arrow riders spoke in trembling voices of the spirits and demons that lurk in this land. They believed it is not a place intended for mortals and I am inclined to agree.'

But the Petrified Forest invigorated Elowen. The Earth-soul soothed her aches and pains, replacing tiredness with vitality. She brushed her hands over the stone tree-trunks, enjoying the tingle on her fingertips and the surges of energy through her body. She knew nothing of the spirits and demons Batu feared, but she divined there were memories woven into the very fabric of the land. Memories of deeds and words long past, of gods worshipped, propitiated and then forsaken. The forest encouraged the imagination to run wild, to concoct speculative histories. Dead and mournful it stood, but once life had thrived and in doing so left a potent presence.

They reached a shallow, U-shaped valley, where the stone trees scattered in far greater numbers. Elowen tried to imagine it as a lush, fertile valley, overflowing with foliage and plants, green and juicy and damp, dusted by pollen and ringing with birdsong and animals cries. Now, it was little more than a desert, although Elowen spotted a stream dribbling along the base of the valley.

They approached a large stone tree, which unlike the others remained upright. Around the tree stood more stones, diamond-shaped with a leathery texture, and with peculiar ridges and protrusions. Elowen counted two dozen of them, some in groups of three or four, others spaced out

142

singularly. The Khiltoi poked some of them with their clubs. Looking at the stones gave Elowen an uncanny sensation. They were just as rich with the Earthsoul as the trees, but they touched her in another, organic way, as though life throbbed through the stones.

One of the Khiltoi pointed up to the sky, watching a group of soaring vultures.

'Not exactly a hopeful sight,' said Diggory

'They won't be feasting on us,' said Batu. 'We should—'

The valley filled with a barrage of hoots and deep, fierce-sounding barks. To Elowen's amazement, all the diamond-shaped stones pulled themselves apart, revealing them not to be stones at all, but winged creatures. Their leathery wings opened up to expose a protruding snout and a furry body with two legs tipped with eagle-like talons. Their eyes were brown and bulbous. Sharp teeth filled their wide mouth. Some of the winged creatures took to the air, hovering above the ground with slow flapping wing beats.

'They are Sciathans!' said Corcoran. 'Blood-sucking fiends!'

Hooting, hissing and bearing their teeth, the Sciathans attacked the Khiltoi vanguard. They grabbed the warriors by their shoulders and pounded on their back with their taloned feet, not breaking the tough, bark-like skin but giving hefty blows. Then the Sciathans retreated and rallied around the upright tree, and there they flailed, stamped and barked.

The Khiltoi responded with insults and war cries. As they readied their weapons, Corcoran said to Batu, 'Orok, strike one of them down to let them know we are not cowed. Once the first demon falls, we'll charge.'

Batu notched an arrow in his bow. Elowen *Linked* with the Sciathans. Emotions flooded her. She experienced their anger and throbbing aggression but nothing like the Wyvern's age-old wickedness. Their hostility came from *fear*. Elowen tasted it. They were mortally afraid. And something else, an instinctive bond, a mood of protectiveness.

Elowen spied amongst the Sciathans several smaller creatures of their kind, clearly their offspring. She understood the reason for the creatures' aggression. Just as Batu drew his bow to fire Elowen shoved his arm, sending the arrow spinning harmlessly to the ground, striking a rock with a puff of dust.

'Have your wits deserted you, Elowen?' said Batu.

'They're not attacking us,' she said. She pointed to the Sciathan's offspring. 'Look, they're protecting their young. They're defending themselves.'

'The ancestors be praised, she's right,' said Bryna. She shouted to the warriors, 'Step back from the tree, lower your weapons.'

'Are you mad?' said Corcoran. Caught between the arguments, the warriors dithered.

'It's the Sciathan's nest,' said Elowen. 'Leave it alone and they won't trouble us.'

'Do as she says,' said Bryna. 'Get away from the tree.'

Corcoran ordered the warriors to back away. They retreated several paces and the Sciathans ceased their hooting and flapping. They surrounded the tree in vigilant silence.

'This is madness,' said Corcoran. 'They are massing for another attack. If we try to get around them they are bound to assault us again. The only way forward is through them.'

'I don't think so,' said Elowen. Without another word, she walked towards the Sciathans. As she approached, the winged creatures stamped and made loud tooth-clacking sounds, but she felt no fear. To her surprise, she realised that Diggory walked beside her. She said to him, 'Go back, it's not safe.'

He looked at her gravely. 'If these things attack you, I want to be by your side.'

Elowen knew she would not be able to persuade him to do otherwise, so decided not to argue. And she was grateful for his presence and support.

The largest Sciathan, with huge wings and mottled white fur, waddled closer to Elowen and Diggory. He gave off an odour that reminded Elowen of a damp dog. She stood still, calmed herself, concentrated and *Linked* with the creature.

I named Tacheía. This is our tree. You not come here.

Elowen bowed, instinctively feeling that it was the right thing to do. 'We are sorry. We mean you no harm.'

Tacheía narrowed his eyes. *You not harm our infants. You not steal our food or water. If you try, we kill.*

'We haven't come to do any of those things,' said Elowen. She glanced at Diggory who was looking at her very strangely, as though he was afraid of her. Dismissing such a thought, she considered what the Sciathan had said about food and delved into her pack. She pulled out a small mouldy apple. She held it out towards the Sciathan and said, 'Please, take this.'

The Sciathan snatched the apple with his hooked thumbs. He sniffed it suspiciously and when satisfied, gave it to one of the infants, who gobbled it down.

145

'Diggory,' said Elowen, her voice a whisper. 'Get more food from the Khiltoi, as much as they're willing to spare.'

'That won't be much.'

'I know, but get what you can.'

He reluctantly plodded back to the Khiltoi and relayed Elowen's request. Even at a distance, Elowen heard Corcoran's cry of astonishment, but at Bryna's urging he yielded a small harvest of nuts, seeds and fruit. Elowen and Diggory placed the food close to the foot of the tree.

At first the Sciathans were cautious. Tacheía scuttled forward and inspected the seeds. Once he had nibbled a few, he squawked to the others, who eagerly shared the food amongst themselves. As they ate, the creatures made soft, happy grunting sounds. Tacheía, whom Elowen decided was their leader, approached and pointed at her. *Friend. We not fight. If you in danger in forest, we help.*

To Elowen's surprise, the Sciathan wrapped his wings loosely around her. Then, he returned to his kin.

Elowen turned to Corcoran. 'We should go. They won't hinder us now.'

'Don't give me orders, child,' he said, resentful at Elowen's role in avoiding a costly and dangerous fight. He motioned for the warriors to move forward, keeping a safe distance from the Sciathan nest.

As they continued on their way, Bryna said to Elowen, 'You are mysterious, Elowen. Where did you learn to imitate the Sciathans' speech?'

Elowen frowned. 'Imitate their speech? I don't know what you mean. Their words came—'

'But you sounded like one of them,' said Bryna.

Elowen looked at Diggory for confirmation. He shrugged and said, 'Aye, it reminded me of when you were with that mangy wolf Ulfur.'

Dumbfounded, Elowen spluttered, 'I…thought…'

'Do not be troubled, Elowen,' said Batu kindly. 'Your skills grow and I think there are more wonders to come from you yet.'

Diggory said, 'Sometimes you scare me. When you use the Earthsoul, I mean.'

'Why?'

'You look…different, you are different. It's like you're possessed.'

'*Possessed!*' said Elowen, startled.

'I know you're not possessed, and I'm grateful for your power. God knows, you've saved me enough times. It's…unsettling.'

'It's still me, it's always me,' said Elowen. 'I control the golden threads, they don't control me.'

He smiled and gave her a long stare. 'I hope so.'

*

Unheimlich hurtled through the Altheart Forest. The scent drove him on; he saw it, like a river of smoke guiding him towards his target. Rich and intoxicating it filled his body, like warm water flowing through cold pipes. He moved with incredible speed, so fast, so quiet that a rabbit nibbling on an exposed root felt his fleeting presence as no more than a momentary breeze on his fur. With every step the smell intensified: he was getting closer.

147

He knew nothing of tiredness, hunger or thirst, but as night fell Unheimlich stopped. He had seen much. His prey was not far away now. Unheimlich stretched his mind to Lord Lucien.

*

Lord Lucien lay in his wagon, tired but not lulled to sleep by the rhythmic rocking of the wooden wheels and the clopping of the horses' hooves. Sleep was a rare gift for him, and on the journey back to the camp at Latibulum, he mulled over many things: training and provisions for the army, preparations and planned dispositions for the battle Prester John said would soon come. But above all, he thought about Elowen. She was strong and resourceful; Lord Lucien worried what would happen if she did find the Tree of Life.

He sat upright, stretching his aching limbs. He found to his consternation that the fresh insertions of Cold Iron encouraged by his physicians no longer eased his pain. He glanced at the mirror. A sense of duty prodded him to contact his Master, to report what he had learnt but he was too tired, and the effort of using the mirror always drained him.

His mind restless, he picked up the nearest book, a 'Book of Hours', the pages curled, the paper speckled brown with age. He turned to the page showing the image of the 'Man of Sorrows'. The angels held up the tortured Saviour's dead body, urging the reader to meditate on his suffering. *Suffering.* Lord Lucien remembered his own suffering well enough, and not just the devouring darkness of his cell. He remembered the pain and humiliation of torture: the rack, reverse hanging, barbed metal lashes, mutilation. The leering faces of leech-skinned priests. FALSE PROPHET. BLASPHEMPER. He slammed the book shut.

As Lord Lucien settled to lie down again, a blinding headache struck, as fierce as a blow to the skull but the pain came from inside his head. Dizzying and stomach-churning shapes and colours hurt his eyes. The shapes and colours coalesced into images he recognised: moonlit trees and snow. He realised what was happening. Unheimlich was making contact.

Although sickened by his mind being in thrall to Hohenheim's abomination, Lord Lucien concentrated on the vision. He saw a river, broad and sparkling, with dreary windswept lands on the far bank. Unheimlich showed him the position of the stars and from them Lord Lucien began to divine his location. South of the Altheart Forest for sure, heading towards the Ágios Mountains.

The connection ceased. Lord Lucien exhaled in relief. The effort and strain had been worse than using the mirror of Prester John. He tried to expand the knowledge given to him by Unheimlich. South. That would mean either taking the pass of Thanásima, or crossing the Petrified Forest. Both hazardous routes, but Lord Lucien judged the latter to be the most likely choice. He knew a detachment of Redeemers patrolled the Petrified Forest, barely a day away from a speedy messenger. They might have a chance…

He got to his feet and shouted for the driver of the wagon to stop.

*

Elowen felt a knot of nerves in her stomach. Something intangible, unknown, troubled her. She detected slight changes in the scents carried on the wind, a stillness that felt somehow unnatural, alien.

Evening approached, the dusky sky a patchwork of reds, yellows and blacks. The wind subsided to a faint murmur. They trudged across a plain strewn with boulders and stone trees. Elowen looked up at the wispy-edged, slow moving clouds, feeling a sense of foreboding. Two days had passed since they had left the Sciathan's valley. She touched her mother's pendant, something she had done many times since leaving Trecadok, a habit, a source of comfort. But now she regretted the action, unconscious though it was, a lapse, a weakness. She kept the pendant as a reminder of everything she did not want to become; to touch it for strength or reassurance felt like a betrayal.

'We can make camp on that peak yonder,' said Corcoran, pointing about a mile ahead, where a hill stood on the other side of a bubbling stream. 'If we set off again at dawn we should be out of the forest by midday. It should—'

A Khiltoi scout cried out, and gestured towards the west. From that direction, following the line of the stream, came several riders. Elowen counted twenty at least. As the riders galloped towards the company throwing up clouds of dust, Elowen recognised with horror their flapping white robes and demon-like black horses. Redeemers.

Corcoran bellowed orders as the Khiltoi warriors readied their weapons. 'Slingers and archers at the front. Take down as many of them as you can before they reach us.'

150

However, the Redeemers lined up along the far side of the stream, out of range of the Khiltoi arrows and slingshots, which splashed vainly into the water.

Batu grabbed Elowen by the arm. 'Stay with Chinua and me.'

The Khiltoi made a deafening cacophony. They yelled out boasts and bloody curses. They beat and rattled their weapons. Their eyes grew wild with battle fury, frightening Elowen with the savage intensity that animated their whole bodies.

Consumed with anger, five Khiltoi broke rank and charged at the Redeemers, waving their clubs and sprinting towards the stream with huge leaping strides. The Redeemers galloped towards them and ran the Khiltoi warriors down, their blades flashing like silver ice. Elowen heard the warriors' death cries and watched in horror as their lifeless bodies slumped into the stream.

The Redeemers broke their line formation and galloped around the company in a wide circle, hurtling so fast that Elowen saw them as little more than white blurs, obscured further by the dust they whipped up. The Khiltoi greeted them with a hail of slingshot and arrows, but the Redeemers somehow evaded every missile.

Elowen heard the crackle of guns and the scream of lead balls cutting through the air. The Redeemers fired pistols and carbines, holding them one-handed as they rode. Two Khiltoi warriors fell.

'They're slaying us one by one,' said Batu as he fired arrow after arrow at the elusive Redeemers, only to miss with every shot.

'We'll be slaughtered!' said Diggory.

To Elowen's dismay, a Redeemer pointed his sword at her and gave a bloodcurdling screech. Flanked by another rider, the Redeemer charged directly at her. Elowen froze in terror, unable to move her limbs or think clearly. Someone stepped in front of her: Chinua. The Orok cut down the first Redeemer from his horse with a brutal slash of his sword. As the second Redeemer held aloft his blade to strike at Elowen, Chinua hurled his full weight against the horse, knocking the Redeemer from his saddle. The Orok drove his sword into the unhorsed Redeemer but a pistol cracked and he shuddered violently, and dropped to his knees, clutching his chest. Blood streamed through his fingers. He pitched forward, face first, and did not move.

Ignoring the hiss of pistol and carbine fire, Batu pushed past Elowen and dragged Chinua back into the circle. Batu cradled his fellow Orok's body and examined his wound. He shook his head despairingly. 'He is dead.'

Diggory cried out in despair. Elowen's legs shook, and she struggled to stay upright.

'Curse them,' said Batu.

The guns crackled again and more Khiltoi warriors fell.

Bryna gripped Elowen's shoulder. 'You have to do something.'

'Me? What can I do?'

'Use the power within you. Use the *bládh*, you are strong enough. You are a *bana-buidhseach*. Only you can save us.'

Elowen saw the terror in the eyes of her friends and the Khiltoi. More would die, perhaps all of them. She steeled herself and walked slowly towards the Redeemers.

152

'Elowen, what are you doing?' she heard Diggory ask. She shook off his grasping hand.

She kept walking but closed her eyes, shutting out the brutal sights and harsh noise of battle. Her thoughts cast back to when she had faced the Wyvern, of how she had controlled the Earthsoul. Remembering those sensations, she connected to the soil, to the stone trees, becoming part of a river of energy. She opened her eyes, watching the golden threads dance and swirl. Elowen felt the ground shuddering beneath the Redeemer's horses. She felt the cracks in the soil, the movement of stones and rocks.

Straining with her mind and body, she stretched out, connecting with ground far away from her physical reach. The closest stone trees vibrated violently and split asunder. The shards blew over the Redeemers, and the ground beneath them opened up into huge fissures, which swallowed some of the horses and riders whole.

An eerie silence followed. The dust and smoke settled. All the Redeemers were unhorsed, their steeds dead or injured. Most of the Redeemers were dead too, but the few survivors rose to their feet, still clasping their pistols and swords. The fight was not over yet.

The Earthsoul still pumped through Elowen—the familiar tingle in her head of *Linking*, followed by a rush of emotions, of thoughts not of her own making. The air filled with birds. No, not birds, as Elowen realised when she looked up. Sciathans. Like hawks swooping down upon a mouse or rabbit, they attacked. Working in pairs, the Sciathans plucked the Redeemers from the ground, lifted them high into the air and let them fall, hooting and screeching as

153

the bodies of their hapless victims dashed on the stones and rocks below. Six Redeemers survived the Sciathan assault. Grievously injured, they tried to crawl away but the Khiltoi were in no mood for mercy. The warriors pounced upon their stricken foes and yelling gleeful battle cries beheaded them with their stone blades. Corcoran held up one of the gory heads, shouting praises to the ancestors as he did so. Some of the horses still lived, although in agony from their injuries. Grim-faced, Batu put them out of their misery, the act as painful to him as it was merciful.

With the battle over, Elowen sank to her knees; she found breathing hard. She thought she was going to faint. A distant voice called out, 'Elowen! Elowen!'

She rubbed her eyes and her vision settled. Trembling, she looked up and saw Diggory. He said, 'Are you hurt?'

'No, I'm just…tired,' she said. Unnerving sensations prickled through her body, and sharp spasms afflicted her muscles. 'Drained would be a better word, in fact.'

'The *bládh* takes a heavy toll,' said Bryna, who stood behind her.

'Are all the Redeemers dead?' said Elowen, squinting in the sinking sun's sharp light. The trembling in her legs and arms began to subside.

Bryna smiled. 'Yes, through your bravery and skill we are saved. Truly you are a *bana-buidhseach*. I have never seen the *bládh* wielded so. You possess a rare power, Elowen, a rare power indeed.'

'You trounced those Redeemers, that's for sure,' said Diggory.

The Sciathans circled, hooting triumphantly. Tacheía descended and landed with surprising elegance in front of Elowen.

You need help. We came.

'Thank you. You saved us.'

You friend. We help friend. Safe now white devils gone. They all dead. You should stay. Other places dangerous. Here is safe.

'We cannot stay, for if we fail, then nowhere will be truly safe,' said Elowen, knowing as she spoke that the Sciathan could not comprehend what she meant.

Tacheía peered at her. *Stay, friend. You belong with the trees.*

Elowen smiled. 'I'm not sure I belong anywhere. But we must go. Thank you again. I hope you remain in peace.'

Tacheía made a deep guttural sound, lifted into the air and swooped away, followed by the other Sciathans, many of them performing acrobatics as they flew.

Elowen turned to Bryna. 'Are there many warriors dead?'

Bryna nodded. 'Yes, and others are wounded, some mortally.'

'And it is to them that you should attend,' said Corcoran, swaggering towards them, still holding the severed head of a Redeemer. 'Your skills as a healer are needed.'

Bryna took a sharp intake of breath. 'My skills? I am not like Bandraoi. I'm not the *taghta.*'

Corcoran gave her a withering look. 'For long years you've studied with Bandraoi, you are deep in her lore and cunning. Enough of our kin have died this day. We must do all we can to save the wounded.'

Bryna looked uncertain, but she agreed and hurried to attend to the Khiltoi casualties. Corcoran lingered. He cleared his throat and while looking up at the sky, said to Elowen,

'Without your…help, we should not have bested the *drouks*.'

Elowen shrugged, not sure how to respond.

'You've felt the harsh side of my tongue,' said Corcoran. 'But we Khiltoi are truth speakers, despite what you may think of me. I've little love for you or your kind, for Men have done untold damage to my people. But I cannot ignore your acts, nor your bravery. Truly you've earned the right to walk alongside our warriors.'

'You honour me,' said Elowen, feeling awkward.

'How do you think the Redeemers found us here?' said Diggory.

'They haunt many lands,' said Corcoran. 'We're just victims of unhappy chance.'

'There is little the Redeemers leave to chance,' said Batu, returning bloodstained from his grisly duty. 'It is dangerous to tarry here.'

'What of the dead?' said Corcoran. 'We cannot leave their bones to be picked dry by the carrion crows.'

'Do not put the living at risk for the dead,' said Batu.

Corcoran opened his mouth to argue but understood the wisdom of the Orok's words. He faced the surviving warriors and said, 'Pay your respects to our dead, but do it swiftly. Then be ready to leave.'

With no time to dig graves, and no wood to form a pyre, the Khiltoi settled on entombing their dead in rough cairns. Elowen stared at the mounds of stones. It was such a lonely place to die, with a tomb never to be visited, never to be remembered, only slowly ground to meal by the relentless work of wind and sun.

156

She saw Batu standing over the cairn built for Chinua. Gingerly, she approached him. He did not turn round.

'I'm sorry,' said Elowen. 'Chinua was very brave. He saved my life.'

'His passing wounds me, but he died courageously, like a true Orok warrior,' said Batu. 'He goes now to the Eternal Blue, to dwell there in peace.'

Elowen pulled out the jade pendant that Batu had given her. 'Chinua should have this. It is a poor offering, I suppose, not worthy of his sacrifice, but it's all I have.'

Batu placed a hand on her shoulder. 'The gesture makes it worthy. This way a piece of Gondwana remains with him forever.'

Elowen slipped the pendant into a gap between the stones. She said, 'We are always surrounded by death.'

'I have seen too much pain and suffering to cry,' said Batu. Elowen noticed he held Chinua's knife, the blade warped by the Egregore's molten ooze. 'You think me cold, perhaps. I have buried so many friends, too many friends. Lives cut short, lives that should have blossomed.'

It shocked Elowen to hear Batu speak so candidly, so emotionally. The Orok went on to say, 'I do not want much from this life. A wife, a child. A simple life, a peaceful life. Perhaps a little land, a strong horse, goats. That would be my chosen reward at the end of all this misery, not gold or glory.'

'You'd be a good father.'

He smiled. 'I hope I have the chance, one day. Sadly, the gods conspire to force me down the road of war. But you encourage me, Elowen. Forgive my morbid words and do

157

not doubt my commitment to your quest. I will defend you, to the death.'

'Let's hope it never comes to that.'

Batu sheathed Chinua's knife. 'I keep this in his memory. May his strength and sacrifice inspire us.'

As darkness rolled across the plains of the Petrified Forest, the weary, grief-stricken company slogged towards the heights on the edge of that dry, forsaken land. The sky was empty of birds. The lizards and insects kept to warm, dry holes. But the company did not cross the bubbling stream unnoticed. Unheimlich crawled over one of the stone trees, his eyes never straying from the company. He drank in the rich scent of the girl. She was so close to him now, so close, a connection no distance could break.

*

The Khiltoi kept a careful watch that evening, doubling their number of sentries. Diggory volunteered to help, and spent three cold hours listening for the dreaded sound of horses' hooves. However, the night drew on and no attack came.

Elowen strolled restlessly through the camp. The land around them slumbered in almost perfect darkness, with only a faint sliver of light pushed out grudgingly from the waning moon. Looking out from the camp offered a view that could have existed in the dawn of time, with no distant firelights, no sign of the existence of Men.

As Elowen wandered she spied a Khiltoi sat cross-legged, far from the warmth of the nearest fire. At first she thought it was one of the sentries but then realised it was Bryna. Listlessly the Khiltoi ran a comb made from antler through her hair. She jumped when Elowen approached.

'I'm sorry, I didn't mean to startle you,' said Elowen.

'No, I'm edgy, it's been…a difficult day,' said Bryna.

Elowen sat beside Bryna, sensing that she wanted to talk. 'How are the injured warriors?'

Bryna rubbed her eyes. 'I've saved some that would have otherwise been lost.'

'That's good.'

'But two others, Drust and Maedoc, were beyond my help and died,' said Bryna. She pointed up at the bright star that still shone with furious intensity, unbroken by day or night. 'I wonder if that star really is an omen. Perhaps it burns for a cause and purpose all of its own. I wonder if we look for signs in the world around us, turning natural phenomena into markers in our lives. I think maybe we should act more on the signs and messages of our own hearts.'

'I think there's much we don't understand,' said Elowen.

Bryna twirled her comb around in her fingers. 'If Bandra-oi had been here, she might've saved Drust and Maedoc. She is *taghta*.'

'As you'll be one day.'

Bryna fidgeted. 'Every time I compare myself to Bandraoi I am found wanting. I know what my people expect of me, but I fear that I'm not strong or wise enough to achieve it.'

'You're being too harsh on yourself,' said Elowen. She found it strange, disconcerting, listening to Bryna's concerns, as they echoed her own so closely.

'The forest has been my home, my world, all my life,' said

159

the Khiltoi, her shoulders slumped. 'But faced with such dangers, everything I've learnt is like thistledown in the wind. In the Altheart I was as swift and fierce as a wild cat. Outside, my strength and courage desert me.'

'I don't believe that,' said Elowen. 'We're all being tested. I'm frightened all of the time.'

'Then what keeps you going?'

Elowen toyed with strands of her hair. 'Hope, I suppose, foolish though it may be. I hope for better days, for an end to fear and suffering.'

'I doubt such days will ever come to pass. But I admire your strength and your conviction.'

The mention of *strength* formed an image of *Burilgi Maa* to flash in Elowen's mind. The words of Lord Lucien echoed at the edge of her consciousness: *Join with me, child. Finish the task that your mother started.* Elowen touched her mother's pendant, before shaking her head, trying to block out such thoughts. 'You think *I'm* strong? I've wanted to run away from all this many times.'

'Then why haven't you?'

'I fight on for my friends, remembering their kindness, and I draw strength from that. Think of your tribe, of your home back at the Dachaigh. Is that not worth fighting for?'

'Yes, indeed it is,' said Bryna. She smiled and tenderly took Elowen's hands in her own. The touch of her skin was rough but warm. 'You're wise beyond your years, Elowen. We are of different races but there is, I feel, a common spirit between us. I swear to be your friend, until the sky falls upon us, or the earth opens up to swallow us, or the sea arises to overwhelm us.'

160

Touched, Elowen said, 'I swear that too.'

'And whatever dangers the days to come may bring, we'll face them, together.'

*

The pain of the connection struck Lord Lucien as though a hand drove into his skull and clasped his brain. Images formed: gouges in the dusty earth, rocks splintered and shattered, winged creatures, abhorrent survivors from primordial bloodlines, scattered bodies of Redeemers, butchered and defiled...

The attack had failed. Elowen had escaped. Lord Lucien broke the connection with Unheimlich, feeling the rush of blood to his head, the sense of life gushing through his veins. The darkness inside the wagon smothered him like a clammy fog. Finding it difficult to breathe, he pulled off his mask, gulping air. He massaged the broken skin on his face, trying to calm himself. For the time being, Elowen was out of his grasp, but he refused to give up. Anger fuelled his determination. Unheimlich would not cease his pursuit. As long as the creature continued to track Elowen, Lord Lucien knew he still had a chance to find her. He needed to be patient, he told himself. God would not betray him now.

*

The weary company set off at dawn, tramping beneath a brooding blood-red sky. The Petrified Forest gave way to the foothills of the Ágios Mountains. Elowen drank in the smells of rich, fresh vegetation: the heady, resinous aroma of pine trees and the light oily scent of olive trees heavy with their black fruit.

From the foothills, a narrow, winding path rose to unseen heights. Ruins spread around the foot of the path. Elowen saw a rectangular door, more than twenty feet in height and fashioned from four blocks of marble. It stood lonely, the building that it once served long since crumbled to dust. There was a colonnade of fluted marble columns joined by their entablature, as well as other scattered columns, some upright with their capitals still attached, others fallen with wiry grass sprouting around the shattered pieces.

Corcoran called a brief rest. Elowen wandered up to the lonely door, running her hands over the marble. As her fingers brushed away dust they revealed symbols, unrecognisable to her, a form of writing she guessed. She wondered who had ever lived in such a remote, desolate region and what had become of them. They would surely be saddened to see their labours dilapidated and abandoned.

A cry of alarm dragged her back into the present, followed by a sound even more terrifying: the pounding of horses' hooves. She spun round. From the east rose a cloud of dust. She heard someone shout, 'REDEEMERS!'

Elowen sprinted back to the company, who readied for another battle. Arrows notched in bows. Smoothed stones placed in slings. Elowen heard the Khiltoi warriors whisper prayers to their ancestors.

Corcoran said, 'Stay together—when the *drouks* are close enough, use every arrow and stone we have. If they charge, stand tall and hack them down with your clubs.'

Elowen's heart thumped. She gulped in air, paralyzed with fear. Still drained after the previous day's battle and the effort of using the Earthsoul, she battled to control her trembling body.

The dust cloud grew taller and the sound of hammering hooves louder. Elowen heard other sounds: the blowing of horns, and booming, lusty singing.

'They're not Redeemers!' said Bryna.

Still obscured by dust, the riders placed themselves between the mountains and the company. As they slowed to a canter, Elowen caught her first clear glimpse of them and she gasped in utter surprise. They each had the body and legs of a potent stallion, and growing from their shoulders the head, arms and torso of a muscular, hirsute man.

'What in God's name are these things?' said Diggory.

'Bandraoi spoke of such a race once,' said Bryna. 'She named them the Marcaiche but I have heard them commonly called Centaurs.'

Diggory said, 'Just when I think I've seen everything—'

Elowen shushed him, overwhelmed by the sight of the Centaurs, magical beings somehow made real. They excited both awe and fear within her. They possessed an untamed wildness mixed with a reasoning intelligence.

The Centaurs came to a halt. One of them, a bulky creature with thick muscle-knotted arms and a reddish brown beard, trotted a little forward. In a rumbling voice he said, 'I am Archontos, and none cross this threshold without my consent. Strangers, what is the word?'

'Address us with more respect and you'll get an answer,' said Corcoran.

163

'By my troth, you are foolish to provoke me with hot words,' said Archontos. The other Centaurs swished their tails, stamped the ground and shouted angrily; some kicked out with their hooves, a show of aggression and threat. Elowen smelt their hot, musky aroma. She feared a fight breaking out.

Batu stepped forward between the Centaurs and the Khiltoi. He bowed towards Archontos. In a slow, soothing voice that reminded Elowen of how he used to speak to his horse, the Orok said, 'You are right to be wary but we have no quarrel here. The word is Omphalos, and we have travelled far and through great danger to answer the summons.'

Upon hearing his words, the Centaurs calmed. Archontos pointed at Batu. 'You speak with sense, my friend. Very well, we shall guide you all into the mountains.'

'We are grateful,' said Batu. 'Have many answered the summons?'

The Centaur flexed his arms. 'Yes, but fewer than we hoped for. Eldar of many lands have arrived. A ragtag group of Men, giants and some blue-skinned beings from across the sea arrived yesterday, but I doubt many more will come.'

'These are dangerous days,' said Batu.

Archontos pointed to the new star. 'Yea, the flaming eye of heaven presages war.'

'Have you heard aught of Oroks?' said Batu.

Archontos blinked and shook his head. 'You are the first of your kind I have seen here. Word reached us of warriors mustering in the east under their new Khan, but even if such tales are true, the warriors have yet to arrive.'

Batu looked disheartened, but did not reply.

'This is the last part of your journey,' said Archontos. 'The going is hard for two-legged beings. The path twists and rises steeply up the mountain.'

'None match the Khiltoi for strength and endurance,' said Corcoran. His closest followers muttered agreement.

'Such boasts will be tested,' said Archontos. 'You are far from the safety of your forest now.'

Sure-footed, the Centaurs trotted up the path, which snaked every bit as much as Archontos had warned. Out of pride, or sheer bravado, Corcoran and the Khiltoi warriors matched the Centaurs' pace, soon forming a gap between them and Elowen, Diggory, Batu and Bryna.

As the path rose, it afforded spectacular views across the Ágios Mountains, giant slabs of limestone carved by aeons of wind, rain, sun and ice. Veins of snow spread down from the frozen peaks. But the land's harsh beauties were lost on Elowen. Her calves, knees and shins ached, while blisters nagged her toes and the soles of her feet. The bitter, eddying wind attacked from all sides. More than once, Elowen peered down in alarm at the vertiginous drops either side of the crooked path.

She plodded on, suffering with every footstep. For a short time, Diggory tried to support her, placing a hand on her back and gently pushing her forward. Yet the exertion proved too much for him and he was forced to funnel all his efforts and strength into his own struggle up the path.

The air thinned and Elowen's pace slowed to little more than a crawl. Bryna stopped and looked at her. 'I can carry you at least some of the way.'

'No,' said Elowen. 'I won't be a burden.'

'Let her carry you,' said Diggory between laboured gasps. 'If not, I'll gladly let her take me instead.'

Elowen finally acceded and allowed Bryna to pick her up, throwing her arms around the Khiltoi's neck to hold on. Bryna carried her until the path disappeared at the foot of a broad slope. It was shadowed by the fearsome peak to the south, and peppered with granite boulders and pitted with ice-filled depressions in the ground. Steps led up to an arched gateway, which marked the highest point of the slope. Four warriors, each carrying a round shield and long spear, guarded the gateway. They wore elaborate armour, with a bronze helmet, corsets of leather, and metal greaves.

As Archontos and the Centaurs approached, the warriors cheered and clattered their shields together in greeting. The Centaurs passed under the gateway and moved out of sight. The rest of the company followed them and Elowen realised with discomfort that the gateway led through to a narrow wooden bridge over a yawning ravine.

The Centaurs crossed confidently, their hooves clattering on the wooden planks. Hoping it would take her weight, Elowen edged across guardedly, her legs shaking. The wind cried with a shrill voice and pounded the creaking bridge with icy gusts. The wooden planks beneath Elowen's feet vibrated. Her stomach lurched as she looked down once at the black nothingness below. She scarcely dared to breathe until she reached the far side, whereby upon a blustery, rocky cliff, Archontos waited for them. They now stood high above the northern end of a valley carpeted by olive trees and shut in by bare, gloomy mountains.

166

'This is the centre of the world,' said Archontos. 'Long ago, under an auspicious constellation, the King of the Gods released two eagles, one from the east and one from the west, and they met at this valley. Omphalos stands on the slopes of this mountain. There you shall find shelter and rest, for a short time. We take the path known to all here as the Sacred Way, follow me.'

The Sacred Way dropped precipitously down the southern side of the mountain. As they descended, Elowen saw that tents sprouted like mushrooms between the ruined columns, headless statues of athletic figures and atrophied buildings. A few Men walked there, and other races too, all named by Archontos. Satyrs, boisterous creatures with the legs, hooves and horns of a goat, but the hairy upper body, arms and head of a man. A tribe of Dwarfs that reminded Elowen of the Brisnings, though blessed with kinder faces. Most startling of all was a group of club-wielding giants, with long hair down to their knees. Archontos named others too, the *imbellis* races as he called them, those that would not fight if it came to war. Woodwoses and Kobolds, all heavily bearded and scarcely reaching a man's waist in height; Dryads, lithe maidens with hair like a canopy of leaves; Fauns, who resembled Satyrs in Elowen's eyes but were smaller, gentler, more graceful, with deer-like features. The *imbellis* answered the summons to Omphalos to share their wisdom and cunning, not to fight.

'Gnothi is waiting for you,' said Archontos as they stepped down a crumbling stone terrace.

'Who is Gnothi?' Elowen heard Corcoran ask suspiciously.

167

'He is the wisest amongst us, the *Protos* is his title. He knows much and peers deep into our souls.'

'You mean he is a *sorcerer*?' said Corcoran.

The Centaur swished his tail and glared at the Khiltoi, his teeth bared. 'Do not speak of things beyond your meagre understanding.'

Archontos said nothing more until they stopped at what the Centaur named as the tholos. Elowen saw a round platform with three steps. Three columns with their entablature survived, though the sprawling pieces of broken masonry suggested that many more had once been mounted there. A man stood motionless in the middle of the platform. He was slender, bald and dark-skinned. He clasped a walking stick, and wore a piece of unstitched cloth wrapped around his torso and legs and knotted at his waist. Despite his threadbare clothes, the cold did not trouble him. He had a fleshy nose and a moustache covered his top lip. He was old, with deep lines across his face, but when he smiled his eyes twinkled with mischief and childish wonderment.

'Ah, the new arrivals are here,' he said. 'I am Gnothi, *Protos* of Omphalos. I welcome you to the navel of the world. Cast aside your fears, for now at least. The pestilence of Prester John spreads unabated, but here, in this most ancient place, we stem the flow.'

'What is the purpose of the summons?' said Corcoran. 'Are we mustering for war?'

'That is still to be decided,' said Gnothi. 'You shall learn more soon, I promise. First, rest and gather your strength. We have only simple quarters but you should be comfortable enough. Archontos will take you to them.'

As the Centaur led the company away, Gnothi took Elowen's arm and gestured for her to remain. He gave her an impish wink. 'I have been looking forward to meeting *you*.'

Diggory hesitated, clearly unhappy at the prospect of leaving Elowen with the stranger. She said, 'Don't worry, I'll catch up.'

Diggory was about to turn when Gnothi said, 'No, boy. Stay with us, it is right that you should remain too. You have both travelled far, I believe, from the island of Helagan?'

Elowen nodded.

'I have never been so far west myself. Long ago, my friend Phytheas journeyed there. He told me of a wild, mysterious, fog-bound island, but I am sure it is more civilised now.'

'You'd know differently if you ever went there,' whispered Diggory.

Gnothi did not hear him, or pretended he did not, as he went on to say, 'I have some people for you both to meet.'

Hobbling with surprising speed, Gnothi led them to a tent with rich embroidery and designs. Mysterious strangers with dark-blue skin, green eyes and webbed hands loitered in the front of the tent. They looked around in surprise as Gnothi, Elowen and Diggory approached, and one of them ducked back into the tent.

'Are these the people who want to meet us?' said Diggory.

'No, they have yet to show themselves,' said Gnothi.

The stranger re-emerged from the tent and this time he was not alone. Two others followed him. Diggory gasped, swore and then laughed. Elowen cried out as soon as she saw them, barely believing her eyes, thinking that somehow a dream had leaked into reality. Wonder mixed with confusion, joy and relief. For in defiance of her deepest fears, her gloomiest thoughts, in front of her stood Black Francis and Prince Asbjorn.

PART TWO

CHAPTER EIGHT

The Oracle

E lowen ran at Black Francis and flung her arms around him. Although still huge to Elowen, he appeared somehow diminished, his eyes deeper set in his face. She sensed his pain but he tried to conceal it. He laughed, lifted her off her feet and plonked her down again. 'I always said I'd see you again, lass.'

Elowen found it hard to talk. She wanted to say so much, but all her words tumbled incoherently on top of each other.

'And Diggory too!' said Black Francis, giving him a hearty slap on the back. 'You're still traipsing along with Elowen?'

'Somebody has to keep an eye on her,' said Diggory.

Elowen noticed that Bo held back a little, though he smiled. He looked older than she had remembered, his face more careworn. She said, 'I'm pleased you're here too.'

He gave her a courtly bow. 'The honour is mine, Elowen. I can scarcely imagine your adventures since we parted.'

'We've got a few stories to tell too!' said Black Francis.

Gnothi quietly reminded everyone of his presence with a delicate cough. 'You have many tales to share, it seems, and it would be wrong for me to ask you all to part again having just become reacquainted. Yet at dusk, Elowen, I must ask you to come with me to see the Oracle.'

'Why?' said Elowen, a little alarmed.

'Do not be afraid,' said Gnothi. 'You may learn much from her, for the Oracle sees things hidden to most. She can give guidance on the trials that await you.'

'Can she see the future?'

'Many windows are open to her,' said Gnothi. 'I leave you for now, I shall return at dusk.'

When Gnothi had gone, Black Francis put his arms around Elowen and Diggory. 'Come, my friends, you must be hungry. We have food and a little wine in our tent. Share it with us while we talk.'

A hot stove warmed the tent, and Elowen and her friends tucked into a meal of crispy bread, olives and mellow wine. They talked breathlessly, as incredible tale followed incredible tale. Elowen's head swam with the details of her friends' exploits. Foreign names, wondrous beasts and exotic lands created a whirlpool of images. The descriptions of the Beauteous Isle astonished her. She shivered at Bo's recollections of the catacombs and of the deadly balebeasts, and thrilled at the story of their defeat of the King of the Sea Beggars. Black Francis told of his imprisonment by the Sea Beggars, and from his hasty descriptions Elowen wondered if he sought to conceal the true horror of what he had suffered.

For their part, Black Francis and Bo appeared equally amazed by the account she and Diggory gave.

Black Francis puffed out his cheeks. 'Oroks, Khiltoi, Elementals. You've been keeping some interesting company.'

174

'The Khiltoi sound like fierce warriors,' said Bo.

'You wouldn't want to fight them,' said Diggory, his mouth full.

'It's clear you've had a hard time,' said Black Francis. He took a deep swig of wine and wiped away the drops that fell into his beard. 'We face difficult days ahead, so I'm glad we're all together. That way we're stronger.'

'What do you make of this place?' said Diggory. 'Are you sure we can trust everyone here?'

Black Francis gave him a knowing look. 'After all you went through at the Sanctuary I understand why you'd be suspicious. But if you watch your step, you've nothing to fear from the folk here.'

'What do you mean, *watch your step*?' said Diggory.

Black Francis said, 'There are some dangerous folk here, good-hearted and foes of Prester John to be sure, but still dangerous. Perhaps dangerous is the wrong word, *wild* might suit better. Many suffered at the hands of Prester John and his cronies, and it's left them angry and unpredictable.'

The tent opened, allowing a gust of cool air to rush in. Gnothi stood there and stretched out a hand. 'It is time, Elowen. Do you have the Mystery of Fire?'

Elowen nodded.

'Good,' said Gnothi. 'The Oracle resides in the main temple, it is not far.'

Elowen followed Gnothi out of the tent. Night had fallen, a cold night with a star-encrusted sky. The bright star that unsettled the Khiltoi continued to burn fiercely. Campfires blazed, and Elowen heard murmurs of conversations, often

175

in tongues utterly alien to her, but no songs, no laughter. A sense of grim expectancy pervaded the camp. A few guards, wrapped up in cloaks against the cold, stomped around, their breath steaming.

As they walked, Elowen said, 'Is the Oracle expecting me?'

'Of course,' said Gnothi, smiling.

'Will she help me with the Mystery?'

'Through her you will learn more, I am sure of it.'

Elowen looked around as she walked, stunned by the scale of the ruins. 'How old is Omphalos?'

'Many buildings here date back thousands of years,' said Gnothi. 'For centuries, before the rise of the Mother Church, the ancestors of the Pertinax people worshipped at the shrines and temples here. Omphalos thrived as a centre of trade, and as a venue for games of athletics and gymnastics too, drawing competitors from lands near and far. Although its gods are forgotten and much of what was built here fell into ruin, Omphalos has remained a haven for those who oppose Prester John's domination, and with the loss of the Sanctuary, it is even more important. It draws freethinkers, followers of the old religions, the persecuted, and the dispossessed. This place is special, Elowen, and I pray to whatever deity listens that it remains so, forever.'

As they approached the temple, they passed votive buildings and treasury houses. Given the time and leisure to do so, Elowen would have loved to explore them, but she knew it was out of the question. Sensing her curiosity, Gnothi pointed to the finest of the treasury houses. At its front stood a portico supported by two enormous caryatid

176

columns, both brightly painted and inlaid with precious metals. Inscriptions on the walls of the treasury house showed battles between gods and giants. Carved with great skill, the figures looked ready to leap out from the stone. Gnothi said, 'This was built to commemorate a famous victory, a victory it is said, founded on the advice given by the Oracle. Many have been rewarded by her guidance, though the unfortunate souls who interpreted her words poorly often fared less well.'

Gnothi increased his pace as they reached the steps of the temple, which was rectangular in plan, with a tall closed door behind a colonnaded portico façade. Relief sculptures portraying gods and eagles decorated the pediment.

Gnothi mounted the steps in only two strides, and rapped on the closed door of the temple with his walking stick. The door opened slowly, although no one emerged to greet them. Without hesitation, Gnothi entered the temple and beckoned Elowen to follow him.

A few hooded and robed priests lurked inside the temple, but they paid no attention to Elowen and Gnothi. Lines of fluted columns divided the temple into a nave flanked by two aisles. A sculptured frieze adorned the top part of the interior of the temple: it showed a series of stories, displaying gods and a host of fabulous beings. At the far end, a gold and ivory statue of a goddess stood upon a plinth and stared down imperiously upon flesh and blood mortals.

Gnothi pointed to a small door beside the statue. 'That leads to the adytum. The Oracle waits for you inside. It is customary to bring a votive offering, but you are a special case. You do not need to seek her favour.'

177

He pushed the door open and stepped back.

'You're not coming with me?' said Elowen.

The *Protos* shook his head. 'The Oracle summoned you.'

Elowen stepped inside. An intoxicating smell filled her nose and left a sweet taste in her mouth. It took a few moments for her eyes to adjust to the dim light. Candles compensated for the absence of natural light. The adytum lacked the formal structure and clean lines of the rest of the temple, with rough walls and an uneven floor. Niches speckled the walls, all filled with an array of votive offerings. Elowen saw small bronze statues of goats, stags and dogs, and lead ornaments portraying warriors with crested helmets and round shields. Most disturbing of all was a shrine filled with hideous clay masks of old, wrinkled women and leering demons.

In the centre of the adytum stood a conical stone with a carving of a knotted net upon its surface. Behind the stone, a round pit fire, circled by mosaics representing unearthly figures, crackled away. Dark brown stains, like courses of filthy rivers, led to the fire from several directions. Beside the fire sat a metal tripod, positioned over a knife-thin chasm in the rocky floor. Vapours rose from the chasm. The Oracle perched upon the tripod. A dish filled with water rested upon her knees and in her left hand, she clasped laurel leaves. She sat motionless gazing into the dish, but as Elowen approached, she said in a croaky voice, 'So, you have arrived at last. Show me the Mystery of Fire.'

Elowen dipped inside her coat and pulled out the Mystery.

'Bring it to me,' said the Oracle, holding out her right hand but still not looking up from the dish.

178

With trepidation, Elowen took a couple of steps forward. The Oracle took the Mystery and looked up, staring straight at Elowen. She was younger than Elowen had expected, scarcely a teenager. She sweated heavily and her eyes were like big black holes, with little colour around the pupils. Her lips curled as she looked at Elowen. 'You are young. But it is my guess your eyes have seen more of life than many greybeards could boast.'

Elowen did not know what to say, so she kept quiet.

The Oracle chuckled and gazed at the Mystery of Fire, bringing it close to her face. 'So, *only the fiery tongues of Omphalos may read me*. Let us see if it is so.'

She stood, deftly placed the dish on the floor and walked to the fire. Her steps were wavering, unsteady, her gait drunken. The Oracle held the Mystery above the fire, the flames singeing her fingers, but she did not flinch. After a few seconds, the Oracle pulled her hand away. She opened her palm to show Elowen the Mystery. It had changed appearance, the outer shell of the stone burned away to leave a pebble marked with tiny writing. 'You see, the flames of this sacred fire reveal the truth of the Mystery.'

'What does the writing say?' said Elowen.

'That is simple: Journey to the Island of the Four Winds.'

'Where is that?'

The Oracle handed her back the Mystery. Despite being subjected to the fire, it remained cool. 'In the eastern waters of the Mednoir Ocean. That is where you must go next. That is where you shall find the Mystery of Air, if you prove worthy, of course. I warn you, obtaining the third Mystery will be your most difficult task yet.'

179

Elowen blinked and tried to hide the fear in her voice. 'Why? What do I have to do?'

'To find the Mystery of Air, you place those close to you in great peril.'

'Why?'

The Oracle's eyes narrowed. 'In time, you'll see. Remember my words, remember the warning within them.'

'I will,' said Elowen, her head spinning a little. 'Thank you.'

'I am not finished yet,' said the Oracle. 'You should not leave here so poorly furnished with advice. The future is not entirely hidden to me, harken to my words.'

She returned to the tripod and, after picking up the dish, sat again. Elowen dithered, not sure what she should do.

'Come closer,' said the Oracle, as she settled the dish on her lap.

She took several deep breaths, the eerie vapours swirling around her. She spoke in a strange language, using a voice that did not sound as if it belonged to her. She rolled her head, fell silent and stared down at the dish, touching the water delicately with her fingertips. The Oracle stood, her arms outstretched. The metal dish clattered to the ground. 'The Tree of Life stands close to death. Only blood will bring it back to life.'

Open-mouthed, confused and more than a little startled, Elowen said, 'I don't understand. What—'

'Only blood will bring it back to life,' said the Oracle. And she kept repeating it. 'Only blood will bring it back to life.'

The Oracle sank to her knees, her whole body quivering. 'You have heard my words, now leave me.'

Elowen hesitated, but saw no other choice but to go. As she reached the adytum door, she turned; the Oracle still knelt on the floor. Elowen pitied her isolation, her loneliness. The Oracle seemed like a prisoner, shackled by her uncanny ability, an instrument for others to use and control.

When she stepped back into the nave of the temple, Elowen found Gnothi waiting there for her. He said, 'Did you find the knowledge you sought?'

'I don't know,' said Elowen. 'What she said confused me.'

Gnothi gave a sympathetic smile. 'Do not be disheartened. In time you may understand the wisdom contained within her words.'

He led Elowen back to the tent and bade her goodnight, saying, 'I shall see you at the council tomorrow.'

Elowen did not know what he meant but, still dazed from her encounter with the Oracle, said nothing.

Once inside the tent, her friends welcomed her happily and bombarded her with questions. Above all, they wanted to know what the Oracle had said to her. When Elowen told them, they looked at her blankly.

'What does that mean?' said Diggory. '*Only blood will bring it back to life?*'

'I assume the Oracle is saying the Tree of Life will only be saved after bloodshed and battle,' said Bo.

Elowen nodded. She had thought the same and found it a far from comforting conclusion. 'What about the Island of the Four Winds? Have any of you heard of such a place?'

Black Francis cracked his knuckles. 'Only in tales and shanties. It's said to be an enchanted island in the eastern waters. I never supposed it to be a real place, just the

181

drunken imaginings of old salts. I've a notion Epios may know the truth.'

'Gnothi said something about a council that was taking place tomorrow,' said Elowen.

'Yes,' said Bo. 'All have been summoned tomorrow to the amphitheatre.'

'Why?' said Diggory.

'We have not been told,' said Bo.

'Well,' sighed Diggory, yawning and stretching out his arms. 'I don't suppose it will lead to anything *pleasant*.'

*

The Pertinax warrior Muthoi yawned widely, his eyes prickling with lack of sleep.

'Three hours until dawn,' he groaned to himself. He looked longingly to the east, searching the sky for the first cracks of light, the sign that his watch would be over. But the sky remained defiantly dark. He stamped his feet and passed his spear from one hand to the other, thrusting his newly freed hand into the deep pocket of his robe. His companion Adexios paced around, his armour clattering. After long hours on guard duty, they had run out of things to say to each other.

Muthoi gulped a lungful of air and stared down the narrow, steep path that he and Adexios guarded. The meagre shadows created by the moon shrouded the path. He saw movement. He blinked, thinking at first that his tired eyes were playing tricks on him. But no, he saw it again. An outline, a silhouette.

'Adexios,' he whispered, pointing at the path. 'Look, there's something down there.'

'What is it?' said Adexios in a hushed voice.

'A person, perhaps. I can't be sure.'

Adexios stared, and after a few seconds said, 'You were dreaming again.'

'I wasn't *dreaming*. Come on, we should check to make sure.'

With spears held low and aimed forward, they moved down the path.

'I told you, there's nothing here,' said Adexios, after they had looked around. 'It's just your imagination.'

Muthoi swore and dismissed Adexios's suggestion with a roll of his eyes. Wearily, but also a little relieved, he plodded back up to the guard post.

As he did so, Muthoi failed to notice Unheimlich, who had curled up behind the rock. When the guards returned to their post, Unheimlich uncoiled his body and continued to sneak up the path.

*

Semi-circle in shape and formed of stone seating in steep terraces, the amphitheatre rested on a natural slope. Bounded by a line of cypress trees, it provided dramatic views across the valley, with the stage framed by the mountain peaks beyond.

To Elowen's surprise, Gnothi insisted she and her friends take seats at the wider, bottom terrace, a gesture intended as a great honour. She felt exposed, conspicuous, and looked up nervously as the other terraces filled. She noticed how those present kept to their racial groups. The Centaurs took one part of the amphitheatre; Dwarfs filled one of the lower rows; the Gigas remained at the back, throwing suspicious glances at the Khiltoi; the Satyrs hollered and sang, drawing displeased glares from the Kojin. Little gatherings of Woodwoses, Dryads, Fauns and Kobolds lurked shyly towards the back; the *imbellis* overshadowed by the more warlike Eldar races. There were tribes of Men too: Pertinax warriors, silent, impassive in simple robes; Janjičari musketeers from Miklagard, dressed in tall hats and red uniforms; warriors of Nyumbani, looking ferocious in wooden helmets and ornate quilter armour.

The cold air tingled with tension. Even Black Francis, who sat one side of Elowen, kept tapping his feet, while Diggory who sat on her other side, fidgeted and gnawed his fingernails. Elowen looked up at the sky, where the bright star burned relentlessly. Something about it troubled her. To her it resembled a lidless eye, always watching her, judging her.

A wall ran behind the stage, with openings framed by columns. Between the openings there were pillars with niches housing marble statues. Stone griffins, weathered and worn by the elements, marked each side of the stage. As Gnothi had led Elowen and her friends to their seats, he had said, 'In peaceful times this stage hosted many wonderful performances. Musical acts to delight the ear and stir the soul. Comedies. Tragedies. This place was a wellspring of art and joy. But perhaps we are soon to witness a drama beyond anything performed on this stage.'

Once the amphitheatre had filled, Gnothi hobbled onto the stage and signalled for silence. He spoke aloud, straining his voice so all could hear. 'Friends, I welcome you to this council, a gathering made in times of profound danger. Only three days ago, Prince Asbjorn, heir to the throne of Prevennis, and his allies crossed the Mednoir Sea to bring us tidings of a secret Patriarchal Edict appalling in its content. For the Edict commands that the Null is forced upon *infants*.'

There were shocked gasps and many cries of anger.

Gnothi nodded, acknowledging the horror of what he had said. 'And this iniquitous scheme is not the end. Prester John has also ordered more Sentinels to be forged, further increasing his power and poisoning the earth.'

'These are dark tidings indeed,' said one of the Centaurs.

'Yes, without doubt,' said Gnothi. 'I am grateful to Prince Asbjorn and his companions for risking so much to bring them to our attention, for knowledge of Prester John's terrible intentions must inform our next steps. And, my friends, we face many challenges. The Brotherhood of Redemption destroyed the Sanctuary. Our old ally, King Olaf of Prevennis is dead, his kingdom seized by the enemy. To the south, the brave Oba of Nyumbani defies Prester John but at an awful cost in life, and his capital is under permanent attack. Ironclads ravage the islands of Kasaba and many there have abandoned their homes and fled west, seeking the New World. Even that destination is not safe, for Prester John prepares a mighty fleet to sail west to claim the New World as his own. One can scarcely conceive of the suffering of the natives there if his plan succeeds. And the Society for the Propagation of Pious Labour feverishly scours the lands for slaves, destroying the poor with wicked devices and lying words. Fearful times indeed, and there is no shortage of prophets and seers to proclaim we are in the Last Days, the edge of an apocalypse. But I ask you not to despair, for as dark as these days are, hope remains.'

'He's optimistic,' whispered Diggory. Elowen nudged him to be silent.

'The arrogance of Prester John has led him to underestimate the threat to his rule, and to overestimate his own power and security,' continued Gnothi. He clapped his hands and two guards appeared through a stage opening. Between them they dragged a short, bow-legged man, who wore a wolf skin and a weasel cap. The guards took him to the front of the stage, where he stood, his head bowed. Gnothi gestured towards the man. 'This is Dolon. He is a spy in the service of Prester John.'

Murmurs of concern rippled through the amphitheatre. Elowen heard the Centaurs stamp their hooves. The Satyrs shouted and made angry gestures at the spy.

'Dolon as you can see is not Nulled,' said Gnothi, tapping his thin walking stick on the stage floor to demand quiet. 'He is one of the Pertinax, who have long resisted Prester John. But for the promise of gold, Dolon turned traitor and agreed to act as a spy for the enemy.'

'Then he should hang!' said a Janjičari.

'Nay, leave him to the Satyrs,' said their Chief, whom Elowen had heard named Silenus. Bald, red-faced and fat, he stomped his goat-like hooves angrily. 'We'll make him suffer!'

186

Gnothi held up a hand. 'Enough! We must not sink to those depths. No doubt, Dolon wished to expose the secrets of Omphalos, yet thankfully, the Pertinax were vigilant and discovered his treachery. Once in our hands he tried to hide behind a web of lies and half-truths, but from these we gleaned much.'

Elowen saw Dolon swallow hard and shake his head, riven by shame. The guards led him away again.

The *Protos* clicked his tongue and straightened himself a little. 'Of all the knowledge we gained from Dolon, one discovery is of primary importance. For we have learnt that Prester John himself, the incontestable ruler of the Holy Empire, has chosen to winter not in the impregnable Ulsacro, but at the Patriarchal retreat—the Inganno Winter Palace. He shall remain there until the *Divine Audience*, which marks the end of the festival of the Ortus, seven days from now. There, in the milder climate, he plans to host the *aristoi*, an assembly of the many kings and rulers who pay him homage. There, he revels in his sovereignty. But there, he is far more vulnerable than he ever dares to imagine.'

Corcoran stood. 'Surely Prester John is well protected?'

'A garrison is stationed at the Winter Palace but we believe it to be less than three thousand men,' said Gnothi.

'What of the Grand Army?' said one of the Centaurs.

Gnothi smiled. 'That is where we have been especially fortunate. We know that Prester John sent the Grand Army north two weeks ago and it is too far away to come to his aid. We have an opportunity, perhaps the last one we will ever get, to strike at Prester John.'

A Dwarf, an elderly greybeard, stood with a wince and a

gasp. 'When we answered the summons, I knew it was the last journey I would ever make, save for the dark one to the lands of death. I believed I was leading my tribe to a place of safety and refuge. Now you speak of leaving here and attacking the enemy. It is madness.'

Gnothi said to the Dwarf, 'Vestri, I understand your fears, but we cannot remain here forever.'

The Dwarf gesticulated all around him. 'With cunning building and fortifications, this refuge could become an impenetrable fortress.'

'And what would the purpose be of our resistance?' said Gnothi. 'What good would we do here, defending these stony hills and ruins, while elsewhere the last embers of resistance are extinguished? Vestri, I understand your fears but if we remain here, we are a caged beast, already Prester John's prisoners. And do not forget the Patriarchal Edict; if we wish to stem the flow of evil, time is very much against us.'

Vestri sat, looking far from convinced. 'If this be the council's will, then bitterly I regret answering the summons, for I've led my tribe into deeper danger.'

'And what would you have us do, beardling?' said Silenus. 'Do you wish to stand back and let Prester John enslave this world?'

'Stand back?' said Vestri, as the other Dwarfs leapt angrily to their feet. 'We've fought for decades against the cruelty of the Holy Empire, forced to live in caves, forced to scrape a miserable existence. We've lost more than most, Silenus. Do you forget our sacrifice at Opfernwald? Four Dwarf tribes fought against the Grand Army of Prester John.

188

Where were the Satyrs on that day? Perhaps if your kind spent less time drinking and singing, you could have done more to defy Prester John.'

The Satyrs howled insults and Silenus said, 'We have fought too, and have only been defeated when betrayed by you cave-dwellers.'

'Lies!' said Vestri. 'We always fulfil our oaths.'

The voice of Archontos rose above the hubbub. 'Once again we endure the tiresome foolishness of the Dwarfs and Satyrs. They are content to waste time on their petty disputes. I despair of ever seeing a time when you put aside your differences and forget the wars you fought against each other so long ago.'

'Hold your tongue, horse-man,' said Silenus. 'While the Centaurs gaze at the stars looking for signs and portents, others are fighting and dying.'

'By my troth, if we did not stand in a sacred place, I'd rip your goat's tongue from your head,' snarled Archontos, his fury kindled by the Satyr.

Arguments broke out between the Dwarfs, Satyrs and Centaurs. Gnothi pleaded for calm but the Eldar ignored him.

'This is lunacy,' said Diggory to Elowen. 'They'll kill each other before even seeing the enemy.'

Before Elowen could reply, a young Nyumbani warrior mounted the stage and bellowed, 'Our Master, the Oba, sent us here to fight alongside the last of the free in the Known World. Yet we see that insanity and fear has infected Omphalos. Why is the council tolerating such idiocy from the Eldar?'

189

Silenus broke from his quarrel with Archontos to say, 'What value is the word of Men in these matters? Never trust Men, that is a lesson I have learnt. They speak with two mouths, and holy words veil their true intentions.'

Corcoran waded into the quarrel. 'You all squabble like children. Perhaps you fight amongst yourselves because you are too frightened to face the servants of the *Moljnir*.'

'Keep to your forests, tree-hanger,' said Vestri. 'These are matters beyond your meagre understanding.'

The arguments drew fresh vigour. Insults, accusations and rebuttals flew like stones. Elowen saw fights breaking out. She trembled, not with fear but with *anger*. A burning rage. She remembered the sorrow, the sacrifice, of so many. The Barbegs' grief at their appalling losses in the battle of the Gladsheim. The grave of Lárwita. The windswept cairn of Chinua. She recalled the many faces of the enemy: the sadistic cruelty of Bishop Serapion, the brutal Society, the merciless Redeemers and above all, Lord Lucien. She stood and stepped on the stage. Hundreds of faces turned towards her in surprise but she did not wither under their stares. Instead, she spoke aloud, her voice not shackled by shyness, guilt or a sense of inferiority. She spoke with the voice of her true heart, the words fuelled by emotions. 'ENOUGH! If we fight amongst ourselves we're doomed. Look how you are acting. Are you not ashamed? All your petty squabbles blind you to the real danger. There's a huge world out there, a world Prester John is going to destroy. Are you going to sit by and let it happen? If we don't make a stand, who else will?'

Her speech silenced the arguments and all eyes fell upon

190

her. Silenus said, 'Who gave you the right to speak here, child?'

'I earned the right to speak here when I led the Wild Host against the army of Prester John. I earned the right when I defied Lord Lucien in the Orok city of Erdene. I am an Adept, and I have seen and survived as many horrors as anyone present here. Yes, I have earned the right to speak.'

Gnothi stood beside Elowen and said, 'She speaks truthfully. We must confront Prester John, for our sake and for the sake of generations to come.'

'But what if those generations turn to evil and forget our sacrifice?' said Vestri.

Gnothi said, 'That is their choice. Our duty is to give them the chance to choose, the *freedom* to choose. Prester John is not like an Imperator of antiquity, concealing his corruption through a reign of bread and circuses, torturing his people for the extent of his mortal years. If he is victorious, he threatens to change this world, irrevocably. Think of the simple pleasures you all enjoy. Birdsong. The sweet flowers of spring. The busy rivers. These are not mere trifles. They sustain life, they make life worth living. If we do not defeat Prester John, all of this is gone, forever. Think of the desolation, the misery that will replace it. We cannot allow that to happen. We must put aside our differences, ignore ancient feuds, for Prester John has exploited them for too long. Fight as one, or fall. I ask you all, will you fight?'

Corcoran leapt to his feet and pounded his chest. 'We Khiltoi have not marched through adversity to sulk here in the mountains. We are warriors. We will fight.'

The other Khiltoi warriors responded to his words with cheers and hollered oaths.

'If the tree-hangers go, we fight too,' said Silenus.

'We Centaurs swore to fight Prester John and we do not waver from that pledge,' said Archontos.

Vestri cleared his throat. 'The Dwarfs shall not refuse this call, if only to stop the Satyrs fleeing in fear once battle begins.'

Silenus scowled. 'Curse you, long-beard. I'll not mourn if all you foul beardlings are slain by the enemy.'

One by one, all the martial races committed to the cause, although many did so with visible reluctance and fear. Gnothi winked at Elowen and allowed himself a smile. 'The will of the council is clear and the course is set: we go to war. Remember, we are not an army of conquest. We do not seek plunder or glory. The Mother Church condemns us as heretics, pagans, *Putidus* as they name us in the Manus language, the Old Believers. It is meant as an insult, a disparagement against those too ignorant to follow the new rituals and beliefs of the Mother Church. I think we should claim this title as our own. The Army of the Old Believers.'

There were cheers of amusement and pride, followed by raucous chants of 'Old Believers! Old Believers!'

Elowen smiled. Gnothi had chosen the name well.

'Whatever the name of this army, it still needs a leader,' said Archontos.

'That is true,' agreed Gnothi. He looked at Bo. 'Prince Asbjorn. You led the Barbegs and their allies against the enemy in the battle of the Gladsheim, I believe?'

'Yes, but—'

'And you were victorious?'

'Only with great help,' he said, signalling towards Elowen.

'Then do you accept the offer to lead us against Prester John?'

A Centaur bellowed, 'You place our army in the hands of this boy?'

'This is madness,' said Corcoran, thumping his chest. 'A powerful warrior should be at the head of the army, someone to strike fear into the heart of the enemy, not this sapling.'

Prince Jeimuzu countered angrily. 'Your words show your ignorance. Prince Asbjorn inspired our people to overthrow our brutal oppressor, the King of the Sea Beggars. If he is to be our leader you should be thankful. I for one shall follow him, and follow him gladly.'

'And I'll second that,' said Black Francis. 'You need a cool head in the days to come and as I look around here, I don't see many others.'

At Gnothi's prompting, Bo stepped onto the stage and faced the crowd. Elowen sensed his tension and nerves but he controlled them well. 'I have fought in battles. I have seen the pain, the misery, the suffering, the death. When I go to war again, it will not be with a light heart. I do not talk of glory, for there is none to be found in war. I have witnessed the cruelty of Prester John and I swear to fight against him, even if death be my reward. I do not demand your allegiance, but I hope to earn it.'

'Very well,' said Gnothi, holding up his hands. 'Are there any objections to my choice of leader?'

Silenus spat into his hands. 'I'm too old and fat to fight

and so must remain here, but if we're all going to die, it might as well be this boy who leads us to our doom.'

Elowen heard other mutterings but no one voiced a strong objection.

'Good,' said Gnothi. 'Prince Asbjorn shall lead the Army of the Old Believers.'

'Do we have a large enough force to be effective?' said Vestri, looking around. 'Even among the martial races here I doubt we can raise more than two thousand. And we lack the cruel weapons used by the forces of Prester John.'

'Indeed we shall be hard pressed but we do not fight alone,' said Gnothi. 'Yesterday a scout from the Orok city of Erdene reached us, promising aid.'

Elowen looked at Batu; a look of relief and joy lit his face.

'The Oroks?' said Silenus. 'Well I remember their butchery during the Great Raid. They ruined cities brick by brick, showing no mercy to their prisoners. They executed the kings of their enemies by pouring molten silver into their eyes and ears. A monstrous race. They care nothing for those outside their borders. I have no faith in their promises.'

Before Batu could react, Gnothi said, 'You judge the Oroks on the past, not on the present. They have a new khan, one that has pledged to fight Prester John.'

'The *Protos* speaks justly,' said Batu, striving to retain his composure and dignity. 'With Arigh Nasan fighting alongside us, our chances of victory are increased. But did the scout give any indication of how many warriors the Khan has mustered?'

'Fewer than he had hoped,' said Gnothi. 'Many tribes re-

194

fused to pledge support to his campaign, understandable in these fearful times. The Oroks spoke of bringing a thousand of their kind, and I am sure each warrior shall fight with the customary skill and courage of your kind.'

Batu bowed at the compliment. 'The Oroks shall not stop fighting until Prester John is defeated, or we are slain.'

'Let us hope it is the former,' said Gnothi. He turned to Bo. 'Prince Asbjorn, begin your muster this afternoon and prepare to march at dawn tomorrow.'

Bo nodded.

'But for all our talk of war, this is not to be our only undertaking,' said Gnothi. 'For even if the battle is won, and Prester John is slain, his infection remains and others, scarcely less terrifying, shall take his place and continue his abasement of this world. I especially fear the Brotherhood of Redemption. In the void left by the death of Prester John, they would surely seize outright control of the Mother Church and its empire. That, Elowen Aubyn, is where *you* come in.'

At Gnothi's insistence, Elowen addressed the crowd and told them more about her quest, her words greeted with many gasps of astonishment. When Elowen had finished, Gnothi said, 'Finding the Tree of Life is of the utmost importance. By attacking Prester John at Inganno we take him by the throat; by finding and saving the Tree of Life, Elowen shall take him by the heart.'

'Much you risk on this legend,' said Vestri. 'What evidence have we this Tree of Life exists?'

'Do you question the Oracle's judgement?' said Gnothi.

Vestri muttered under his breath and sat.

195

'I don't understand this,' said Silenus, rubbing his stomach. 'Even if the girl succeeds, what would be gained?'

Gnothi said, 'If the Tree of Life is reborn and the Earthsoul replenished, then the power of Prester John, and much of the damage he has wrought, would be undone. Cold Iron is strong, but the Earthsoul is stronger still.'

'What of those with the Null?' said Archontos. 'How would they be affected?'

'That I do not know,' said Gnothi. 'I hope they would be liberated from the control of Prester John, but nothing is certain. Do not underestimate the danger of this quest. Elowen will have need of companions.'

Diggory stood. 'I'm with Elowen, to the very end.'

She whispered, 'You don't have to go. You'd be safer staying here. I wouldn't blame you if you didn't come.'

Diggory folded his arms. 'I'm going with you, no argument. You'd have to tie me in chains to stop me.'

Touched by his loyalty, Elowen smiled. 'I'm glad. I'm safer with you beside me.'

Black Francis spoke next. 'It's been my privilege to travel many miles with Bo, but I think my path lies now with Elowen.'

'You've risked so much for me already,' said Elowen to Black Francis. 'I'd feel guilty for putting your life in danger again.'

'I looked death straight in the face, lass. Such an experience shakes a man, *changes* him. I'd always fancied I'd be too clever for death, but the reaper's more cunning than I'd supposed. If I'd have died on the Beauteous Isle, I'd have left so much undone, so many bad deeds unredeemed. I want to leave a mark, a good mark, on this world. To give rather than take. I don't know how much time I've got left, but I'm determined to use it wisely. And right now, that means helping you, lass. If Bo takes no offence, of course.'

'I have valued your support and wisdom, my friend, and am sad at the thought of our parting,' said Bo. 'But you are making the right decision.'

'And you, Batu?' said Gnothi. 'What is your intent? I assume you plan to ride to war with the Oroks.'

The Orok rose to his feet. 'I remain loyal to Arigh Nasan until death, but I have sworn to protect Elowen, and with her leave, I shall remain at her side.'

Elowen beamed and nodded happily.

'I wish to go with Elowen too,' said Bryna.

Corcoran looked furious. 'Impossible. I won't hear of it. We need you for the battle to come.'

'The battle will not be won or lost by my presence,' she said.

'You are destined to be *taghta* and your place is with your people,' Corcoran said. 'That is your duty.'

'And that duty is best served by helping Elowen,' said Bryna. 'For if she fails, all will fail, all will be lost, whether you win in battle or not. I do not part from you and our kin lightly, in fact the very thought of it rips at my heart. But I am sure in my choice.'

Corcoran shook his head and gave her a dismissive wave. 'By the ancestors, you are headstrong and foolish, Bryna. If you decide to abandon your people then it's your choice. Do as you will, I care not.'

'The time for talk is over,' said Gnothi. 'The course is set.

197

I compel none of you to act against your will. If you wish to remain here, you have my blessing and I do not judge you ill. For the rest of you, a dark and dangerous path awaits, but be emboldened by the justness of your cause. Everything, my friends, is at stake.'

*

The last hints of light drained from the sky, the sun hidden by the tips of the mountains. Omphalos buzzed with activity. Warriors gathered weapons and provisions, repaired and cleaned armour, and participated in prayers and blessings. The attitudes of the different races fascinated Elowen. Some, such as the Centaurs, Dwarfs and the Khiltoi fired themselves up with boisterous war songs and swore unbreakable oaths of vengeance against the enemy. The Satyrs drank heavily, singing and swearing, and participating in mock combat that looked to Elowen horribly close to the real thing. Others were quieter. The huge Gigas, who frightened Elowen a little, remained together in thoughtful silence. The Kojin prepared incessantly, checking their weapons and complicated armour in well-rehearsed drills.

'You know, I don't envy them,' said Diggory. He leant with Elowen upon a ruined wall close to the amphitheatre, watching the army prepare for their march north. 'I don't want to see another battle.'

'I doubt what awaits us will be any better,' said Elowen.

'Perhaps not,' he shrugged. 'But we've got some fine folk with us. Batu, for a start. And now Black Francis again and his crew. Bryna's a tough fighter.'

'Epios is coming with us too,' said Elowen, not sure if that was a good thing or not.

Diggory frowned. 'He's an odd one, I can't fathom him out. I asked Black Francis where they found him. He winked and said he came from the sea. What do you make of that?'

'Bo told me that Epios is…a shape-shifter,' said Elowen.

Diggory looked horrified. 'A *what*? You mean, like a werewolf.'

'Not a *werewolf*. But he can change form, into a bird or a fish.'

Diggory shook his head. 'The more I see of this world, the less I understand. A shape-shifter, by God. Can we trust him?'

'Black Francis and Bo trust him. That's enough for me.'

'Well, I guess they know what they're doing,' said Diggory, looking far from convinced.

Following Gnothi's advice, Elowen and her companions planned to set off for the *Husker Du* straight away. Despite the danger, the thought of travelling again with Black Francis lifted Elowen's spirits a little. The Captain was nearby, readying packs along with Bryna and Batu. He called out to Elowen and Diggory, 'Come on, you two. It's time we were leaving.'

With some reluctance, Elowen slung a heavy pack over her shoulder, aware of the hardship the journey ahead was likely to bring. Gnothi appeared, hobbling along with the aid of his walking stick, accompanied by the mysterious Epios. The *Protos* said, 'I have arranged for Pertinax warriors to escort you back to your ship.'

199

'Thank you,' said Black Francis. 'Before you know it we'll be on-board the *Husker Du*.'

Batu looked unusually pensive. 'I have never sailed before.'

Black Francis gave him an encouraging tap on the arm. 'You'll be safe in my hands, don't fear.'

'Safe except for storms, sea monsters and Ironclads, that is,' said Diggory.

Black Francis laughed at his cheek. 'Aye, but there are perils on land too.'

'That is certainly true,' said Bryna in a low voice.

Epios surprised Elowen by taking her hand and kissing it. 'I am honoured to make this journey with you.'

'Thank you,' said Elowen, a little startled.

'Can you really change shape?' said Diggory bluntly.

Epios raised an eyebrow. 'You are direct in your speech, young man. That is no sin, I suppose. Yes, I can take other forms, when the time is right.'

Diggory opened his mouth but Epios second-guessed his question. 'No, the time is not right. When the waves are curling and the air is rich with salt, perhaps I shall demonstrate my curious capability.'

Diggory looked disappointed but said nothing further on the matter.

'Polite words of parting are inadequate for the gravity of the situation,' said Gnothi. 'But know that the goodwill of all free people go with you, from this moment until the end.'

'Whatever that end may be,' said Diggory.

Elowen remembered something. She dug into her pack

and pulled out Lárwita's book. She passed it to Gnothi and explained what it was. He flicked through the pages, his face alight with interest. He said, 'Fascinating! Your friend had an extraordinary mind!'

'There wasn't anyone cleverer in the Sanctuary,' said Elowen.

'I don't doubt it. I have never seen anything like it. Flying machines. Hydraulic devices. Equipment for breathing underwater. His mind was a treasure trove. Remarkable.'

'I don't want his work to be forgotten,' said Elowen.

Gnothi smiled and tapped the book. 'This will be of profound interest to our natural philosophers, I promise you. Prester John has sought to suppress science, save for when he uses it for his own twisted purposes. If we ever come to better times, your friend's book may be the spark to fire a thousand imaginations.'

'I hope so,' said Elowen.

'Come on, lubbers,' said Black Francis. 'Gather your gear, let's get moving. The sea's calling me back.'

Elowen felt someone tap her back. She turned and was surprised to see Bo standing there.

'I wanted to say farewell and wish you good luck,' he said. 'We seem destined to meet…only fleetingly.'

A little flustered, Elowen said, 'So it would seem.'

He opened his mouth but checked himself. Finally, he said, 'Look after Black Francis will you?'

Elowen laughed. 'I'll try.'

'And…yourself, look after yourself, I mean. I hope this will not be our last meeting.'

There was an awkward silence. For a second he leaned

forward as though to embrace her, a timid movement broken by the booming voice of Black Francis. 'Come to see us off, lad?'

Bo flashed a quick regretful look at Elowen before the Captain hugged him like a bear smothering its victim. 'Good luck, lad. Give Prester John hell from me. And stay in one piece, as I expect to hear the full tale when next we meet.'

A flicker of a smile passed over Bo's face, an appreciative but rueful smile. 'I will look forward to it.'

And so at last, Elowen and her companions began their journey, trudging down the long path out of the mountains and towards the sea.

*

High up in a cypress tree, hidden from view, Unheimlich lurked. He had watched Elowen for hours, moving unseen from one concealed vantage point to another. He had watched her transfixed; some intangible quality of hers absorbed him. He felt sensations that pained him, their sweetness so alien to his body, a tantalising hint of emotions that he could never truly feel. He licked his lips and prepared to follow the girl, no longer compelled simply by Hohenheim's orders, but also by his own fascination.

- CHAPTER NINE -

A Long March

B o stared at the mountain peaks, but saw only Elowen's eyes, the moment of their parting carved into his memory. He wondered if he would ever see her again.

'Are you going to stand there all day, or are we going to do some work?' said Valbrand.

Bo stood upon the steps of the tholos, the three graceful columns behind him, watching the army make its final preparations. It was a fresh dawn, with a blood-red sky. He looked down. Valbrand stood at the foot of the steps, hands on hips. He looked irritable, his short fuse already smouldering. Bo said, 'How goes the muster?'

Valbrand kicked at the ground. 'They're ready, leastways as ready as they're ever going to be. It would be easier if we had a proper army rather than this rabble of tribes all jabbering away in languages I don't understand. Those so-called Captains have got their hands full.'

Bo winced. Gnothi had appointed Archontos, Prince Jeimuzu and Corcoran as Captains for the campaign. Archontos and Jeimuzu were natural leaders, but the choice of Corcoran rankled with Bo, who had marked the Khiltoi down as a hothead and troublemaker. Bo had acquiesced with Gnothi's decision but now regretted not pushing his viewpoint more vigorously. Doubt and insecurity had held his tongue and he cursed his indecision and weakness. Trying to bury his concern, he said, 'As long as they are ready to fight when the time comes, that is all that matters.'

'Aye, they'll fight all right,' said Valbrand. 'I'm worried they'll end up fighting each other before we get to Inganno. You've got a tough job.'

'I know that,' said Bo. 'Much depends on the Oroks, for we need more warriors. Valbrand, have I taken on too much here?'

Valbrand shrugged. 'Perhaps, but you're the best we've got. If anyone can lead this mob, it's you.'

'Was that a compliment?'

'Aye, but it was well hidden. Now, I had better help Archontos marshal those cursed Satyrs. By the gods they're tough, but it's whether they'll get to the battlefield sober that troubles me.'

'As a paragon of abstinence, I am sure you are the right man to deal with them.'

Valbrand laughed as he walked away and flicked an insulting hand gesture to the Prince, who smiled at his friend's cheek.

Something Gnothi had said at the council nagged at Bo. *He plans to host the aristoi, an assembly of the many kings and rulers who pay him homage.* Would his mother, the ruling Queen of Prevennis, be there? There was so much he wanted to say to her, so much anger he longed to vent. He wondered if she ever thought of him. She had seldom shown him any

204

love or affection. Perhaps she believed him to be dead. Whatever the truth of it, she would never forgive him for slaying Haakon, her beloved firstborn.

And he knew that if they defeated Prester John, however remote a possibility that might be, it dangled the prospect of him seizing the crown from his mother, the crown she usurped by murdering his father.

'The hour is almost upon us.'

Bo had not heard Gnothi approach. He turned and said, 'Yes, a long journey awaits us.'

'Remember the route we discussed,' said the *Protos*. 'Head northwest and then follow the coast northwards until you reach the Colossi of the Dawn Ruler. There, you should meet with the Orok army. The Khan's messenger promised they would be there within three days. From the Colossi, it is about three more days' march to the Winter Palace. You have no time to lose.'

'But is there not a shorter route?' said Bo, his teeth chattering in the cold. 'The longer the army is on the march, the more exposed it will be. We risk all surprise being lost. There must be another way.'

Gnothi shook his head. 'To pass through the Petrified Forest is no longer possible, as clearly the enemy watches that route.'

'What about the pass of Thanásima?' said Bo.

'Too dangerous and far too close to the city of Thlipsis, which is loyal to Prester John. The Brotherhood of Redemption patrols those lands. The only other path, the shortest path, takes you through the forest of Kakos, an evil place where all fear to tread. You cannot go *that* way.'

205

'Then the coastal path is the only one open to us,' said Bo. He looked upon the forces he was commanding with trepidation and no small feeling of puzzlement. All the military lessons drilled into him as a scholar meant little now. He saw few modern weapons: only the tiny contingent of Janjičari carried muskets. The Centaurs paraded with long spears and curved swords, the Dwarfs with hammers and axes. The Khiltoi and the Pertinax were like warriors from a long forgotten age. Even the Kojin, fearsome in their full armour, looked anachronistic. Bo tried to push the doubts out of his mind. He had to believe they could succeed. Seeing Elowen again had given him a surge of hope. If she had survived all of the terrors ranged against her, they surely had a chance of victory against Prester John. The months apart had not dulled his fascination with her. Their brief reunion felt bittersweet. She passed through his life like a spring flower, blooming briefly and then lost, surviving only in memory.

Valbrand stomped up the steps of the tholos. He gestured to the army behind him, who had fallen silent. 'Well, we're ready to leave, God help us.'

'They wait for you,' said Gnothi to Bo. 'A leader should make the first step.'

Feeling self-conscious, feeling like a fraud, Bo stepped forward, and in an instinctive gesture, raised his sword. To his surprise, the army cheered, 'Old Believers!'

The *Protos* gave a stiff bow and said, 'May fortune shine upon you, Prince Asbjorn, and those that fight alongside you. Remember, when you have secured victory, send a raven here to Omphalos to bring news.'

'I pray I shall have cause to do so,' said Bo. Feeling hundreds of pairs of eyes trained upon him, he sheathed his sword and took the first steps of his long march. The Army of the Old Believers followed him.

*

Lord Lucien writhed on his bed. Spasms of pain still shuddered through his body, though at last they receded. The fresh Cold Iron within his skin heightened his sensitivity, increasing the intensity of his connections with the creature Unheimlich. Every vein, every muscle, every bone cried out in agony, a pain so intense he thought at times it must surely overwhelm him. He had not wanted to do it. He knew the toll that the Cold Iron took. But he needed it.

Slowly his breathing returned to normal. His pain subsided to a dull ache. The memory of the visions he shared with Unheimlich, the dizzy rush of sounds and images, remained vivid. He had seen much, all of Elowen's plans laid bare before him. Excitement replaced the last residues of pain. He sat up. So, Elowen planned to travel south by sea. He needed to follow her, and follow her swiftly for she had a considerable head start. He pushed open the doors of his wagon and stepped outside. He shouted, 'Send for Brother Carrasco.'

Two of the Redeemers guarding his wagon sprinted off towards the main camp. They returned moments later with another Redeemer. He stood as tall as Lord Lucien. His spotless white robes gleamed, and from his belt hung a rapier and a parrying dagger, the emblems of a gentleman, a vestigial of Carrasco's life before he took the vows of the Brotherhood.

'Carrasco,' said Lord Lucien. 'I have vital orders for you.'

Carrasco knelt on one knee. 'Command me, Lord.'

Lord Lucien looked down at the Redeemer, glad that his mask concealed his look of disdain. Something about Brother Carrasco unsettled him; untroubled by remorse or pity, he was loyal and brutally efficient. Yet Lord Lucien sensed that Brother Carrasco's obsequious manner concealed boundless ambition, and a greed for power. His relentless inquisition against the pagans in Gamlejord proved his worth, and had seen him rise to rank of *Legatus*, second only to Lord Lucien himself in the Brotherhood.

'Prepare a detachment of twenty of our Brotherhood,' said Lucien. 'Tell them they are leaving for the port of Partenza.'

'It will be done,' said Carrasco, his head still bowed.

'And send your swiftest scout to Partenza, ahead of the Brotherhood. Tell him to bring orders to the Admiral of the Fleet that three Ironclads are to be made ready without delay and fully crewed.'

'I shall arrange it, my lord.'

'Good, I have one more command,' said Lord Lucien, gesturing for Carrasco to stand. 'Prepare my horse; I will accompany the detachment south. I leave the army in your command. You have my battle plan, you know what to do when the signal is given.'

'You honour me,' said Carrasco, his eagerness and bloodlust vivid in his tone. He clenched the grip of his rapier. Lord Lucien knew that he would enjoy leading the slaughter to come. 'I shall not fail you, my Lord. Though I am grieved to learn you will miss our victory, one that owes so much to your genius.'

'It is unavoidable, I must fulfil the Patriarch's wishes,' said Lord Lucien, knowing that Carrasco would never question the falsehood, such would be his joy at assuming command of the army. He dismissed the Redeemer from his presence and stepped back inside his wagon. He glared at the mirror, in particular the vicious claws that surrounded it. He did not intend to take it south. He wanted no distractions, not even from Prester John.

Guilt at defying and *deceiving* his Master wounded Lord Lucien, as it ripped away the deeply knotted cords formed by years of unquestioning service. For much of his life, he defined his very being by his loyalty to Prester John. His Master had saved him from torment and torture, rescued him from the brutal hands of the ignorant. He had nurtured his skills, given him the tools with which to enact his vengeance. Lord Lucien owed him everything. But that understanding withered when confronted by his urge to find Elowen, to right a terrible wrong. He had never felt so complete as when Athena Parthenos had been beside him. He did not think it love. He doubted he possessed the capacity to love. But in her intensity and burning desire for retribution against those who had wronged her, Lord Lucien had discovered a kinship, a connection that eluded him in the rest of his life. Together they established a balance, a corrective to the godless disorder of so much of the world. They achieved illustrious things and would have achieved much more had she lived longer. Her death fractured his soul. He wanted to feel whole, not broken. Now, with Elowen, he hoped for the same connection. Oh, how the world would tremble if Lord Lucien and the daughter of Athena Parthenos strode forth, united in purpose!

His mind sparkled with thrilling plans and possibilities. Lights, as lustrous as stars, flashed in front of his eyes, giddy with excitement. He clasped his hands together in prayer and begged the Almighty to guide him, and to give him the strength and fortitude to succeed.

*

Two days after leaving Omphalos, Bo and the Army of the Old Believers reached the old coast road. They trudged along wide sandy beaches fringed by dunes, and past salt marshes busy with wintering waders and wildfowl. Bo often found himself gazing out to sea, watching the grey waves break lazily, dispersing in foamy puddles and snaking rivulets across the flat expanse of sand.

Bo's sense of passing time sounded in his head like a persistent drumbeat, marking every second. He had hoped to reach the coast sooner but their descent down the narrow mountain tracks had been slow. Tiredness fuelled arguments amongst the Old Believers, and Bo had to resolve a number of petty disputes, distractions that drained his energy and confidence. The column trudged like a line of rowdy, ill-ordered cattle. He hoped now that they were on flatter ground, their progress would prove swifter and harmonious.

Bo had feared harassment from Redeemers or Egregores,

210

but they saw no trace of the enemy. Indeed, the land the army passed through appeared barren and empty. They came upon a number of small, long-abandoned settlements, all half-buried by the dust and sand whipped up by the unceasing wind. Trees were few and all were storm-ravaged and mournful.

'This is a godforsaken country,' said Valbrand, looking around as they walked.

'Few Men ever settled here,' said Corcoran. 'The soil is poor and Men lacked the wisdom to turn it to a good yield. If they had had the skills of the Khiltoi, perhaps things would've been different, but Men are so slow to learn.'

Corcoran revelled in his appointed role of Captain and insisted on walking with Bo, which annoyed the Prince as he found the Khiltoi warrior bumptious and argumentative.

'At least Men have discovered how to use metal,' said Valbrand, tapping the blade of his sword for emphasis.

Corcoran scowled. 'We Khiltoi are above using such materials, wood and stone suit our purpose.'

'Noble sentiments, but they won't protect you from Prester John,' said Valbrand. He was spoiling for an argument; Bo was used to detecting the signs.

'My people have endured well enough so far,' said Corcoran.

'Aye, *so far*,' said Valbrand, clearly enjoying riling the Khiltoi.

'That's enough,' said Bo. He spoke slowly and deeply, trying to sound authoritative, trying to mask his voice, which he feared still sounded boyish. 'We have no time for squabbling. We fight together or we fail.'

'Aye, you're right,' said Valbrand, though he sounded reluctant. He flashed a surly glance at Corcoran who returned it but remained quiet.

That night they made camp close to a marshy area adjacent to a long strip of sandy beach. As Bo commanded, the army set up a stockade to protect them against attack, digging a narrow trench around their camp, strengthened by sharpened stakes pushed into the ground. He posted perimeter guards to keep watch.

A subdued atmosphere pervaded the camp. Bo wandered past tents filled with weary, hungry and footsore warriors. Many ate simple meals, others slept. As he walked, Bo passed a blazing campfire, around which sat Corcoran and a group of Khiltoi, Dwarf, Satyr and Centaur warriors. Corcoran dominated the conversation, telling boastful stories of slaying Redeemers. His audience nodded and muttered admiringly at his tales. As he watched Corcoran framed by the fire's busy flames, Bo thought the Khiltoi looked as mighty a warrior as he had ever seen, a warrior even those loyal to Prester John would surely fear.

How Bo wanted to swagger up to them, confident as their respected and loved leader, and join in with their revelry. But a more plausible outcome formed in his mind: silence would greet his presence, soon followed by whispers and sneers. Fearing humiliation, Bo turned away and, feeling a failure, feeling like a coward, he headed towards his tent. Deep in thought, the voice of Prince Jeimuzu made him jump.

'I thought you would be resting,' said the Kojin Prince. 'You look troubled. Please, sit with me for a time.'

Jeimuzu sat cross-legged and alone, his sword beside him and a hinged lacquered wooden box lay open on his lap. Bo sat beside the Kojin Prince and pointed at the box. 'What is that?'

Jeimuzu looked reluctant to explain, but he turned and opened the box to allow Bo to see. Decorated with gold leaf, the box contained small figurines of seated Kojin; some sat with their hands clasped together, others held books or scrolls. 'It is a shrine, fashioned by monks. There are thirty protective deities, one for each day of the month. For much of my life I neglected the deities and the ancestors, but the challenge of these times reconnects me with them somehow. This surprises you, perhaps?'

Bo smiled. 'You sound more like a priest than a warrior.'

'I have never been described so before,' said Jeimuzu, laughing. He closed the wooden box and placed his unsheathed sword across his lap. 'In recent weeks, I have witnessed countless strange things, many of which challenge my understanding of this world: the *Kodai-no*, the Gigas and Epios, perhaps *him* most of all. The problems of this world are too complicated to be solved by fighting alone. Yet, fight we must. I ask for the ancestors' guidance, but it is through my sword hand that I shall dictate my destiny.

Bo stared at Jeimuzu's gleaming sword. He saw the wave pattern in the grain of the steel. 'I believe you are right. And I have not yet thanked you for your words of support at the council. They were a comfort to me.'

'You may have cause not to thank me, for the duty to which you have been appointed is onerous.'

'We face many dangers.'

213

'Yes and not all of them from the enemy. I do not envy you, Prince Asbjorn. Simply keeping this army together will be a tremendous task. The Centaurs and Satyrs are unruly, and the Khiltoi are full of boasts and aggression. You can trust the Kojin though, you know this?'

'Yes, of course.'

Jeimuzu bowed his head. 'We have not always spoken kind words to each other, you and I, but I meant what I said at the council.'

Bo thanked him again, got to his feet and strode towards his tent. Jeimuzu reopened his little shrine.

*

At first light, the Army of the Old Believers continued their march. The grey sky and cold wind brought Bo little cheer as he trudged forward at the head of the long snaking column. One of the Khiltoi scouts returned, running fast. He pointed behind him and spoke swiftly to Corcoran in their native language.

Corcoran turned to Bo and translated the scout's words. 'He says that there's something ahead, a fortress perhaps.'

Trying to keep calm, Bo signalled for the column to halt. 'I need to see what is happening. Valbrand, Jeimuzu, Corcoran, Archontos, come with me.'

Led by the scout, they hurried towards a hill that ran at an angle to the coast road. As Bo and the others climbed the hill, the carpet of fern and heather gradually gave way to rocky outcrops and scree that proved difficult to scramble over. Once at the top of the hill, blocks of weathered stone

214

marked the summit and offered a hidden vantage point from which to view the land ahead.

'It's not a fortress, it's a monastery,' said Valbrand. 'A monastery of the Brotherhood of Redemption.'

It stood directly in front of them, some two miles away. Bo saw a church, surrounded by a thick curtain wall marked by two octagonal towers, both decorated with patterned brickwork and topped with a flag of the double-headed eagle. The monastery abutted the sea, with a small crescent-shaped beach and a jetty stretching out into the water.

Bo knew that once such places had been bastions of learning and charity; now seized by the Brotherhood of Redemption, they were strongholds where the young were taken to receive the Holy Null.

'This wasn't on any of the maps given to us by Gnothi,' said Valbrand, scratching his bald dome.

'This presents a problem,' said Jeimuzu. 'The road runs close to the monastery. We can hardly hope to get past it without being seen.'

'We could wait until nightfall,' said Valbrand.

'They'll still see or hear us,' said Corcoran.

'If they send word to Prester John, all surprise will be lost,' said Archontos. 'They could also harass our column from the rear.'

'Then we should head inland,' said Jeimuzu. 'March east for a time before turning back north and then northwest again.'

Archontos grunted. 'That is a long way round. We'd be late meeting the Oroks at the Colossi and we'd never reach Inganno before the end of the feast of Ortus. I also doubt our supplies will last us that long. We are already running low on food, and there is precious little to scavenge in these lands. And to the east of here is a festering, disease-ridden marsh, and beyond that lies the city of Thlipsis, which is even more important to avoid.'

'What do you suggest?' said Valbrand.

'Attack,' said Archontos. 'I studied the stars last night and they presaged battle. Tis a good omen. We have surprise and the numbers to overwhelm the enemy.'

'Aye, but not without heavy losses, losses we can ill afford,' said Valbrand. 'Battles are not decided by the *stars*.'

'I agree with the Centaur,' said Corcoran. 'If one Redeemer, or any other scout, escapes from the monastery with news of our army our plan is ruined. We should storm the monastery. It is the only way to be sure.'

'The walls look thick and tall,' said Jeimuzu.

'Not to the Gigas,' said Archontos. 'And the Khiltoi could scale those walls.'

Corcoran slapped his chest proudly. 'Have no doubt of it.'

'Cool your blood, this is all far too risky,' said Valbrand. 'We have no idea of the enemy's strength. Attacking that monastery is like sticking your head inside a wasps' nest. We should head east and avoid it all together.'

'Frightened, are you?' said Corcoran.

Valbrand glared at him. 'As I live and breathe, I am not afraid of battle, and I call anyone who says different a liar. But I've seen enough of war to know that blundering into a battle you've no need to fight is folly.'

Archontos scrapped at the ground with his hooves. 'Prince Asbjorn, you are our leader. What are your orders?'

216

Bo felt pressure, like a tightening band around his skull. He wanted time to think, he *needed* time, but time was the one thing he did not have. He hated the thought of attacking the monastery. He wanted to circumvent it if possible, but his stomach churned at the delay that would cause; he was already afraid that despite all their efforts they would arrive at Inganno far too late to attack Prester John. And he was afraid the Captains would think he was weak if he did not order an assault. He swallowed, his throat dry. 'We will attack. But before we do, I need to know everything your scout has seen.'

The scout knelt and sketched out a plan of the monastery in the sandy soil. Corcoran translated the scout's words. 'There is a gate on the east wall, and it opens to a cobbled road.'

Bo studied the scribbled plan. 'This is going to require most of our army. The gate worries me. We will need to move quickly to prevent anyone escaping that way.'

'We Centaurs can achieve that,' said Archontos. 'None gallop faster and we'll be at the gate before the main attack commences. No one will escape our watch.'

'Very well,' said Bo. He turned next to Jeimuzu. 'I want your warriors to support the Centaurs.'

The Kojin Prince's expression was impassive, but he accepted the order with a nod.

'The Gigas can deal with the walls, either by breaking a gap in them or lifting others into the monastery,' said Bo. 'The Khiltoi can help them. Once the walls are breeched, the rest of the army can attack.'

'Those walls are bound to be strongly defended,' said

217

Valbrand, plainly unhappy with Bo's decision to attack. 'To reach the monastery we'll have to cross over a mile of open flat land, dangerous if the defenders have muskets or cannon.'

His anxiety building, Bo ran his fingers through his hair. He wanted Valbrand's support and the fact that he lacked it left him feeling more uncertain of his decision to attack. He tried to be logical and reasoned, 'We will suffer causalities, it cannot be avoided. I do not like it any more than you, but losses are inevitable if we take arms against Prester John.'

'You sound too free with the lives of your warriors,' said Valbrand. He shook his head and turned his back.

His reaction unsettled Bo. He struggled to think lucidly. His mind buzzing with a hundred different things, he said, 'Prepare the army.'

'When should the attack start?' said Jeimuzu.

Bo looked up at the darkening sky. 'We wait until nightfall. That should give us the best chance of success. If we are lucky, we might catch them on their evening prayers.'

'If you ask me, it's us that need to pray,' said Valbrand.

*

Bo crouched on the summit of the hill, staring at the monastery, straining to see what was going on. He chewed his fingernails, a dormant habit from childhood that sometimes re-emerged under stress. He muttered to himself, 'Please God, let this work.'

Valbrand knelt beside him, silent, sullen, unsmiling. He fought off every question from Bo with a curt grunt.

Led by Paleos, the Gigas advanced, striding forward as fast as they could manage, followed by the Khiltoi. They moved as dark shadows beneath the silvery moon. Bo turned and said to Archontos, 'Go—secure the gate.'

The Centaurs reacted with snorting and blowing sounds, their tails raised high in the air. They galloped off, whooping and singing.

'I fear the gift of surprise is soon to be lost,' said Moriko, shaking her head. She followed Jeimuzu, who led the small band of Kojin warriors on foot after the Centaurs.

Meanwhile, the Gigas reached the wall, and came under fire. Bo saw musket flashes and heard the crackle of small artillery pieces.

'I think all hell has broken loose,' said Valbrand, the first words he had spoken for over an hour.

Bo leant forward, desperately trying to see what was happening. But smoke and darkness obscured the scene. He stood, and with his sword aloft shouted, 'CHARGE!'

He sprinted down the slope, hurtling towards the monastery. His heart hammered with excitement and fear, adrenalin pumping through his body. The rest of the army followed him. Valbrand ran at his side, yelling battle cries, gorging on the frenzy of battle.

As they came to the wall, they entered a fierce struggle. The familiar sensations of war thrust themselves upon Bo. The screams, the shouts. The smell of sweat and blood. The Janjičari fired their muskets, trying to suppress the artillery mounted on the walls. One of the Gigas lay dead, sprawled out on his back, his face a ruin from cannon shot. The surviving Gigas lifted dozens of Khiltoi over the wall and onto the battlements above, where they fought hand-to-hand with guards.

Bo gestured to Paleos. 'Help me up.'

Bo was hoisted off his feet so swiftly that he felt as though he was going to be thrown over the wall, but he landed with his feet planted firmly on the narrow battlements. He surveyed the scene. The church loomed in front of him, built of bricks, weathered to a grim brown colour. The church's spire rose far above the rest of the monastery, like the sharp end of a deadly spear thrust into the sky. There was a huge arch over the church's western door, which reminded Bo of a gaping mouth. Smaller buildings, stores, a refectory and chapels, surrounded the church.

The Gigas lifted more and more warriors onto the battlements and soon the south wall was secure. Exhilarated and relieved that his plan was working, Bo shouted, 'Follow me, down into the courtyard!'

He descended the steep stairway leading down from the battlements. The church's west door swung open, and from it spewed Redeemers. Bo quickly counted them. Five. Ten. Twenty. Thirty. The Khiltoi reacted with a hail of arrows and slingshot. The Janjičari fired a musket volley. None of the Redeemers fell and they fanned out to advance in a straight line, striding forward at great pace.

'Let's cut their throats,' said Corcoran.

'No, not yet!' said Bo. He did not want the Khiltoi to do anything rash, but their battle lust overrode any cool, logical thoughts and they sprinted at the Redeemers. Bo watched helplessly as the cruel blades of Cold Iron cut down warrior after warrior. He panicked. He froze. He did not know what to do. Some of the Satyrs and Dwarfs joined the attack, but the Redeemers slew them piteously. Valbrand fired shots from his crossbow but although he hit his targets, it had no effect. He said to Bo, 'We have to retreat, now!'

Bo was about to give the order when the ground beneath his feet shook. He turned. Led by Paleos, the Gigas had scaled the walls and jumped down into the courtyard. With their clubs swinging, they charged into the enemy. Some of the Redeemers broke away from the line and confronted the giants. To Bo's horror, they avoided the wild, angry club swings of a Gigas and slashed at his legs until he fell. As he toppled down onto his knees, they ran their swords through him. But it proved an empty victory, for seeing one of their kind butchered inflamed the anger of the Gigas. With vicious club swings they crushed many of the Redeemers, leaving a grisly trail of broken bodies.

The rest of the Old Believers found new heart and flung themselves into the fray. Bo joined the fight, with Valbrand at his side cursing and swearing. A Redeemer reared up in front of them, his white cloak splashed with blood. He gave a chilling scream but Bo brought his sword down towards the Redeemer's head. The Redeemer blocked the blow but the impact forced him backwards. Bo heard Valbrand's crossbow twang and the bolt struck the Redeemer in the throat. He tottered backwards, clutching his throat and gurgling. Bo finished him with a brutal cut to the midriff.

Surrendering was inconceivable to the Redeemers and each fought until slain. With the last of the enemy killed, the Khiltoi, maddened by their losses, rampaged. Led by Corcoran, they charged into the church and Bo heard the sound

221

of breaking glass. Valbrand grabbed his arm and shouted, 'Get those savages under control!'

Bo hurried after them. Their eyes alight with fury, the Khiltoi charged through the church's cavernous nave like frenzied wild beasts. They upturned candles and used them to set fire to tapestries, the choir pulpit and the altar screen. They smashed windows, whooping with delight as shards of stained glass showered the nave floor.

'Stop this!' said Bo. 'It is senseless and achieves nothing.'

'This is our *revenge*,' said Corcoran. 'We burn their church as they burned our villages and groves. They destroyed living creatures and living things; we smash only stone and glass.'

Bo again ordered them to stop but the Khiltoi ignored him. Only when the fire raged too dangerously for them to remain in the church did they leave, singing as they emerged outside, the air full of their proud boasts. Others joined in. Soon many monastery buildings were ablaze. The Satyrs looted some wine and drank copiously, which in turned fuelled their aggression. Bo wandered around like a parent who has lost control of unruly children, ordering, begging them all to stop but to no avail.

Valbrand pulled Bo away and pointed to a small squat brick building to the side of the church. Without making eye contact, Valbrand said, 'You have to see this.'

'I cannot ignore what they are doing,' said Bo, waving his hand around at the rampaging Khiltoi and Satyrs.

'For now it is out of your control,' said Valbrand. 'Let it play out, there's nothing you can do. Besides, you must see this.'

The door to the building hung on its hinges, kicked open. It opened to a single room, low-ceilinged and dark. As soon as Bo stepped inside a coldness entered his body, a sense this was a place of evil, of suffering. A furnace stood cold. Crude instruments hung on the wall, all with cruel hooks and barbs. Dark brown stains plastered the tiled floor and a putrid smell lingered. Bloated flies hummed evilly.

'What is this place?' said Bo, shivering. 'Is it a dungeon for torturing prisoners?'

Valbrand shook his head. 'Not exactly. I think it is where children are brought to be Nulled. This is where they have their freedom taken away from them. Perhaps that is torture, the very worst kind.'

Bo thought about the terrified children who must have suffered here, deceived and tortured by those they believed to be protecting them. 'So, this is the blessing of the Holy Null.'

'This is one place we *should* set on fire,' said Valbrand.

Sick to his stomach, Bo said, 'I have seen enough.'

As they came out into the smoky, flame-licked courtyard, Valbrand said, 'We have thirty dead at least and more than twice that number injured. And with this place burning, we've announced ourselves for miles around.'

'We should be long gone before anyone else comes here,' said Bo. 'By God, Valbrand, if you are angry with me just say it. I grow tired of your sniping. If you no longer wish to fight alongside me then go back to Omphalos, or find a tavern and spend your time drinking away your sorrows. I need your help. I need you to be a *friend*.'

'I *am* your friend, you fool,' said Valbrand. 'A friend's only

223

worthy if they speak the truth. I respect you but I won't pander to you. You allowed those Eldar hotheads to dictate your decisions, decisions you knew damn well were wrong. Bad counsel comes to a bad end. Archontos is wise and honourable, but like all Centaurs, he loves war. Corcoran's a tough warrior and we need him, but he's as dim as a sheep. He isn't shrewd. You need to be. You're a prince, not some bootless knave. Seems to me like you were more worried about proving how strong you were, rather than making the right decisions.'

'What do you know about it? It is easy enough for you. All you have to do is fight. I have to make the difficult decisions. I have to be a leader and a leader must be strong.'

'I may not know much, but I know that when a leader stops listening to harsh truths he's walking a path to ruin. A flatterer is no friend. You'll find plenty of folk to flatter you, not I.'

With that, Valbrand spat on the floor and stormed off, shaking his head. Bo stood still and watched him. Valbrand's words infuriated because, deep down, he knew that he was right. He had wanted to prove himself. He had wanted to show that he was strong. He cursed his stupidity and lack of judgement.

The fires burned furiously but hunger and tiredness finally brought the looting to a halt. Trying to compose himself, Bo managed to persuade the Old Believers to get out of the fire-wasted monastery. They carried the casualties on rickety, bloodstained makeshift stretchers. Brief prayers were spoken over the fallen but there was no time to bury them.

As the army filed out of the monastery through the gate,

Archontos and the Centaurs hailed them with triumphant cheers. The Kojin hung back.

'Did anyone escape the monastery?' said Bo to Archontos, dreading the answer.

'None got out,' said the Centaur.

'Good,' said Bo, glad for any small success. 'We need to get away from the monastery and find somewhere to camp.'

'We have just fought a battle,' said Corcoran, strutting around with a wineskin in his hand. 'We need rest.'

'And more wine!' said a Satyr, sparking laughter.

His cheeks flushed, Bo tried to stand firm. 'Do as I command. I am in charge of this army.'

He walked on and the Old Believers reluctantly followed him, but he swore he heard Corcoran mutter, '*For now.*'

CHAPTER TEN

The Colossi of the Dawn Ruler

The Army of the Old Believers finally camped in the ruins of a cliff-top stronghold, some five miles north of the monastery. Haphazard walls built of a mix of sandstone blocks and unfired bricks crisscrossed the site, while a single gate flanked by two trapezoidal towers kept a lonely vigil.

Bo stood on the edge of the cliff; far below him the waves churned and foamed. A natural limestone arch formed by the sea's relentless action reached out from the cliff into the water. Its chalky exterior reminded Bo of flesh-stripped bones. He rubbed his tired, juddering eyes and looked to the south; there the burning monastery glowed like a candle in a dark room. He wondered if other eyes, unfriendly eyes, surveyed the same flames. A beacon to proclaim his recklessness.

Bo turned back and faced the camp, an ill-ordered city of tents hastily erected around the crumbling stones. He had posted sentries on the perimeter of the camp, and some perched precariously in the gate towers. Those not on sentry duties either slept or drank, enjoying wine looted from the monastery. Their songs and laughter carried on the keen sea breezes. Earlier Bo had heard other sounds: the moans and cries of the wounded as the surgeons and healers struggled to save them, moans and cries that agonized him, guilt and pity jabbing at him like the relentless pokes of a spear. He had lost control of the army. He had failed as a leader. Perhaps if he had not attacked…if he had waited…The words of Valbrand reverberated in his mind: *Seems to me like you were more worried about proving how strong you were, rather than making the right decisions.*

Since the attack on the monastery, Bo had seen little of Valbrand, so little that he suspected his friend was deliberately avoiding him. Bo realised how much he missed his jokes, barbed comments and gruff support. He cast his eyes upwards, staring at the cloud-devoured sky, and whispered, 'I've been a fool.'

'Ah, here is our heroic leader.'

The sarcastic voice chilled Bo's blood. Corcoran, with a wineskin in his hand, approached him, flanked by several other Khiltoi. 'You are not joining our revels?'

'I am hoping to sleep, perhaps you should do the same. We need to conserve our strength.'

Corcoran emptied the remains of the wineskin in a single swig and dropped it on the ground. 'Is that an *order*, little white-skinned Prince?'

'If you want to take it that way, yes, it is,' said Bo. He tried to control his voice, to hide his fear and embarrassment behind a stony expression. To others he probably appeared aloof, cold; only he knew the turmoil within him.

'I grow tired of your orders,' said Corcoran, getting louder

227

with every word. 'You looked like a startled rabbit during the battle. It's a miracle you did not wet yourself! You're no leader.'

The Khiltoi's booming voice drew onlookers like wasps to a mouldering, fermenting apple. Bo noticed Valbrand amongst them. His heart pounding, Bo said, 'You are drunk, Corcoran, so I will overlook your words.'

Corcoran laughed. 'Overlook my words? What choice do you have? Your orders mean nothing, little Prince. It's time that a true warrior led this army.'

All of the Khiltoi cheered their approval, as did some of the Satyrs and Centaurs. Panic rising within him, Bo flashed a look at Valbrand who glared back, stony-faced. Bo turned to Corcoran. 'I will not lightly stand aside. Gnothi appointed me to lead this army, and I intend to do so.'

'Then we have a problem,' said Corcoran. 'But it can be resolved simply enough. If you wish to remain leader, you have to prove your strength to me and the rest of the Old Believers.'

'I have nothing to prove,' said Bo. 'Gnothi appointed—'

'Gnothi is not here,' said Corcoran wolfishly. 'I offer you a duel. A duel to the death. The one left standing shall be declared the leader.'

There were cheers and roars of approval. Bo felt events crushing him. He knew if he refused the duel, he would lose all credibility and would have to surrender the leadership. But to fight…could he defeat the Khiltoi warrior? He had no option. He took a deep breath and said, 'Very well, we fight.'

Archontos pushed through the crowd and said, 'This is

madness. We fight each other, wasting energy that should be unleashed against Prester John. Prince Asbjorn, do not indulge this dangerous folly.'

'It is all right, Archontos,' said Bo, wanting so much to follow the Centaur's advice, but knowing if he did so then Corcoran would win anyway. He lied and said, 'I know what I'm doing.'

Archontos retreated, cursing and swishing his tail. As the Centaur did so, Prince Jeimuzu, flanked by Moriko, called out to Bo. 'Archontos is right. This is dishonourable. However, if it must alas come to combat, one challenged to a duel can nominate a champion to fight in his stead. Give me this honour, Prince Asbjorn. Your life is too precious, and I have no doubt that I have the beating of this Khiltoi.'

Bo felt a flicker of pleasure, at least he had some friends, some measure of support, but he could not accept someone else fighting for him. He raised his trembling hands. 'That will not be necessary, Prince Jeimuzu, though I am grateful and honoured by your offer.'

'You might live to regret that, or more likely you won't,' said Corcoran. He held his arms aloft and gestured for those watching to stand back and form a wide circle. 'This will not take long. Little Prince, you've no chance against me.'

'We shall see,' said Bo, trying to sound confident, but he was shaking with fear. With trembling hands, he unsheathed his sword.

A Khiltoi warrior handed Corcoran his obsidian-bladed club and he twirled it in his fingers. He stroked his moustache in a vain, preening manner. He circled Bo, readying himself for an attack. He licked his lips. 'You'd have been wiser to flee.'

Bo took slow, deliberate steps, keeping his balance, and his distance from the prowling Khiltoi. He tried not to let the Corcoran's words distract him. He needed to focus, to block out the world around him. He knew if he panicked he was doomed. He waited for Corcoran to make the first move. It was not long in coming. Growing visibly impatient, Corcoran leapt forward and swung his club at Bo, who ducked to miss the blow and blocked a follow-up attack with his sword. His whole body juddered with the impact.

'You're weaker than I thought,' said Corcoran.

Bo shut out the Khiltoi's words. He focused on Corcoran's movements, on how he shifted his weight, on how he carried his weapon. He needed to anticipate his opponent's actions.

Corcoran attacked again, howling and lunging forward. Bo sidestepped but before he could strike with his sword, Corcoran used his greater size and reach to land a heavy punch on Bo's shoulder. Bo staggered to the edge of the circle, only for the eager, baying Khiltoi warriors to push him back towards Corcoran. Bo managed to steady himself, although his shoulder throbbed with pain.

'The time has come to finish this,' said Corcoran, urged on by the onlookers. He charged but Bo moved faster and brought a slashing cut that struck the Khiltoi on the hip. Corcoran gasped in pain and anger, and in his drunken fury, lurched wildly at Bo, his eyes ablaze with hate.

But Bo now had the measure of his opponent. He swayed

to miss a brutal club swing and then whipped a chopping cut down onto Corcoran's left arm. The blade did not cut deeply but the Khiltoi dropped his weapon. Before Corcoran could react, Bo slashed at his legs, scoring a scything blow into the Khiltoi's left thigh.

Corcoran groaned and sank to his knees. Bo brought his blade to the Khiltoi's throat. The onlookers fell silent, the boisterous songs and chants ceased.

Bo looked at Corcoran. He knew he could kill him with one stroke, he *wanted* to. He wanted revenge for Corcoran's attempts to humiliate him. He wanted to prove he was strong. He wanted those who doubted him to be afraid. His fingers tightened on the handle of his sword, his muscles tensed.

Corcoran spat. 'Do you wish to torture me? Kill me and have it done with.'

Bo felt the impatient eyes of the army upon him. They waited to see what he, their leader, would do. He knew his actions would define their view of him. Did he want to kill out of anger, out of vengeance? Did he want to be a leader who ruled by fear?

He sheathed his sword. 'Get up, Corcoran. I'm not going to kill you. You fought well. And I have need of strong fighters in the days to come.'

Corcoran scowled at him. 'I don't need your pity.'

'And I do not give it to you. You questioned my leadership and I have demonstrated my strength. Now it is time for you to show me your character. Put aside these petty grudges. Fight instead those who seek to enslave your people. I swear I shall fight to my dying breath to defeat Prester

231

John, but I should feel happier if you and your kin fight alongside me.'

Corcoran bowed his head. Many Khiltoi nodded, clearly in agreement with Bo's words. Bo turned to the crowd and said, 'I am your leader. I do not promise victory. But let us stand together, let us show Prester John we are not afraid.'

To his amazement, many of them cheered, and some chanted, 'Asbjorn! Asbjorn!'

Wincing, Corcoran rose to his feet. He gestured for everyone to be quiet and faced Bo. 'I don't like you, Prince Asbjorn, but you're a warrior, that I concede, despite your spindly frame. You won today and I'll hold my tongue for now, though I do not say that our quarrelling is done.'

Bo impulsively held out a hand. To his surprise, Corcoran shook it, albeit hesitantly. Bo said, 'You should have the surgeons see to your wounds.'

Corcoran shrugged. 'We Khiltoi are not troubled by mere *flesh wounds*. I'll be marching tomorrow and ready to fight, don't worry about that.'

Limping, but pushing away all offers of help from the other Khiltoi, Corcoran made for his tent. The rest of the onlookers dispersed too, seeking food or sleep.

Bo felt a tap on his shoulder. It was Valbrand. 'I have to admit it, you handled that quite well.'

'Thank you,' said Bo. He trembled a little as the adrenaline, the rush of aggression, soaked away from his body. He had been so close to losing command of the army, so close to losing his life.

'I was tempted to step in and help you, but you had the situation under control.'

'It did not feel so to me,' said Bo. He looked at Valbrand. 'I'm glad you are talking to me, at least.'

'If you think I'm going to apologise for chewing off your ear earlier you're in for a disappointment. I meant what I said before and I was right in what I said. But you showed proper guts in standing up to that tree dweller, and good judgement to spare his oversized neck. Speaking plainly, if I'd been in your place I'd have skewered him but a man in your position needs to take a broader view of events.'

'I think you're right. And although you have no need to apologise, I certainly do. I do not question your friendship. I value it highly. I have seen enough of treachery and deceit to know and understand the value of a true friend.'

Valbrand squinted at Bo. 'You're not planning on giving me some kind of *embrace* are you?'

Bo laughed. 'No, you're quite safe.'

'That's fine then,' said Valbrand with a smile. He gave Bo a friendly punch on the arm. 'I'm off for some sleep, so I can forget about all this madness for an hour or two.'

With that, Valbrand sauntered away. Bo looked out to sea again. It stretched out like a black desert, without end, timeless. His fears, his sense of weakness and inferiority still tormented him. The responsibility of leading the army weighed heavily upon him. It would bring him no glory, no comfort, no joy, but he understood his responsibility, his higher duty and did not resent the cost. Bo trembled and to his shame he fought back tears, tears he was glad the night concealed.

*

233

As dawn broke and the Old Believers followed the road further inland, the weather showed a different face. Thick black clouds, like smudges on a canvas, rolled over the sky and leered down. Working with the remorseless cold wind, they soon brought slanting, horizontal, deluges of rain. The army sloshed through slimy mud. They suffered the hardships endured by every army in history: blisters, hunger, thirst and lice. Despite the miserable conditions, Bo urged the army forward. Time ran short. They were still far from Inganno and had to meet with the Oroks before they could offer battle with any hope of victory.

It rained until late afternoon, when the alliance between the black clouds and capricious wind finally sundered, leaving a sky pink with dusk's delicate touch. The Old Believers marched on, the road gradually turning from a muddy track to a cobbled avenue that led them through a cluster of ruins. Built in long rows were numerous square tombs, each carved out of the rock and embellished with decorated cornices and doorways.

'What is this place?' said Bo.

'The necropolis of the Turskum, a civilisation of Men that flourished here in antiquity,' said Archontos as he trotted alongside Bo and Valbrand. 'They were peaceful folk who grew rich from mining and farming. They were famed for their metalwork and love of banqueting.'

'Did Prester John destroy them?' said Bo.

'No, they vanished centuries before his rise, abandoned by their gods. The Imperators conquered this land, swallowing it as part of their empire, though of course in time that empire fell too, as do they all.'

'I fear the Holy Empire of Prester John will break that trend,' said Valbrand.

Once through the necropolis, the road followed a steep gradient and it brought them to a breath-taking spectacle. Ahead loomed two sandstone statues; each stood twice the height of any of the nearby trees. Both depicted a figure seated upon a throne, hands rested on their knees and staring forwards. The statues showed signs of weathering and deliberate damage; few features from above the waist were recognisable, giving them a blank, sinister appearance.

'Would you look at *that*,' said Valbrand with an admiring whistle.

'The Colossi of the Dawn Ruler,' said Bo. 'They are well named.'

'This feels like a place that has seen sorrow and death,' said Valbrand. 'I don't like it, but at least the Oroks shouldn't have any problems finding us here.'

'I hope we are not too late,' said Bo.

Archontos looked around anxiously. 'Gnothi said to expect them by Ortus Eve. They should be here already.'

A Khiltoi scout shouted and pointed at a ridge to the west. A rider waited there, staring down at the army, a silhouette back lit by the falling sun. The rider came down the ridge and rode steadily towards them. As he drew close, Bo saw that he wore an iron helmet with a leather neck-protector, and a heavy woollen coat over a lamellar-armour cuirass. A bow and a quiver full of arrows were strapped to his back. His leathery face was broad and flat, with high-set cheekbones and a stubby nose. A red scar marked his face. He rode a short, stocky horse.

The rider dismounted close to the Colossi. In a deep, heavily accented drawl, he said, 'I am a messenger of the Khan. Who leads this army?'

Bo stepped forward. 'I am Prince Asbjorn. What news do you bring? Has your Khan brought his warriors?'

The Orok smiled. 'I suppose before answering the question I should seek proof that you are indeed the army sent forth from Omphalos. Yet as I look upon you all, I see such an alliance as could not be imagined coming from any other place.'

'I can assure you we are not imposters,' said Bo.

'I am assured,' said the Orok. 'And to answer your question, yes, the Khan has brought his warriors.'

The Orok remounted his horse and sat up in the stirrups. He waved towards the east. Within seconds, a line of riders appeared on the ridge. Dozens, then hundreds of them, like a snake crawling across the edge of the ridge. The Orok turned to Bo and said, 'We have ridden many miles across harsh lands.'

'Tell the Khan we are grateful,' said Bo.

The Orok laughed. 'You already have. I am Arigh Nasan, Khan of the Orok tribes.'

'What deceit is this?' said Archontos, stamping his hooves. 'You said you were a messenger, and now you claim to be the Khan. I do not trust this Orok's tongue.'

'Please forgive my deception, but I had to be sure you were who you claimed to be before I revealed my warriors to you. Prester John's followers are not above using traps.'

Valbrand laughed. 'This Orok has guts and cheek. He's my sort of fellow.'

236

'I am honoured by your kind words,' said Arigh Nasan, his face inscrutable so Bo could not tell if he was joking. The Orok said to Bo, 'I am glad to see you though I had hoped you would come sooner and in larger numbers.'

Bo shrugged. 'Prester John's grip is tightening. Many that would have come to Omphalos were prevented from doing so. And we have already fought one battle.'

'Alas, I too bring fewer warriors than I had hoped. I called a Kiyot, but not all the tribes supported my plan. They preferred to protect their own lands rather than send warriors west to confront Prester John. I do not condemn them, but it means I have gathered barely a thousand riders. In the golden age of the Orok Empire, khans commanded vast armies, strengthened by catapults, trebuchets and giant crossbows. Alas, in these withered times, our muster is meagre in comparison. I appealed to the Eldar races of the distant east, the Dvorovoi, the Ovinnik and the Banniks, but they are suspicious and distrustful, and refused to join our expedition, just as they ignored the summons to Omphalos.'

'Each of your warriors bolsters our hopes for the battle to come, for the Oroks' fighting prowess is legendary,' said Bo, but his heart sank a little. He had hoped that the Oroks would bring many more to augment the dwindling numbers of the Old Believers.

'But perhaps talk of battle is over hopeful,' said Arigh Nasan. 'You are a day late, to have even a slim chance of reaching Inganno in time we must leave immediately.'

Bo shook his head. 'That is impossible. We have been marching all day. The army has to rest.'

237

Arigh Nasan gave him a hard look. 'If we delay, we shall miss this chance to attack Prester John.'

'If there was a swifter road I would take it,' said Bo.

'There is a swifter road,' said Corcoran. 'In Omphalos I heard talk of a road that runs straight through the ancient forest of Kakos. It's not far from here and if we take that road, we should reach Inganno within two days.'

'Gnothi warned me against going that way,' said Bo.

'And with good reason,' said Archontos. He inclined his head. 'Those woods are deadly.'

Corcoran gave a derisive snort. 'We Khiltoi do not fear any woods.'

'Then you're more foolish than I supposed,' said Archontos. He said to Bo. 'If we go through the forest, we are throwing our lives away. Don't agree to this, I beg you.'

'Tales of Kakos reached Orok ears,' said Arigh Nasan. 'And they are tales of shocking evil. It is said that a witch dwells there, a foul sorceress named Zanash who devours any traveller unfortunate enough to cross her path.'

'It is the only way to reach Inganno in time,' said Corcoran, crossing his arms defiantly. 'If you are too frightened to go that way then we might as well turn back.'

Valbrand turned to Bo and said, 'I think you should decide.'

Bo tried to swallow but his mouth was dry. He looked up at the Colossi. Their blank, crumbling faces stared back at him. The warning of Gnothi echoed in his mind and the very thought of venturing into the forest to confront Zanash terrified him. But there was truth in Corcoran's words. If they followed the planned route, they could not reach

238

Inganno before Prester John left. If the road through the forest was the only way to get to Inganno in time, they had to try it, regardless of the danger. He drew in a deep breath and said words he did not want to say, and words he knew most of those around him did not want to hear. 'I have decided. We shall take the forest road.'

*

The army camped roughly, barely bothering to set up tents. They slept until just before dawn, setting off while it was still dark. Leaving the Colossi to continue their silent, centuries long, vigil, the Old Believers turned north-west, towards the forest of Kakos. Looking fresh and full of vigour, the Oroks protected the flanks of the weary, lice-ridden army.

The Khan rode alongside Bo. Looking down from his horse, he said, 'I have heard your name before, Prince Asbjorn. Elowen Aubyn spoke of you. She praised your courage.'

Bo failed to prevent a little smile. 'Elowen's bravery far outstrips mine.'

Arigh Nasan looked at Bo solemnly. 'I cannot judge that, but in many ways I pity her. Elowen has suffered so much. I fear too much is being asked of her.'

'I would not underestimate her strength.'

'Indeed not, but the foes she faces are so terrible,' said Arigh Nasan.

As the day began to brighten, they splashed across a shallow, whispering stream and into a dry, lifeless land studded

239

with sombre hills and craters. There was no grass, and clusters of ash-grey rocks stood like markers of buried tombs. A handful of trees reached upwards, but they were unlike any trees Bo had seen before, with weirdly twisted trunks and branches. He scarcely believed it possible that any trees could root in such parched, dusty soil. Strewn incongruously on some of the hills were the ruins of chimneys and wheelhouses, relics from long-abandoned mining. The wind whipped up clouds of dust, turning the army into a column of grey, ghostly figures.

The desolate, rocky landscape reminded Bo of the tales of the scientists in the Preven court who had viewed the moon through various fantastical lenses. They spoke about wonders they had observed, or claimed to have observed: a barren, heavily cratered world.

'What a depressing place,' said Valbrand, scratching himself in the endless struggle against lice.

'Once many fair trees grew here,' said Archontos. 'Many sang of the beauty of the groves, but no more.'

'What happened?' said Bo.

Archontos looked uneasy. 'From the beginning of time, Zanash protected the forest, nurturing life, enriching the Earthsoul. Yet the forest did not satisfy her. It is said she yearned for more than just protecting life, she wanted to *create* life. In her eagerness for the knowledge to achieve this, she eventually turned to one she should have feared, one she should have resisted.'

'Prester John,' said Valbrand, spitting as he said the name.

'Yes, so it was,' said Archontos. 'Keenly he worked with her, drawing out her wisdom, using her for his own malevolent purposes. He poisoned this land and, so it is claimed, the soul of the guardian. Realising she had been duped, Zanash withdrew to the heart of the forest, locking it away like a prison, forbidding any to travel through on its dark paths. It is a cursed, evil place. Eldritch creatures dwell there now, unnatural, misshapen beings.'

As much as he tried to ignore such tales, Bo doubted his decision. Was he being reckless? If Kakos proved as dangerous as Archontos believed, blindly leading the army into the forest would be disastrous. But it was the swiftest way to Inganno. So however terrible the risk, the situation compelled him to take it. He had to be bold.

After several more hours plodding through the stark hills, they came to a rise from which they beheld at distance a black and brooding forest. Fumes rose from the tightly packed trees. As they drew closer to the forest, they saw that thick hedges and ivy-clad trees formed a solid wall, impenetrable against all intruders. However, a huge wooden gate, carved with intricate swirling, spiralling patterns, offered the possibility of a way into the forest.

Bo ordered the Old Believers to rest on the broad slope facing the forest. He called the Captains, Valbrand and Arigh Nasan together. 'We need to get into the forest, but I'm reluctant to lead all the army through at once.'

'You will not get inside without the permission of Zanash,' said Archontos.

'And how do we do that?' said Valbrand. 'Just knock on the gate?'

'We could break the gate down and force our way through,' said Corcoran.

241

'There will be no *breaking*,' said Bo. 'We have no idea of what we are facing. I will approach alone. That way, we do not risk losing the whole army.'

'I see the sense of your plan, but you should not be risked, Prince Asbjorn,' said Arigh Nasan. 'You are too valuable.'

'Yes, the Orok is right, it is too dangerous,' said Archontos. 'We Centaurs would say Zanash carries fire in one hand and water in the other. She is not to be trusted. I am Eldar; Zanash will look more kindly upon me. I should go.'

'No,' said Bo. 'I am in charge. It is my responsibility.'

To avoid any further argument, Bo set off immediately. Conscious of having the eyes of the army upon him, he tried to keep his pace unhurried as he approached the gate. He did not want to reveal his fear. The weirdly carved gate loomed larger with each step. He felt like an infant, preparing to enter an adult world.

When he reached the gate, he stopped and looked back. The Old Believers lined the slope, distant now, reminding Bo of the little toy soldiers he had played with as a child. Odd calls and howls drifted from the forest, muffled by the densely growing trees.

He stared at the gate, absorbing the details; he saw symbols of the sun, birds, beasts and trees, all parts of restless, flowing patterns. Bo leant forward to knock on the gate but before he could do so, a voice from inside the forest rang out. 'Who disturbs the peace of this land?'

Bo took a second to compose himself. 'I am Prince Asbjorn of Prevennis.'

'And why have you come here, *Prince Asbjorn of Prevennis*?'

'To ask Zanash's permission to pass through the forest.'

242

Cold, hollow laughter greeted his words. 'What madness drives you to make such a bold and foolish request? Are you eager to meet your death?'

Bo settled on saying, 'That is something I will only discuss with the guardian.'

'So be it.'

Releasing a waft of damp decaying vegetation, the gate opened outwards, forcing Bo to step back smartly. A figure stood in front of him. Robes covered his body and a wooden mask, long and with frightening, exaggerated features, concealed his face. He held out a hand towards Bo. 'Come with me, Prince Asbjorn.'

The opened gate offered the first glimpse inside the forest and the sight chilled Bo's heart. From the gate, a road ran straight, like a pale outstretched arm. Around it and over it, hideously malformed trees grew, their thorny branches intertwined in a permanent struggle for light.

An emerald glow emanated from the cramped spaces between the trees, eerie and unnatural. A thin mist floated spectrally above the road and every now and Bo thought he spied fast-moving amorphous shapes, with the hints of arms and legs. The dank air was like a poison that entered his mouth and slipped into his body, passing its pestilence along his veins.

But he could not turn back. There was no other way. He had promised to try to find passage through the forest. He had to see it through. He took a slow, reluctant step across the threshold. Moved by hands or forces unseen, the gate slammed shut behind him.

- CHAPTER ELEVEN -

Kakos

The masked figure said to Bo, 'I am Shëmtuar. Follow me, and do not step off the road.'

He turned and strode down the pale road. Bo said, 'Is it far? I do not have much time.'

Shëmtuar laughed. 'In the forest, it is Zanash who decides how much time you have.'

As he followed the masked figure, Bo kept peering into the forest, his eyes drawn by darting, shadowy movements. More than once he thought he saw eyes staring back at him. Overhead came the sound of birdsong, but the calls were alien to him, sounding strangled, gargled.

Shëmtuar turned onto a path that branched off from the road. Here, the trees were much closer, and as Bo walked, he brushed against their branches. The cloying smell of rotting leaves filled his nostrils, and the ground beneath his feet squelched. He heard the pitter-patter of moisture on the leaves but no rain fell. It appeared that the trees themselves secreted an oily resin, which dropped from the branches like melted wax.

The sights, the smells, the sounds of the forest nibbled away at Bo's sense of reality, almost convincing him that it existed only as a figment of his imagination, a fantasy born in sleep or madness. As he tried to catch up with the masked figure, he glanced to his left. From within the mass of branches, limp leaves and draping lichen, a pair of green eyes glared at him. Bo stopped and squinted, trying to get a closer look at the creature. He saw only an outline, vague and misshapen. He heard shallow, gurgled breathing.

The creature retreated, swallowed by the forest's darkness. Shëmtuar yanked Bo's arm. 'There is nothing in there you need to see.'

They came to a wide clearing, and faced an ivy-clad stone tower, twisted, climbing skyward in sinuous curves. Its irregular, impossible shape heightened Bo's disorientation. Four steep steps led up to a wooden door; Shëmtuar mounted them and pounded his fist on the door. It opened inwards, creaking and groaning, hurling out a stink that made Bo think of a hot, smoking cannon. Before entering, Shëmtuar turned to Bo and said, 'This is your final chance to turn back.'

Bo shook his head but kept it lowered; he did not want his guide to detect his fear.

'So be it,' said Shëmtuar. 'She is waiting for you.'

Once inside the tower, they ascended a narrow, winding staircase, and as they reached the top, Shëmtuar stepped aside, ushered Bo through an open door, and hurried back down the steps like a startled spider, a development both unexpected and unsettling. Bo edged his way along a windowless corridor, illuminated only by a faint glow ahead.

With his heart pounding, Bo stepped warily through a low archway, ducking as he did so, and emerged into a smoky

245

oval-shaped room, his footsteps tapping on the tiled floor. There were no windows although a shard of light speared down from a hole in the ceiling. Shelves covered every wall, all filled with dust-veiled bottles, pots, flasks and phials. Bo heard a weird sound, a kind of singing, like the strained me-owing of a cat.

Peering through the wispy smoke, Bo spotted a figure seated upon a wooden throne. The figure called out, 'Come closer. I wish to see you.'

With the wailing still ringing in his ears, Bo edged towards the throne, and saw more clearly who awaited him. Zanash. She had a white, doll-like face framed by a tangle of long, curly black hair. Her small mouth remained closed and her eyes peered out from beneath thick, coal-black eyebrows. Bo saw no wrinkles on her porcelain face, no sign of old age, yet her voice sounded venerable and weary.

Two creatures sat around the throne. Although they showed human proportions and limbs, they appeared blended with other animals. One of them had the long snout of a dog, with patches of fur on his hands and face. The other, whom Bo guessed had been singing, showed more feline features, including a tail that rested on his legs. Disturbed, Bo shivered as he stared at the creatures. The cat-child stopped singing. He stared at Bo, and whispered to his companion.

Zanash stroked the heads of both creatures and gave Bo a haughty look. 'If you are reckless enough to come into my chamber, you should at least bow.'

Cursing his stupidity, Bo sank to one knee. 'Forgive me.'

'That is better,' she said, her small mouth shaping a cruel, mocking smile. The dog-like creature scuttled towards Bo, and sniffed him. Zanash ordered it to back away and gestured for Bo to stand up. 'So, what brings you before me?'

'I am here to seek passage through the forest,' he said as he rose to his feet. 'I have need of haste, and cannot be delayed.'

'What is the cause of your haste?' she said, leaning back.

He took a deep breath. 'I lead an army north.'

The guardian's eyes narrowed. 'An *army*? You want me to allow an *army* to pass through the forest? Why would I agree to such folly?'

'We march against Prester John.'

Zanash glared at him. A change came over her face, giving her harsher, animal-like features. She stood. 'If this be a jest then I shall slay you with my own hands.'

'It is no jest,' said Bo, his throat tinder dry.

'You cannot prevail against the evil one. There is no power strong enough to defeat him.'

'With respect, I disagree. We have total surprise, but only if we strike swiftly. And this is why we must have passage through the forest.'

Her stare intensified. 'If I agree to your request and you are crushed, will that not bring the fury of Prester John down upon my land? He has blighted it enough already.'

Bo remembered what Archontos had told him about Prester John's betrayal of the guardian. 'He has wronged you before. Do you not wish for revenge? Do you not wish to see him ruined, and his works undone?'

Her eyes flickered, taking a wilder aspect that Bo found disconcerting. 'Yes, I do desire revenge.'

'By helping us you might achieve it.'

Zanash nodded and circled Bo, ready to pounce. She smelt strongly of lavender, and yet he detected it concealed a stench of corruption, of decay. 'Prester John took so much from me. Together we achieved great things, wonderful things. We created *life*. The deadly Sicarius Tree, the Succo Spider and mightiest of all, the giant Carnifex. The glory of the Creator ran through my fingers. Look at my beautiful children, Aelurus and Canispuer, are they not delightful?'

The two creatures cooed and slobbered at her attention.

'But all the time he feigned friendship,' she continued. 'Prester John stole from me, betrayed me, destroyed many of my creations and almost destroyed my land. He grew strong as my power withered. Yes, revenge would be the sweetest nectar on my lips. You have my permission.'

Barely believing his good fortune, Bo hastily bowed again. 'I am grateful beyond words.'

'You get ahead of yourself. My permission I give, but it is not without conditions.'

'Name them,' said Bo, trying to hide his concern.

Zanash paused, as though savouring the moment. 'None pass through this forest without a sacrifice. In exchange for my permission, I demand a life.'

Bo trembled and his eyes juddered. With his voice reduced to a mouse-like squeak, he said, 'If there must be a sacrifice, I offer my own life.'

She frowned, an exaggerated gesture, a clear sign that she was enjoying herself. 'No, I would rather your strength is spent on fighting the accursed Prester John. Offer me one of your warriors. I am reasonable. I ask for only one. Offer me a life and I shall gladly spare yours.'

Although the idea sounded abhorrent to Bo, his mind spun connections. Who could take his place? He was tempted. He did not want to sacrifice himself. If there was someone else, someone…

No, he fought the temptation. He could not ask another to give their life so cheaply. He rubbed his eyes and pulled himself to his full height. 'No, it is my duty and mine alone.'

Zanash rubbed her face and smiled. 'A pity, but perhaps there is another way.'

She strode over to a shelf and rummaged amongst the countless dusty containers. At length she pulled out a small green phial. Aelurus and Canispuer yapped and howled excitedly. Zanash turned to Bo. 'This is a slow-working poison. Drink this and from the moment it passes your lips you are doomed. But it will take days, maybe as many as seven days if you are as strong, to work its sorcery. Until the end you will feel few ill-effects, and you should be granted enough time and strength to lead your attack against Prester John. But, do not be fooled: it will claim your life in the end. This is my final offer to you.'

She uncorked the phial and passed it to Bo. It felt warm in his palm, and a rancid smell escaped from inside. Every impulse, every instinct, warned him against drinking the poison. He wanted to throw it away. He did not want to die. Then another force within him took shape. He remembered what they were fighting against, what they stood to lose if they failed. He thought of the vile building inside the monastery, the place of suffering for so many children, and

249

there were dozens, maybe hundreds more such places across the Known World. Bo knew of no greater proof of Prester John's evil. He had accepted the chance to lead the army. He would do whatever was needed for victory, even if it cost him his life. He had to do it. He had to swallow the poison.

Closing his eyes, he brought the phial to his lips and drank the contents with one swig. It left a foul, burning taste in his mouth and he choked and spluttered. Zanash gently traced her fingers down his throat towards his stomach. 'I can feel it entering you. It is patient, it shall bide its time. There is no remedy, there is no cure. Search for one if you wish but you search in vain. You are now the walking dead.'

Bo glared at her, struggling to focus, his head swimming. He almost choked as he said, 'And passage through the forest?'

'It is granted,' she said. 'Go now. Shëmtuar is waiting for you outside, ready to lead you back to the front gate. There, assemble your army and lead them through the forest.'

'I have your word that we shall not be hindered?'

'Of course,' she said. 'Only advise your followers to keep to the road. If they stray and disturb those who dwell here, I cannot protect them. There are restless souls amongst the trees, and once stirred, they are beyond my control. And this you must know too: dark the forest is, but light no fires. To do so invites dreadful peril.'

'I will tell them,' said Bo, disturbed by Zanash's warning.

'Good. I urge you to go then, for in all ways, Prince Asbjorn, time is not on your side.'

With those troubling words ringing in his ears, Bo rushed

back towards the army. The poison's bitter taste lingered in his mouth, coating his tongue. He had seven days at most. Seven more dawns. He had known of course he was likely to be slain in the battle against Prester John, but he had retained a flicker of hope that he would survive. Now, his bargain with Zanash extinguished that hope. Part of him now *wanted* to die in battle, it was surely a better fate than the slow death caused by the workings of the poison. But he knew he could not needlessly throw his life away, not while he still had breath to draw and a duty to fulfil. He needed to be strong. He would hide it from the others. The knowledge of his sacrifice would not help them.

As Bo returned to the army and summoned the Captains, Valbrand greeted him with a hearty slap on the back. 'You look worried, my friend. Did you succeed?'

He forced a smile and nodded, 'Yes, and we must go now.'

'It is said that Zanash seldom grants favours to mortals,' said Archontos. 'How did you persuade her?'

Bo hesitated, not wanting to reveal the truth. He settled on saying, 'She has little love for Prester John.'

'Then we are fortunate,' said Corcoran. 'It's a shame she did not choose to march alongside us. She'd make the enemy's bowels tremble.'

'If you had beheld her, you would not wish for such a thing,' said Bo.

'You believe Zanash will keep her word?' said Arigh Nasan. 'In the forest we are vulnerable to ambush.'

'She will keep her word,' said Bo, thinking of the little phial of poison. 'She will not betray us.'

251

'Then what are we waiting for?' said Valbrand.

Bo said, 'Follow me into the forest, but give warning to all to stay on the road, and light no fires.'

The army marched towards the forest. At first boasts and songs filled the air, but a hush fell as they reached the shadows of the trees. Shëmtuar stood to one side of the open gate, as motionless as a statue, impervious to the stares and fearful mutterings of the Old Believers. Bo nodded to him as he passed into the forest but received no reaction. He went first, at the head of the army. He did so out of duty, but he battled to contain his fear. The army filed into the forest's open mouth and one by one, the forest swallowed them.

Mist drifted over the road and the air was stuffy, rank with decomposing vegetation. Chilling cries echoed around the trees. Bo heard scuffling and rustling. Shadows flitted here and there, glimpses of abnormal shapes. Bo thought he heard not only the calls of animals, but whispers and chilly laughter too.

The Oroks struggled to settle their horses, who neighed, whinnied and swished their tails. Only with soothing words practised over generations did they manage to coax their steeds to move. Apart from the jangling of their equipment and the occasional hushed conversation, the rest of the army marched in near silence.

As they plunged deeper into the forest, the branches of the trees established a dense canopy above the road, blocking out all but the few spindly spears of sunlight fortunate enough to find a route through the entanglements of branches, leaves, lichen and thorns. Bo remembered the guardian's words. *Dark the forest is, but light no fires. To do so invites dreadful peril.*

Moisture dripped from the trees and coated the road with sticky, stinking ooze. Bo longed for the wind's cold touch and the brightness of the winter sun. He heard raised voices behind. He stopped and turned. Three Satyrs pointed at the trees. They shouted excitedly, their eyes wide.

'What the devil is up with them?' said Valbrand.

Before Bo could reply, one of the Satyrs stepped off the road and leant forward into the trees.

'COME BACK!' said Bo.

But the Satyr ignored him, and edged closer to the trees. Without warning, and with horrific speed, arms of several creatures burst through the boughs and the bushes and pulled the Satyr screaming into the darkness. He let out one last hollow, despairing cry. The other Satyrs hurriedly backed away and began loosening their arrows wildly into the trees.

'STOP THAT!' said Bo, desperate to avoid any unnecessary bloodshed.

The Satyrs lowered their bows. Sheepishly, one of them said, 'We saw something glistening in the trees, something golden.'

'A trick of the demons that dwell here,' said Valbrand.

'Whatever it was, do not stray from the path again,' said Bo.

Corcoran strode up to him, his club gripped tightly. 'Why have we stopped? Are you *afraid*, Prince Asbjorn?'

Bo smiled at the provocation. 'We must be careful. This forest is dangerous. Do not underestimate the forces here.'

253

'We Khiltoi are never afraid when amongst the trees. We—'

The trees shook, as though animated by a violent gust of wind. A huge shape crawled out from the darkness and squatted in the road in front of the army. Bo turned to see a creature hideous enough to drive any mortal insane with terror. The height of a mature oak tree, bipedal, forward-stooping, and with extended arms, saliva dripped from its drooling, canine mouth and its red eyes shone like fire. Tufts of hair burst through its scabrous, mould-caked body. It ripped at the ground with repulsive paws.

Bo heard yells and screams of alarm from the army. Even the Gigas stood frozen in fear, unable to comprehend the monstrosity. Corcoran cried out in the Khiltoi tongue and retreated several paces. The creature growled and swung a paw towards Bo. The blow missed by several feet, but Bo felt the rush of air onto his face. He drew his sword and stood still, facing the creature. Behind him, panic rattled through the army, with some of the warriors bolting back down the road. Bo knew he needed to keep the army's discipline. He had to face the creature.

The creature glared at him, all the time wheezing and drooling. Despite his fear, Bo felt a morsel of pity. It was surely one of Zanash's demented creations. He remembered what the guardian had said: *the giant Carnifex*. It suffered by being alive. It lived in agony, its ill-fitting limbs and bones punishing it with every breath.

But pain made it more dangerous.

Carnifex lurched forward, grasping for Bo. He side-stepped and chopped at the creature's paws with his sword,

254

scoring a deep cut. Carnifex howled in pain and, stooping even further, tried to bite him. Bo almost fell backwards but steadied himself enough to slash a glancing blow at the creature's jaw. Bo heard the twang of Valbrand's crossbow and a shot struck the creature on the shoulder. As Carnifex prodded in confusion at this fresh wound, Bo saw his chance. He ducked beneath a half-hearted swipe of a paw and drove his sword into the creature's stomach. The monstrosity clutched its gut, and with a wail of despair, fell forwards. Carnifex took one last rattling breath.

Valbrand slapped his thigh. 'I'll be hanged, that was a piece of dragon slaying to match the best tales.'

'It was no dragon,' said Bo. His heart drumming, he looked at Corcoran, who hung back, embarrassed by his own reaction when faced with Carnifex. Bo said to him, 'You see now, I am not afraid.'

The Khiltoi sneered.

'There might be more of these cursed swine,' said Valbrand. 'We shouldn't tarry here.'

Skirting round the slain creature, the army pushed on and the canopy above them thinned, surrendering to beams of reddish sunlight. The prospect of escaping the forest quickened everyone's step. Ahead, Bo spotted a gate, taller than the one through which they had entered the forest. The gate was heavy, but with a hard push from two of the Gigas, it opened, allowing a flood of light and cool air to wash over the army. They poured through the gate, each blinking in the light and swallowing a lungful of clean air. The Centaurs blew war horns in triumph and the Satyrs yelled out throaty, bawdy songs. Some even chanted, 'Asbjorn! Asbjorn!'

Bo felt a surge of excitement and pride, but immediately he recalled the price of his bargain: the remorseless poison that stalked his veins. Any joy drained away. He looked up at the sky, where the fading sun coloured the swirling clouds in a range of oranges and browns. Evening was close. He would not see many more. Tortured by the knowledge of his death sentence, he wanted to cry, he wanted to scream out, but he could do neither. He had to keep his composure and fulfil his duty.

After resting for a few hours, the army set off again before first light, aided by a fortuitous full moon. They marched northwest across a limestone region of hills, gorges, caves, and lakes fed by underground rivers. Oak woods nestled in more sheltered spots, and Bo found them a refreshing and wholesome sight after the horrors of Kakos. The easterly wind brought a warmer edge, and a hint of the onset of spring.

As the afternoon merged into dusk, they turned west and directly ahead of them ran a line of barren hills. Hollering gulls wheeled overhead and the fitful southern wind air carried a salty scent. Bo ordered Prince Jeimuzu to scout ahead with his warriors and they returned within the hour. The Kojin looked excited and spoke to Bo in a hasty, jabbering voice. 'The Winter Palace is over those hills, barely three miles away.'

Bo swallowed, excitement and fear bubbling inside him. Eagerly he asked, 'Were you spotted?'

Jeimuzu shook his head. 'We Kojin know how to move without being seen. Guards patrolled outside the main gate, but we saw no other soldiers, no stockade, no watchtowers.'

256

'That sounds hopeful,' said Arigh Nasan. 'Yet there is bound to be a garrison.'

'I have not told you the most important part yet,' said Jeimuzu. 'Above the highest tower flies a golden flag of the double-headed eagle.'

'So, Prester John is still there,' said Bo.

'We must attack straight away,' said Corcoran.

Bo took a moment to think. 'We cannot attack blindly. I need to see the Winter Palace and the surrounding land so I can make the dispositions for battle.'

'I'll come along too,' said Valbrand.

'Very well,' said Bo. He turned to Arigh Nasan, Corcoran and Archontos. 'Keep the army out of sight behind this hill; we do not want to lose the advantage of surprise. Set guards and lookouts. Give all the warriors a decent meal from whatever provisions we still have—they will need all their strength.'

Following Jeimuzu, Bo and Valbrand hurried to the summit, which was marked by a standing stone, deeply incised with disc, cup and serpent shapes. Bo finally saw the destination they had worked so hard to reach. A flat plain, roughly circular in shape stretched out in front of them. Low hills surrounded it on all sides except to the south, where a slight gradient led down a sandy beach. In the centre of the plain stood the Winter Palace of the Patriarch. Fashioned from wood and pinpricked with hundreds of windows, the palace was a huge complex, a mass of towers, cupolas, gilded double-headed eagles, spires and ogee-shaped roofs. Opulent, fanciful, imperial, the sheer scale of the palace left Bo awestruck and intimidated.

257

'There's no doubt we've found the right place,' said Valbrand.

Bo tried to put aside the palace's overwhelming dimensions and formulate a plan of attack. His imagination placed images over the reality in front of him, sending Oroks charging across the plain, supported by the Centaurs, with the rest of the warriors following on foot. In order to reach their objective, Bo knew that his army would need to cross at least a mile of flat, open land. That would leave them exposed to cannon-fire and, when they got closer to the palace, musket-fire. However, to his surprise and relief, no exterior defences protected the palace: no curtain wall, no barricades, no ditches. Although he did not doubt that hundreds, if not thousands, of soldiers lurked within the palace, it was obviously not designed as a fortress. Wooden walls and glass windows would prove little obstacle.

And above all, they possessed the advantage of surprise. He thought of Prester John, sitting in his throne, secure in his power, in *his* mind unassailable, invincible. Well, soon he would receive an almighty shock.

Bo turned to Jeimuzu and Valbrand. 'I have seen enough. Begin the preparations. We attack at first light.'

- CHAPTER TWELVE -

The Clashing Rocks

Helped by a favourable wind, the *Husker Du* sliced smoothly through the gently rolling waves. Elowen paced up and down the ship. It had been two days since they had set sail from the cove of Ekrixi and she was still trying to regain her sea legs.

Far above the ship, Epios, having taken the form of a gull, flew to keep watch, thriving on the chance to soar on the lusty air currents. However, on-board the atmosphere was gloomy. The crew of the *Husker Du* worked at their many and varied duties, but with miserable faces and no accompanying songs and laughter. Even Black Francis carried a distracted air, endlessly poring and frowning over charts.

Only Bryna looked happy. She found the sea a source of endless delights, from the taste and touch of briny spray on her face, to the endlessly rolling and twisting waves, to the occasional glimpses of whales and dolphins. She laughed and gasped excitedly as she witnessed each new wonder. The crew remained wary of the Khiltoi. Lost in the marvels around her, Bryna did not seem to notice, or care, about the crew's frostiness.

Elowen well understood the despondent mood on the

259

ship. They sailed into dangerous, uncharted waters. A sense of menace, of unseen enemies closing in, was palpable.

She tried to clear her mind, to live in the moment, experiencing only the rich physical sensations of the journey. But she found it impossible. One thought always broke through: *Only blood will bring it back to life.*

The Oracle's enigmatic words haunted her, poking into her consciousness. She agonized over their meaning, trying to find a glint of hope within the words, but failing to do so. She plodded over towards Diggory and Batu. Diggory's face had taken a sickly shade of green not long after boarding the ship. He had spent most of the voyage sitting quietly with his head in his hands, or running to the side of the ship to vomit. To distract Diggory, Batu had engaged him in a game of knucklebones. They played listlessly, the Orok scarcely happier than Diggory to be on the ship. As Elowen approached, they both looked up from their game. Batu gestured towards the bones. 'Do you want to play, Elowen?'

In no mood for games, she shook her head.

Diggory rubbed his stomach. 'How much longer do you think it will be before we get to the Island of the Four Winds?'

Elowen shrugged. 'I don't know. Not *much* longer, according to Black Francis, but I'm not sure he knows either. He says these are strange seas.'

'All seas are strange to Oroks,' said Batu. 'We have little love of boats.'

'Ah, you are missing out, my friend.'

Black Francis appeared. He looked pensive and scratched his beard distractedly. He greeted them all with a half-

260

hearted smile. 'Are the joys of sailing upon the open sea lost on you all?'

'I haven't found any joys yet,' said Diggory.

'I see you've not changed your mind since we sailed from Dinas Hein to Prevennis, all those months ago,' said Black Francis. He looked at Elowen. 'And what about you, lass? How are you bearing up?'

'I'm fine.'

'Well if that's the case, you're better off than me,' he said. 'My head is so full of troubles it's a marvel it doesn't burst.'

'Are you sure you know where this island is?' said Diggory.

Black Francis harrumphed. 'Well, it isn't on any *map*, lad. I'm navigating from tales I've heard, and from a little common sense. Trust this old salt, lad, we'll find the island. Though what we'll find when we get there, well, that I don't have a clue about. We're far from any trade routes and I know as little about these waters as a lubber.'

As Batu and Diggory played their game, Elowen steered Black Francis away from them. 'With everything that's been going on, I haven't had a chance to properly thank you for taking us on this voyage. I understand how perilous it is for yourself and your crew.'

'The peril's real enough, but I want to help you, Elowen. If I'd had a daughter, I'd have been proud if she was like you. There's no one to remember me, even the crew, those barnacle scrubbers bless 'em, will forget me soon enough when I'm gone, Shrimp apart, of course.'

'I don't think that's true,' said Elowen, surprised by his candour.

'There are dark places in every man's heart,' he said. He tapped his chest. 'A man may hide them, even to himself, but they're still there and they eat away at the soul. You see, it's selfish in a way. By helping you I'm helping myself, washing away the stains of the past. You've given me a purpose, something grander than I've had before.'

He gave Elowen a hearty slap on her back before saying, 'We'll find this island, lass, I swear it.'

*

Unheimlich licked the rat's blood on his lips. He toyed with the dead, half-eaten rodent in his hands, moving its floppy legs in mimicry of life. He did not need to eat, but sometimes found pleasure and comfort in the act. He especially enjoyed the taste and texture of fresh blood; it made his body tingle pleasantly, and gave a soothing sensation of warmth.

He sat curled up within the ship's bilge. The perpetual motion he found calming—the stinking, festering water did not trouble him. His nostrils still tingled with the girl's scent, blocking out all other smells. He recognised her footsteps on the wooden planks, sensing her weight and movement. The connection was strong now, too strong to be broken.

He had followed the girl from the mountains to the sea, unseen by her and the others. Avoiding detection on the ship proved easy enough, he found many holes and nooks to hide in. Night was his favourite time. Hidden by darkness, he haunted the ship like a restless ghost. The girl had

262

slept on deck one night, allowing Unheimlich the chance to creep close to her, so close that her every breath sounded like a rushing wind. He had resisted the temptation to reach out and touch her. O, how he had wanted to! But he could not risk revealing himself.

Repeatedly during the sea voyage, he connected to Lord Lucien, guiding him ever closer with visions. Unheimlich detected his desperation, his yearning to find the girl.

Unheimlich grew bored of playing with the rat and let it drop from his fingers, watching with detachment as the corpse slithered to a resting place on the slippery, oily planks. He waited for darkness, for the chance to scurry up to the top deck, to drink in the girl's delicious smell. Even in his mind, undeveloped as it was, he sensed that she would not live for long. He wanted to enjoy watching her while he still could.

*

The kind wind continued for some hours but as they sailed further south, Elowen noticed a change in the sky. Bloated clouds rolled slowly above them, occasionally illuminated by eerie sparks of light, like fireworks. Even the vivid new star disappeared from view. The sea grew darker, the waves choppier, as though some hidden presence in the unimaginable depths below stirred restlessly.

A lookout in the rigging shouted, 'Land ahoy!'

Elowen and many of the crew rushed to the bow of the ship. Ahead, a small island glowed in the setting sun. Towering golden-brown cliffs, topped with tufts of vegetation, enclosed a dark grove of cypresses. Doorways to dark passages unseen peered out from the rock faces, framed by smooth marble. The wind died, and the sea around the island turned calm, mirror-like.

'Is this it?' said Diggory. 'Is this the Island of the Four Winds?'

Black Francis nodded. 'That's what I'm guessing. What say you, Elowen?'

'Yes, this is the island,' said Elowen. She stared at the cliffs, a mixture of fear and anticipation churned in her stomach. If the Oracle's warning was true, within the depths of the island must lurk some terror worse than she had encountered before. The Oracle's warning returned to Elowen: *To find the Mystery of Air, you place those close to you in great peril.* She did not want to put her friends in any more danger. It was clear what she had to do. She said, 'I need to go there, alone.'

'That's madness!' said Diggory.

'Diggory is right,' said Batu. 'You cannot go alone.'

'I can and I must,' she said. Fearing how her friends might react, she did not want to explain her reasons. She turned to Black Francis, 'You have to trust me on this. All I ask is that one of your crew takes me across in the dinghy.'

Black Francis folded his arms. 'If your mind's made up, I guess there's nothing more to say. Although I'll be the one to take you there, I insist.'

As they lowered the dinghy and Elowen prepared to climb down, Diggory said, 'Please let me come ashore with you.'

She shook her head and began to descend into the dinghy. 'Not this time. You've risked enough for me already, and

I've no doubt you'll risk your life again. But let me do this alone.'

The *Husker Du* had anchored close to the island, so with Black Francis at the oars of the dinghy they speedily covered the distance. In the form of a dolphin, Epios accompanied them as far as the island. He swam alongside the dinghy, bouncing in and out of the water with ease.

Waves lapped listlessly against half-submerged rocks as the dinghy grounded on the tiny shingle beach at the foot of the island. The sun vanished, leaving the inky blue sky smeared by brown clouds.

Black Francis helped Elowen out of the dinghy. 'I'll wait for you here, lass. If you need help, yell. I'll come to you.'

Elowen felt tiny beneath the cliffs. She looked around. She had no firm idea of where she needed to go but the doorways clearly had to lead *somewhere*. Leaving the shingle beach and the murmuring sea, she climbed up a set of precipitous, crumbling, weed-splintered steps, until she reached the largest doorways. There she paused, trying to catch her breath. She looked down at the beach. Black Francis and the dinghy were now far below her. Even if she had to shout for help, she doubted he could hear her from so far away.

She peered into the doorway. She could see only darkness. A scent flowed from it, not foul but fragranced, a gentle sweet smell. She steeled herself to step inside, to edge into the darkness.

She was about to go forward when a voice boomed out. 'BE GONE, INTRUDER. YOUR KIND DOES NOT BELONG HERE.'

265

The voice bellowed, swirled and echoed; dust and sand shook from the cliffs. Shards of lightning ripped across the darkening sky. Thunder cracked and the ground shuddered. Although shaken, Elowen refused to be cowed. 'Show yourself, if you're so strong.'

'HOW DARE YOU TRESPASS ON MY DOMAIN, MORTAL? WHY ARE YOU HERE?'

'To seek the Mystery of Air,' she said, trying to keep her voice firm and unwavering.

'YOU ARE NOT WORTHY. GO, OR YOU WILL BE IN GREAT DANGER.'

Elowen held up the Mystery of Fire. 'This shows I am worthy. I have come for the Mystery of Air and I won't leave without it.'

She heard laughter, cruel, cold laughter, followed by the sound of footsteps crunching on gravel. A startling figure emerged from the doorway. He wore a mask with manic, wide eyes, wild tangled hair and a mouth of razor-sharp teeth locked in a frenzied grin. From a simple headpiece protruded a large feather. He wore a robe that billowed in the wind and he clasped a conch shell. The swirling winds calmed. The sky brightened. He whipped away his mask to reveal a beaming, ruddy face, framed by untidy white hair and a shaggy beard. But Elowen barely registered such details, for one feature above all stunned her: the old man had a pair of white-feathered wings. At first Elowen thought they were part of a costume, reminding her of the actors who performed grim Miracle tales on festival days in Trecadok, but a closer look revealed that they were flesh, bone and blood. She wondered if he was an angel, recalling the paintings and stained glass windows she had often stared at in church.

'So, the Mystery of Fire has been claimed and now you come for the Mystery of Air,' he said in a melodious, whispery voice. 'I am Ventus and I sense you have a strong connection with the Earthsoul. I feel its energy around you. Tell me, how is old Cholos?'

She searched for the right words. 'He is…was…well when last I saw him.'

'You speak with care. Cholos showed you little kindness I am guessing. That was ever his way. Fire in his veins, there is no denying it. For that reason alone, I am surprised that he agreed to give up the Mystery.'

'He did not give it up. I…took it.'

Ventus stretched out his wings and took to the air, swooping over Elowen in wide circles. He said repeatedly, 'You *took* it from him.'

After several more circles he landed beside her, still laughing, his eyes wet with tears. 'Truly you are courageous, for Cholos is fierce. And mighty sore must he have been too, though that does not sadden me, as he is a bitter old wretch. I have not seen him for centuries and that causes me no grief. Although we are kin, both being Elementals, I have little liking for him. However, I think I like you, child. Tell me your name.'

She told him.

'Well, Elowen Aubyn, I see no reason to tarry,' he said, wiping his damp eyes and folding his wings. From his robes, he pulled out a leather bag tied with silver string and passed it to Elowen.

267

She held it, feeling the soft material of the almost weightless bag. Recalling the Oracle's terrible warnings, she looked at Ventus in surprise. 'You are just giving this to me?'

He laughed. 'Do not be deceived, for this is not the Mystery of Air. Although I like you, you must earn the prize of the Mystery. The bag is in itself of little value, I have thousands more, but it may help you in the test to come. Take this bag and with your companions sail due south from here. Soon, you shall come to the Clashing Rocks.'

'What are they?'

His smile faded. 'They are a pair of enormous rocks that mark the safest passage south. Either side of them are treacherous reefs and whirlpools. You must sail through the gap between the rocks.'

'We have a good Captain,' said Elowen. 'He'll know how to get through.'

The Elemental fluttered his wings, a nervous gesture. 'Ah, but I have not told you all. Well named are the Clashing Rocks, for as any vessel approaches, they smash together at tremendous speed. No ship can survive the impact. No ship has ever sailed through them and survived. The Clashing Rocks have been the death of many cunning captains and experienced crews.'

Elowen finally understood the Oracle's warning. *To find the Mystery of Air, you place those close to you in great peril.* The danger was not on the island, it was the Clashing Rocks, a danger that threatened not only her life, but the lives of her friends, and all on-board the *Husker Du*.

Ventus pointed to the bag. 'Open that and you shall unleash a gust strong enough to propel your ship forward.

With skill and good judgement, it may be enough to see you through the Clashing Rocks, but you will have little time. The Clashing Rocks give no second chances. Choose wisely the right time to open the bag and you may be fortunate. Fail and you and all your companions are doomed.'

'If we succeed, what then?' said Elowen.

Ventus smiled kindly, as though he detected the desperate hope in her words, and sympathised. 'If you survive the devouring jaws of the Clashing Rocks, it is said they will lock together forever, and no longer be a danger to ships. What is more, triumph over those perilous rocks, and I swear the Mystery of Air will be yours.'

'How will I get it?'

He laughed, as though her question amazed and amused him in equal measure. 'Allow me that little surprise at least. Once you have the Mystery of Air, continue southwards and you shall come to the sunken city of Shuruppak.'

'Sunken city?' said Elowen.

'When you see it you will understand,' he said. 'If you are fortunate, the tower of Cleito, the very highest point of the city, shall be revealed to you. But I warn you, it cannot be reached by a boat. The currents around it are said to be deadly enough to devour any vessel.'

Elowen struggled to comprehend what he was saying. He spoke in riddles. 'How am I to reach it?'

'Give the Mystery of Air to the waves and the path shall be revealed,' he said.

'But—'

The Elemental's smile faded a little. 'No more questions. I am master of the winds and storms in this ocean. I promise to help guide you to the Clashing Rocks, but once you are there, I can intervene no further. Go now, and use wisely what I have given you.'

Ventus bowed and retreated through the doorway to melt back into the darkness.

Clutching the bag, Elowen hastily descended the steps. Ventus's description of the Clashing Rocks terrified her, but what troubled her more was the thought of placing her friends in such peril. She had to tell them, and give them the chance to turn back.

Black Francis waited for her on the beach, smiling broadly with relief when he saw her return. He spoke quickly, the words tumbling out of his mouth. 'By the gods, I'm glad to see you safe. This is a fearful place. Did you hear that evil voice within that storm? It made the island shake. What's that you're carrying?'

Elowen told him what Ventus had said to her. When she mentioned the Clashing Rocks, Black Francis gasped. He said, 'They are spoken of with terror by all who sail the oceans. Is there no other way?'

'No, Ventus assured me of that. I do not ask you or your crew to do this. If you don't want to go on, I understand.'

Black Francis clasped his hands together and growled, 'I don't want to turn back now, though the very name of the Clashing Rocks fills my old heart with fear. But there's wisdom in what you say. I'm the crew's Captain and although they'd argue different, I'm no tyrant. If they want to turn back, I'll honour their wishes. I'm going to put it to a vote—the majority wins.'

*

270

'So, that's what we're up against.'

In ashen-faced silence, the *Husker Du*'s crew stood in a circle and stared at Black Francis. With Elowen positioned behind him, he had just finished telling them about the Clashing Rocks. He went on to say, 'I can't do this without you. I refuse to command you to go, that's why I've asked for a vote. If you don't wish to go south, you must speak up and speak honestly. I condemn no-one for voting against me, and that's the truth. If the majority votes against, we won't go that way.'

Elowen scanned the faces of the crew. Black Francis had spoken candidly of the dangers of the Clashing Rocks, and their chances of success. The crew were tough, hardy souls, not easily frightened, but it was clear to Elowen they had little enthusiasm for such a voyage. She felt sure they would vote against the plan. Some exchanged glances, as though searching for support. Elowen clutched the bag given to her by Ventus; some of the crew stared at it, as though dubious of the claims made of its power. With a look of grim-faced determination, Diggory stepped forward. 'Where Elowen goes, I go too.'

Elowen smiled gratefully. Batu and Bryna stepped forward too.

Limpet, the ship's cook, stood with his arms crossed and said, 'I do not wish to go. I've faced battles and monsters, but I'm not volunteering to go on a voyage that only leads to certain death.'

Several of the crew murmured agreement. Some looked disapprovingly at Elowen, shaking their heads. They would vote against going south, Elowen felt sure of it. She had to

271

speak. 'I know this is a lot to ask of you all. I wish there was another way, a safer way, but there isn't.'

'Well, that's what you say,' said Limpet. 'You're trusting the word of some lunatic hermit on an island. Perhaps he's wrong, or lying.'

'I don't think he's lying,' said Elowen.

Limpet remained unconvinced. 'Whatever the truth, I say there must be another way. If not, we don't go at all.'

Elowen lowered her head. She wanted to disappear. Doubt held her tongue.

Shrimp, the ship's coxswain, called for silence. He stood in front of the crew. 'That we live and breathe this day is down to the courage and kindness of Black Francis. When he found us we were destined for the mines of Gorefayne, destined for the Null. Black Francis saved us all. Yes, we've suffered hardships, but we've had adventures, we've seen wondrous lands, and we've been *free*. If helping Elowen gives us the chance to fight for the freedom of all, then I say we must accept it, whatever the risks to ourselves.'

'God's wounds, have we not risked enough,' said Limpet. 'Captured by the Sea Beggars? Fighting Ironclads? Our pool of good fortune surely runs dry.'

'We've not survived due to good fortune,' said Shrimp. 'Rather courage, strength and skill have seen us through. And that's been true of every one of you. Think on this: if you retreat now, if you turn away from Black Francis at this most desperate hour, aye, you might live a little longer, but will you be able to live with yourselves? We're the crew of the *Husker Du*, we've never shirked a challenge and I for one won't start today.'

272

When he had finished, Shrimp lowered his head and stepped back into the circle. There was no reaction. The silence remained, only broken when Black Francis said in a cracked voice, 'If there's nothing else anyone wishes to say, we should vote. Anyone who wishes to return to the mainland, raise your hand.'

Limpet's hand shot into the air. A few others joined him.

'And now those in favour of facing the Clashing Rocks, raise your hands.'

All of Elowen's companions voted in favour, as did most of the crew. She felt a deep surge of relief.

'So be it, we go south to the Clashing Rocks,' said Black Francis, puffing out his cheeks. He clapped his hands and shouted, 'Come on, you swabbies, no slacking. You've had a rest, now back to work. Look alive, I'll hear no bleating!'

Elowen watched as the crew scrambled to their duties. They slipped into work patterns shaped through the experience of many journeys. Any emotions that leaked out during the vote vanished in the heat of their physical labours, fear washed away by sweat, doubts hidden under calloused skin. She wondered what they really thought of the voyage, and the terrible danger, they all faced. She felt guilty. Did they blame her? Did they hate her?

'I'm sorry to put you through that.'

Elowen realised that Black Francis was talking to her. She stuttered, 'It...it is fine. You did the right thing.'

'Indeed you did,' said Bryna, cutting into the conversation. 'You do not treat the lives of your followers lightly. For that you win their respect and loyalty.'

Black Francis laughed. 'They might not see it that way.

I'm a simple man of the sea, and as such I rely on a mix of wits and luck.'

'If so, they serve you well,' said Bryna.

'What can I do?' said Batu. 'I am tired of being little more than a saddlebag.'

Black Francis rubbed his beard. 'The eyes of Oroks are keen. And we'll need lookouts. We're sailing into hazardous waters.'

'I can do that,' said Batu, looking pleased. He turned to Diggory. 'You can help me, my friend.'

From the way his shoulders sank, Diggory appeared far from enamoured with the prospect but did not protest.

Shrimp hurried up to Black Francis, a wry grin on his face. 'We're ready to weigh anchor.'

'Good, we need to crack on,' said Black Francis. More softly, he added, 'I think your little speech made all the difference.'

'Aye, my skill with words was always superior to yours,' said Shrimp. 'What I said was true, though. I meant it.'

'I know,' said Black Francis.

Just as Shrimp strode away, Epios, who had last been seen as a gull soaring far above the island, playing on the fickle air currents, landed on deck. He changed back into an old man and said, 'Why do you tarry?'

'We'll be under sail soon enough, my friend,' said Black Francis.

'I am glad to hear it. The weather seems fair, although I fancy that may soon change.'

As soon as they set sail, a southerly wind blew. Elowen recalled Ventus's promise. *I am master of the winds and storms in this ocean.* I promise to help guide you to the Clashing Rocks. She thought she heard his laughter above the wind, but concluded it was her imagination. Huge black rainclouds darkened the sky. A squally wind thrashed the sea, forcing the *Husker Du* to lurch through swollen, foam-tipped waves.

The crew worked furiously. Bryna wandered around deck, her arms outstretched, lost in her own world, enjoying the storm's violence: the hissing rain, the rampaging wind, the sense of relentless, violent movement, of nature unleashed and untamed. Her clothes soaked by sea spray, Elowen remained on deck too, anxious for her first glimpse of the Clashing Rocks. She struggled to keep her feet as the ship lifted and dropped, climbing and descending the hills and valleys created by the waves. The *Husker Du*'s timbers creaked and shuddered. After several hours, the howling wind ceased and the ship settled. The sea calmed, the wind reduced to a murmur. The clouds cleared, exposing patches of blue sky. The crew gathered at the ship's prow, pointing forward. Others prayed. Some trembled in fear. Elowen soon saw what attracted their attention.

Straight ahead from the prow of the *Husker Du*, two tall, roughly egg-shaped rocky islands floated, with barely a mile between them. On either side of the islands bellowing maelstroms tormented the sea's surface. Debris floated on the choppy waves: rope and planks of old rotting wood, the remains of a hundred shipwrecks. A mouldy plank, which peeked out of the water like a shark's fin, bobbed closer and closer to the islands. As the plank reached the space between the islands, there was a deafening roar; the islands

275

first trembled and then moved towards each other at great speed, crashing together with an explosion of displaced water. They held for a second, before slowly recoiling to their former position. Elowen strained to breathe, fear pushed upon her chest.

'There's no hope, we must turn around,' said one of the crew.

'Have courage, we don't flee from danger,' said Black Francis. He looked at Elowen and nodded towards the bag she carried. 'It's time, lass.'

Before she could answer, Epios cut in. 'The gift of Ventus is not enough to survive the Clashing Rocks.'

'You tell us this *now*?' said Black Francis.

'Hear me out,' said Epios, holding his hands up defensively. 'You need other help too. You need *me*.'

'Unless you can turn yourself into a leviathan and hold the rocks apart with your tail, I don't think there's much you can do,' said Black Francis.

Epios shook his head. 'I promise you, in a more modest form I can aid you and repay my debt to your kindness and mercy on our first meeting.'

'I don't understand,' said Black Francis.

'Observe the islands,' said Epios, striding around the deck like a schoolteacher. 'They sense movement between them, and come together to crush it. The trick is to attempt your passage at the perfect time.'

'Which is?'

Epios smacked his hands together. 'Just after they have slammed into each other. Without fail, they move slowly back to their usual position before they can move together

276

again. With a kind wind, you should have enough time to get through.'

Black Francis exhaled slowly. 'How on earth can we control that? We can move towards the islands at speed but we can't make them come together *just* before we get there.'

Epios gave a mischievous grin. 'Ah, but I can.'

*

Slowly, inexorably, the *Husker Du* approached the Clashing Rocks, dragging every ounce of energy from the slothful wind. In the form of a gull, Epios soared above the ship. Elowen looked up at him, her whole body tingling with fear and anxiety.

Diggory bit his lip. 'Is there any way this can work?'

'We've got only one chance,' said Elowen, looking down at the bag she cradled in her hands.

'I was hoping for a more optimistic answer,' said Diggory.

After waving away all offers of help, Black Francis took hold of the tiller in his chunky hands. He shouted to the crew, 'Ease out the mainsail. When Elowen opens that bag, we'll be running before the wind.'

The crew darted to carry out his commands. The Clashing Rocks loomed ever larger. Black Francis bellowed to Elowen, 'It's time, lass. Open the bag.'

Elowen untied the silver string and pulled open the neck of the bag. She expected a reaction. The clouds above them to part in a violent surge of wind. A dizzying rush of air. A blast of lightning. An ear-splitting roar of thunder. But there was just a flat bag in her hands.

277

She looked despairingly at Diggory. He shook his head and said, 'It was all a trick. Ventus lied to you.'

The *Husker Du* drew ever closer to the Clashing Rocks, which began to shudder ominously. Elowen realised everyone was staring at her. She felt a fool, taken in by Ventus. He had probably laughed as he watched them sail away. Perhaps he was an agent of Prester John, or perhaps a wicked old soul like Cholos, his heart infected by centuries of malice. In despair, she turned to Black Francis. 'We have to turn back. It's not working.'

He looked at her, his face like carved stone. 'Not yet, we must keep trying.'

The shuddering of the Clashing Rocks grew louder and louder, excited by the hapless victims approaching their hungry jaws. Elowen felt wind caress her hair and stroke her face. It strengthened, blowing harder, sweeping the ship towards the Clashing Rocks. She looked round, facing northwards. Feasting on the wind, the *Husker Du*'s sails bulged.

'You've done it!' said Diggory, his voice almost stolen by the wind. 'It's working!'

Black Francis let out a yell of joy. He gripped the tiller, using all his strength to steer the *Husker Du* towards the Clashing Rocks.

Overhead, buoyed by the wind, Epios raced in front of the *Husker Du*, heading towards the Clashing Rocks. He lowered height to fly between them. The Clashing Rocks sensed the intruder and surged towards each other.

Elowen cried out, thinking the two stone giants must surely crush Epios, but at the moment of impact, which

278

sounded louder than any explosion she had ever heard, she spotted the tiny figure of the gull flying free.

Epios wheeled round and flew back to the *Husker Du*. He transformed back into a man, in mid-air and landed feet first on the deck. 'Now, Black Francis, steer between the Rocks!'

The Clashing Rocks, as though being wound backwards by giant pulleys, began to return to their original positions. A tiny but growing gap, a splinter of light, materialized. With the force of the wind, the *Husker Du* picked up speed. Black Francis yelled and cursed as he struggled to use the tiller to control the direction of the ship. They drifted too wide, bringing them too close to one of the Rocks.

'Straighter! You must go straighter!' came the yell from one of the lookouts.

The Clashing Rocks almost reached their original position, just as the *Husker Du*'s prow drew level with them.

'We're too late!' said Diggory.

The Clashing Rocks stopped and trembled ferociously, as though conscious of the trick being played on them.

The *Husker Du* pushed forward, the whole length of the ship now horizontal with the rocks. With a terrifying roar, the Clashing Rocks thundered towards each other, groaning and creaking, moving with malevolent speed and intent, each forcing out a huge bow wave. Many of the crew screamed. Some covered their faces, unable to watch the entity that would surely slay them all.

Closer and closer the Rocks came, swallowing dozens of yards in seconds.

We won't make it, thought Elowen. I've failed. All is lost.

279

The Clashing Rocks thundered together, grazing the *Husker Dü*'s stern and showering the deck with spray and sharp fragments of stone. But the ship sailed on. They were through.

Elowen breathed again and laughed giddily. The crew cheered and embraced each other. Black Francis let go of the tiller and sank to his feet, his lips moving in a silent prayer.

CHAPTER THIRTEEN

The City Beneath the Sea

The fierce wind eased. The *Husker Du* drifted as the surface of the ocean became more like a pond, the waves lulled by some unseen force. Behind them, the defeated Clashing Rocks remained stationary, just as Ventus had predicted. They looked forlorn, monuments to forgotten glory and triumphs, their hideous menace vanished. The maelstroms calmed, their monstrous roaring forever silenced.

As the stress of the passage through the Clashing Rocks seeped from her body, Elowen's legs shook and her ears buzzed as though populated by insects. She felt a firm slap on her back and became conscious of Black Francis standing beside her. Between laboured breaths, he said, 'You did it, lass.'

Her hearing still fuzzy, she smiled. 'I just opened a bag, you steered us through.'

'Aye, me and this crew of clods and swabbies,' he said, smiling. He looked back at the Clashing Rocks. 'It was mighty close though. Did you ever imagine such horrors?'

Diggory said, 'I've a feeling in my gut we'll be seeing much worse.'

281

Black Francis laughed. 'Cheer up, lad. We're all still breathing, and that's a miracle considering what we've been through.'

Elowen's skin tingled with the energy of the Earthsoul. The golden threads danced above the *Husker Du*. A sudden spinning wind dashed over the ship, and upon it floated a single feather. Elowen scooped it up as it landed on the deck.

'That's an ostrich feather,' said Black Francis with a short laugh.

'What's an ostrich?' said Diggory.

Black Francis scratched his head in bemusement. 'Big flightless bird. I've seen them at markets and menageries. Can't think how one of their feathers got all the way out here.'

Elowen grasped the feather and slowly she recognised where she had seen it before: in Ventus's headdress. Excitedly she said, '*This* is the Mystery of Air.'

Epios strode along the deck, his face beaming. He looked at the feather. 'This is a thing of wonder, child. You are blessed, but you have earned your blessings. We have beaten the Clashing Rocks. A grave curse has been removed from the seas.'

'We would not have survived without you,' said Black Francis.

'I believe that to be true, if you forgive my immodesty,' said Epios and he did a little dance. 'And in doing so, I have repaid my debt to you.'

Black Francis shifted his weight awkwardly. 'Aye, there's no arguing with that.'

282

'So, it is time for me to bid you all farewell,' said Epios.

'You're leaving?' said Diggory. 'But we need you.'

Epios bowed. 'I am flattered you believe so, but I have other matters to attend to.'

'More important than what we are trying to do?' said Diggory.

'Not necessarily, but they are important still. The oceans are wide and deep, and my concerns are many. I face other battles, other struggles with which I must contend. I cannot linger in one place for too long.'

Black Francis said, 'Well, I'm sore at the thought of you leaving us, but I see it must be so.'

Epios nodded. 'By staying with you, others may suffer for my neglect, and that I cannot allow. It is the way of things. I judge there is strength enough on-board this ship to complete the quest. So, my friends, farewell. Perhaps we shall meet again. Such things are hidden to me, for the sea is mysterious, forever beyond our true understanding.'

With that, he leapt overboard, and in the instant his body splashed into the water, he became a dolphin. He disappeared beneath the surface for a second and reappeared in a joyful, exuberant leap. To Elowen's surprise, Epios *Linked* with her.

Approach the Elemental protecting the Mystery of Water with caution, child. She will try to tempt you, show you glories and riches. Be strong.

Epios dipped beneath the water again and swam away. Disturbed by his warning, Elowen wondered why he had not spoken of the Elemental before. Perhaps he did not want to alarm the crew.

283

'That's a shame,' said Diggory as Epios disappeared from sight. 'We could've done with his help.'

'He's done enough for us already,' said Black Francis. 'We should be thankful, not sad.'

Batu and Bryna joined them, both visibly shaken by the passage through the rocks. Batu said, 'So, what now?'

Elowen said, 'Ventus said to continue south, to the sunken city of Shuruppak.'

'Every sailor has heard tales about the sunken city,' said Black Francis. 'It was supposed to be the greatest city on earth, a magnificent place. A fertile land, set amid sheltering mountains, with vast fields of crops and enormous herds of tame cattle that grazed on the rich pastureland. The city was said to be impregnable, defended by a formidable army and fleet.'

'Tales of the sunken city have reached the Oroks too,' said Batu. 'We name it T'aghum. Our storytellers say the kings of the city sent emissaries and armies across many lands, passing knowledge to some, conquering others.'

Black Francis nodded. 'Aye, legends say they never lost a battle. Some called them invincible.'

'What happened to the city?' said Elowen, eager to learn more, both to help her quest and to satisfy her curiosity.

Black Francis paused, like the skilled hesitation of an actor or orator, trying to squeeze every moment of emotion and drama from his words. 'I've heard many different accounts, all of them terrible, all of them tragic. Some say that their power and conquests angered God, and so he sent a horrendous deluge to punish their insolence. Others say that the folk of that city discovered a forbidden secret, some knowledge that led to their downfall. Whatever the truth of it, all the stories agree on one detail, that without warning gigantic waves swallowed Shuruppak and it has been hidden ever since.'

'But if it's beneath the sea, how will we find it?' said Diggory.

Elowen shrugged. 'Ventus said we'd see the tower of Cleito. That's where we have to reach. We have to believe what he said. We have to trust him.'

Black Francis looked unconvinced but he turned to Shrimp. 'There are no charts for these waters. I want extra lookouts in the rigging and tell them to keep their eyes peeled. Give Crab the sounding line and tell him to keep checking the depth. Tell him if we run aground, I'll have his guts.'

Even under full sail, the going proved slow. The wind murmured and whispered, seemingly exhausted by its earlier exertions. Mist, wispy, ghost-like, drifted over the ship, untouched by the gentle wind. Mysterious sounds echoed. A nervous silence fell upon the crew. Black Francis strode anxiously around deck, looking out to sea. The crew chattered uneasily. Elowen shared their anxiety, their sense of looming dread.

They sailed on for close to an hour, when the mist finally cleared. Clear blue skies, a warm wind and a keen sun came as a shock after the gloom, and Elowen squinted and shielded her eyes. There were shouts and cries from the lookouts.

A spire protruded from the sea. Carved from marble, it gleamed like a ray of pure white light. Stairs rose from the foamy water and curled around the spire, ending at an arched doorway at the top of the tower. The spire's cold, clinical lines frightened Elowen.

Black Francis took Elowen by the arm and said, 'We've found it. The tower of Cleito. Drop anchor! Don't get any nearer.'

'What are you afraid of?' said Elowen.

'There's something hidden in these waters,' said Black Francis. 'By the look of those currents, it's probably a nasty rock or reef. This is as close as we're going to get. I'll use the dinghy to take you across, it'll be hard going, mind.'

'No,' said Elowen. She recalled what Ventus had said about the path being revealed. 'I think there's another way.'

'What do you mean?'

'Just…a hunch,' said Elowen. She held up the feather, the Mystery of Air. 'Ventus said that if I give this to the ocean, the way will be clear.'

Black Francis peered at the feather. 'Well, if you believe it will help, I suppose we ought to try.'

Conscious of her friends and the crew watching, Elowen walked to the ship's prow, leant over the edge and let the feather drop into the water, where it floated unremarkably on the surface. She waited. Nothing happened. She heard a few sniggers from the crew. Her cheeks flushed furiously. She felt like an idiot.

Then, she heard a deep rumbling sound from beneath the ship. In a straight line between the *Husker Du* and the tower of Cleito, the water hissed and boiled. Black Francis pulled Elowen back from the edge of the ship. To her amazement, the sea parted, revealing a straight bridge of marble, running

286

from the prow of the anchored *Husker Du*, directly to the tower. She turned to Black Francis and said, 'I have to cross the bridge.'

He scratched his beard. 'Aye, seems like the only way. I'll come with you, lass.'

'Are you mad?' said Diggory. 'It's most likely a trap, and God knows what's lurking in that water.'

'Elowen has greater intuition than you know,' said Bryna. 'You must not doubt her.'

'I don't *doubt* her,' said Diggory. 'Well, if she's risking her neck, I'm going too.'

'No,' said Elowen. 'There's no sense in you risking your life as well.'

'I'm not arguing with you,' said Diggory, crossing his arms. 'I'm going'

'I'll go too,' said Bryna.

Batu cleared his throat. 'I shall accompany Elowen also.'

Elowen's first instinct was to protest, but she realised that she did not want to go alone. She needed their help. 'All right, let's start.'

The crew lowered ropes from the ship down to the bridge. Elowen watched as Bryna and Batu speedily descended. Rather slower and far less elegantly, Diggory and Black Francis followed. Elowen went last. She gripped onto the rope with all her strength, barely daring to lower herself lest she slip. She heard well-meaning but unhelpful shouts of 'hold tight!' and 'don't fall!'

She lowered herself enough for Bryna to reach up and help her down. Elowen exhaled with relief when her feet touched the marble of the bridge. She composed herself, and impulsively took the lead and headed for the tower. Bubbly, milky waves lapped over the edge of the bridge, and Elowen's feet splashed as she walked. She concentrated on keeping her balance and not slipping, but she glanced to her side and saw a face in the water staring back at her. She was beginning to think she had imagined it when she saw another face, and then many more. Female faces, beautiful, framed by flowing hair, with eyes like glowing sapphires. Two of them broke the surface, laughing, and singing. Although each had the head, torso and arms of a woman, they also had a fish tail.

'What are they?' said Batu, unsheathing his sword.

Elowen stopped and pointed down at the water.

'Mermaids!' said Black Francis, pointing at them.

The mermaids playfully splashed their tails, showering Elowen and her friends with water. They gestured for them to jump into the sea.

'Ignore them!' said Bryna. 'They're far more dangerous than they appear. There is darkness in their hearts.'

The mermaids responded to her words with spits and hisses, before diving down and out of sight.

'I think you upset them,' said Diggory.

Bryna scowled. 'I care not.'

They continued along the bridge, walking in the menacing shadow of the tower of Cleito. As they approached the foot of the steps that coiled around the tower, a spout of sparkling water spewed out of the sea in a perfect arc that landed on the end of the bridge. The water took the shape of a woman. She strode towards Elowen and her companions, stopping only a few feet away. She stood six foot tall, with flowing silver-grey hair. A simple robe covered most of her body, but Elowen noticed that silvery fish scales coated her shoulders and neck. She stretched out her arm and pointed at Elowen. She spoke, her voice fluid, soft and swift. 'I am Leucothea. Only she enters the tower.'

'Where Elowen goes, we go,' said Bryna.

Leucothea laughed, and the tone of her voice harshened. 'I forgive your insolence, as it is born from a simple mind. Defy me again though, and nothing will save you from the storm.'

The power of her words silenced Bryna. Leucothea spoke to Elowen. 'You have come for the Mystery of Water, I believe.'

Elowen nodded. 'Are you the water Elemental?'

'Yes, and I have sensed your coming,' she said, her voice calm again. 'So, you conquered the Clashing Rocks. Their restlessness and anger have pulsed through the waters of this sea for years beyond count. For you to have reached this far proves your courage, or perhaps your luck. Whatever the truth, if you wish to claim the Mystery of Water, you must follow me. I permit your friends to remain here. No harm shall come to them, though they would be wise to avoid the Daughters of the Sea, for they are cunning and full of wiles.'

Diggory gave Elowen a despairing look. Guessing what he was about to say, she got in first. 'It'll be all right.'

Elowen followed Leucothea up the stairway. The steps were narrow and steep, and Elowen harboured a stomach-churning fear of falling. Mounting step after step, she puffed and wheezed, her back damp with sweat, her head dizzy. Finally they came to the arched entrance Elowen had spotted earlier. They stepped into a circular room. The room was bare of furniture, although a mosaic covered the floor with sparkling images of dolphins, fish and birds. Elowen stared at the mosaic, stunned by the vivid colours and intricate detail.

Elowen saw four windows, positioned like the main points of the compass. Leucothea went over to the southern window, and motioned for Elowen to join her. The window looked out over the ocean, which stretched to the horizon, a vast expanse of glistening blue.

'Is this tower all that's left of Shuruppak?' said Elowen.

Leucothea smiled. 'No, not all. Do you wish to behold the city, Elowen?'

'Well, yes, but how?'

'Let me show you,' said the Elemental. She raised her hands and spoke, her voice so powerful it sounded disembodied, mustered from the depths of the ocean itself. Elowen covered her ears and her whole body vibrated.

Leucothea fell into silence and pointed out of the window. Elowen followed the direction of the Elemental's hand. As she did so, she thought Leucothea had cast a spell to trick her eyes, to show her things that could not possibly exist. For the sea to the south of the tower began to part, peeling backwards in four enormous cliffs of water. As they did so, they exposed the seabed, and Elowen spotted the remnants of what had once been a city. She saw battlemented walls, the outline of streets and avenues, beehive-shaped tombs, and the ruins of buildings, some small, others of an unimaginable size. There were a number of pyramids, but one tow-

290

ered above them all—an enormous step pyramid, which filled the southern end of the city.

'I know what you are thinking,' said Leucothea. 'You believe this is a dream. I assure you, Elowen, it is not. You look upon the lost city of Shuruppak, hidden from the eyes of mortals since the deluge that devoured it.'

Elowen shook her head. 'This is…I…'

'If you could find words you believed adequate to explain what you are experiencing, Elowen, I would think less of you. What you are experiencing now is beyond words.'

The sea stopped retreating, the walls of water miraculously held in place, leaving a vast rectangular part of the seabed visible.

'The Mystery of Water lies within the city,' said Leucothea. 'If you wish to claim it, and discover the location of the Tree of Life, down there you must go.'

'*Into* the city?' said Elowen.

'Do not fear the sea here,' said the Elemental. 'Nothing happens in these waters without my design. Come, child.'

After descending to the lowest level of the tower, Leucothea led Elowen through a narrow passage in the wall of water. Elowen found it a terrifying, disconcerting experience. Despite Leucothea's assurances, she feared the water would crash down on them. She saw shapes and shadows behind the wall, fish, dolphins, and a whale. A shark swam against the wall, pressing its snout and opening its jaws, only inches away from Elowen, who stepped back and shouted out in fear.

'They cannot break through the water,' said Leucothea. 'Keep moving.'

The passage led into the city, passing through a huge entrance. A relief surmounted the colossal lintel, which showed a column flanked by two lions, although the head of one of the carved beasts was missing. Leucothea said, 'Once gates of shining bronze stood here, but the merciless sea ripped them away.'

Now at ground level, Elowen realised that the roads and avenues were much wider than she had anticipated. Banks of sand half-buried many of the buildings, while others looked as though they had been gnawed at from above, with roofs vanished and the tops of the walls ground down.

'Where are we going?' Elowen said as Leucothea strode ahead, following the route of the straight wide road that bisected the city.

The Elemental did not turn but pointed ahead, to the immense step pyramid. 'To the Temple of the Sun.'

'Is the Mystery of Water in the temple?' said Elowen.

'Yes, if you choose to claim it,' said Leucothea.

'Why would I not claim the Mystery?' said Elowen.

'We shall see.'

They reached a wide square, surrounded by ruins of temples, palaces and assembly halls. Elowen was disturbed to see a black obelisk in the centre of the square. When she stopped, Leucothea said, 'It is not a Sentinel. The pestilent hand of Prester John has not infected this place.'

After the Elemental beckoned her to take a closer look, Elowen gazed at the obelisk, seeing that it was made not from Cold Iron but from fine-grain black limestone. There were panels on each of the four sides of the obelisk, depicting scenes of battle and tribute.

'Proud were the kings of this city,' said Leucothea. 'They liked to record their victories, believing that they would be remembered for eternity. Little did they know of the true nature of the world, nor of the immensity of time. Their supremacy lasted little more than the blink of an eye.'

She pointed to a statue close to the obelisk. Stood upon a pedestal of reddish stone, it portrayed a king with his hair and beard worn long. He held a sickle in his right hand and a mace in his left. Elowen noticed carved inscriptions in a mysterious language across his chest. She stared at his face, seeing pride, ambition and cruelty. 'Who is that?'

'Ul-amburiash, the last King of Shuruppak, who was not burdened by modesty or humility,' said Leucothea. She pointed to the inscriptions and read aloud, '*I am the weapon of the Great Gods, with no equal among the princes of the four quarters of the world. I have subjugated all of mankind, and have conquered cities and mountains to the farthest extent.* Such exalted pronouncements! Such proud boasts! Yet those who fool themselves into believing they are god-like and invulnerable are often only at the cusp of annihilation. Ul-amburiash is now only dust, for such is the fate of all mortals.'

'Why was the city destroyed? I heard God punished them for their pride and arrogance with a flood.'

'The rulers did grow proud and arrogant, but this city's fate was not a punishment. Violent is this world, ever-changing. There are forces beyond the knowledge of Men, and they have no sense of right and wrong, of good and evil. They follow motions set in place at the beginning of time. Those within this city were unfortunate. The flood was tragic, but it was not driven by a conscious will.'

293

They pushed on to the pyramid. An imposing stairway of broad, deep steps led to the entrance, three levels up from the ground, flanked by two stone sculptures of winged, human-headed lions. Elowen looked up nervously at the sculptures, troubled by their blank, lifeless eyes and the enigmatic smile their lips formed.

From the entrance, they came into the great hall, or *megaron* as Leucothea named it. Water dripped from the ceiling and briny puddles covered the floor. Rectangular in shape, stone panels decorated its walls. They told the narrative of battles and rituals long forgotten. Elowen saw motifs repeated: eagle-headed spirits, a god in a winged disc, and a king in a variety of dignified poses. She noticed faint traces of paint, and guessed what was now worn and sandy, had once been a show of colour. They showed the intricate details of a world forgotten, a world the inhabitants of the city must have believed eternal.

The largest collection of panels drew Elowen's attention. They showed a king driving a chariot and leading his warriors during a hunt. The panels told a story from the discovery of lions in the forest, to the ferocious pursuit and eventual slaying of the animals. Elowen stared at a panel depicting a lioness in its death throes, pierced with many arrows, its agony tangible as life ebbed from its body. Elowen felt pity and sadness as she stared at the lioness, its life ripped away for mere sport, slain to prove a king's prowess and strength.

'Men often treat animals with wickedness,' said Leucothea. She stepped closer to Elowen and stroked her hair. 'You are not like them, Elowen.'

Uncomfortable with the Elemental's touch, Elowen tensed her body and focused her attention on the panels. She noticed that one of them showed a king on either side of a Sacred Tree, with a winged disc above and protective spirits behind. 'Is that the Tree of Life?'

Without answering her question, Leucothea steered her away from the panels and towards a dozen enormous chests that lay in a line against the wall. Leucothea knelt down beside the largest chest. She smiled knowingly at Elowen. 'Famous was the wealth of the kings of this city. Many vassal lands paid rich tribute. These chests are watertight, and contain fabulous treasures. Do you wish to see?'

Intrigued, Elowen nodded eagerly.

Leucothea lifted the lid of the chest, revealing that it was full of gold, silver and lapis lazuli. 'For centuries these riches have lain here, beautiful, priceless, but useless. Out of the hands of even the most desperate and grasping thief. I doubt Prester John possesses wealth to match the contents of these chests.'

Elowen struggled to comprehend the scale of the treasure in front of her. She yearned to touch it, to hold it, to see the glittering jewels in her hands, to feel the smooth lines of gold. She imagined being a ruler, a queen, draped in jewellery, rich enough to acquire and own *anything*. Such wealth would provide power, unlimited power. She could build palaces, raise armies, crush enemies. Elowen's heart pounded with excitement.

The Elemental slammed the chest shut; the sound reverberated around the *megaron* and broke Elowen's reverie.

'Is the Mystery of Water kept in one of these chests?' said

Elowen, clearing her head from the cloud conjured by the treasure.

Leucothea shook her head. 'No, it is not in here. Come with me.'

The Elemental led Elowen across the *megaron* and out through a door on the far side. Elowen had expected to enter an anteroom or private chamber, but she found herself on a balcony, looking down onto a cavernous space, lit only by light wells in the ceiling. As Elowen stared down at the room, and realised that its floor had been carved into a chart: she recognised the shapes of countries, islands, seas and rivers.

'This is the Map Room,' said Leucothea. 'Built by King Ul-amburiash to flaunt the extent of his dominions, it shows the Middle Sea, and the surrounding lands. Now, I use it for a different purpose. Here, you may discover the secret location of the Tree of Life. What you have searched for is here, if only you choose to take the Mystery of Water.'

Elowen hesitated, wary of a trick. 'Of course I choose to take it. I have to find the Tree of Life.'

Leucothea held up her hands. 'Do not be hasty, child. I have not yet given you the other choice. You *could* take the Mystery and learn the location of the Tree of Life, that would be simple, or I could reward you in another way. Do you recall King Ul-amburiash's treasure in the *megaron*?'

'Yes,' said Elowen.

'If you so choose then the treasure is yours, all yours. But if you take it, you cannot have the Mystery of Water. Likewise, if you choose to take the Mystery, you cannot have the treasure. A difficult choice awaits you, Elowen.'

'I cannot…cannot give up on the quest,' she said, hating herself for the indecision in her voice. The potent memory of the treasure lingered.

'But think what this quest could cost you,' said Leucothea. 'You are brave, Elowen. You have defeated many enemies and endured many trials. You have inspired those around you. And yet you have paid a heavy price. You need not suffer any more. Let others continue the struggle against Prester John, you have already played your part. If you take the treasure, I promise to take you to a land far from here, safe from the grasping reach of Prester John and those who serve him. For the rest of your days you shall live in luxury and peace. No more want. No more pain. You deserve it. You have earned it. Let me help you, Elowen.'

'But…my friends. What about them?'

'They will understand, Elowen. They cannot go with you, of course. But they will not condemn your choice. They will be happy for you, as true friends should be.'

Leucothea stepped closer to Elowen. She gently took her arm and tried to steer her away from the Map Room and back into the megaron. Elowen allowed Leucothea to guide her away. The Elemental's words echoed in her mind. *For the rest of your days you shall live in luxury and peace.* She thought again of the treasure, of the shiny gold, the glistening jewels. *No more want. No more pain.*

She stopped at the door of the *megaron*. She could see the treasure chests. Leucothea said, 'They will be yours, all yours. Go in, claim them. You deserve them.'

Something made Elowen turn. She looked back at the Map Room. She was so close to the Mystery of Water, so close to finding the location of the Tree of Life. She had been through so much to get to this point. She remembered her friends, and all they had given and risked for her. Yes, she had suffered, but so had many others, and some had even paid with their lives. Tom Hickathrift, Lárwita, Baba Yaga and Chinua had died to protect her. To turn away from the task she had been given was a betrayal of their sacrifice. And what use were jewels in a world ruled by Prester John? How could she enjoy precious stones and piles of gold coins, all the time knowing she had abandoned the duty entrusted to her, and abandoned her friends?

She slipped her arm out of Leucothea's grip. 'I do not want the treasure. I've come here for the Mystery of Water, that's all.'

'Do not toy with me, child. Do you really believe in this cause you fight for? Think of the cruelty of Men: are they worth saving? You would risk your life for them? I offer the treasure only once. Reject it now and lose it forever. Do not be foolish. Think about what I am offering you.'

'I know what you are offering me, and the temptation pulls at my heart. But I know too that it is wrong. I have to find the Tree of Life.'

'At the expense of your own life?'

'If that is what it takes, yes,' said Elowen, her voice shaking. 'The only gift I want is the Mystery of Water, the treasure can remain here. I want no part of it.'

A smile cracked Leucothea's hard face and she laughed, a sound as joyous and musical as the flow of a bubbling mountain brook. 'Worthy indeed, you are. I declare that you pass the test.'

298

'This was all a *test*?'

Leucothea laughed again. 'By resisting the allure of the treasure, of the easy, comfortable path in life, you proved worthy to claim the final Mystery.'

'But I *was* tempted. I nearly chose to take the riches.'

'Ah, but that merely proves you are mortal,' said the Elemental with a wink. 'Elowen, give me your right hand.'

Elowen frowned. 'Why?'

'Please, do as I ask,' said Leucothea, her tone friendly but insistent.

Gingerly, Elowen held out her right hand; Leucothea cupped it in her hands and rubbed her fingertips across Elowen's palm. Elowen felt the tickling of Leucothea's fingernails, followed by a warm, tingling sensation, which she had scarcely registered before it turned into an intense burning feeling. Elowen yelped and withdrew her hand.

'What are you doing?' she said, shocked and incensed.

'The task is done,' said Leucothea. She looked at Elowen, regret etched on her face. 'I am sorry to cause you pain but it was necessary. Look at your palm.'

Elowen did so. Upon her palm, she saw the shape of an inverted triangle, marked out by three lines of reddened skin.

'The pain shall pass in moments,' said Leucothea. 'This mark is the Mystery of Water, and you will need it to pass the final threshold. But first, let me show you where the Tree of Life can be found.'

They returned to the edge of the balcony, looking once more across the vast sculptured map. Leucothea held her arms aloft and chanted. An opening in the ceiling high above them cracked open, though how it moved Elowen could not guess. A shaft of light speared down, illuminating a small portion of the map. The shaft slowly tracked across the map, growing in strength and luminosity. Finally, it struck a part of the map carved as a tree-trunk shaped mountain; it sparkled when the light touched it, gleaming like a torch.

'That is the Mountain of Haramu,' said Leucothea. 'It is sacred to the people of that land, being at the heart of their Ancestral Realm. There, on the mountain's northern slopes, you shall find the Tree of Life.'

*

Elowen's friends were still waiting for her when, accompanied by Leucothea, she returned to the bridge. The walls of water gently subsided, once again drowning Shuruppak. Elowen allowed herself a wry smile when she noticed her friends' open-mouthed looks of terrified amazement as they watched the ocean settle.

When they saw Elowen, their amazement turned to joy, and Diggory ran to embrace her. 'We thought you'd been swallowed up by the sea.'

'I'm quite well, as you can see,' said Elowen, almost suffocated by his embrace.

'By the ancestors, what happened to you?' said Bryna.

'There's so much…later, I'll tell you later.'

'Do you have the Mystery?' said Batu, giving Leucothea a suspicious sideways look.

Elowen held her palm open.

'Curious,' said Batu, his eyes narrowed.

'Is that it?' said Diggory. 'I expected a jewel or—'

'Not everything of value glistens or sparkles,' said Leucothea.

'And I know where the Tree of Life can be found,' said Elowen. She went on to tell them about the mountain.

'You should not delay seeking it,' said Leucothea.

'On that we are agreed,' said Black Francis.

'If you wish to follow my advice, make for the city of Nyumbani,' said Leucothea. 'It is ruled by the Oba, and is one of the few regions not in thrall to Prester John. If such a thing exists, it is a safe port. From Nyumbani, head southwest, until you reach the Mountain of Haramu. Go now, with all speed. I wish you good fortune, the *best* fortune, for if you fail, Elowen, everything fails.'

With that, Leucothea took Elowen's hand, gently kissed it, and strolled back to the tower, walking freely, as though without a single care in the world.

PART THREE

- CHAPTER FOURTEEN -

The Wild Coast

A s they sailed south, the wind grew warmer and the sun stronger. Keen to avoid the heat and to get some rest, Elowen retreated below deck. Curling up on her bunk, she ran her fingers over the mark in her palm, the Mystery of Water. The Tree of Life felt real to her now, not just a mythical, abstract destination. She slowly drifted to sleep, the worlds of waking and dream fused. The ship's timbers creaked, singing in a secret wooden language.

In her emerging dream, the sounds mixed with shadowy, flitting images of Shuruppak. The walls of water. The Map Room. The enigmatic smile of Leucothea.

Something else overpowered her dream. A face, hideous to behold. A hairless head, with protruding, probing eyes and skin that looked cold and wet to the touch. Dribble oozed from its lips, a glimpse of rodent-like teeth. Cold fingers touched her face…

Elowen woke with a start, her heart hammering. She rubbed her eyes. She looked around; she was still in the small, plain cabin. As her breathing and heart calmed, she lay down again, closed her eyes and settled back to sleep.

*

Beneath her bed, contorted into a small space, Unheimlich licked his fingertips. He quivered with excitement, the sensation of the touch still pulsing through him. He wanted to touch her again; he needed to touch her again. He listened to her slow, rhythmic breathing. Slowly, he untwisted his body, crawling out from beneath the bed like a spider, his legs and arms misshapen. He pulled himself to his full height, staring at the girl. His face only inches away—her breath felt like a soft warm wind on his face. She shuddered a couple of times, her legs jerking as she dived deeper into sleep.

He licked the string of drool that hung down from his lips. He would touch her face with one hand, and stroke her hair with the other. He reached out his hand, closer…closer…

The girl awoke, coming round so quickly that she surprised Unheimlich, blunting his usual razor-sharp reactions. They stared at each other, in mutual shock, then the girl screamed.

*

Elowen screamed as she looked at Unheimlich and realised she was fully awake, and not deep in a hideous nightmare. Tiny, thin and hairless, it seemed impossible that it could be alive, and not the macabre creation of a demented doll maker. But it breathed, and its eyes glistened with unnatural life. Instinctively she tried to *Link* with the creature, but rather than the Earthsoul's warm energy, she felt only coldness, like a deep dark hole.

'Who are you?' she said. '*What* are you?'

Unheimlich hissed, but before he made any move, the door to the cabin burst open, and Batu and Diggory charged inside. They looked at the creature and Diggory gasped, 'What the hell is—'

Unheimlich scuttled up and along the wall on all fours and made for the opened door. Just in time, Batu kicked the door shut. He grabbed the creature by the legs. Elowen thought that the strong Orok would swiftly overcome the creature, but she was wrong. It bent back Batu's fingers, making the Orok howl in pain, and wriggled free of his grip. Diggory moved towards it but Unheimlich sprung at his chest and knocked him backwards.

Panting heavily, the creature turned to the door, which creaked open again. It was Bryna. Unheimlich hurtled towards the gap but the Khiltoi seized him with a grip that the creature's attempts at pulling and biting could not dislodge. Black Francis stood behind Bryna, his eyes wide in shock and amazement.

'Kill it!' said Batu, his face red with anger. 'It is a demon.'

Trapped in Bryna's grip, Unheimlich wriggled furiously and in vain. The Khiltoi said, 'Yes, this is a being of pure evil, it deserves to die.'

'NO!' said Elowen. She pulled herself off the bed and stepped closer to Bryna and the creature she held. 'Don't kill it. We don't know what it is yet.'

'We came at once when we heard your scream,' said Diggory. He pointed at the creature. 'Had we not, this brute would have murdered you.'

'I don't think so,' said Elowen, fascinated by Unheimlich's

307

tiny ugly features. He reached out towards her with his free hand and made a gesture.

'It wants me to lower my head,' said Elowen, now more curious than afraid.

'It's a trick,' said Diggory. 'Don't give it a chance to hurt you.'

Elowen ignored him and edged a little closer. She lowered her head. Unheimlich stretched out his hand and with his cold fingertips gently touched her forehead. A second later, a powerful sensation overwhelmed her, much stronger than any experience of *Linking*. Colours, lights, shapes raced around her, gradually coalescing into images she recognised. Three ships, black marks against the horizon, smudges of choking smoke spewing out of tall chimneys. Ironclads. Her vision jerked painfully, throwing her inside one of the ships. She smelt hot metal, oil and smoke. She saw men working, doused in sweat and grease.

Then she saw him.

He sat alone in a small room, his head lowered. The way his robes draped over his motionless body gave the impression of him being a statue, not flesh and blood. Then he lifted his head. He wore his mask, his eyes like black holes. He recognised her and knew she was watching. He mouthed one word. 'You.'

The visions broke. Elowen looked around, her head throbbing, her sight still shaky. Unheimlich stared at her, his eyes wide. Still in Bryna's grip, he gave her a look of sadness, perhaps even regret. Then he violently twisted his neck. Elowen heard a sickening click and the creature's body went limp.

Bryna let the lifeless body drop to the floor, cursing in disgust. Diggory bent down and peered at the body. 'It's dead. It killed itself somehow.'

'But what was it?' said Bryna. 'And what was it doing here?'

'A spy of Lord Lucien,' said Elowen. She told them about her vision, and added, 'It had some kind of connection with Lord Lucien. When it touched me, I felt the connection too. I saw Lord Lucien, and he saw me. He's in a ship, an Ironclad, and he's pursuing us.'

'If that's right, then through this infernal creature Lord Lucien has seen and heard everything,' said Black Francis. 'He'll know where we've been, and he'll know where we're going.'

'Then we'll have to go a different way to the Ancestral Realm,' said Bryna.

Black Francis sucked his teeth. 'You make it sound as though it's easy. Nyumbani is the only safe anchorage in these waters.'

Rubbing his chin, Batu said, 'What of the Wild Coast? Could we not land there? It would be the swiftest route.'

'The swiftest route to disaster and death perhaps,' said Black Francis. 'The Wild Coast is justly named. Violent storms drive ships onto rocky reefs, or rogue waves swallow other vessels whole. Few ships sail in those waters and with good reason.'

'They'll be less chance of being found by Lord Lucien if we go that way,' said Bryna. 'He won't expect it.'

'That's true,' said Elowen, still troubled by the haunting vision of Lord Lucien. 'We have to elude him.'

Black Francis winced and scratched his head. 'I don't like it, not one bit. But there's sense in what you're saying. If we sail due south from here, it should bring us to the site of the old city of Emaeke.'

'I remember that city from the Holy Book,' said Diggory. 'The Saviour cast down the temples of the heathens there.'

'Aye, so it's said. I doubt there are many heathens there now, or folk of any kind. It's closer to Haramu than Nyumbani, which is one advantage I guess. My boys won't be pleased to go that way, and not just because they'll miss the taverns of Nyumbani. They'll know the tales of the Wild Coast. They'll go if needed and do their duty, but it'll be with heavy hearts. Elowen, this is a desperate risk.'

'Desperate risk or not, we have to go that way. It's the only way to escape Lord Lucien.'

Black Francis rubbed his beard. 'Then so be it.'

*

Severed from his connection with Unheimlich, Lord Lucien lurched back into full consciousness. He sat in his small, unfurnished, windowless cabin on the Ironclad's gun deck. Only thin walls separated him from the rest of the vessel, and he heard again the engines' incessant metallic pounding and the shouts of the crew. The smell of oil, grease and smoke polluted the air.

But as he cursed the ill fortune of Unheimlich's discovery, other sensations came to him: a faint whisper of Elowen's breathing, blurred images of her cabin. At first he thought they were echoes of the mental union with Unheimlich, but

310

then he realised the creature had performed one last service: he had passed his connection to Elowen onto Lord Lucien.

His legs trembling, Lord Lucien dragged himself upright. He pulled open the cabin door and yelled for the Captain. He sat back down, the door closing behind him. Images, blurry and flickering, appeared as he blinked. It was not his imagination. The connection existed. It was faint, but if he could control it, tame it…

There was a soft, tentative knock on his door.

'Enter,' said Lord Lucien.

The door edged open and the ship's Captain stepped hesitantly inside. He wore a loose, shapeless garment and a cocked hat, the only visible sign of his rank. He nimbly removed the hat and bowed. 'You asked for me, my Lord?'

His mind still fogged, Lord Lucien rubbed the back of his neck. 'We cannot allow our quarry to escape. I need this ship to travel faster.'

The Captain toyed nervously with his hat. 'My Lord, all the men are exhausted. We've been sailing for two days without rest. I also believe it'd be prudent to port at Mistrieh, to check for any damage and to take fresh provisions—'

Lord Lucien held up a hand to stop the captain mid-flow. By his command the ship, and the other two Ironclads that sailed with them, drove remorselessly south, pushing the ship, and the crew, to the limit of endurance. 'You speak of damage. We have not been involved in a battle. Is the vessel not working as hoped?

'It is but—'

'And you speak of provisions. Have we enough rations?'

'If the crew eats and drinks sparingly, perhaps but—'

'Then eat and drink sparingly they must. Until we have found the enemy, we do not delay. We do not rest. The welfare of the crew does not concern me. It is your duty to ensure they continue to work, by whatever means seem best to you, but I exhort you to not be bound by kindness or concern. Do not spare the whip. If you fail in this duty, I shall replace you. I need hardly spell out what that would mean for you. I trust you understand my meaning?'

The Captain gulped and stood as straight as he could. He saluted Lord Lucien. 'Perfectly, my Lord. I assure you, the men will work to the full extent of their strength. I won't fail you, Lord Lucien.'

'I am relieved to hear it. Now, leave me. Return to your post.'

In his eagerness to escape Lord Lucien's presence, the Captain almost walked into the half-open door. He bundled through the gap, and closed the door behind him.

It angered Lord Lucien to have to endure such feeble servants. Soon, he hoped, such concerns would be irrelevant. The Cold Iron in his veins tingled. He closed his eyes, took three deep breaths and prepared to reach out to Elowen.

*

The rising sun turned the sea the colour of copper. The crew were quiet. Elowen heard no songs. No laughter. She shared their unease. The encounter with the creature brought back a fear she thought she had lost, the fear of

312

Lord Lucien pursuing her. Somehow he must have learnt that she had survived the fall in the labyrinth of Bai Ulgan. Lord Lucien knew she was alive and he was pursuing her.

Standing beside Diggory, Elowen took a place on the prow, grateful for the cool wind but as the sun dragged itself above the horizon, a thick bank of mist formed in front of them. She heard one of the crew cry, 'This is a demonic fog.'

'It's just sea mist, lad,' said Black Francis. 'The hot air from the dry lands is hitting the colder ocean winds. The Wild Coast is near.'

They laboured through the fog, the ship creaking and groaning. Slowly, the fog dissolved enough for the coastline to come into view. Elowen saw a long beach of dusty grey sand, which rose steeply to a bank of dunes. Beyond the dunes, wispy columns of black smoke drifted skywards. At the lower shore, the sea boiled and dashed against half-drowned rocks. A huge detached cliff thrust out into the ocean, with a giant opening carved out by the waves.

'This is it, lass,' said Black Francis, clasping Elowen's shoulders with his huge hands. 'We go ashore here, though I confess I little like the idea of setting foot on this coast.'

'You're coming with us?' said Elowen.

'Aye, I can't let you go without me. Shrimp will keep the ship and crew safe while I'm gone, I'm sure of that.'

Leaving the *Husker Du* anchored and under the command of Shrimp, Black Francis rowed the dinghy to the beach. As well as the Captain, Bryna, Batu and Diggory accompanied Elowen. A greasy mist danced along the beach, making shapes indistinct, ghostly. A cloying, unnatural smell wafted.

313

Elowen heard a distant but unrelenting wailing, like the call of an animal in distress.

'What do you suppose is making that sound?' said Diggory.

'It's the wind, nothing more,' replied Black Francis.

As they drew closer to the shore, Elowen spied the mouldy wrecks of several ships, their rotten hulls like exposed ribcages. On the uppermost beach, the head of an enormous statue protruded from the sand, its body either lost or buried deeply. The statue portrayed a king wearing a tall conical crown with a bulbous end. With immense almond-shaped eyes, enlarged lips and high cheekbones, the king's expression was imperious, as though he viewed his realm with complete conviction of his authority and invulnerability—a jarring contrast with his ruined state.

As soon as they drew close to the beach, Black Francis grabbed his musket and two pistols. He growled, 'Gather your weapons and keep your eyes peeled. We don't—'

He never finished the sentence. In the corner of her eye, Elowen saw a shadow swoop towards them. It crashed into the middle of the dinghy, smashing through the wooden planks before rising upwards. Elowen watched as the shadow climbed. It was a flying creature, with wide membranous wings, an elongated neck and long spear-like jaws. The dinghy began to lurch and sink. Black Francis grabbed his musket and pistols. 'Everybody out!'

Following the others, Elowen plunged into the water, which came up to her chest. Spluttering and spitting out brine, she pushed towards the beach. In seconds, the dinghy slipped beneath the surface like a weighed-down corpse. She finally flopped onto the sand, but Batu dragged her roughly to her feet and said, 'We are not safe yet.'

Bryna prepared her sling. Elowen saw Black Francis frantically load his musket and pass a pistol into Diggory's trembling hands. 'Take this, lad. Mind now, it's loaded.'

Diggory looked unsure. 'I've never fired one of these things.'

Black Francis scowled. 'There's no time for a lesson, lad. When the time comes, aim, squeeze the trigger and hope to God you hit your target.'

Batu said, 'It is coming back! And there are more of them!'

Soaking wet and blinded by the salt water, Elowen tried to look around. As her eyes adjusted, she spotted three of the flying creatures skimming over the beach towards them, their wings fully outstretched. They reminded her of the Sciathans but were bigger and as she *Linked* with them, malevolence flooded her body. Feelings of pure hate.

The creatures approached, screeching furiously. Batu fired an arrow but it fell short of its target. Black Francis's musket cracked and then Diggory shot, the recoil jerking him backwards. Bryna released a slingshot and it brushed the tail of one of the creatures. The creatures screeched in alarm and soared away, heading inland.

'What in God's name are those things?' said Diggory, panting and shaking heavily.

'I don't know and I'm not sure I want to find out,' said Black Francis, hastily reloading his musket. 'They've gone and we should be thankful for that.'

'I'm starting to understand why they call this the Wild

315

Coast,' said Diggory, staring at the smoking pistol in his hands.

'What about the dinghy?' said Batu.

'It's lost,' said Black Francis. 'It's a curse to be sure, but there's nothing I can do about it.'

'How will we get back to the *Husker Du*?' said Diggory.

Black Francis paused before answering. 'Let's worry about that after we've found the Tree of Life.'

All anxiously peering up into the sky, Elowen and her companions hurried up the beach, skirting away from the wrecked ships. They scrambled up the dunes, the sickly sweet smell worsening with every step. The warm, clammy air made Elowen breathless and hot. Disconcertingly, the mournful wailing they had heard on their approach to the shore continued.

They mounted the dunes and looked ahead. Elowen saw a plain stretching for about a mile, where it abruptly ended at a lofty wall, crudely fashioned from uncut stone, rubble, and banks of sand and wood. The wall ran without obvious end, blocking the land beyond from the coast. A single gate, formed by assorted pieces of wood nailed together, offered the only way through the wall. Between the dunes and the wall were wedged stone tombs, many partially swallowed by the drifting sand, around which stood flimsy wooden shacks and straw-roofed mud huts. Elowen spied several patches of cultivated land, where enfeebled crops toiled to pull free of the ground. A series of enclosures, like wooden cages, held a few emaciated sheep, pigs and chickens. Scattered about the settlement were small bonfires of oily wood, all hurling out spirals of black smoke.

316

'Who would choose to live *here*?' said Diggory.

Batu pointed to the wall. 'Perhaps they have no choice.'

'Those fires are strange,' said Bryna. 'Perhaps they are a kind of signal.'

'Let's hope whoever lives here is friendly,' said Black Francis.

Elowen noticed with a chill that a Sentinel stood on the edge of the settlement. Veins of sickened soil radiated from it like the spokes of a wheel. Broken tools and rocks circled the Sentinel and some of the earth around it had been gouged, as if dug away by a fraught animal.

Black Francis tapped his musket. 'If the folk here are Nulled, this could be tricky.'

A cold tingle played down Elowen's neck and spine. She looked up and saw in the sky three black shapes hurtling towards them. She screamed, 'THEY'RE COMING BACK!'

Cursing and swearing, Black Francis lifted and aimed his musket. Batu notched an arrow in his bow and prepared to fire. Bryna placed herself protectively in front of Elowen, with Diggory alongside her holding the pistol in both hands with a palpable lack of confidence.

The creatures dived, their spear-like jaws ready to impale and tear. Elowen tried to summon the Earthsoul's power but the golden threads were faint and, blemished by the Sentinel, would not easily submit to her command. She heard the creatures' terrible squawking. With their wings opened, they filled and darkened the sky. They were close. Seconds away. Black Francis fired but missed.

An ear-splitting cry rang out, but it did not come from the

317

creatures, who changed direction and scudded away and over the wall. Figures emerged from the wooden shacks. None of them were Nulled but they advanced ominously. Wiry, tall, dark-skinned, with handsome, intelligent faces, they carried shields made from hide, wood and basketwork, curved at the top and straight at the bottom, large enough to protect a man kneeling. They wore leather armour and protective armlets festooned with symbols of the sun and moon. Most of the warriors carried slender, iron-tipped spears of hardwood, but Elowen spotted that two of them grasped flintlock muskets.

The warriors shouted at Elowen and her friends and made aggressive motions with their spears. Black Francis held out his hands in a submissive gesture, but his intervention made little impact. Just as the warriors' shouts reached a crescendo, an older man pushed his way through. Hobbling on a walking stick, his face was as wrinkled and pitted as bark, but his eyes shone bright and keen. He spoke to the warriors and they immediately quietened and lowered their weapons. The old man rested on his walking stick; an expression of disgust curdled his face. 'Who are you? Why do you disturb our land and provoke the *Kongamato*? I am Ayanmwen, Chief of our tribe. Answer me or die.'

'Greetings, friend,' said Black Francis. 'Please accept our gratitude for saving us from those brutes.'

'We're more interested in keeping them away from our village than saving you,' said the old man. His head moved jerkily as he spoke, reminding Elowen of the motions of a pecking bird. 'And you have not answered my question. Why are you here?'

318

Black Francis said, 'We're travellers, seeking to journey south. The *Kongamato* as you name them attacked us and sunk our boat as we came ashore.'

Ayanmwen spat and the globule landed near the feet of Black Francis. 'Yes, they'll attack any boat that tries to land here, or any that tries to leave. Why are you intent on going south? That way leads only to the Ancestral Realm, which is not a land fit for mortals.'

'Aye, and that is the land we seek,' said Black Francis.

'Is it, indeed?' said Ayanmwen, rubbing his beak-like nose. 'Are you in league with Prester John? I do not see the Null but it might be part of your deception.'

'We are his foes,' said Batu.

'As a spy might very well say,' said Ayanmwen.

'No one calls me a spy of Prester John,' said Diggory. 'Not after what I have been through, not after what we have all been through.'

Black Francis gripped Diggory's arm and pulled him back. 'Ayanmwen, please forgive the hot hasty words of the young. But he is right in what he says, we are not spies, I swear on my grave.'

'I'll hold my judgement on that, for you are outlandish folk,' said Ayanmwen. He peered at Bryna. 'This one is strangest of all, with skin like the bark of a tree. What is it?'

Bryna's hands made fists. She snarled, 'You should show more courtesy—'

Batu stepped in front of her, gesturing for her to be quiet. She relented and took a calm, deliberate step back. Batu turned to the old man. 'We are all tired from a long journey and the fright of the attack of the *Kongamato*, and tiredness

319

can fray the most even of tempers. Besides, the welcome we have received here is less than kind.'

Ayanmwen snorted. 'We are ever vigilant, and with good reason. Ironclads haunt this coast. They keep their distance, but they appear every few weeks, prowling like a lion stalking its wounded prey. Perhaps you're here to spy on us, to prepare for an attack. Be assured, strangers, I'll protect my people, whatever the cost.'

The warriors formed a circle around Elowen and her companions. They raised their spears threateningly. She had to act. The sense of delay, of not being able to push forward made her tense, her whole body coiled up, ready to spring. She clenched her jaw in frustration. She remembered the visions the strange creature had given her; she knew that Lord Lucien pursued them, and that he would never rest until he found her. For the first time since landing on the Wild Coast, she truly felt the Earthsoul's energy, faint though it still was. She said to Ayanmwen, 'Please, we mean you no harm, and we are certainly not allies or spies of Prester John. I am an Adept. The Illuminati and the Oracle of Omphalos have charged me with a mission of immense importance, a mission that if successful, could break Prester John's power forever. If you thwart us, all you'll achieve is your own destruction.'

Startled by the power in Elowen's voice, Ayanmwen's mouth gaped open. Bewilderment, even fear, replaced his aggression. 'You are an *Adept*? I believed—'

'That Prester John had destroyed them all? No.'

One of the warriors thumped his spear on the ground and muttered, 'Witch.'

320

'If you think me guilty of witchcraft, then you speak with the tongue of the Mother Church,' said Elowen. She glared at Ayanmwen. 'I know you serve your people, and would die to protect them. Trust your instincts. Do I look evil, do I seem evil?'

Ayanmwen took a deep breath and uttered a single word command to the warriors, who lowered their spears and stood back. The Chief said, 'No, I doubt you no longer. Forgive my fiery tongue. We are not used to friendly visitors.'

'There's nothing to forgive,' said Elowen.

'Come with me,' said Ayanmwen. 'Honour us by accepting our hospitality. You'll want to dry out and eat. We have little food to spare, but we'll give you enough to fill your bellies.'

Black Francis puffed out his cheeks and winked at Elowen. 'You're very persuasive when you put your mind to it.'

'A *bana-buidhseach* does not always resort to fighting in order to prevail,' said Bryna, looking admiringly at Elowen.

Ayanmwen led them down into the settlement, hurrying alongside an open drain and past the motley collection of mud huts and shacks. A few people leant out of low doorways to peer at the visitors, but they quickly recoiled and slipped back into the darkness of their homes. Elowen noticed many of the houses had beside their door a wooden sculpture of a similar design: a woman standing with elaborate scarification on her front and back. She pointed to one of the sculptures and said, 'What is it?'

'They are left outside our dwellings as protection against evil,' said Ayanmwen.

321

'Do they work?' said Diggory.

'We have hope, even when reason argues against it,' said Ayanmwen.

More than once Elowen noticed vaporous figures flitting around the tombs. She thought it was a trick of the light or her tired eyes deceiving her, but no, again she saw them. They had tools in their hands: baskets, mattocks and hoes. She stopped and said in alarm, 'There's something hiding there.'

Ayanmwen gave a knowing smile. 'They are the *Shabtis*, servants of the kings buried here, made to do their bidding in the afterlife. However, the Sentinel has disturbed their rest, and they plague us with their wailing.'

'They're *ghosts*?' said Diggory, his voice wavering.

'They are a constant nuisance but they'll do you no harm,' said Ayanmwen, urging them all to carry on. He led them towards the largest wooden shack, an unsightly structure built around three tombs and a toppled colonnade of pillars. Many gutter-pipes and spouts projected from the rickety roof. As they reached the shack, Ayanmwen turned and said, 'This is the Grand Hall, but as you can see it is but a mockery of the name.'

They ducked through a doorway, the lintel of which displayed a disturbing carving showing birds attacking a human face. They came into a wider space than Elowen had expected. Many wooden beams supported the roof, and onto the beams were nailed bronze plaques. Exquisitely made, they showed scenes of battle and rituals of courtly life. Elowen saw portrayed kings, warriors, farmers, merchants, sailors, priests, mothers and children, some with

322

their hands reaching out from the plaques. They formed a city of people cast in bronze, a panorama of life. A number of small shrines nestled in alcoves. Within each shrine stood a statue, a brass head wearing decorative neck ornaments and a crown. Elowen thought she heard distant voices, ghostly whispers, but concluded it must be some peculiar effect of the hall.

Dozens of people lingered inside the hall. All were thin and looked hungry. Their clothes were little more than rags, and they wore sandals made from woven cord. They stared at Elowen and her companions in bemusement, perhaps too hungry, too low in spirit to be afraid. The appearance of the children shocked Elowen most: half-starved, haggard and eyes like pebbles pushed into the ground.

Following Ayanmwen's fussy orders, two men laid out a ring of cushions in the middle of the hall and brought out a little food held in pottery vessels made from unpolished, undecorated clay. Ayanmwen gestured to Elowen, 'Please, you and your friends must rest your feet here. I wish we had more hospitality to offer, forgive our desperate state.'

'You are generous,' said Elowen. 'We are grateful for your kindness.'

As they sat, Black Francis said to Ayanmwen, 'This is a dangerous land. I'm surprised you've managed to survive.'

Ayanmwen, who sat cross-legged in front of his guests, sighed and said, 'The Wild Coast is a place of woe and ill-fortune brought us here. We left Nyumbani nigh on two years ago, seeking to escape war and the threat of the Null, seeking a better life for our children. Cruel winds drove us to this shore, but at first, we believed it to be a blessing. In

323

the times of the Dual King a city flourished here, founded by settlers from the Delta.'

'Emaeke it was named,' said Black Francis. 'It is well recorded in the Holy Book and other histories.'

'That is true,' said Ayanmwen. 'When we came here, we found nothing but ruins. Yet although the city vanished long ago, we thought we would be happy here, in a fruitful land, close to the Ancestral Realm. We thought this a fine place to start our colony. We named it Wokovu, which in the common tongue translates to *Salvation*. But days after our arrival, the forces of the Mother Church found us.'

'How?' said Batu.

Ayanmwen coughed and ran his tongue over his lips. 'Little escapes the attention of Prester John. An Ironclad discovered our settlement. We fought the enemy off with frightful loss, but before they fled, they planted that cursed Sentinel. It poisoned the land and brought foul miasmas. The Sentinel drove the *Kongamato* wild; maddened by the Cold Iron, they attacked us when we tried to leave. The *Kongamato* destroyed the ships you saw on the beach yonder. We are stranded here now.'

'Why have you not fled inland?' said Batu.

Ayanmwen shrugged. 'Mortals cannot dwell within the Ancestral Realm.'

'Is that why you built the wall?' said Diggory.

'We built the wall to stop the pestilence of the Cold Iron spreading to the Ancestral Realm. Here at least we can contain it, although we have no chance of escape.'

'And yet you suffer for it,' said Black Francis. 'That is a noble but terrible sacrifice.'

Ayanmwen pointed to his forehead. 'We escaped the Null, only to find another prison.'

'Why haven't you destroyed the Sentinel?' said Diggory.

'We tried, and some of my kinsmen died in the attempt,' said Ayanmwen, to the nods of his tribesmen and women. 'Our weapons made no impact on it. It is too strong.'

Pity gushed through Elowen as she looked around the hall, seeing the hungry people, their meagre belongings, their absence of hope. She stared at a young girl, her face skeletal, her arms and legs like brittle twigs. To see the girl's suffering sickened and infuriated Elowen. The tyranny of Prester John imprisoned the folk of Salvation. Elowen could not ignore it. She remembered what Tom Hickathrift had once said about Adepts. *They worked to protect the world around them and to sustain the Earthsoul.* She stood and said, 'I'll destroy the Sentinel.'

Ayanmwen frowned. 'Destroy the Sentinel? With what? Your bare hands? I have heard tales of the great powers of Adepts, but trust me: this is a task beyond your kind.'

Elowen rubbed her hands together. 'We'll see.'

Leaving the Grand Hall, Elowen strode purposively towards the Sentinel. She walked as though she was the head of a snake, with her companions and the whole tribe behind her as the sinuous body. Diggory and Black Francis followed a pace behind her and urged her to reconsider.

'You're being reckless, lass,' said Black Francis.

'He's right,' said Diggory. 'You know how dangerous these Sentinels are.'

'I know, but I can destroy it, I'm sure of it,' she said, though her conviction wavered with each step. It was the tallest Sentinel she had seen, dwarfing the one she had grown so used to seeing in Trecadok.

Diggory persisted. 'But what if Lord Lucien senses it somehow? These Sentinels are queer things. They seem to call to the Redeemers.'

Elowen had a discomforting feeling he might be right but her mind remained set.

Black Francis tried a different tack. 'I feel sorry for the people here but it's not our problem. We cannot afford this delay. Thanks to that monstrosity we found on the *Husker Du*, Lord Lucien probably knows where the Tree of Life is. We have to get there before him.'

'But I can't abandon these people, not if it's in my power to help them,' said Elowen.

She increased her pace, signalling her intent to end the conversation. She stopped five paces away from the Sentinel. The ground around the obelisk felt spongy underfoot, and hissed and steamed.

Trying to shut her mind to all distractions, Elowen closed her eyes and knelt. She settled her breathing and relaxed her muscles. She reached out with her mind. The Earthsoul's energy channelled through the dying, desiccated soil. Although she remained still, Elowen felt as though her hands moved through the earth. Her head throbbed. Her neck muscles strained and ached. Fighting off the pain, she pushed out further, expanding with her mind, finding and touching the cold void of the Sentinel. Even with her eyes closed, images came to her, dreamlike, hazy. The golden threads strengthened, coiling around the Sentinel, squeezing, twisting. Elowen's agony increased. Her body burned, and a sound like thunder roared in her ears. She wanted to let go, escape the tortuous pain...

Out of the swirling colours and images, the face of the girl she had seen in Salvation came to her. Starved. Frightened. Eyes without hope. Elowen knew she could not fail her. Reaching out with every ounce of energy, she drove the golden threads at the Sentinel. She heard a ferocious CRACK and opened her eyes in time to see the Sentinel topple backwards and smash into several pieces.

Before Elowen could move, a vision struck her, it *consumed* her, drowning all her senses. The face of Lord Lucien appeared in front of her, as though it were inches from her own. She saw the scratches of his mask. She saw his eyes. Words formed in her consciousness.

I see you, child. You reveal yourself to me. I will find you.

The vision ended. Elowen heard shouting but it sounded muffled, distant. She tried to stand up but was too dizzy to do so, the ground and sky spinning around. Her ears rang and her eyesight blurred. She felt a sharp ache in her stomach and vomited.

She sensed Diggory by her side. He said, 'You did it, Elowen. By God, you did it. Look!'

With enormous effort, she opened her eyes again. The Sentinel lay strewn in charred, steaming pieces. The greasy fog dispersed, unveiling the sky. The sun's heat poured through and silenced the wailing of the *Shabtis*.

Diggory and Black Francis helped her stand. She turned round to see the people of the settlement laughing and cheering. Ayanmwen rushed to embrace her. 'It is a miracle! You have delivered us!'

327

'Don't crowd her,' said Black Francis. 'She needs to rest, don't you, Elowen?'

The vision of Lord Lucien remained with her, overshadowing everything else. Fear raced through her. 'No, I can't rest. We have to keep moving. I saw him again. He saw me.'

'But you are exhausted,' said Black Francis.

She shook her head. 'There's no time. He's hunting us. Do you think Lord Lucien will rest?'

'But can you manage to walk?' said Diggory.

'I have to manage,' said Elowen. 'I'm strong enough, I promise. We have to leave, and leave now.'

*

The imposing timber gate gaped open like a mouth, the world beyond dark, impenetrable. Elowen and her companions waited as Ayanmwen brought them packs of food and wineskins filled with water. He also gave them necklaces made from coral beads and amulets. He said, 'These can bring you good fortune.'

'Thank you,' said Elowen. 'Your people have shown us great kindness.'

When Diggory peered hopefully inside the packs of food, he screwed up his face in disgust. 'What are those?'

'Fried lizards,' said Black Francis.

'And that's food?' said Diggory.

'If you're hungry enough,' said Black Francis. 'They taste like chicken, or so I've heard.'

'I hope I won't be hungry enough to want to eat those,' said Diggory, retching.

328

'I hope so too,' said Black Francis. He rummaged through the packs and said, 'Look, there's plenty more food here, yams, nuts and beans. These people have been generous, especially as they have so little to spare. We won't starve if we manage our supplies carefully.'

The inhabitants of Salvation celebrated the destruction of the Sentinel. With pipes and skin-covered hand drums, they played feverish rhythms. Elowen heard the stamp and shuffle of bare feet, loud cries and yells, and the sharp sounds of clapping sticks. Along with her companions, she had resisted Ayanmwen's offer to stay and enjoy the festivities. She had no choice. To delay further risked disaster. They had no idea how close Lord Lucien was to them.

Ayanmwen said, 'Go due south from here until you reach the bend in the Great Fish River. Then follow the course of the river to the southwest, it'll lead you to the mountain you seek.'

Strapping their packs to their backs and fastening their weapons, Elowen and her companions trudged through the open gate and into the Ancestral Realm.

- CHAPTER FIFTEEN -

A Living God

Bo stood upon the summit of the hill and leant against the standing stone. He looked west towards the Inganno Winter Palace. Surrounded on three sides by the cinder grey hills, the gaudy, decorated building looked incongruous, as though it had wandered in from another time, another place. To the south, the grey-blue sea churned, and heavy waves rolled onto the sandy beach.

Bo turned and stared at the Old Believers, all gathered on the other side of the hill, hidden from the enemy. Men, Oroks, Centaurs, Satyrs, Kojin, Gigas, Dwarfs, Khiltoi, and hundreds of horses. Weapons sharpened. Armour cleaned and repaired. Oaths taken. Prayers offered. Their anticipation, excitement, and fear formed a tangible essence.

'I think we're ready,' said Valbrand, who knelt beside him. He placed a hand on Bo's shoulder. 'You're ready too. This is your moment, your victory.'

Doubt circled every decision Bo made. He went over his plan again and again, looking for weaknesses and finding many. As much as he appreciated it, Bo did not share Valbrand's optimism, but whatever his fate, he needed to win the battle. He gripped his sword, trying to draw on its lineage, thinking of the dozens of hands that had wielded the blade. Its sharp edge had slain countless foes over the centuries, and he hoped he would prove worthy of the sword in the battle to come. He drew a deep breath and said, 'Very well, let's begin the attack.'

'You need to address the army first,' said Valbrand.

'Do you think so?' said Bo.

'Definitely.'

'What should I say?'

Valbrand tapped him in the chest, exactly above his heart. 'Tell them whatever you are feeling in there.'

Bo nodded. He knew Valbrand was right. Clenching his hands, he stepped down the weathered limestone terraces towards the waiting army. Absorbed in preparations, no one noticed him as he approached. He stopped on an outcrop of rock, which stood above the army like a pulpit. Feeling self-conscious and ridiculous, he cleared his throat and called for silence. His nervous, phlegmy throat turned his words into little more than a squeak. Cursing silently, he steeled himself and then, in a shout louder than he had ever believed he could make, announced, 'HEAR ME NOW!'

His words carried on the wind, booming out, and they silenced the army. Hundreds of heads turned his way. Summoning all the strength in his voice, he said, 'My friends, this is the day we have waited for. The cruelty of Prester John has touched us all. We have lost loved ones, we have lost homes. We have all suffered. Now, we have the chance for vengeance, to make Prester John pay for his crimes. I am honoured and humbled to lead you. I know you will fight with courage and honour. Fight for yourselves, fight for your comrades. Fight for the loved ones you have lost, and for your loved ones that live still. Fight for the victory you deserve.'

When Bo finished talking, silence greeted him. His stomach churned. Had he said the wrong thing? Had his words been too strong, or too weak? He wanted to run away, to erase the moment from his memory…

He heard a cheer, followed by another. Hundreds of cheers, growing louder and louder. The whole army cheered. They waved their swords above their heads, jabbed their spears skywards. They began to chant, 'Victory! Victory!', then the chant changed to 'ASBJORN! ASBJORN!'

Tears welled in Bo's eyes. He held his sword aloft and bellowed, 'VICTORY!'

Valbrand patted his back. 'You found the right words.'

'I hope so,' said Bo, his heart pounding with excitement. 'And now, my friend, it is time to fight.'

*

The Army of the Old Believers climbed over the brow of the hill. The Centaurs led the way, closely followed by the mounted Oroks. The Gigas plodded behind them, and the rest of the warriors waited as the reserve ready to strike once the battle was underway. Bo trembled, an action of his body he could not master and one he hoped his clothes concealed. He remembered the chaos of the attack upon the monastery. He had failed to control his forces as the frenzy and madness of battle exploded. This time he needed to be stronger, more decisive.

Trying to block out such discouraging thoughts, Bo watched as the Centaurs, Oroks and Gigas readied to charge. He looked for signs of enemy activity and saw nothing.

'They're probably still asleep,' said Corcoran. 'We'll ring Prester John's neck before he can squeal for help.'

Prince Jeimuzu added, 'Yes, I doubt we will be facing true fighting men, just palace guards, soft-hearted gluttons.'

'Maybe, but they will be Nulled so they will be no pushover,' said Bo.

Valbrand looked at Bo. 'You need to give the signal.'

Bo nodded. His whole body shook. He lifted his sword, brought it down and shouted, 'CHARGE!'

At his word, the Centaurs hurtled forward, bellowing and cursing. The Oroks, protected by coats of mail and iron helmets, galloped after them, their colourful flags billowing in the wind. The Gigas went next. They ran slowly, but their huge legs swallowed up the distance.

Alarm bells and horns sounded from inside the palace. Imperial Guards rushed through the main gate. Musketeers and pikemen formed a defensive line in front of the palace. Many of the windows pushed open, where Bo guessed musketeers and bowmen would take position.

As the Centaurs came within range, the musketeers fired, puffs of grey smoke like flowers opening for the sun. A few of the Centaurs fell but the rest charged relentlessly. The pikemen lowered their weapons but the Centaurs crashed through them. As the Oroks joined the battle, the enemy broke up into small, isolated groups of infantry. The grim orchestra of battle carried on the air: screams, shouts, the

333

clashing of steel, and the crackle of muskets. But the Old Believers clearly held the advantage, overwhelming the enemy with their strength and fury.

'This is a walkover, not a battle,' said Corcoran. He turned to Bo. 'When can my warriors join the fray? If we delay, there'll be no one left to kill.'

'Wait for my order,' said Bo, wanting to focus on the unfolding battle, fearful of rushing his manoeuvres. He sensed the Khiltoi's pounding bloodlust. He knew they would think him weak if he did not rush his forces into the battle, but he had to risk that. Corcoran scowled at him but Bo refused to change his mind. He was in charge. He refused to be intimidated.

Horns sounded again, and at that signal, the surviving Imperial Guards retreated, fleeing back through the main gate. There were cheers from the Centaurs and Oroks.

Beside Bo, Prince Jeimuzu laughed. 'I thought the Nulled warriors would fight to the death. If they flee, there is nothing that can save Prester John now.'

Bo wished he could share the sense of jubilation, but something nagged at him, a feeling that it was going too well, that the enemy submitted too easily. With the infantry driven from the field, the Centaurs and Oroks formed lines in front of the palace, leaving gaps for the lumbering Gigas to burst through. Musketeers fired from windows, but Bo saw only a few wisps of gun smoke. Perhaps the enemy truly was defeated. Hope rose within him.

The Gigas prepared to assault the palace, readying their huge heavy clubs. Bo said aloud to his reserve, 'Advance!'

There were jubilant cries from the warriors as they began

to march towards the palace. Bo ran with the vanguard of his foot soldiers; Valbrand kept at his side, like a guard dog.

Ahead, Bo saw hundreds of corpses, some Orok, some Centaur, but mostly Imperial guards, their once gleaming armour dented, broken and sprayed with blood and mud. Bo wondered what horrors awaited him in the palace. He could not believe Prester John would submit easily.

As they caught up with the patrolling Centaurs and Oroks, Bo turned to Valbrand and said, 'Get word to Archontos and Arigh Nasan to form a tight defensive ring. I do not want anyone to escape. Once we are—'

The sound of horns silenced him. This time the horns did not come from inside the palace, and not just horns, but trumpets and drums too. Bo followed the source of the sounds to the hills to the north. His every nightmare about the battle took physical form. Cavalry, musketeers, pike-men, archers, artillery, passing like a slow wave of black water over the hill. The Grand Army.

'There must be thousands of them,' said Corcoran, for once almost lost for words.

'This is impossible,' said Arigh Nasan, riding back to confer with Bo. 'Gnothi sent us word that the Grand Army was far to the north'

'They knew we were coming all along,' said Valbrand, as the ground trembled under the advancing army. 'We've walked into a trap.'

They came under heavier fire from the palace. From every window came shots from muskets, carbines or crossbows.

Between heavy breaths, Arigh Nasan said, 'We have to retreat. The battle is lost. We face a foe too great in number.'

'No,' said Bo, trying to take control of the situation, trying to use his knowledge and experience of battle to make decisions, rather than relying on his emotions. 'If we try to run it will descend into a rout. Do you think the enemy will allow us simply to flee the battlefield? They would hunt us down without mercy.'

'What then, we stand and fight?' said Corcoran, pointing at the Grand Army. 'Fight against *that*?'

Bo tried to think, he had so little time to formulate a plan. Judging the enemy's strength and positions, he said, 'Yes, we must fight, but not just stand. We have to advance against the Grand Army.'

Gasps of astonishment greeted his words.

'Have you lost your wits?' said Corcoran.

Bo attempted to remain calm, authoritative. 'Look, they have brought heavy cannon. If we stand our ground, adopt a defensive formation, they can pound us from a distance with impunity. We must charge them head on, negate any advantage their artillery gives them. We might be able to disrupt them before they complete their dispositions.'

'That's a desperate plan,' said Archontos.

'This is a desperate situation,' said Bo. 'We *must* attack, straight away.'

'But to what end?' said Corcoran. 'There's no hope. We are hugely outnumbered.'

'If we flee, all is lost. When again shall so many races muster to fight side by side in battle? This is our only chance to defeat Prester John.'

'And if we are slaughtered?' said Jeimuzu.

'We always knew the risk. I do not compel you to join me,

336

you are free to choose. If you wish to flee, then flee. You have all proven your courage to me.'

Valbrand said, 'I always thought you'd be the death of me, and it seems I was right. I'm with you, lad.'

'We Kojin shall fight, as you command,' said Jeimuzu.

'There seems no good choice here,' said Arigh Nasan. 'But the smallest hope is worth holding on to. The Oroks shall do as you order.'

Archontos said, 'To victory or death.'

Only Corcoran remained silent. Finally, he took a deep breath and said, 'Never let it be told that the Khiltoi fly in the face of danger. We fight.'

Bo turned to Archontos. 'Will you lead the charge again?'

The Centaur held his sword aloft. 'Our place is always at the front.'

Bo bowed with respect.

'We shall follow,' said Arigh Nasan.

'Good, though you must protect our flanks,' said Bo. 'I am concerned about their cavalry. They have cuirassiers in full armour, and dragoons will support them in large numbers. We are doomed if they overrun our flanks.'

'I understand,' said Arigh Nasan, ordering his warriors to relay his command using their flags.

'Good,' said Bo. 'Those on foot must follow behind.'

The first detachments of the Grand Army, infantry flanked by armoured cuirassiers, reached the plain. On the slopes above them, gunners worked furiously to prepare their artillery. Bo knew they had to move quickly to avoid advancing into a hall of cannon fire. He turned to Archontos. 'Begin the advance.'

337

Archontos bellowed a chest-beating challenge to the Grand Army, a gesture matched by the other Centaurs. As their shouts and boasts grew to a crescendo, they charged. Already running himself, Bo watched as the Centaurs and Oroks barrelled towards the enemy lines, with the Gigas plodding behind them. Bo felt giddy, manic, his body was ready to explode through adrenalin and fear.

Ahead, the Grand Army hastily prepared its formations, and Bo thought, or at least hoped, he detected surprise in their movements, as though the attack he had ordered had disrupted their plans a little. Musketeers created untidy lines, only partially protected by rows of pikemen. The cuirassiers struggled to control their steeds, which appeared unnerved by the din and chaos of the impending attack.

On and on the Old Believers advanced. Sweat dripped into Bo's eyes; he wiped it clear, frantic to see what was happening ahead. The Centaurs, now barely two hundred yards from the enemy's front line, galloped with a flurry of hoof beats, throwing up thick clods of earth. The musketeers opened fire. Bo saw musket flashes and thick dark plumes of powder smoke. Some of the Centaurs fell in cruel, untidy heaps of broken limbs and broken bodies. But many of them reached the line, and leapt over the pikes, crashing into the enemy, trampling on them or cutting them down with swords. The pikemen formed tight defensive clusters like enormous hedgehogs. But this usually sound tactic proved no defence against the Gigas, who pushed through them with brutal sweeps of their clubs.

As the Centaurs and the Gigas drove into the enemy, the Oroks followed, sweeping towards the flanks to clash with the squadrons of cuirassiers, their blades flashing. Protected by thick armour and atop mighty steeds, the cuirassiers looked more like machines, automatons brought to life by some mysterious sorcery. Yet the smaller, lightly armoured Oroks had their measure, using their speed and horse-riding skills to parry charges and drive their own attacks, stinging at them like furious wasps. Precisely fired arrows felled many cuirassiers, with others slain or unhorsed by swords and javelins.

Confident the flanks were, for a time at least, secure, Bo led the rest of the army into the enemy's lines. Wheezing and blowing hard, Valbrand still ran at his side. The Kojin kept close too, their fearsome armour rattling. As Bo ran directly into the battle and into a choking cloud of dust and powder smoke, he heard the angry hiss of red-hot lead shot all around him. He trod on abandoned muskets, snapped pikes, smashed armour and slippery corpses.

With their front lines shattered, fragmented groups of musketeers and pikemen fought for their lives. With no time to reload, the musketeers drew swords or turned their weapons around to use the handles like clubs. An unhorsed dragoon pushed through the smoke to lunge at Bo with his sword. Bo parried and brought a slashing cut down against his enemy's chest, but the metal body armour deflected the blow. The dragoon yelled triumphantly and drove Bo back with two vicious thrusts; he lifted his sword to inflict a killing blow but he underestimated Bo's speed, who stabbed the tip of his blade into the man's unprotected throat. The dragoon gave a gurgling gasp and fell. A musketeer then assailed Bo, swinging his heavy flintlock musket. Bo ducked to miss the blow and then slew his opponent with a slash to the stomach.

Panting heavily and drenched with blood, Bo looked around to try to understand the state of the battle. Valbrand and the Kojin, the latter terrifying in their demon-like masks, engaged opponents in vicious duels. The Centaurs pushed back the enemy further and further. Close behind them, the Khiltoi fought in full battle frenzy, their size and strength defeating countless enemies, and they received valiant support from the acrobatic Satyrs, the hammer-wielding Dwarfs and the grim Pertinax who dashed forward with relentless ferocity, killing with sword and spear. The Oroks steadfastly held the flanks, beating off determined attacks from cuirassiers and dragoons. A thought, startling in its optimism, formed in Bo's mind: could they win?

The trumpets of the Grand Army blared out and their shaken front formations retreated, sprinting up the slopes in a chaotic retreat.

'They're running!' Bo heard Corcoran cry. The Khiltoi warrior gestured to the rest of the army. 'Let's drive the scum from the field!'

'No, not yet!' said Bo. He feared the retreat was a feint, and took no satisfaction when he saw his hunch proved correct. The musketeers and pikemen reformed their lines on a higher slope, strengthened by thousands of fresh troops brought up from the rear. Bo spied heavy cannon, as well as smaller culverins and falconets. Valbrand grabbed his shoulder and pulled him to look to the east. There, squadrons of light cavalry galloped across the hills, heading for the rear of the Old Believers. Bo swiftly gathered his

340

Captains. Paleos, who bled from several small wounds, also joined them.

'If we stay here we'll be encircled,' said Valbrand. 'We have to retreat.'

'Where to?' said Jeimuzu, his voice muffled behind his mask. 'The sea is to our south.'

Valbrand sniffed. 'Better to fight with our backs to the sea than to be encircled. It'll funnel the enemy directly to us, which may reduce the impact of their greater numbers.'

'Valbrand is right,' said Bo. 'We have advanced as far as we can. We must retreat to the sea. The beach seems like as good a place as any.'

'For what?' said Corcoran.

'A last stand,' said Valbrand.

'We need a rear-guard to prevent a rout,' said Bo.

'We Gigas can hold the line for a short time,' said Paleos. 'It is what I have come to propose.'

'It is certain death,' said Bo.

Paleos glared at him. 'I prefer to call it *sacrifice*. Do not be fooled, we Gigas do not wish for death. But we have lived long, so if our time has come, it is perhaps not unjust. Once before our vigilance failed, and many suffered for it. It is time for the Gigas to repay our debt, to erase the stain of our past failings. We shall give you time enough to withdraw.'

Valbrand gave Bo a 'what are we waiting for?' look and tried to steer him backwards.

Bo ignored him and said to Paleos, 'The nobility and valour of the Gigas are beyond compare. It has been an honour to fight alongside you. And I swear, if we win through

341

this day, I shall do all I can to ensure that the tombs of the Neofermenos are protected.'

Paleos bowed and stroked his long beard. 'Let us hope that a better world comes from this horror, even if we Gigas do not live to see it.'

With that, Paleos turned and mustered the surviving Gigas. They charged headlong into the enemy's lines. Their clubs swept aside infantry and cavalry. In seconds, piles of injured and slain men and horses piled up around each Gigas. Desperate to take advantage of the time earned by the Gigas, Bo said, 'RETREAT TO THE SEA!'

As the Old Believers withdrew, Bo looked back at the Gigas. They fought with fury, gouging swathes out of the enemy formations, but the Grand Army did not succumb easily. Gunners brought up cannon, and from close range they sprayed the Gigas with hateful blasts. One by one the giants fell, limbs ripped, skin shredded. Paleos stood last, to the end swinging his club. Only as a volley of musket-fire tore into him did he perish, toppling over like a magnificent oak cut down by axes. As the body of the Gigas crashed onto the ground, Bo realised that he had witnessed the end of a race; their kind would never again walk the earth. He hoped they would be remembered somehow, if only in tales and songs, if only as a legend.

A near miss from a musket shot brought Bo back to his duty. He had hoped for a smooth withdrawal, but the Old Believers retreated in a rush of stampeding hooves and sprinting warriors, pushing and jostling. As they passed the palace, a hail of arrows, bolts and musket balls rained down on them, further thinning their ranks. Running as fast and hard as he could, Bo tried to urge his warriors on. Fighting for breath, he said, 'FASTER! FASTER!'

He looked to the eastern hills and saw the enemy cavalry rushing to attack the rear of the Old Believers and cut them off, to complete an encirclement Bo knew would mean a massacre. But ahead of them, the Centaurs and mounted Oroks reached the beach, their hooves sending up small explosions of damp sand. They turned and readied to defend themselves. Thwarted in their mission to surround the Old Believers, the enemy cavalry slowed to a trot and waited at a safe distance for the rest of the Grand Army to catch up.

At last, the weary, shaken survivors stumbled onto the beach. Bo gauged that they had lost at least a third of their strength.

Valbrand peered at the churning sea. 'Perhaps we could swim for it.'

'This is no time for jokes,' said Bo.

'I guess you're right,' said Valbrand. 'You haven't failed, you know.'

'What do you mean? The battle is lost. We are all going to die here.'

'Aye, but a lesser man wouldn't have got us this far.'

Bo closed his eyes, wanting to shut out the horrors around him, if only for the briefest of moments. 'But what was the point? We're going to be massacred.'

'The point is we stood up to Prester John,' said Valbrand. 'That means something, whatever happens to us now.'

The Grand Army stopped its advance several hundred yards away, forming a wall of soldiers, horses and weapons.

343

Bo thought about a forlorn, desperate charge, one last gesture of defiance. But those around him were too weary for such a move. All they could try to do was hold their ground.

The enemy waited in silence. One horseman advanced from their ranks, trotting slowly towards the river. A Redeemer, draped in resplendent white robes. When he came within two hundred yards, he stopped and lifted his hand. 'I ask for a parley. Who commands this puny rabble?'

Valbrand gripped Bo's arm. 'Let's kill him and get on with the battle.'

Bo shook his head. 'No, if he wants to talk, let me at least hear what he has to say.'

Trying to appear confident, Bo strode towards the Redeemer, halting a safe distance from him. A hood hid most of the Redeemer's face, leaving only a slight glimpse of deathly pale, purple-streaked skin and a mouth of cracked, swollen lips and misshapen teeth. Bo sheathed his sword but kept his hand firmly on its grip. 'I am Prince Asbjorn, and I lead this army. You ask for a parley, what is it you wish to say before you are defeated?'

The Redeemer laughed. 'Defeated? You either jest or are deluded. You can have no victory this day, as I guess you well know, *Prince* Asbjorn. Yes, I know your name. A leader of rogues and brigands in the north, I believed you to be. Well, you should have stayed there. You have got involved in affairs far beyond the reach of your power or wisdom.'

'Do you wish to insult me, or do you have something valuable for me to hear?' said Bo, trying to control himself, trying not to react to the provocation.

344

'I am Legatus Carrasco, commander of the Grand Army. I offer terms, if you are sensible enough to hear them.'

Bo hesitated. He wanted to dismiss any offer made by the enemy, but he knew he should at least listen to what the Redeemer had to say. If nothing else, it bought a little time, though time for what he could not guess. He had no faith in miracles. 'Tell me the terms you offer.'

'Surrender and the lives of your warriors shall be spared. There will of course be punishment. There *must* be a penalty for your rebellion and sedition.'

'What punishment?'

The Redeemer paused, as if to savour the sound and texture of his reply. 'To serve both God and Prester John, in the mines of Gorefayne. And of course, you and the other Men shall be given the blessing of the Holy Null.'

'You are truly magnanimous. But you speak only of Men, there are others amongst us. What of them?'

Carrasco gave a dismissive snort. 'They are soulless creatures, a pestilence cursed in the eyes of God. They will work until death claims them but they do not deserve the honour of the Null.'

'I pity your ignorance, for you have allowed your mind to be twisted by the poison of Prester John,' said Bo. 'This army fights for all free people, for all races. We fight as one. For that reason, and countless others, I reject your terms. Being slain in battle is better than the humiliation and slow death of slavery.'

Carrasco gripped the reins of his horse. He spat out his words. 'Half-witted fool. Your sacrifice is meaningless. You shall all die grievous deaths. You shall not be buried, but

345

left as dung upon the earth. Carrion shall feast on the flesh from your rotting corpses. Nothing stands in the way of Prester John's final victory. God wills it.'

'If you believe you know the will of God, then you are the half-witted fool.'

'This parley is over,' said Carrasco, wheeling his horse around. 'The Brotherhood of Redemption does not know the meaning of mercy, Prince Asbjorn.'

'We do, and that is why we will always be stronger than you,' said Bo, his voice fluttering as he spoke, as though his body treacherously fought to display the weakness and doubt he tried so very hard to conceal.

The Redeemer saw only Bo's defiance. He cursed and galloped back to his lines.

Bo returned to the Old Believers. He hoped, he prayed, he had done the right thing. It was easy enough for him to reject surrender; thanks to the poison of Zanash he had only days to live. Was he being selfish, reckless with the lives of others? What would the others say? Would they have accepted the Redeemer's terms?

'So, did he agree to surrender?' said Valbrand.

'No, he did not,' said Bo, in no mood for humour, black or not.

'That's a shame,' said Valbrand. 'It would save us a lot of trouble.'

'We're in for trouble, that's for sure,' said Bo.

'What did the Redeemer say?' said Arigh Nasan.

Bo stared at those around him, preparing himself for their reaction. 'He offered to spare our lives, if we agree to be their slaves and serve in Gorefayne.'

Archontos pointed to the Grand Army. 'By the way they prepare to attack, it is my guess you rejected their offer.'

'Then you did well, Prince Asbjorn,' said Corcoran, slapping Bo on the back. 'We Khiltoi would rather die than live as slaves.'

'I concur,' said Arigh Nasan. 'I once endured the horror of the mines and wish no such fate for any of my kin. If it is our fate to fall on the battlefield, then I shall feel no shame.'

'Death with honour,' said Jeimuzu, bowing to the other commanders.

'What's all this talk of dying?' said Valbrand, loading his crossbow. 'We should be worrying about making the enemy die, rather than fret about our own ends. There's breath in me yet, and plenty of fight too. I say enough talking; let's get on with this battle.'

The enemy's trumpets blasted and their formations moved. Bo heard shouts of 'God wills it!'

Bo said to Valbrand, 'I think you have your wish.'

*

From the main window of the Winter Palace's Golden Chamber, Prester John watched the battle unfold with satisfaction. In a voice old and raspy, he announced, 'The fools refuse to surrender but it matters not. Our victory is at hand.'

Prester John no longer wore simple clothes. A habit, lavishly ornamented with jewels, replaced the cowl and cape of coarse wool that he had worn for years. His jewelled crown proved his confidence. He had no need to be humble now.

347

He smiled, aglow with satisfaction. Victory was nothing new to him, but to be able to witness this triumph at first hand gave him immeasurable pleasure. He had waited for this moment, to watch the death throes of those who had defied him for years. Eldar. Heretics. Illuminati. How arrogant they had been, thinking that they had surprise, that they would catch the Patriarch of the Mother Church unguarded. As if he would allow himself to be defeated so easily! His plan, carefully conceived, executed perfectly, proved his genius. From this day forward, there would be no resistance to his rule. He bestrode the world like a God.

He turned and looked back into the room, not even glancing at his mirror; he did not need to reach out to other lands, he controlled everything. Frescoes with a golden background decorated the room. In one corner, his throne sat on a richly carpeted dais. To the right of the throne stood an icon of the Saviour, crowned and holding a sceptre: a prize ripped from the Church of Holy Wisdom in heretical Miklagard. Velvet-covered benches ran along the walls. Upon the benches sat the *aristoi*: kings, queens and bishops, the most powerful rulers in the Known World such as King Henri, Duke Pizarro, Cardinal Theodulf, Alcuin of Helagan and King Philippus, all assembled for the *Divine Audience*, a chance to be in the presence of the Patriarch. They sat silent and motionless, and watched his every move, listened intently to his every word. Fawning, obsequious, their lust for power made them insecure and anxious. Prester John smiled. The *aristoi* served a purpose. He needed them for now. Perhaps he would not need them in the future. The relentless energy of Cold Iron throbbed through his body. He felt so strong, strong enough to live for a thousand years, perhaps strong enough to defeat death all together.

He walked back into the centre of the room and stood with his arms outstretched. 'God be praised, this day shall be forever remembered in the histories.'

In the corner of his eye, Prester John saw someone rise to their feet. He turned to see Queen Isabella of Prevennis standing with her hands clasped in front of her chest. Within her dark hair, a tiara sparkled. She said with a pious air, 'You have led us on a path blessed by the Almighty. Through your wisdom and strength, we enter a new age of paradise. I vow to remain your faithful servant, until death takes me.'

'In your struggles to subdue the northern rebels, you have shown me your loyalty, dear Queen,' said Prester John. Her eagerness, her *desperation* to prove herself both amused and sickened him.

Lapping up his words, Queen Isabella beamed, and curtseyed to him. 'To serve you, my Lord, is a reward beyond value.'

'I thank you,' said Prester John. 'And yet it troubles me that it is your whelp who leads this army of heretics. My spies confirmed it to be true. Troubling tidings indeed.'

The effect of his words was as dramatic as the violent ripples of a stone dropped into a still pond. The Queen trembled and her face whitened. She lowered her head and hurriedly returned to her seat. With her head bowed, she said, 'He is no son of mine. I reject and disown him utterly.'

'The same blood runs through his veins as yours,' said

349

Prester John, taking pleasure from her discomfort. 'I hope you never seek to emulate his sedition.'

The Queen bolted out of her seat and threw herself at his feet. 'I shall never forsake you, my Lord.'

Prester John tapped her head and gestured for her to rise. She faced him with moist eyes and quivering lips. She was a puppet in his hands and he enjoyed toying with her. He controlled her utterly. She could never betray him. As with thousands of others, the Null ensured her loyalty. In a soft, fatherly voice, he said, 'Be seated, Queen. Be at peace.'

She backed away, her hands clenched together, whispering prayers.

Prester John addressed the *aristoi*. 'We should each offer a silent prayer, to give thanks to God for our glorious triumph.'

When the prayers finished, Alcuin of Helagan stood and said, 'It is sad Lord Lucien is not here to share in this moment, for he has done so much to serve the mission of God.'

The very mention of Lord Lucien stabbed at Prester John, troubled as ever by his closest servant's obsession with the daughter of Athena Parthenos. Prester John wanted to find and destroy the Tree of Life, but he believed Lord Lucien's fixation on that mission above all other concerns to be misguided. Through the mirror, he had searched for Lord Lucien, trying to find him, trying to persuade him to return. But his attempts failed, finding only silence. It confused him, irritated him. A nagging concern took root. Did he detect a wilful defiance in the silence? Disloyalty? No, he refused to believe that of Lord Lucien.

Prester John returned to the window. The battle raged. His eyes feasted on the sight. The Grand Army, the Heavenly Host as some named it, smiting the union of heretics and unclean spirits. He wanted to watch the final moments, to see the end of his greatest enemies. With victory, all the Known World was his. Unchallenged, unassailable, he planned to stretch his dominion into lands as yet undiscovered, so wherever the sun rose and set, mortals would live and die under his rule, the rule of a living God.

- CHAPTER SIXTEEN -

Across the Ancestral Realm

Elowen looked up at a night sky filled with stars and constellations unfamiliar to her, although the new star burned with increased intensity. The cold wind carried unfamiliar scents. Leading the company, Batu marched ahead, tracking, watching, listening, primed for violence like a stalking cat. He carried a flaming torch, which bobbed in front of them, a chilling reminder of the Lantern Men Elowen had seen so many months before in the Mengoon. Black Francis and Diggory flanked Elowen, while Bryna walked at the rear. Elowen knew they deliberately adopted such a formation to protect her.

The icy starlight formed uncanny shadows, which distorted the contours of the land. As they walked, Elowen heard animal calls, and scurrying and scratching. Several times, Batu turned towards a troubling sound and held his torch aloft, and in its glare flashed the eyes of nocturnal creatures, some very small, some worryingly large. To the relief of Elowen and her companions, the creatures bolted when the light fell upon them.

'What are they?' said Elowen.

'I reckon we're better off not knowing, lass,' said Black Francis.

'We ought to put out that torch,' said Diggory, fear making him talk a little louder. 'It's bound to attract trouble. If Lord Lucien is following us, he could see us from miles away.'

'Without this torch we shall blunder around in the dark,' said Batu. 'Most beasts fear fire, so it gives us protection. Trust me, Diggory, I have journeyed through many wild places. I do nothing lightly, or without care.'

Even in the stifling, overpowering darkness, Elowen perceived a sense of the size and scale of the land around them. She felt the Earthsoul strongly, waves of energy pulsating through her body. It refreshed her, washing away aches and pains, giving vigour to her muscles and limbs. The Earthsoul whetted her senses too. She detected subtle differences between the heady night scents. Sounds, even small ones, such as the crackling of Batu's torch, the hum of insects, her companions' breathing, resonated loudly.

Gradually, the black canopy above them cracked, allowing red light to leak across the sky. Dawn revealed a landscape of undulating plains of brown grass, dotted by dense clusters of trees and tall shrubs. A few outcrops of reddish rock reared in lonely, windswept arrangements. The soil, baked hard in some places, dusty in others, was iron-red in colour.

As the sun rose, the temperature climbed rapidly. Elowen's hair dampened with sweat and her mouth became dry. She swigged water from her wineskin but heeded Batu's warning to conserve her supply. She squinted in the harsh

353

light, and the horizon shimmered. Countless flies buzzed in the air, a relentless nuisance as they landed on her face and crawled in her hair. But for all the physical discomfort, the Earthsoul's potency remained undimmed, and the golden threads whirled over many of the rocks and trees.

'What I'd give for a mug of ale and a cool sea breeze,' said Black Francis, wiping his forehead. 'I thought the Beauteous Isle to be hot, but this country is a furnace.'

'This is worse than the steppes,' said Diggory, before nodding apologetically at Batu. 'No offence, of course.'

Batu turned round and smiled wryly. 'I agree with you, my friend. This is not a land for the living.'

'You're wrong,' said Bryna. 'I feel the life here. Keenly I sense the threads of the *bládh*. Do you feel it too, Elowen?'

'Yes, I do. There are memories here, ancient memories.'

'Aye, but memories of who, or what?' said Black Francis.

The company climbed a long, low-lying hill. Left parched and dusty by the sun, the flat summit stretched for a mile. Four groups of stone pillars marked the summit. Formed from red, iron-rich rock, they were polygonal in shape and each stood the height of a man. Golden threads shimmered around many of the pillars.

'Did people make these?' said Diggory, tapping a pillar.

'I believe so,' said Batu. 'Winds did not shape these stones. Clever hands made them, and for a purpose.'

'What purpose?' said Bryna.

'The answer to that is long lost,' said Batu. 'This place will hold its secrets until the end of the world.'

'That might not be too far away,' said Diggory.

The summit provided a vantage point of the route ahead.

354

The monotonous arid plains gave way to a sandstone region, through which a broad, lazily flowing river carved gorges and towering cliffs. Directly in front of the hill, the river formed a wide bend before curving to the west.

'This must be the Great Fish River,' said Batu. He pointed further to the south, where a solitary mountain was visible. 'And that must be our destination.'

Elowen recognised the shape of the mountain from the Map Room in the Temple of the Sun, its distinctive shape fastened in her mind. Haramu. Somewhere within its clefts and folds of stone stood the Tree of Life, the very thing that had drawn her across the Known World, spinning her life into directions she could never have imagined. And now she approached the final stages of that journey, she wanted it to be over, she wanted an end.

They descended the hill and followed the river on its eastern bank, heading southwards. Elowen looked across the river and saw a number of fearsome creatures lying on the far bank. Dark bronze in colour, each creature had four short splayed legs, a long powerful tail and a scaly hide. Their elongated snouts contained a fierce pair of jaws. One of them waddled towards the river and slid into the water.

'Are they dragons?' said Elowen, pointing across the river at the creatures. The rest of the company stopped to look.

'No, but they are deadly,' said Black Francis. 'They're crocodiles, common in hot lands. I've seen them before. Man-eating brutes.'

Batu nodded sagely. 'It is said that no blow can hurt them, such is the hardness of their skin. In Orok legend, they are amongst the oldest of all beasts.'

355

Without trying to, Elowen *Linked* with the crocodiles. She could not make out words, only a flavour of their feelings, not malevolence, but primal instincts, chilling in their brutal simplicity. They wanted to kill not for evil, not for power but to sustain themselves.

Groups of plovers hopped amongst the crocodiles, pecking at the ground. Elowen said, 'Those birds don't seem to be afraid.'

Black Francis laughed. 'They're braver than me.'

'We'd best keep well out of those monsters' way,' said Diggory.

'Yes, this land teems with predators,' said Bryna.

'And the very worst predators of all are hunting for us,' said Elowen, the thought of Lord Lucien never far from her mind.

Further south, the riverbank grew more thickly wooded. Watered by the river, the stinking slimy ground beneath their feet squelched and bubbled. Gnarled roots of ugly, ungainly trees drove into the mud and stretched out like tentacles into the river. Biting insects swarmed around the branches, eager to feast on living flesh and blood. Cursing and swearing, the company pushed on, finally reaching drier ground free of the insects.

As the day waned, they found themselves scrambling up rocky hillsides; far below, the river charged through a winding gorge. Trees clung precariously to cliff sides, some with roots splitting through the rock and leaning over the river, as though readying to jump into the waters below. The cliffs throbbed with life. Birds chattered and chirruped in the trees and shrubs. Lizards darted from rock to rock. To

Elowen's alarm, snakes slithered beneath shrubs or lounged over rocks coloured by lichen.

They walked until dusk. By that time, Elowen struggled to put one foot in front of the other. Weary, thirsty and hungry, even the Earthsoul failed to provide succour. She craved sleep. Batu found a shallow cave and after a brief inspection led them all inside. Bryna lit a small fire and the light revealed a host of paintings on the cave walls. Elowen saw figures of people and beasts, all rendered in vibrant colours, bursting with energy and movement. Primitive and powerful, they offered a glimpse into a vanished world.

Keeping guard, Batu positioned himself at the mouth of the cave, his sword and bow at the ready. Bryna sat and leant against the wall, her head lowered. Grumbling, Diggory curled up on the stony floor of the cave and went to sleep. Black Francis did likewise. Elowen lay down close to the fire, enjoying its warmth, watching the dancing flames and the restless shadows they threw onto the wall. Sleep came quickly to her, but it proved uncomfortable, unsettling, stalked by fragmented dreams. She saw the jaws of a crocodile, its long pointed snout and vicious teeth. It leant towards her; she was powerless to move, gripped by an invisible force. The face of the crocodile warped into the mask of Lord Lucien. He spoke to her, the same words he had spoken to her in the labyrinth beneath Bai Ulgan. *If you take your place by my side, you shall be worshipped, and your thoughts shall guide the actions of Men for generations to come.*

The mask disappeared. Elowen felt someone gently tapping her face. She opened her eyes and saw Bryna leaning over her. 'It's time to go, Elowen.'

357

'So soon?' she said, feeling groggy and a little sick. The words of Lord Lucien echoed in her mind.

'Yes, we can't wait for dawn,' she heard Batu say.

She sat up and saw Diggory and Black Francis rising to their feet, moving like old men. With glazed eyes, Diggory peered at Elowen. 'I could sleep for a hundred years.'

'You may have the chance to rest one day, but not today,' said Batu.

Diggory laughed and said to Elowen, 'I wish we had Lárwita's balloon! We'd get to the Tree of Life in no time.'

'I think our *flying* days are over,' said Elowen, giggling at the memory of their dramatic escape from the Sanctuary. The image of Lárwita's shy smile flashed in front of her. A happy memory, but one veiled by the brutal manner of his death. He had given his life to protect his friends. Determined to be worthy of his sacrifice, Elowen stood, trying to throw off the shackles of tiredness. She wanted to push on.

They gathered their belongings, extinguished the fire and Batu led them outside into the chilly night. Once again, the Orok held aloft his torch as a light to guide them. Eerie animal cries echoed around the cliffs and far below the river churned and thundered. The swirling light of the torch revealed rustling bushes, evidence of creatures scampering for safety. In the darkness, the shrubs and trees took on a grotesque, menacing aspect, with their twisted branches stretched out like malformed limbs.

The frigid night air cleared a little of the fog in Elowen's mind but her brief sleep had hardly refreshed her. Her eyes stung with tiredness. She heard flapping above her head and as she looked up she saw dark shapes moving.

'Odd to see so many birds at night,' said Diggory.

'They are not birds,' said Batu. 'They are bats.'

'Bats!' said Diggory. He waved his hands around, swiping away at the bats.

'Be quiet,' said Batu. 'Do not draw attention to us, for sound carries far in such a silent land.'

'I don't like bats,' said Diggory.

'They are no danger to you,' said Batu.

Diggory snorted. 'If that's the case, they'll be the only things living here that aren't.'

Dawn brought relief from the oppressive darkness, although Elowen and her companions welcomed the sun's burning heat far less. They came to the lip of an escarpment and ahead of them stood the Haramu Mountain. Brooding, sinister, it rose dramatically above the few low hills around its base. An immense natural wall of stone encircled the mountain, resembling the ramparts of a fortress, and in front of the wall ran a gorge. Ruins filled much of the dusty plain between the escarpment and the mountain. Elowen saw temples, tombs, columns and statues, a nameless city long abandoned.

'Half a day from here,' said Bryna, pointing ahead to the mountain.

'As a Khiltoi strides, perhaps,' said Black Francis, red-faced and rubbing his knees. 'Not at the speed I walk.'

Bryna smiled. 'I'll try to carry you if you wish.'

'If I had less pride, I'd take you up on that offer,' he said, half-laughing, half-grimacing.

Taking advantage of a deep gash in the escarpment, they managed to clamber down to the plain below. Elowen

359

looked around, feeling horribly small and horribly exposed. The hot wind screeched across the plain, flinging clouds of dust that made Elowen's eyes water. More than once, she felt a supportive hand from Bryna on her back, and the Khiltoi whispered, 'Just keep going, Elowen.'

They traipsed on. Plagued by the incessant flies, and pummelled by the pitiless sun, each step forward required effort, each step meant more pain. They rationed the water carefully, drinking with tiny sips. Conserving their energy, they spoke little.

The closer they came to the mountain, the more Elowen felt the Earthsoul's power. The golden threads emanated from the mountain in wide arcs. Their strength made her tingle but they also tired her, as though their energy proved too much for her body to contain.

They reached a gateway of monumental size, the entrance to the nameless city. Elowen stopped to stare in wonder. She saw many carven figures on the gateway, though any colour had long been rubbed away by the wind and sun. A winged disc adorned the cornice and Elowen recognised symbols of the Tree of Life, just as she had seen in Shuruppak. They were close now…

A high-pitched yelling echoed all around. From out of the ruins burst a host of terrifying figures. Clad in garments made of scarlet-coloured leaves, each wore a mask made from bark, and carried a sharpened blade of stone in one hand and a wooden stick in the other. Elowen counted at least twenty of them, and they rapidly formed a circle around her and her companions. They stomped, yelled and waved their stone blades menacingly, in wild, elaborate rhythmic motions like a frightening, intoxicated dance. But for all their aggressive movements and noise, they did not attack.

'Who are they?' said Black Francis, scrambling to ready his musket.

'Spies of Prester John, I reckon,' said Diggory.

'No,' said Bryna. 'You are wrong.'

The masked figures stopped and stood motionless. One of them, his mask adorned with animal horns, said aloud, 'You can come no further. Go back. You do not belong here.'

'You speak the Common Tongue?' said Black Francis with surprise.

'I speak all tongues,' said the man with the horned mask. 'It is our gift. For we do not know where imposters may come from, and the message must be the same for all.'

'What message?' said Batu.

'That you are not welcome here. Go now and go quickly.'

Bryna spoke angrily to him in the Khiltoi language. She gasped in surprise when he replied in the same tongue. He then said, 'Do not test our patience. Leave now, or be slain.'

Batu held up his hands. 'Please, we are no danger to you. We merely wish to reach the mountain yonder.'

'The mountain is forbidden to all, unless you have the Mark.'

'The Mark?' said Diggory.

Elowen remembered. The Mystery of Water. She looked down at her hand, staring at the triangle formed by the red lines in her palm. She held up her hand. 'Is this what you mean?'

The horned figure lowered his head, staring at her hand. He strode forward and grabbed her wrist. All of Elowen's companions moved to defend her but she said, 'NO! Let him look.'

Holding her wrist in a tight grip, the figure pressed his fingers into her palm. As he did, he chanted to himself in a low whisper. He released her wrist, took a step back and bowed. He removed his mask. Wrinkles crisscrossed the dark skin of his face. His brown eyes showed the weight and wisdom of long years, mixed with a mischievous quality. 'My name is Ifueko. Forgive me, *Okhuoba*, we have waited long for your coming.'

The other strangers bowed too. Elowen watched them, puzzled and faintly embarrassed.

'Who the hell is *Ok-hu-oba*?' said Diggory.

Ifueko pointed to Elowen. 'She has come, as has been long prophesised. We are the *Etisa*. We have guarded The Way for centuries beyond count, as we swore to do.'

Chanting '*Okhuoba*', the rest of the *Etisa* removed their masks, revealing both men and women. Then Ifueko said, 'We hoped this day was close. Ever the Tree of Life sickens, and soon it may fail and forever be lost to the world.'

'That won't happen,' said Elowen, forcing words out of her dry throat. She was about to say more when pain exploded in her leg, exactly where she had been stabbed by the Redeemer in Dinas Hein many months before. Hideous horns hollered above the wind, followed by the noise of pounding hooves. Wraithlike within a cloud of dust and sand, a dozen Redeemers mounted on huge horses galloped towards them.

362

Elowen cried out in pain and fear. She would have fallen had Diggory not supported her.

'This is a trap,' said Black Francis, pointing accusingly at the *Etisa*.

'We knew nothing of their presence and they are odious to our eyes,' said Ifueko. '*Okhuoba*, let me guide you to the Tree of Life, before it is too late.'

Elowen dismissed the idea with a wave of her hand. 'I won't abandon my friends. We fight together.'

'Your best chance of saving them is to go to the Tree of Life,' said Ifueko.

'He's right, Elowen,' said Black Francis. 'Go with him, and Diggory too.'

'The Tree of Life is the most important thing,' said Batu, notching an arrow in his bow.

'What about you?'

'We'll hold them as long as we can,' said Black Francis.

'They'll kill you,' said Elowen.

Black Francis gripped his musket and winked. 'Have you so little faith in us, lass?'

The dust cloud moved closer. The Redeemers' white robes billowed like demented flapping wings. Black Francis, Bryna, Batu and the other *Etisa* stood in a line, defiant, determined, but surely doomed.

'They're coming, Elowen,' said Diggory, pointing frantically at the Redeemers. 'We can't wait. Look, Ifueko is already heading towards the mountain.'

Tormented by guilt, Elowen turned away, and with Diggory beside her, began to run after Ifueko. As she did so, she heard the first crack of Black Francis's musket, and the whooshing of arrows and slingshots. She ran, half-blinded by sand and hot tears. She repeated to herself, 'I'm a coward. A *coward*.'

They followed Ifueko into the complex of temples, tombs and courtyards. Statues of striding kings with elaborate crowns stood amongst decorated sandstone pillars and columns with flower-shaped capitals. Ifueko dashed along a straight causeway, which was flanked by statues of reclining, ram-headed creatures, who watched the progress of the visitors to their realm with cruel, aloof detachment.

As Elowen, Diggory and Ifueko drew closer to the mountain, the avenue diminished into a dusty track, and the statues, lofty columns and tombs gave way to primitive standing stones, irregular in shape and carved with many ring and cup markings. Most striking of all to Elowen's eyes, was a line of four clay statues, all representing beasts with the body of a lion, and the head, beak and wings of an eagle. Each statue was fashioned with intricate details: erect ears, sharp talons and feathered breast. Diggory nodded at the statues and said, 'Who made such horrible things?'

Ifueko gave a grim laugh. 'They are griffins, protectors of the Tree of Life, but little life flows through them now. They have all but returned to the earth that birthed them. You need not fear them.'

Elowen glanced again at the statues. 'You mean, they're *alive*?'

'Keep running, *Okhuoba*,' said Ifueko.

The track ended abruptly at the gorge that stood between the city and the mountain. Like silent witnesses, curious rock formations, lurked around the final yards of the track.

To Elowen's surprise, a narrow stone bridge spanned the gorge.

'Are we going to have to cross using *that*?' said Diggory in alarm, pointing at the bridge. 'Will it take our weight? It looks like it might crumble beneath our very first footstep.'

'It will serve,' said Ifueko. 'Come, cross swiftly and we'll be out of the reach of your enemies.'

'I would not be so sure,' said a voice from further away. Elowen flinched as soon as she heard it. From behind the standing stones emerged four white-robed Redeemers and Lord Lucien. A pistol shot rang out. Ifueko jolted violently, gasped and fell to his knees. He held his hand to his shoulder, and blood dripped through his fingers.

A Redeemer seized Elowen, his hands like icy clasps on her shoulders. She tried to summon the Earthsoul's power, but her thoughts were too scrambled, and the golden threads eluded her. Diggory lifted the pistol Black Francis had given him and fired at Lord Lucien, but his shot was hasty and missed. Before he could reload, two of the Redeemers overpowered him and forced him to the ground.

'ENOUGH!' said Lord Lucien. 'Stop resisting, boy. Do not make us slaughter you.'

'I'd rather fight to the death than give in to you,' spat Diggory, his face pushed into the ground.

Lord Lucien laughed. 'You still have spirit, boy, but you are a fool. I do not wish to kill any of you, Elowen least of all.'

'You were happy to try before,' said Diggory, struggling in vain with the Redeemer who held him. 'You tried to hang us in Bai Ulgan.'

'Only because it was convenient to let the Khan deal with you, now it is different. I have no desire to slay you, as long as you submit to my will and give me what I want. Elowen, do you want to see all your friends slain?'

'Ignore him, Elowen,' said Diggory. 'He's a liar.'

'Elowen,' said Lord Lucien, his tone softened. 'Listen to me. You discovered the alchemist's creature, did you not?'

Elowen's skin crawled as she remembered it. 'Yes.'

'Before Unheimlich died, he passed the connection I shared with him to you. I can bend my sight far beyond the naked eye. That is how I found you. Now you should see what I have seen.'

He touched the top of her head. Elowen experienced a violent white flash. Although her feet remained firmly planted on the ground, she had the sensation of movement. A vision formed. Through a cloud of dust and sand, she saw Black Francis, Batu, Bryna and the *Etisa* fighting the Redeemers. It was a desperate, unequal struggle. Outnumbered, her friends and the *Etisa* fought for their lives, a fight Elowen knew would be in vain. The Redeemers would show no mercy.

The vision ended. The real world returned.

Lord Lucien said, 'You see clearly that your friends are doomed. I do not want to kill you or them. You remember what I told you before. We need not be enemies. Surrender and all your friends will be spared.'

She trusted none of the words that came out of Lord Lucien's mouth, but she could not let her friends die in a fight she knew to be hopeless. In a hoarse voice, she said, 'I surrender.'

'Good, you have made a wise choice,' said Lord Lucien, sounding pleased. He gestured to one of the Redeemers. 'Take word to our brothers to capture the others unharmed and bring them to me.'

'It will be done, my Lord,' said the Redeemer, who hastened away.

Lord Lucien looked at Elowen. 'Once before I offered you the hand of friendship, to take your place by my side, just as your mother Athena Parthenos did. That offer still stands.'

'Never,' she said evenly.

He paused. 'And what of the Tree of Life? You have come so far to seek it, but surely you see that you have lost. I shall destroy the Tree of Life, once and for all.'

'But first you have to reach it,' said Ifueko. 'The Way is blocked to you.'

'Perhaps, but not to her,' said Lord Lucien, pointing to Elowen. 'She will take me to the Tree of Life.'

Elowen laughed grimly and shook her head. 'I'd rather die.'

'Your defiance is tedious. You think you are strong, but against the power of Prester John, you are a straw in the wind.'

'You'll soon discover Prester John is not as strong as you imagined,' said Elowen.

Lord Lucien gave a short, bitter laugh. 'Of course, I had forgotten. The *secret* attack on the Winter Palace.'

Elowen's blood ran cold. How did Lord Lucien know? She looked at Diggory and his face registered the same horrified shock.

'Did you honestly think this so-called attack was a surprise?' said Lord Lucien. 'Your feeble army has fallen into a trap, one long-prepared. Yes, my Master waits at the Winter Palace at Inganno, but he is not alone. Only a few miles away stands the Grand Army ready to defend him as soon as your rabble of heretics launch their assault. A spy we sent into the arms of the Illuminati, the name of Dolon. He brought you news of Prester John, did he not? You do not answer, but from your expression, it is clear his name is known to you. Your army does not march to victory; it marches only to defeat, and none shall be spared.'

Elowen lowered her head, trying to shield her tears from the mocking eyes of Lord Lucien.

'This is all lies,' said Diggory, as the Redeemers yanked him back on his feet. 'He's trying to deceive us again.'

'No,' said Elowen. 'He's telling the truth.'

Lord Lucien reached out a hand. His icy fingertips stroked her forehead, toyed with her hair. In a hushed voice, like a devoted father speaking to his child, he said, 'Armed with this knowledge, do you still defy me? Your cause is lost. Even if you revive the Tree of Life, what would be achieved? The Illuminati are crushed, your army massacred. My Master has won total victory. Serve him. Stand by my side. Rule, as you were meant to rule. You shall be well rewarded, I swear it.'

'I don't want any *rewards*,' said Elowen. 'I want nothing from you.'

'Ah, but you do not mean that,' said Lord Lucien, his words lulling, hypnotic. 'This world needs control, Elowen. The Eldar are dangerous, fickle. Men cannot be trusted.'

'It's you that can't be trusted,' said Elowen.

Lord Lucien shook his head. 'We are divine, Elowen, you and I, Messengers. To rule is our destiny. Do you believe the Eldar and Illuminati are your *friends*? They praise you, admire you, for you are their instrument. Even if you succeed, they will turn on you, punish you. Your choice is simple, Elowen. In this life, you either control, or allow yourself to be controlled. There is no middle ground. You have sensed your power, your mastery of the Earthsoul. Think of what it gives you. Think of how you feel when the golden threads react to your control. You could have more, Elowen, more power, more strength, just as your mother possessed before she was murdered. Follow her path, Elowen. Complete what she started. Take me to the Tree of Life.'

Something about his words, his tone transfixed Elowen. She *did* remember what it was like to control the Earthsoul, to feel as though she mastered everything around her. She remembered the rush of energy and power, the exhilaration. Her mother had led armies, her name feared across the lands. She could do the same…

No. She pushed the thought out of her mind. Her mother had been cruel, a monster. Elowen wanted to be different. She did not want power. She did not want dominion over others. Death she thought preferable. She looked up at Lord Lucien. 'No, I will not be another *Burilgi Maa*.'

He sighed. 'You are foolish, girl. I could cut off your hand, and use the Mark that way.'

Elowen physically jolted in alarm.

Ifueko coughed and wheezed, 'That would not help you. Only living flesh can open The Way.'

369

'Are you trying to trick me?' said Lord Lucien. 'Perhaps I should remove her hand to expose your bluff.'

Ifueko gave an enigmatic smile. 'If you do so, you will lose any chance of getting to the Tree of Life. You could ignore me, of course, but are you prepared to take such a risk?'

'Perhaps not, but there is another way, I believe. Elowen, you are certain in your refusal? This is the last offer I shall make.'

'I won't help you, kill me if you wish, but I won't help you. Nothing you can say can change my mind.'

'We shall see,' said Lord Lucien. He pulled a knife from his robes, strode toward Diggory and thrust the blade into the boy's stomach.

Diggory's mouth opened and he exhaled a rattling gasp. His face turned white and he fell, clutching his stomach.

'DIGGORY!' said Elowen. She knelt beside him, cradling him as he yelled in pain. Crying, she looked up at Lord Lucien. 'WHY? WHY KILL HIM?'

Lord Lucien appeared unmoved by her response. As he wiped his knife clean, he said to Ifueko, 'Is it not told that the fruit of the Tree of Life hold special properties?'

'Yes, so it is believed. Some have spoken of immortality, but that is nonsense. However, its juice can heal all wounds, cure any sickness.'

Lord Lucien turned to Elowen. 'Then I believe we have a way of saving your friend's life. Take me to the Tree of Life and as a reward, I shall allow you to take one fruit, just one, enough to heal the boy's injury.'

'How can I trust you?' said Elowen, wiping away her tears.

'What choice do you have if you wish to save your friend's

life? I took care where I stabbed him, but I doubt he has much more than an hour to live. He is far beyond the aid of any healer now. Only the wondrous fruit of the Tree of Life can save him. If you refuse, your punishment shall be to watch him die slowly, and in unimaginable agony. So, will you come with me?'

Elowen looked down at Diggory, his face pale and misshapen by pain. She did not trust the word of Lord Lucien. She did not want to lead him to the Tree of Life; she knew he would destroy it. But she could not watch her best friend die. If she refused any chance, however slim, to save Diggory's life, then all her struggles, all her trials, were wasted. She wiped hot tears from her eyes and said to Lord Lucien, 'Very well. Let us find the Tree of Life.'

CHAPTER SEVENTEEN

The Tree of Life

Holding her arms out for balance, Elowen edged across the narrow bridge. She glanced down but could not see the bottom; the gorge plunged into impenetrable darkness.

Lord Lucien followed Elowen—an unwelcome shadow. She hated being so close to him. He had caused her so much suffering, so much pain. Yet what hurt most of all was that his offer to join him, to betray all she had fought for, tempted her. She tried to deny it to herself, but a part of her, a part she detested, *had* wanted to seize the power he had offered. Such weakness had consumed her mother, and Elowen loathed herself for almost succumbing to the same temptation. Lord Lucien not only represented the worst aspects of any person, intolerance, cruelty, a naked lust for power, but somehow he brought out the darkest aspects of her character too. She considered trying to push him from the bridge, but she knew he was too strong. He would kill her, and in so doing condemn Diggory to certain death. For the sake of her friend, she had to carry on.

Gusty dry winds buffeted Elowen, nudging her to the edge of the bridge. Walking cagily, she avoided toppling into the gorge. However, by the time she reached the far side, her legs shook with a life of their own. To calm herself, she closed her eyes and slowed her breathing. When she felt her muscles relax a little, she opened her eyes and saw the enormous wall of stone that girdled the mountain, an impenetrable slab blocking their path forward.

'Do not tarry, Elowen,' said Lord Lucien. 'The boy bleeds freely and his death is near.'

'But there's no way through.'

'You give up too easily,' said Lord Lucien. He walked up to the wall. He swept his hands over the rock, dislodging a cloud of dust. He took a step backwards and said, 'Look, there is a sign.'

Elowen came closer to the wall and saw carved into it an inverted triangle, matching precisely in proportions the shape burnt into her palm.

Lord Lucien pointed at her hand. 'If I guess correctly, that Mark is our way through the wall.'

Elowen remembered what Ifueko had said about the Mark. She placed the palm of her hand over the triangle carved into the wall. At first, the touch felt cold, then her hand warmed and beams of light burst through tiny cracks in the wall.

'Stand back, Elowen,' said Lord Lucien.

She did as he said, walking backwards, still staring at the wall. The beams of sharp light formed the outline of an arched door. Elowen heard a tremendous roar of stone grinding against stone, and to her amazement, the door opened outward, pushing out a wave of sand and rocks as it did so.

373

'*Well done*, Elowen,' said Lord Lucien. 'Let us advance.'

He strode through the open doorway, from which a path wound up a steep rock-strewn slope. Other than the whispering wind, there was silence. No birdsong. No calls or cries of animals. Elowen hurried to keep up, conscious that she had so little time left; she hoped she would be back in time to save Diggory, though she knew all else was lost.

*

Bo watched in despair as cannonballs ripped lanes through the ranks of the Old Believers. Smaller artillery pieces showered them with a deadly red-hot rain. Waves splashed around their legs, the foam coloured pink by blood. Crimson streams crisscrossed the beach. Corpses floated in the water. The horror of battle drove most of the Oroks' horses mad, and they scattered, running hither and thither. Using the last of their ammunition, the Janjičari fired a final, desultory musket volley. Bo yelled to the Satyr and Orok archers to keep firing, but their arrows made little impact on the overwhelming numbers of the enemy. Obscured by the acrid cloud of grey smoke, the Grand Army waited.

'This is a slaughter, not a battle,' said Valbrand to Bo, ducking as another cannonball roared overhead to land with a hiss in the sea.

'There is nothing we can do about their artillery,' said Bo. 'We have to wait until the barrage ends.'

'There might not be any of us left by the time that happens,' said Valbrand, firing another crossbow bolt towards the enemy ranks.

But the barrage ceased. From behind the swirling smoky mist, shouted orders echoed. Bo heard the clanking of armour and the thumping of thousands of booted feet. Then out of the mist, Bo saw line after line of pikemen, advancing in tightly controlled formations, marching to the rhythmic tempo pounded out by drummers.

Valbrand spat onto the ground, wiped his mouth and fastened the silk ribbon around his neck. 'Aye, this is more like it. We'll all die this day, but I'm taking some of these devils with me.'

The archers fired more arrows, felling a few of the pikemen but not enough to slow or break their lines. At the last, the pikemen sped their advance, the sharpened tips of their weapons thrusting into the defending ranks. Bo saw many of his warriors skewered by the pikes, their sickening cries ringing in the air. He narrowly dodged one pike, ducked under another and stabbed his sword into the nearest opponent, slaying him with the blow. Others followed his example, driving into the enemy with swords and axes. Bo heard the throaty yells and curses of the Khiltoi as they charged and leapt at the enemy, routing foes with their sheer strength and fury, their battle-lust at its peak. Valbrand, Jeimuzu and Moriko fought by his side; and Bo grasped they did so to protect and guard him.

Shaken by the ferocious counter-attack, the pikemen retreated several yards, leaving space for bands of musketeers to push through and fire a volley. Bo felt a sting in his leg; a lead ball had scraped his skin and a patch of blood widened. He had no time to think about it. Relying on raw fear and strength, he fought foe after foe, each struggle a brutal fight to the death. He stabbed, hacked, slashed, kicked, punched and gouged. Blood spattered his face, and left his hands slimy. He heard cries of anger and pain. Driven by the primal desire to survive, he ceased to view those he fought as living beings—they were only hateful things to be butchered.

At last, a little space on the battlefield cleared around him, and he had a chance, just a few precious seconds, to try to work out what was happening in the battle. A core of the surviving Old Believers kept formation, but the rest had broken into smaller, far more vulnerable groups. Above them, ink-black clouds grew, hanging above the battle like massive weights ready to drop down.

Bo tried to formulate a plan to disrupt the enemy but as he did so, the musketeers and pikemen reformed to leave a clear lane through their ranks. Along the lane floated a head made of stone, a head without a body or limbs. Fiery, filthy smoke issued from its nostrils. The Khiltoi wailed in despair as it approached, and Bo heard their cries of '*Námhaid*! *Námhaid*!'

Bo knew another name for the stone monstrosity: Egregore. The Old Believers backed away from the Egregore, their courage draining. Some Oroks loosened their precious remaining arrows at the Egregore, as did the Khiltoi with their slingshots, but the missiles bounced harmlessly off the grotesque stone head and did nothing to hinder its advance.

The Egregore's eyelids opened to reveal two repulsive glowing orbs and its lips parted. A scream struck Bo's head like a punch. The rest of the Old Believers were similarly afflicted—many fell to the ground, writhing in agony and misery. The Grand Army advanced, ready to crush their helpless, defenceless opponents. One thought came to Bo. 'All is lost.'

Deafened and confused, movement caught his eye. He saw a Khiltoi warrior sprinting towards the Egregore, yelling as though to push away the pain. Corcoran. With an athletic leap, he threw himself at the stone head and climbed on top. He brandished his club and with savage swings, ruined both of the Egregore's eyes. Hissing molten metal spurted out of the eye-sockets, and smoke and pungent vapours erupted from the gaping mouth. With an angry moan, the Egregore dropped to the ground, and Corcoran just leapt off in time to avoid being crushed as it rolled over several times before it stopped.

Spared the agony of the Egregore's screams, Bo and the rest of the Old Believers cheered. Corcoran raised his broken, charred club in triumph. But three white shapes moved towards him as swiftly as smoke carried by wind. Redeemers. The Khiltoi beat off the first attack and sent one of the Redeemers sprawling with a kick to the midriff, but the other two were upon him. Bo saw the wintry, silvery glint of their swords as they hacked Corcoran down.

The other Khiltoi warriors howled and moaned in despair, but Bo barely had time to absorb the loss when he saw dozens more Redeemers striding through the ranks of musketeers and pikemen.

'This is the final assault, Prince Asbjorn,' said Arigh Nasan. Unhorsed, the Khan's face and hands were smeared with blood. 'If you have a master strategy, this would be a good time to deploy it.'

Bo looked on in despair. The remnants of his army huddled in a tight group, now numbering hundreds rather than thousands. The Redeemers advanced, closely followed by rank after rank of pikemen, dragoons and musketeers. Drums pounded. Trumpets shrieked. The enemy sang triumphant hymns.

'At least this business is going to be over, once and for all,' said Valbrand.

'Their numbers are too great, and our warriors are spent,' said Jeimuzu as he rallied the surviving Kojin warriors around him. 'There is no hope for us now.'

'Then we must fight without hope,' said Bo. Perhaps the certainty of defeat and death made him reckless; with his doom decided, there was nothing left to fear. He drew a deep breath and bellowed, a shout of anger, of frustration, but above all, of defiance. He waved his sword, his father's sword, the sword of a king. With his comrades following, he charged into the enemy.

*

Lord Lucien broke into a run. Elowen drove herself to keep up with him, sweating heavily and breathing hard. The Earthsoul pulsed through her, so strong that it sent painful spasms into her muscles and bones. Her head pounded. But need pressed her forward, and she whispered to herself, 'For Diggory—keep going for Diggory.'

Lord Lucien stopped. He stood motionless, his back to her, his robes rustled in the wind. Elowen scrambled up the slope towards him, and there in front of her, in a sunken, circular dell, stood the Tree of Life. Her excitement, her relief, vanished, as the tree's appearance did not match her imagination. It stood forlorn, leafless, stark and sepulchral, with branches, knotted and dry like sun-bleached bones. Peeled gouges of bark hung limply from the bloated trunk. Elowen felt the life of the tree, but only faint, nimble flickers of energy pushed through its deep roots, like flickering candles glimpsed from afar.

Lord Lucien unsheathed his sword. 'So, this is the secret hidden for so long. This tree has grown since the formation of the world, helping to spawn monstrosities and demons that have cursed the Mother Church and mocked the Almighty. No more. When the tree is dead, there shall be order, with nature finally shackled and tamed. I dream of roads stretching across the Known World, slicing through pestilent forests, linking great cities. I have seen plans of machines that can transport people and cargo faster than any boat or horse-drawn cart. This is the future, Elowen. Men protected by the benevolent rule of Prester John.'

Elowen ignored his words and pointed despairingly at the barren Tree of Life. 'There's no fruit.'

'So it seems,' said Lord Lucien.

'But how can I help Diggory now?'

'You cannot. Do not look at me so harshly. His death is *your* fault.'

'You stabbed him, you're the murderer.'

'I did what was necessary to reach the Tree of Life. Your stubbornness led to this. The likes of Lord Hereward and Baba Yaga filled your mind with fantasies, lies and corrupted versions of history. You have not the sense to judge

379

what is right and what is wrong. You have shown yourself unworthy of your mother. You have strayed from the path you were meant to take.'

Elowen wiped tears from her face. She stepped closer to Lord Lucien. His metallic scent filled her nostrils. 'My mother was *Burilgi Maa*, a willing servant of Prester John, and so I'm proud to be unworthy of her. You are the corrupted one; you seek only to enslave, to destroy everything that you cannot control. You say you are a Messenger, but you've spread nothing but hate and ignorance. *You* strayed from the path. You were meant to bring peace, to help people.'

Lord Lucien pointed the tip of his sword at Elowen's chest. 'Why should I help anyone after what happened to me? When the Church discovered my identity, that I was a Messenger, they tortured me. When Prester John rescued and restored the Church to its true mission, he saved me from a brutal death. I have seen the true face of Man—it is bestial, devoid of mercy.'

'You think you're the only one who has suffered?' said Elowen. She rolled up her sleeves to show the scars on her arms. '*I* have suffered. My friends suffered, some killed. But unlike you I have not given up. You're weak, a coward. I'm stronger than you.'

Lord Lucien laughed. 'Your insults mean nothing to me. I have triumphed, Elowen.'

The anger building within Elowen finally broke. She wanted to kill him. With all her strength, she tried to summon the Earthsoul's power. She saw the golden threads weaving and spinning around her. Focusing her mind, she tried to direct all the energy towards Lord Lucien, she wanted to crush him, destroy him. But her fury impaired her control; the golden threads resisted her, slipping through her fingers like water...

She lay flat on her back, groggy, confused. Her ears hissed. Her vision blurred. She lifted her head, hearing the cold, hollow laughter of Lord Lucien. He stood over her. 'You underestimate me, child. With the infusion of Cold Iron, I am stronger than ever, too strong for your golden threads.'

'Then why don't you kill me, and have it over with?'

'I wish to see your reaction as I slay your precious Tree of Life. You are a witness to the birth of a new world, though not one you will live long enough to enjoy.'

With that, he marched down towards the tree, brandishing his sword. He chanted in *Manus* as he advanced, his intent clear: to plunge his hideous blade of Cold Iron into the bark, to kill the Tree of Life. Still weak, still dizzy, Elowen scrambled after him; she knew she had to stop him.

Lord Lucien stopped directly in front of the Tree of Life. He placed both his hands on the handle of his sword and swung it backwards, ready to strike the trunk. Elowen charged at him. Her vision altered. Instead of the greys and browns of the world around her, the golden threads burst into incandescence. They formed a halo around the tree. She saw a dark shape, a silhouette: Lord Lucien. His movements were slow, as though he moved through deep water. His blade formed a spectral outline, a void. With all the force she could muster, she hurled herself between the sword and the tree. She felt a tremendous blow against her right arm and torso, which knocked the breath from her body. The golden threads extinguished. The real world flooded back. Elowen opened her eyes, trying to make sense of the images around her. Lord Lucien stood over her, his sword still in his hand. In a wavering voice, he said, 'How…you moved so swiftly…how…'

Rivulets of blood splashed the lower trunk of the tree and dripped down towards the base and roots. A sickening realisation struck Elowen. Blood. *Her* blood. The blade had wounded her, not the tree. She looked at her body. A gash ripped across her right arm and chest. Blood splattered across her clothes; she saw pieces of ruined skin, or broken bones. She felt violent, mind-numbing pain. She felt cold, an iciness that touched her every muscle, bone and limb. Her vision faded…

She experienced a jolt, a surge of energy. The ground beneath her rumbled and trembled. The tree began to transform. The bark replenished, shedding old flaking pieces as a snake sheds a skin. Buds and leaves burst from every branch, all happening as though time moved from winter to summer in an instant. Golden threads danced around the trunk, their movements joyful. The Oracle's words returned to her. *Only blood will bring it back to life.*

Elowen heard a murmur, a mournful cry. 'NO!'

Lord Lucien fell to his knees. The sword dropped from his trembling hands. He pawed for it, trying to pick it up. He shivered fiercely. He ripped away his mask and once more Elowen looked upon his ruined face. His bloodshot eyes now widened in terror and confusion. His skin, already pasty, crinkled and slivers fell away. His body shrank, his bones cracked and snapped. He reached out his hands towards her, a gesture of pleading, but no further words came from his mouth, only a gruesome death rattle. Within seconds, his body crumbled to dust. Elowen saw pieces of Cold Iron within the dust, but they steamed, hissed, and melted. His white robes and mask remained—the only visible signs of his existence.

'I have done the deed,' whispered Elowen. Death would be her reward, deliverance from worldly pain. She had no more strength to resist. She closed her eyes. The darkness was a comfort. There would be no return: only the eternal sleep of death, and release from the torment of her wounds.

As life seeped from her, Elowen thought of her friends. She hoped they would be safe. And Diggory. *Diggory.* His name jogged a memory. She wanted to hear his voice again, laugh with him. She could not let him die, not while she still might be able to save him. She had to try. She opened her eyes and pulled herself to her knees, gasping with pain. She looked up at the tree. At first she saw only leaves and branches, but then, yes, not far above her, she spotted a splash of reddish orange. A fruit, just one. She managed to stand, her right arm hanging limply. Striving to remain conscious, she stretched out with her good arm and pulled the fruit from the branch. It filled her hand, shaped like a pear but bigger, softer and juicy to the touch. She held the fruit to her lips and took a small bite, juice dribbling down her chin. She dripped a little of the juice onto her wounds. For a second it stung abominably, but soon the pain dulled. Her skin fizzed and stretched to repair her wound. Soon, no sign of her injuries remained.

'I'll live,' she murmured, saying it to convince herself. The pain ceased. The fruit of the tree had healed her. She had to get back to Diggory as fast as she could. So, clasping the fruit like a precious holy relic, she left the Tree of Life and headed back to her friends.

*

The fever of battle consumed Bo. It distorted the world, leaving only the blunt sensations of the mayhem around him: crashing metal, the reek of blood, screams of the dying. Like the jaws of a glutinous predator, the ranks of the Grand Army slowly closed upon Bo and the Old Believers, and the Redeemers formed the vicious white teeth of those jaws. The Captains tried to marshal the fatigued warriors. At the heart of the battle, Jeimuzu and his fellow Kojin warriors cut swathes through the enemy. The Oroks rallied around Arigh Nasan, the Khan visible through the clouds of dust, smoke and heaving bodies. He felled opponent after opponent, inspiring those who followed him to fight on. Still bellowing orders to the Satyrs, Dwarfs and the other Centaurs, Archontos tussled with his foes, using sword, fists and hooves. Deprived of space in which to gallop, the Centaur fought as a wild animal caged.

A Redeemer confronted Bo, a cadaverous face with bloodshot eyes visible beneath his hood, his stench of putrefaction sickening. The Redeemer tried to decapitate Bo with his gleaming blade of Cold Iron, but in the cramped maelstrom of battle, he struggled to position himself and Bo managed to deflect the poorly aimed blow. With a vig-

384

our born of anger and desperation, Bo drove his own sword into his assailant's chest. The violent impact threw back the Redeemer's hood to reveal his white, hairless head. He made no visible or audible sign of pain, though blood dribbled from the corner of his mouth. Bo ripped out his sword and hacked the Redeemer's head from his shoulders.

However, any sense of relief for Bo proved to be fleeting, as the slaying of the Redeemer drew in more of the Brotherhood. In seconds, Bo found himself facing seven Redeemers, but he was not alone.

'Stand back, Prince Asbjorn!' came a muffled cry. Jeimuzu leapt in front of him, accompanied by Moriko. They charged the Redeemers, their long slender swords moving so swiftly Bo's eyes strained to follow their movement. They cut down one Redeemer, and a second, but for all the Kojins' fighting skills and courage, the Brotherhood were not easily daunted, and they had other weapons. As the two Kojin fought back to back, a Redeemer drew a carbine from his robes. As Bo saw him load the weapon, he cried out a warning to Jeimuzu and Moriko, but to no avail. The Redeemer fired the carbine at close range. An ear-splitting shot rang out. Bo watched in horror as the shot struck Jeimuzu in the neck, breaking through the leather armour. He fell. Moriko fought on alone. The Redeemers swarmed around her, like white waves ready to drown her.

Yelling in rage, Bo rushed at the Redeemers, waving his sword like a madman. He swung his sword at the nearest Redeemer but clouded by anger he judged his attack badly, and his opponent blocked the blow and knocked the blade from Bo's hand. Bo felt the flat side of the Redeemer's

385

sword strike him hard on the back and he fell to his knees. Icy hands gripped his neck from behind, he could not move. The Redeemer stood over him and in a loathsome voice said, 'Time to die, heretic.'

The Redeemer held the sword aloft, ready to bring it crashing down onto the top of Bo's head. Bo refused to close his eyes. He did not want to show fear. At the final moment of his life he wanted to be strong, defiant.

The Redeemer jerked, and the sword slipped from his trembling fingers, narrowly missing Bo's head. Gagging, retching, convulsing, the Redeemer fell to his knees. He stretched out his hands and moaned. To Bo's astonishment, the Redeemer's body withered; his limbs shrivelled and his bones cracked like dry tinder. And he was not alone—all the Redeemers succumbed, dying in seconds, diminished to gruesome piles of shrunken limbs and smoking ashes. An eerie silence descended over the battlefield. The ugly, boiling clouds above them broke apart, as though ruptured by strong winds but the wind had died. The Grand Army wavered, fear in the eyes of every musketeer, pikeman and dragoon, and they began to back away.

Valbrand dragged Bo to his feet. 'Look at them! Something's happening!'

Dazed, Bo said, 'She has done it! Elowen has completed her quest. She has saved the Tree of Life!'

*

Prester John watched as the Grand Army commenced the final surge against their treacherous foe. It would not be

386

long now. Soon, the heretic horde would be slain or driven into the sea. They would not be remembered. No monument, no tomb would mark their sacrifice. Without turning from the window, Prester John said to the *aristoi*, 'This is the moment of glory, the moment of providence.'

In response, the *aristoi* clapped and gave prayers of thanks.

A searing pain ripped away Prester John's smile and the breath from his body. The *aristoi* fell into stunned silence as the Patriarch staggered back several paces. The Cold Iron within him burned; steam issued through growing holes and splits in his flaking skin. With horror, he looked at his hands as they shrivelled to the size of an infant's, the dead skin dropping off like melted wax. Beside him, the surface of the mirror cracked and its frame buckled and snapped.

In the last agonising moments of his life, Prester John understood what was happening. As his brain played out its terminal functions, he formed one final image. The Tree of Life, reborn, rejuvenated. His mouth opened for the last time and he gasped, 'No, I cannot die.'

His crumbling body disintegrated, and death took the Patriarch of the Holy Mother Church.

*

The retreat of the Grand Army descended into a panicky rout. Many cast aside weapons and trampled over comrades in their desperation to flee. Others huddled together like frightened, bewildered children, wakened from a dream and struggling to cope with the glare of the conscious world.

'The power of the Null is broken!' Bo heard Valbrand

387

shout. 'They're free of Prester John, and they don't want to fight now!'

However, the Old Believers showed little mercy for their stricken enemy. Bo watched in horror as the battle-frenzied Oroks, Khiltoi, Satyrs, Dwarfs and Centaurs hacked down fleeing soldiers. He understood their lust for blood and revenge. They had seen friends and kin slaughtered, but Bo did not want cold-bloodied murder to tarnish their victory. He screamed out orders, 'Hold! Do not advance! Let them run!'

Eventually, his orders got through, but only after vengeful warriors slew dozens of the fleeing enemy. As the Army of the Old Believers gathered around him, Bo heard exultant shouts of 'victory!' and 'Prince Asbjorn!'

Casting aside old enmities, many Old Believers embraced warmly, or sang songs that rejoiced in their triumph and deliverance. Bo could not join in with them. As he scanned the battlefield and saw the countless corpses, the grisly aftermath left him empty and ashamed. So much blood spilt, so much loss, so much suffering. Now that the battle had passed, he felt once more the effects of the slow-working poison in his body: a gnawing pain in his stomach and a thirst no amount of water quenched. They had won the battle, and for that, he felt glad and relieved beyond words. Yet the future belonged to others.

A hearty slap on his back brought Bo back to the present.

'I would've thought the conquering hero might have a smile on his face,' said Valbrand.

'I am not a conquering hero,' said Bo. 'Many earned this victory, not least Elowen.'

'Aye, there's truth in that,' said Valbrand. 'But you kept us together when everything was falling apart. That any of us lived to savour this moment is down to you.'

Uncomfortable as ever with praise, Bo sought to change the subject. 'We must disarm the prisoners.'

Valbrand nodded. 'That should be easy enough. I don't think they've got much fight left in them.'

'And arrange for a raven to be sent to Omphalos,' continued Bo. 'We must bring tidings of our victory to Gnothi.'

Arigh Nasan, now mounted on one of the few surviving horses, rode up to them, accompanied by Archontos. 'Hail, Prince Asbjorn. The reign of Prester John has ended, a day I had feared would never come. This is a victory to resonate through the ages. However, I'm anxious about the Winter Palace. It is not yet conquered.'

'With the Grand Army vanquished, the enemy's stronghold should prove easy to storm,' said Archontos.

'I want no more bloodshed unless it cannot be avoided,' said Bo. 'Archontos, send a herald to the main gates and order him to request a parley.'

The Centaur looked uncertain. 'If that is your command.'

'It is. Perhaps we can achieve more by talk than by the sword.'

'Then I'll see it done,' said Archontos, before galloping away.

They herded the survivors of the Grand Army into closely guarded groups and soon hills of abandoned swords, pikes and muskets mushroomed across the battlefield. Meanwhile, escorted by Valbrand, Bo combed through the macabre debris of battle looking for Prince Jeimuzu. He had

389

seen the Kojin fall and wanted to take his body for a proper burial at least. After a brief search, they found him, with the few remaining Kojin warriors circled about him. To Bo's amazement, the Prince lived still, but any relief passed as he realised the Kojin's injuries were mortal.

Moriko sat beside her brother, holding his hand, chanting softly. Bo knelt next to her. Jeimuzu turned his head and said in a low voice, 'Prince Asbjorn, is the battle over?'

'Yes, your Highness,' said Bo. 'We have won a famous victory and the Kojin earned great renown.'

'The ancestors be praised,' said Jeimuzu, wincing as it was clear that every word pained him. Blood dribbled from his mouth. He forced a smile. 'The way of the Kojin warrior is death, and my death is not in vain.'

At first, Bo did not know how to reply. He stumbled over his words before finally saying, 'When songs and tales are told of this battle, you shall rightly be hailed as a hero, and the courage and war-skill of the Kojin shall be famous across many lands.'

'There are worse ways to be remembered,' he said, his voice fading. He used all his remaining strength to talk. He gripped his sister's hands and murmured, 'I go now to the Pure Land. This world grows dark. Only this I ask: return my body, and those of all Kojin warriors slain in this battle, to the Beauteous Isle, to be buried in the chambers of our hallowed forebears.'

Moriko wiped her eyes. 'You have more than earned that honour, dear brother. And I shall see it done.'

Jeimuzu smiled at his sister and said in the faintest whisper, 'The sea. I can hear the sea. She calls to me…'

390

And with that, Prince Jeimuzu died.

Moriko wept and laid her head upon his still chest, clutching her brother's sword. The other Kojin recited prayers, their faces stern.

'This is a bitter sacrifice,' said Bo.

Moriko straightened. 'Yes, but one my brother was prepared to make. Through his death and those of our fellow warriors, he helped our people to survive.'

'And not just your people,' said Bo. 'All have cause to thank the Kojin for the role you have played in this struggle. I hope now your people can dwell in peace, a peace you have given so much to earn.'

'I hope so,' said Moriko. 'My brother respected you, Prince Asbjorn, more than he ever told you.'

'I was privileged to have known and fought alongside him,' said Bo, his eyes misting with tears. 'You once told me you wanted to control your destiny. Well, you have done so, and have proven your valour and worth. I do not know what the story of the Kojin tribe will be in this new age we enter, but Princess Moriko, I know that you shall be at the heart of the story, and guiding all that is good about your people.'

Moriko took his hands in hers. 'I pray you become King of Prevennis, Asbjorn, and when such a day dawns, I pledge eternal friendship between your people and the Kojin.'

'The people of Prevennis could not receive a gift of greater value,' he said. King of Prevennis. The poison in his body ensured that it would remain a dream only, a mirage, *fairy gold* as his old nurse would have said. He looked at the corpse of Jeimuzu, shuddering as his mind struggled to comprehend that in a short time he too would lie lifeless. His throat dry, he said to Moriko, 'Know my prayers are with you and all the Kojin tribe.'

Bo stood, bowed to the fallen Prince, and left the Kojin to grieve. Accompanied by Valbrand, he strode away, his head lowered in thought.

Valbrand said, 'I had a few run-ins with that Prince Jeimuzu but he was a fine warrior.'

'Yes, the loss we have suffered bitters the taste of victory.'

Bo heard the heavy thump of hooves approaching. He looked up to see Archontos. The Centaur stopped in front of him. 'Our herald has returned and he brings important tidings. Prester John is no more. He died along with his foul Redeemers. His long tyranny is over.'

Valbrand gave out a hearty, war-like cheer. Bo's heart skipped. Prester John was dead. Could it be real? He tried to remain calm, rational. 'We need proof of his passing before we accept such a claim. And what of the *aristoi*? Do they offer surrender?'

Archontos' face soured. 'They have agreed to a parley, although they insist you go to the Winter Palace to meet them.'

Valbrand's face darkened. 'Sounds like a trick to me.'

'Let us hear what the *aristoi* have to say first,' said Bo. 'The power of the Null is finished, who knows how that will change things?'

'Null or not, some of them kings and queens are plain wicked,' said Valbrand. 'I say burn the cesspit down and have done with it. If they want to stay inside while that happens, I'll shed no tears.'

'No more fighting and killing,' said Bo. 'I shall go to the *aristoi*.'

'If it is a trick, you'll be vulnerable,' said Valbrand. 'You should not go in alone. I'll come with you.'

'Can I trust you to behave?'

Valbrand laughed. 'When have I ever let you down?'

Not entirely reassured, Bo said, 'Very well, but others should come too. We have fought in the name of the free peoples of this world, and they should be present at this moment. Send word to Arigh Nasan, he should represent the Oroks. Archontos, you must attend on behalf of the Eldar.'

The Centaur bowed. 'It would be an honour.'

Bo looked up at the Winter Palace, which gave the impression of being larger and more formidable than before. He felt shooting pains through his stomach; the poison worked its dark magic. Bo knew his time was running out.

- CHAPTER EIGHTEEN -

Flight to the Sea

Exhilarated, Elowen ran, feeling no fatigue, no pain. The mountain shook, as though some overwhelming force from the bowels of the earth strained to reach skyward.

The golden threads danced around her, urging her forward, filling her with strength and vitality. She sprinted across the narrow bridge, sure in her every footstep, sure in her balance and control. The bridge trembled as she crossed and when she reached the far side of the gorge, she turned to see it collapse. She had no time to consider it further though, as she spotted her friends and the *Etisa*. She yelled out in joy when she realised they were still alive. Elowen saw the remains of the Redeemers: white robes, smouldering piles of dust, burnt bones.

Diggory lay cradled by Batu and Bryna. When he realised Elowen had returned, Black Francis went to embrace her, but she ignored him and came to Diggory's side. His face was pale and his breathing shallow. He looked at her and opened his eyes, slits only. 'You…came.'

'He is close to the end,' said Ifueko, his own wound heavily bandaged.

'I can save him,' said Elowen. She held the fruit over the wound in his stomach and squeezed.

'Be sparing,' said Ifueko. 'We may need more.'

Heeding his words, Elowen allowed a little more juice to fall onto Diggory's wound. She opened his mouth and dripped more into his mouth. He winced and groaned, but colour returned to his cheeks and his wound healed, just as Elowen's had done.

'By God, it's a miracle,' said Black Francis.

Still shaking and clearly confused, Diggory looked at Elowen. 'Am I dead?'

She laughed, and cried happy tears. 'No, not yet.'

'Truly you are the *Okhuoba*,' said Ifueko.

'What about Lord Lucien?' said Batu.

Elowen told them what happened at the Tree of Life. Black Francis grinned, 'So that's what befell the Redeemers. I shan't mourn them, or Lord Lucien for that matter.'

'I wonder what this means?' said Batu. 'Dare we hope that all Redeemers are so afflicted?'

'And what about the battle?' said Bryna. 'Perhaps Prester John himself is dead.'

'It is to be hoped so,' said Batu.

'Come, Ifueko,' said Elowen. 'Let me heal your wound.'

'No, it is not serious and it will mend well enough,' said the *Etisa*. He pointed to the fruit. 'Save it for someone more gravely wounded. The Way is now blocked to you, Elowen, and you can never return to the Tree of Life. That fruit is all you have left. It'll stay fresh for a few days to come at least, and in that time, you may cure many wounds. Use it wisely.'

395

Ifueko gestured to the other *Etisa*, who brought bags filled with gold and jewels.

Black Francis gasped and joked, 'Have you been raiding the tombs?'

Ifueko gave him a hard look. 'The tombs are sacred and remain forever untouched and unblemished by our hands. These riches come from the treasury houses, left in vanity by wealthy supplicants of civilisations long gone to buy favour in this life from their gods. They are wasted here, and could be used for a greater purpose. *Okhuoba*, I give these to you.'

'There must be a fortune there!' said Diggory.

'Yes, with such riches, one could live in luxury, but that is not why I give them to you,' said Ifueko. 'I believe you will use this wealth for good, to help others, and not spend rashly or hoard greedily. It is an important responsibility.'

Elowen nodded.

'And this you must take too, for the fruit,' he said, passing Elowen a painted clay jar. 'The juice of this fruit is more valuable than any riches, remember that, *Okhuoba*.'

'I will,' said Elowen. She placed the fruit inside the jar.

Black Francis said, 'I hate to rush things along, knowing you're all tired, but I'm mighty anxious to get back to the *Husker Du*. If Lord Lucien and those Redeemers found us here, there's a chance they landed at the same place in the Wild Coast we did, and that could put my boys in terrible danger.'

'Yes, it is time for you all to leave this place,' said Ifueko.

'Aren't you coming with us?' said Elowen. 'Surely your duty is finished?'

396

'You no longer need our aid, but we continue to guard the Way, as we always have. Our vigilance never ceases. You have saved the Tree of Life, but other perils will emerge in the ages to come. Too easily forgotten are the gifts of Earthsoul.'

As they prepared to leave, Elowen said to Diggory, 'Are you sure you can manage?'

'I'm fine,' said Diggory.

'But it's a long and hard walk back to the coast,' said Elowen.

Ifueko cleared his throat. 'There is no need to walk.'

He rose to his feet and stood in front of the statues of the four griffins. He spoke to them using words that made the ground shake and a cloud of dust shook from the statues. Their sun-baked surface changed, the reddish clay turning into feathers and skin. The griffins stretched their taloned legs and spread their wings wide. They glared at Elowen and her companions, their expressions haughty and pitiless.

'Everybody run!' said Black Francis, but Ifueko signalled him to keep still.

'Stay where you are, they will not harm you,' said the *Etisa*. '*Okhuoba*, you must approach.'

Diggory clasped her arm. 'Don't do it, Elowen.'

'Trust me,' said Ifueko. 'You are safe. As the Tree of Life is reborn, so life flows through them once more.'

Slowly, reluctantly, Elowen approached the griffins. As she did so, to her surprise they lowered their heads.

'They recognise you as the *Okhuoba*,' said Ifueko.

Elowen stroked the feathered chest of one of the griffins and she *Linked* with the creature.

397

You save tree. You give us life.

The griffin spread his wings again. Daunted by the creature's size and power, Elowen backed away a little.

We want to fly. Too long since we last flew. We help you perhaps.

'Could you carry us to the coast?' said Elowen.

Yes. Swifter and stronger than eagles are we.

Elowen turned to her companions, unable to resist a smile. To Diggory she said, 'I was wrong earlier. It looks as though our flying days aren't over.'

*

Elowen whooped and yelled in delight. The griffin soared at tremendous speed, the world below distant, the hills, trees and plains impossibly small, like a child's toys. The griffin's intoxicating energy raced through Elowen. The rhythmic *whoosh, whoosh* beat of its wings rose above the roaring wind. Its glossy feathers shone like stars.

She clung to the griffin's back, just behind its wing joint. The bags of gold and jewels, and the clay jar containing the fruit from the Tree of Life, were tucked in beneath her. Diggory in turn held tightly to Elowen's back, his arms wrapped round her and eyes firmly shut. He repeated, 'We're going to fall. We're going to fall.'

Giddy with the flight, and from the freedom and jubilation of completing her quest, Elowen laughed. The griffin took her away from the Tree of Life, and from months of terror and anguish. The rest of the griffins followed, each carrying one of Elowen's other companions. She wondered what Bryna, Batu and Black Francis made of their journey.

398

Soon the coast came into sight and Elowen spotted the settlement of Salvation and the surf-beaten shore. Further out, and tiny upon the blue waves, bobbed the *Husker Du.* It was safe. She turned excitedly to Black Francis but movement in the sky caught her eye and from the west she saw three dark spots approaching. She felt a stab of fear as she recognised them: *Kongamato.*

The griffin sensed her fear and *Linked* with her.

They no hurt you.

The griffin's confidence was well founded. Rather than attack, the *Kongamato* performed acrobatics, climbing and diving at breath-taking speed, even flying upside down for stretches. They rejoiced in the appearance of the griffins, as if balance had returned to their world.

The griffin landed close to the wall. The inhabitants of Salvation emerged, their fear replaced by astonishment and joy as they watched Elowen and Diggory dismount.

Diggory puffed out his cheeks. 'And I thought Lárwita's balloon was frightening.'

Elowen laughed and placed a steadying hand on his arm. 'It was quite an experience.'

The other griffins landed, and with varying degrees of difficulty, their passengers dismounted. Bryna and Batu looked too stunned to speak. Black Francis, red-faced and wide-eyed, said, 'In all my days…never seen…in all my days…'

As one, all four griffins lowered their heads, and in a smooth motion leapt skywards and flew back inland.

Ayanmwen approached Elowen with outstretched arms and knelt at her feet, clasping her hands. 'You are our deliverer, a bringer of miracles.'

399

Elowen gently pulled him upright and passed him one of the bags. 'This will help you in the days to come.'

Ayanmwen unfastened the bag and gasped when he looked at the contents. 'You give this to us freely?'

'Freely and happily,' said Elowen. 'When your ships are rebuilt and you trade again, it will help you to build your colony here—a proper home, a safe place for your children, for the generations to come.

Ayanmwen leant forward and kissed Elowen on both cheeks. 'There are no words…'

Black Francis roared with joy when he saw the *Husker Du* still moored out to sea. 'Ah, seeing her again cures any aches or pains. We need to get to her but that won't be easy with our dinghy sunk.'

'We have a canoe,' said Ayanmwen. 'It is crude, fashioned from a hollowed-out tree trunk. We never dared use it when the *Kongamato* haunted us, but it is sturdy and should serve your purpose well enough.'

A sudden disturbance gripped Elowen, and the golden threads, which had lain as a subtle glowing edge to all living things, exploded into radiance. The world around her peeled away. Visions came to her. She saw an immense palace of wood surrounded by the ghastly debris of war: dead bodies, injured horses, blood-smeared grass. She saw Khiltoi. She saw Oroks. But she saw nothing of the enemy. Then she knew: the battle was won.

The vision jolted her again, drawing her to a figure prostrate on the ground. It was Bo. He looked close to death, with his normally white skin a sickly green pallor. A cold feeling trickled through her body, a poisonous sensation.

400

The vision ceased with a blinding but mercifully brief pain in her head.

She said aloud, 'I have to save him.'

Her companions looked at her with alarm and concern. Diggory grasped her arms to steady her and said, 'Elowen, what's wrong?'

'It's Bo, he is in danger.'

'But…how would you know that?' said Diggory.

'I have seen it.'

Black Francis said, 'You are tired, it's a swoon, perhaps you are sickening—'

'I am not sick,' said Elowen. 'I saw Bo. It was real. It was not a dream.'

'I believe her,' said Bryna to the others. 'Through the power *bládh*, she can see far. Elowen is a *bana-buidhseach*, if she says her sight carries across oceans, I do not doubt her.'

'Even if Bo is in danger, what can we do about it?' said Diggory.

'We have to go to the Winter Palace at Inganno,' said Elowen.

'Elowen, you cannot save everyone,' said Batu. 'If it is Prince Asbjorn's fate to die bravely in battle, it must be so. Many have had worse partings from this life.'

'I do not accept *fate*,' she said. 'And I do not think he suffers from the wounds of battle. Something else ails him, something from which he can be saved.'

'How?' said Diggory.

'With this,' said Elowen, tapping the clay jar she carried.

Black Francis scratched his beard. 'I've learnt not to dismiss your words, Elowen. If Bo is in danger, that troubles me more than I can say, and I for one won't stand back if there's anything we can do to save him. We'll do what we can, lass, that I promise you.'

*

The enormous wooden gates of the Winter Palace swung open. With some trepidation, Bo, Valbrand, Archontos and Arigh Nasan approached.

'If they mean us harm we're caught like rats in a trap,' said Valbrand.

'We shall find out soon enough,' said Bo. He felt weak, and knew it was not fatigue from the battle. The poison spread through his body, corrupting and destroying it from within. He licked his parched lips, and a foul salty taste filled his mouth.

A man greeted them. He sported a knee-length shirt worn over his trousers and tied at his waist by a leather belt. He fiddled nervously with the cords of his coarse linen cape. He bowed low, his forehead almost touching the ground. 'I welcome you, Prince Asbjorn, noble leader and victorious commander. And of course, I extend my welcome to your worthy companions.'

The warm words surprised Bo and it took him a moment to gather his thoughts. 'The *aristoi* asked to speak to me, I believe.'

'Yes, it is so, my Lord,' said the man. 'I am but a humble servant, pray let me take you to their Excellencies.'

The servant turned and gestured for Bo and his companions to follow. Guards loitered by the gates; nervous and edgy, they kept their distance like shy children, all with the same glazed, puzzled expressions. Bo noticed how the guards picked at their Nulls, as though they had only noticed them for the first time.

Once through the gates, Bo and Valbrand walked into a huge courtyard thrown into shade by the palace. Bo peered up at the towers, spires and cupolas. On the walls above, the ironwork gutter spouts had been carved into leering devil's heads.

Hundreds of soldiers—dusty, bloodied survivors of the battle—loitered in the courtyard. They stepped aside to let the visitors pass, content to watch in uneasy silence.

'Look at their faces, they are like scared lambs,' said Archontos. 'We have nothing to fear from them.'

'We cannot be sure,' said Bo. 'Just because they have been released from the power of the Null it does not mean they will be any less hostile. Remain vigilant.'

The servant led them into the palace and along a wide corridor richly adorned with tapestries and carpets. Crystal chandeliers hung from the ceiling. Icons of Prester John and the Saviour, all made from gold and ornamented with jewels, filled the many alcoves. Bo, his clothes stained with mud and blood, felt like a beggar.

Archontos trotted through the corridor, smirking at the mess left by his muddy hooves. Arigh Nasan glared at the riches around them; sickened visibly by such ostentation and decadence. For his part, Valbrand appeared rapt by the treasures they passed. Wide-eyed, he whispered to Bo, 'There's gold enough here to keep a man rich for a hundred lifetimes.'

403

'We are not here for *gold*,' said Bo.

'More's the pity,' said Valbrand.

They followed the servant up a steep, broad stairway. Archontos ascended awkwardly, his hooves clattering. The servant stopped in front of a tall doorway. 'The *aristoi* await you inside.'

The servant turned to leave but Bo grabbed his arm. 'Is there a scribe here?'

He looked at Bo with a puzzled expression. 'Yes, Old Verfasser serves that function for the *aristoi*.'

'Then bring him here, please,' said Bo. 'Tell him to bring quill, ink and parchment, and tell him to wait by this door until I call for him.'

Looking perplexed, the servant nodded and slipped away. Bo said to his companions, 'It would be best if you let me do the talking. I'll go in first.'

Bo knew he faced another battle, his final battle, but one that would be fought with wits and words rather than swords. His body toiled against the poison, but he steeled himself. Taking a deep breath, he stepped inside. In opulence, the room surpassed everything they had seen before. Frescoes of dazzling design and intricate detail. An icon of the Saviour, which glistened as though fire burned within it. A throne perched upon a carpeted dais, and at the far end of the room, windows allowed shards of dusty golden light to enter. A sickly smell of burning hung in the air.

Kings, queens, bishops and lords from lands afar filled the room, all stood in expectant silence. As Bo entered, they bowed or curtseyed politely, and one within their number said, 'Welcome, Prince Asbjorn.'

The voice belonged to a tall man with a prominent, jutting jaw. He wore a black patterned doublet with full black breeches, black stockings, and flat black shoes. In one hand, he carried a wide-brimmed black hat. With the other hand, he picked at the red skin around his Null. 'Greetings, Prince Asbjorn. I am King Philippus of Salvinia.'

Bo had heard the name of Philippus of Salvinia before. He recalled distant childhood conversations. *Philippus*. His mother's brother. 'I never expected to meet you, Uncle.'

King Philippus smiled. 'I am gratified you recognise my name, dear nephew. Sadly your father's adherence to the heretic faith kept us apart during your childhood, but I give praise to the Almighty that finally we meet.'

'You have an odd family, Bo,' said Valbrand as he swaggered into the room, shadowed by Arigh Nasan and Archontos.

The façade of politeness maintained by the *aristoi* fractured as Bo's companions entered, especially when they beheld Archontos. Bo noticed their sneers and ill-favoured whispers. A bishop said, 'We invited only you, Prince Asbjorn, not these…others.'

'Whatever you have to say to me, you must say to them too,' said Bo. 'They are here on behalf of all those who have suffered under the scourge of Prester John. If you refuse to speak with them present, this assembly is over.'

King Philippus held up his hands. 'Let us not be hasty. We are here to talk, not to fight. There is much to be resolved, and hot words can only lead to regret later on.'

'We have received tidings that Prester John is dead,' said Bo. 'Have you proof of his demise?'

405

'God forgive me for saying it, but little of the Patriarch remains,' said Philippus. He gestured for the other *aristoi* to stand back. There, in front of the window, Bo saw a melted lump of metal and glass. Beside it lay a pile of dust, withered bones, steaming fragments of metal and a bejewelled habit.

'So, he truly is dead,' said Valbrand. He looked at Philippus and tapped his forehead. 'How does it feel now, with Prester John gone and the Null powerless?'

'The Patriarch has ascended to heaven and we mourn his loss,' said Philippus, his head lowered. 'A new age is upon us, one full of uncertainty and fear. Without the wisdom of Prester John to guide us, I fear disharmony, war and famine. In such times we need leadership, we need one who is strong enough to steer us through the difficulties ahead, and to ensure the sanctity of the Mother Church. We need a new Patriarch.'

'You want another tyrant?' said Bo. 'And I suppose you are offering to take the throne?'

'It is for God to choose the successor to Prester John,' said a bishop. 'It is through His providence that we *aristoi* work.'

'I am King of Salvinia, but it is not God's will that I should wear the Patriarch's crown,' said Philippus. 'Another must continue the work of Prester John.'

'His time is over,' said Arigh Nasan. 'Why speak of continuing his legacy? The thrall of Cold Iron is broken. You are free now, as are all who wear the Null. Why do you wish to return to oppression?'

'Because they are afraid,' said Archontos. 'For years the

406

aristoi assented to the word of Prester John, who told them what to do, whatever the cost. They gained power, and now they fear that it is going to be taken away.'

'Be silent,' said Philippus. 'Your kind are not welcome here, *Centaur*. Through mere fortune you have triumphed, but do not think the Mother Church and Holy Empire will tolerate your infestation. The work Prester John started shall be finished. God wills it.'

Archontos reared up on his hind legs in fury, and only a shout from Bo prevented the Centaur from charging at the King. Bo said, 'This does not help, my friend. Do not rise to their provocation.'

'Prince Asbjorn, how can you bear to keep such company?' said Philippus. 'You do not belong with them. You have demonstrated your strength, your leadership. Join with us. We are prepared to offer you power greater than you have ever imagined.'

'I only came here to receive your surrender,' said Bo. 'Now it seems my time has been wasted, as you offer only foolish words.'

King Philippus shook his head. 'I have failed to persuade you, but there is one who might be able to make you see sense. Good Queen, dear sister, show yourself.'

From behind a group of bishops and lords, a figure to that moment unseen by Bo, slipped through to stand beside King Philippus. When he beheld her, Bo was dumbstruck. A single word escaped from his mouth. 'Mother!'

'Yes, my son, I am here,' she said. She carried a crown.

The sight of his mother inflamed so many emotions within Bo that he did not know how to react. Anger, hatred, guilt, shock and, in the smallest of doses, love assaulted him. He tried to find words but failed. He felt the mere presence of his mother stripped away his identity of being a man, a warrior, a leader. He returned to being a child.

In a voice soft and soothing, a voice he had never heard as a child except for when she spoke to her firstborn Haakon, she said, 'You have been through so much, Asbjorn. It has wounded my heart to think of your suffering. Truly, there can be no deeper pain for a mother than to be parted from her child, from her own flesh and blood.'

'You…you allowed Haakon to sentence me to death.'

'It was a difficult time after your father died—'

'You murdered him.'

She clasped her hands together. 'I understand your anger but there were so many…misunderstandings. We all spoke harsh words unmeant and performed deeds ill-considered. But by the grace and mercy of God you, my only living son, are returned to me. And how you have risen in stature. A feared warrior, the head of an army. Truly you are worthy.'

'Worthy of what?' said Bo.

Smiling, she held up the crown. 'Worthy to wear this. Worthy to become Patriarch of the Mother Church.'

Bo laughed bitterly. 'I think you have lost your wits, Mother.'

'Take the crown and with it shall come power beyond measure. Your every wish fulfilled. Rule, my son, rule with me by your side. For who could have a wiser, more trusted adviser than his very own mother?'

'Your mother speaks the truth, Asbjorn,' said King Philippus. 'And you can always trust on the support of the

Crown of Salvinia. The Ulsacro will be yours, along with armies and navies to command. Think not only of the Known World, but also of uncharted lands. Consider the New World, far to the west, a realm of godless, unlettered savages. You could lead them towards the enlightenment of the Almighty. Your name shall be worshipped across every land and every sea. Reject these heretics and Eldar demons that have such a hold on you. Complete the mission started by Prester John.'

Bo's head swam. Whether it was the effect of the poison, or the shock of all that he had heard, he could not tell. He found it hard to stand, and felt as though the floor moved. Patriarch of the Mother Church. He only had to reach out his hands and it was his. He would be the most powerful man in the Known World, his every desire, every whim within his grasp. Every surgeon, physician, herbalist and healer could be summoned to defeat the poison in his veins. Then freed of the poison, he would rule unchallenged, like a god, never again to be afraid, never again to feel inferior. It tempted him, but he knew it meant nothing, almost laughable, the crown offered to a dead man. The poison in his veins rendered the offer meaningless. He had but days to live. No crown, no throne, no armies could save him, and it would be vain and wasteful to try. For accepting the crown, even for a few days, would legitimize the rule of Prester John, and when Bo died, who would seize power in the vacuum that would surely follow? And even if life stretched out in front of him, did he want to take what was being handed to him so freely? To rule as a despot, as Prester John had done? What power would he have? Would he be the puppet of his mother and his uncle as they made their last, frantic reach for dominion? He said to his mother, 'Hand me the crown.'

The Queen's face lighted with joy. With eager, trembling hands, she passed the crown to Bo. He held it, running his fingers over the jewels and the smooth golden curves. Then slowly, deliberately, he dropped it at his feet. Bo heard gasps of alarm but ignored them. He stepped back, drew his sword and with all his strength brought it down upon the crown. The hard steel of his blade cut through the golden crown, slicing it into two pieces.

'Madman!' said King Philippus. 'What have you done?'

Bo scooped up the two pieces of the crown and hurled them at the King, who ducked in time. 'The *aristoi* are disbanded.'

'What right do you have to make such an edict?' said Philippus.

'The victorious army outside gives me the right,' said Bo. 'If you refuse to surrender, I swear to give the order for the Old Believers to attack, and you will not escape with your lives.'

His mother made one last attempt to persuade him. 'My son, these ill-bred swine have poisoned your mind. Why do you side with *them*? Should you not stand alongside your own kind?'

'*My own kind?*' said Bo, his voice rising. He refused to be intimidated. In the past, he would have cowered in front of such company. They were older, more powerful, blessed with the confidence of those born to rule. An innate deference would have controlled him. No longer. He had sur-

410

vived battles, witnessed things the *aristoi* could scarcely conceive. He had no reason to be afraid. No reason to back down. He said, 'Yes, I have witnessed what my own kind has done to this world. Enslavement. Corruption. Brutality. Intolerance. I want no part of it.'

'And you are so very different?' said Philippus. 'Behind your façade of righteousness, do you not plot to seize power?'

'I wish to claim nothing that is not mine to take,' said Bo, out of breath. 'If you surrender, you may return to your lands. I do not want your crowns or titles.'

'You would simply let us go?' said Philippus.

'Yes, for I do not want this war to continue. But perhaps those who followed you blindly during the tyranny of Prester John may now look upon your reign with a more critical eye. Be wary, *Uncle.*'

'You dare to threaten us?' said Philippus.

'Not at all,' said Bo. 'Your demise shall not come at my hand. But continue to neglect or ill-treat your own people, and perhaps they shall not be so forgiving.'

Bo heard a hushed voice from behind. It was Archontos. 'Bo, what are you doing? You are letting them go?'

'I refuse to end one war by beginning another,' said Bo. 'If this truly is a new age, I do not want to mark its birth with murder. Let their own people decide whether these kings are worthy to rule. So, I say to the *aristoi*, are my terms acceptable to you? Do you agree to return to your lands in peace? And above all, do you agree not to persecute the Eldar, those you refer to as *tainted ones*, and to allow them the freedom to live unmolested?'

411

The low, resentful murmurs turned into nods and mumbled agreements. Bo said, 'Then I am glad, but of course, such a pledge must be recorded, lest the promises you make today fade swiftly in your memories. Scribe, it is time!'

Verfasser, an old man dishevelled in poorly shaped robes, limped into the room. He carried a roll of parchment and squinted at Bo with small, rheumy eyes.

'I want you to record the conditions of this treaty,' said Bo.

The scribe unfolded the parchment over one of the tables and prepared to write.

'Treaty? Why do you speak of a *treaty*?' said Philippus.

'A treaty to bind you to the promises you have made and to protect the rights of all from oppression,' said Bo. He began to dictate the terms, which Verfasser diligently recorded.

'You expect us to freely sign this treaty?' said a bishop, once Bo finished.

'Yes, and remember you do so in the eyes of God. If you refuse, then the battle is not over and the forces that surround you shall be unleashed. If that happens, do not expect mercy.'

Bo watched as the *aristoi* muttered amongst themselves. He heard angry whispers; he sensed their frustration and thwarted ambitions. Bishops, queens and kings stared at him, with eyes resentful and full of hatred. Detecting their weakness, Bo decided to push them, to test their resolve. Despite the power of the *aristoi*, he knew he held the upper hand. 'My patience runs thin. Should I give my army the order to attack? They still thirst for blood.'

After one last look at the rest of the *aristoi*, as if to confirm his understanding of their will, Philippus lowered his head. 'No, the war is over. Scribe, give me the quill.'

With a lingering sigh, the King of Salvinia signed the treaty, his flowery signature rippled across the bottom of the parchment. One by one, the rest of the *aristoi* signed. When Queen Isabella approached to add her signature, Bo stepped in front of her. 'You have no need to sign.'

'I am exempt from this folly?'

'Yes, because from this day you are no longer the ruler of Prevennis.'

She looked at him with outrage and hatred. 'You seek to usurp me?'

'You betrayed the rightful King of Prevennis, and therefore have no right to sit upon the throne.'

'A throne you doubtless wish to seize.'

'That is not my decision,' he said, knowing that with so little time left to live, he would never be the King. 'In times past, the *Althing* of Prevennis elected a ruler, and so it shall be again.'

'What is to become of me?' she said, her lips trembling. 'Am I destined for the gibbet?'

'It would be deserved, perhaps, but I do not condemn you to death. Exile is your punishment, never to cross the borders of Prevennis again. I am sure that your brother will shelter you in this time of need.'

Queen Isabella spat at Bo. 'You were always hateful in my eyes, weak and foolish like your father. How I curse that you live and my Haakon is dead. It should not be so.'

'It is clear that the loss of the Null has not softened your

413

heart,' said Bo. 'I hope in exile you might learn some humility.'

'You show precious little mercy,' she said.

Bo smiled. 'I learnt that from my mother.'

*

Bo stood with Valbrand on the dunes that fringed the beach, watching as the long trail of monarchs, bishops, courtiers, servants and soldiers coiled out of the Winter Palace and headed for the lands beyond, the lights of their lamps flickering in the growing dark.

'Do you think this treaty of yours has any worth?' said Valbrand.

'I can only hope so,' said Bo, trying to conceal a wince as vicious pain knifed in his stomach. 'I hope that a few strokes of a quill can achieve more than a thousand strokes of a sword.'

'You know, some might say you were too merciful.'

'There are worse things to be accused of,' said Bo.

Valbrand puffed out his cheeks. 'Not for a leader, not in *these* times.'

'I hope we are coming into *better* times,' said Bo.

Valbrand snorted. 'You're always optimistic. But above all, I don't understand why you haven't claimed the throne. You're the rightful King of Prevennis, surely?'

Pain stabbed at Bo and he paused before answering. He wanted to tell Valbrand the truth, but struggled to find the right words. 'It is not as simple as that.'

'Perhaps such matters are beyond me,' said Valbrand. 'I

look forward to returning to Prevennis though. I've seen enough of foreign lands. Don't you want to go back?'

'Yes, more than anything,' said Bo, fighting through the pain to vocalise each word. The poison grew stronger. He had to tell Valbrand the truth. If he failed to do so now, he may never get another chance. 'But I will not see Prevennis again.'

'What? Do you have another adventure planned? By the crow's stinky wings, I would've thought—'

'I am dying, my friend,' Bo said, blurting out the words.

Valbrand looked at him as though he suspected a joke. 'That's not something to say lightly.'

'I do not say it lightly, it is the truth,' Bo said. He told Valbrand what had happened in Kakos, who stared at him open-mouthed.

'I do not believe this,' said Valbrand, clasping Bo's shoulders. 'There must be a cure for this poison. We have surgeons, healers, cunning-men—'

'It would do no good,' said Bo, the world around him starting to grow faint. 'I accepted the bargain offered by Zanash, and must take the consequences. I am afraid, but I am not bitter. The battle is won. Prester John is vanquished. I do not regret the bargain.'

Valbrand protested. 'But we cannot give up.'

He went on to say more but Bo could not hear him. His head pounded, a crashing sound thumped in his ears. His eyes juddered and he lost all focus. Vaguely, he thought he felt Valbrand holding him. He heard distant shouts of 'BO! BO!' And then he heard no more.

415

CHAPTER NINETEEN

Elowen's Choice

The *Husker Du* ploughed through the waves, sailing north, leaving the sun-baked lands of the Wild Coast behind.

Since their departure, the lusty winds proved kind, and in their howling, Elowen often fancied she heard the words and laughter of Epios and Ventus.

But for all their progress, Elowen's anxiety did not ease. She stood at the ship's prow, always looking forward. She longed to see land. She longed to reach the place where Bo lay stricken. She tapped the clay jar, and whispered a silent prayer that its contents would save his life.

'If these winds continue, we'll be at Inganno much sooner than I expected,' said Black Francis, joining her at the prow. 'My boys may be rum-soaked wastrels at times, but they're working as though the devil himself is chasing us. And this wind is like a gift from the gods.'

'I'm grateful to you and your crew,' said Elowen. 'I hope we get there in time to save Bo.'

'Aye, you'll get no arguments from me. I hold that lad in high esteem. I'd be mighty sore to lose him.'

The rest of the journey proved uneventful, and at last, as

the sun began to light up the sky one morning, a yell from the crow's nest announced, 'Land ahoy!'

Elowen strained to see. A vaporous icy fog skulked over the coast. As the *Husker Du* approached, Elowen saw a shape take form: a huge edifice, with towers, spires and wooden walls. She heard the heavy footsteps of Black Francis and without turning said, 'Is that the Winter Palace?'

'Aye, that it is,' said Black Francis. 'I don't want to take any risks so we'll anchor a safe distance away.'

Once the *Husker Du* had anchored, Elowen went ashore, accompanied by Black Francis, Diggory, Batu and Bryna who had all insisted on going along. Before they had left the Wild Coast, Ayanmwen gave them the canoe as a gift to replace the dinghy destroyed by the *Kongamato*. Thick, high waves rolled towards the beach and the journey was rough, with the canoe lurching and dropping in an alarming fashion. Salty sea spray splashed onto Elowen's face. With his sweat steaming in the chilly air, Black Francis worked his paddle with fury and broke through the watery chains that tried to drag them into the depths.

At last, the canoe's keel grounded upon the beach. Elowen leapt out, her feet sinking in the foam and wet sand. Shadowy figures stood on the beach, their features indistinct. As they approached, Elowen recognised they were Orok warriors. Batu hailed them and the Oroks welcomed him. To Elowen's joy, Arigh Nasan was amongst them.

'Elowen, you are a walking, breathing miracle,' said the Khan, embracing her. 'You have saved us all.'

'I played a small part,' said Elowen.

'You are modest, and I have no doubt Diggory aided you

417

with distinction,' said Arigh Nasan. 'The Khiltoi brought me tidings of Chinua. I mourn him greatly.'

'He died as a warrior and shall be feted by the ancestors,' said Batu.

Arigh Nasan nodded. 'Elowen, your arrival is timely, for word reached us that Gnothi is coming here with a host from Omphalos. Your courage is sure to be celebrated, as is deserved.'

'Forgive me, Arigh Nasan, but I am anxious to find Prince Asbjorn,' said Elowen.

The Khan's face darkened. 'I have grave tidings.'

Elowen's stomach lurched as she saw the expression on his face. 'Is he…dead?'

'No, but he has only hours remaining and I fear those hours will bring him little but pain and torment. He fights the poison bravely, but bravery is not enough. Tirelessly our healers have worked, yet no medicine, no charm, no prayers have helped him.'

'What happened?' said Black Francis.

Arigh Nasan told him of Bo's bargain. 'The poison is of an ancient brew, and one we are powerless to cure. I am sorry, there is no hope. His triumph will cost him his life. He said nothing of the bargain he made until the poison began to consume him.'

'I must see him,' said Elowen.

They hastened over the dunes. Beside the palace spread a camp of tents, shelters and campfires. Mounds of freshly dug soil lined the foot of the hills to the north. Patches of earth were scorched and gouged, the scars left by the battle.

Arigh Nasan led them to a small, plain tent at the heart of

the camp. Guards stood in front of the tent. A Khiltoi. An Orok. A Satyr. A Centaur.

'They are an honour guard for Prince Asbjorn, a sign of respect and gratitude,' said Arigh Nasan. 'I will not interfere. I leave you to give your respects.'

Inside, Bo lay upon a bed of loose blankets. Valbrand sat cross-legged beside him, grim-faced, silent. Elowen looked at Bo with despair. Clammy sweat matted his white hair. His lips were black, cracked and bleeding. His pink eyes opened a little. In a frail, shallow voice, he said, 'Elowen, is it you? Are you real, or is this a dream to torment me?'

'It is me,' she said, forcing a smile. She knelt down and took his hand. It was deathly cold. 'And Black Francis is here too.'

He coughed. 'Then you survived too, you old rogue. I am glad.'

'Not as glad as I am,' said Black Francis, trying to be cheerful, but Elowen saw that tears moistened his eyes. 'Be strong, lad. You'll pull through.'

'Not this time. Death calls me.'

Elowen fumbled for the clay jar. 'I won't let that happen.'

'No, it is too late for me,' he said, closing his eyes. 'The poison has done its work.'

'Drink this,' she said as she removed the lid from the jar.

He winced and groaned, but opened his mouth wide enough to swallow a little of the juice. Drops fizzed as they touched his lips and skin. Elowen poured a little more into his mouth. 'Swallow, Bo. Please.'

Wincing with pain, he did so. He jerked violently and yelled out, his eyes wide open.

419

'What's happening to him?' said Valbrand, jumping to his feet. He glared accusingly at Elowen.

'I don't know,' she said, looking on in horror as Bo thrashed around as though assailed by an invisible terror. His writhing stopped abruptly and he lay on his back, eyes closed, motionless.

'Is he dead?' said Black Francis.

Valbrand leant over Bo and said, 'He's not breathing.'

'My God, he's dead,' said Elowen. She had failed. If only she had been quicker…

Bo inhaled, a deep rattling gasp. He opened his eyes. The green tinge to his skin faded. His cracked lips healed. In a whisper he said, 'The pain...the pain has gone.'

He tried to sit up. Valbrand said, 'Steady there, lad.'

Bo waved away his protests. 'Please, Valbrand, I am fine. There is no pain.'

Black Francis patted Elowen on the back. 'It worked, lass, it worked.'

Glassy-eyed, Bo stared at Elowen. 'What did you do?'

Shyly she held up the jar. 'This juice came from the fruit of the Tree of Life.'

'So you did get there,' he said, the strength in his voice returning. 'I knew you would. You have triumphed, Elowen. Against all their armies, all their strength you triumphed. And Lord Lucien, is he dead?'

The mere mention of his name chilled Elowen. She rubbed the hair from her face. 'Yes, he is no more.'

'That is a blessing,' said Bo. He looked at Black Francis and laughed, 'And you, old buccaneer, I am beginning to think you are indestructible.'

420

'What can I say? People keep trying to kill me and every time they fail.'

Arigh Nasan cleared his throat and pointed at Elowen's clay jar. 'Forgive me, Elowen, but we have many injured, some close to death from wounds or infection. If a few drops are enough to heal Prince Asbjorn, then I feel we should try to save more casualties.'

'Of course, you're right,' said Elowen, sealing the lid back on to the jar. She knew it was her duty to help as many as she could.

'Thank you, Elowen,' said Arigh Nasan. He opened the entrance to the tent and said, 'Follow me to the tent of healing.'

As she stepped half outside the tent, Elowen looked back, catching Bo's eye. He smiled, holding her gaze for a few seconds.

'Come, Elowen,' said Arigh Nasan.

She smiled and hurried back outside.

*

Bo watched Elowen leave with a heavy heart. He wanted to say so much to her, though his gratitude went beyond words. Since leaving the forest of Kakos, he had lived with the certainty of the poison killing him. The knowledge shadowed his every thought. Elowen had not just cured his body; she had cleansed his mind, wiping away fear and despair. He had a future again. He wondered what horrors she had passed through. He thought he glimpsed an echo of them in her eyes, a hint of sadness and pain.

421

The image of her face stayed with him, a picture placed over the waking world. He wanted to trace his fingers across her face, he wanted to talk to her, about everything and nothing. He wanted the rest of the world to melt away to silence, so he had nothing else to think about, nothing else to focus on, only her.

'I sometimes wonder if there'll ever be any rest for that lass,' said Black Francis, bringing Bo back to the present.

'I...don't know,' said Bo, his thoughts scrambled.

Batu said, 'I leave you to rest, Prince Asbjorn, and I have much to discuss with the Khan. Come, Diggory.'

The Orok gave a stiff bow and slipped out of the tent, followed by Diggory.

'How do you feel now?' said Valbrand to Bo.

'Stronger than I have for many a day.'

'Then the girl's worked a miracle and no mistake,' said Valbrand. 'And now you're recovered, do you intend to claim the crown of Prevennis?'

Bo shrugged. 'I meant what I said to the aristoi. I shall leave it to the *Althing* to decide.'

Valbrand frowned. 'You shouldn't hesitate to claim your birth right.'

'I will accept it if offered,' said Bo. 'I do *hope* to be offered it, but I want to be sure I have my people's support first.'

'They'll support you,' said Valbrand. 'I'm certain of that.'

'Aye, he's right, lad,' said Black Francis. 'Your folk will see sense. You'll soon have that crown atop your head.'

Bo took a deep breath. 'Well, if that is so, I want to have people around me I trust. Valbrand, will you return with me to Prevennis?'

Valbrand gave an exaggerated gasp. 'How would you survive without me?'

Bo laughed. 'Indeed!'

'And considering that you'd be a king and all high and mighty, would it be presumptuous to think that a comfortable apartment in the Hammersund Palace is a suitable reward for such a loyal companion and servant?'

'I never think of you as a *servant*, that is for sure,' said Bo. 'If I become King of Prevennis, I have more in mind for you than just relaxing in luxury. I want you to be head of the Kingsguard.'

Valbrand's grin died. He tugged at the silk ribbon around his neck and glowered at Bo. 'How could you suggest such a thing? You know what the Kingsguard did to me, what they took from me. I could never join them.'

'I am not asking you to *join* them, I am asking you to command them,' said Bo. 'The Kingsguard need an honest Captain, someone to ensure they are never again tarnished by murder and corruption. Even if the power of kingship twisted me, as it has done to others, I know you would never use the Kingsguard as a tool of terror against our own people. A king can have no better friend than one who tells him when he is wrong. If I am the King, I want you to protect our land, and stop me becoming the very worst that I could be. You could not save your wife and child, but you could protect countless others. Please, accept this duty.'

Valbrand rubbed his eyes. A smile slowly appeared on his lips. 'Curse you, lad, you've grown a silvery tongue. I'll accept your offer. And you're damned right that I'll keep you in line. I've got my eye on you already.'

'I am glad to hear it,' said Bo. 'Your wife and child would have been proud of you.'

Valbrand cast his eyes down. 'I hope so.'

Bo turned to Black Francis. 'And you, my friend, I have much to ask of you too.'

'Me? I'm an old salt. The King of Prevennis would have no use for the likes of me.'

'I disagree,' said Bo. 'Prevennis is a sea-faring nation, and yet our navy was all but destroyed by Prester John's Iron-clads. If I become the King, I want you to rebuild it. I want ships for trade, ships for exploration, and warships to protect them. I want sailors trained and treated properly, no more pressgangs.'

Black Francis puffed out his cheeks. 'That's a tall order for one man.'

'Yes, it is. But I believe you are shrewd enough to ensure it gets done. And before you ask, you will be well rewarded, of course, as will your courageous crew too.'

'When you put it that way, how could I refuse?' said Black Francis with a broad smile.

'By the gods,' said Valbrand. 'You'll have a bandit leading the Kingsguard and a pirate in charge of your navy. What sort of kingdom are you hoping to build, Prince Asbjorn?'

Bo smiled. 'A better one, I hope.'

*

Once inside the tent of healing, Elowen used the remaining juice from the fruit as wisely and sparingly as she could, trying to save those most severely wounded. She saw awful

424

sights. Satyrs, Men, Oroks, Dwarfs and many others—some slashed or stabbed by blades, some burnt, others disfigured by cannon fire and musket shot. Broken bodies. Shattered limbs. Many cried out in pain and distress, curses and prayers sounded in many different accents and languages, as though their despair spanned the world.

Elowen saved many, but she knew that for every casualty she helped, another would die. Bryna assisted Elowen, using her skills as a healer. She had greeted the news of Corcoran's death quietly, without tears. Elowen wondered if she volunteered to help the injured to distract her from grief.

With sweet-smelling herbs, healers tried to mask the stench of blood, sweat, excrement and urine. But Elowen gagged several times, and her eyes watered. Although racked with guilt, she felt relieved when she used the last drops of the juice and could do no more to help the injured. She stepped outside, gulping in the salty air. Bryna followed her and said, 'It is difficult, is it not, to see such suffering?'

Elowen sniffed. 'Yes, war is hateful. So many lives lost, or damaged. I just hope with Prester John gone, there can be an end to war.'

Bryna gave a bitter laugh. 'An end to war? Elowen, such a thing will never come to pass. Prester John is slain, and for that, I rejoice, but in time, other oppressors will emerge. So it is with Men. Slow they are to learn from their history, swift to be seduced by the prospect of power and conquest. Others will emerge offering paradise, and in their blindness, Men will follow them into death and despair.'

'I hope you're wrong,' said Elowen.

'So do I. Time will tell.'

425

'I am sorry about Corcoran,' said Elowen. 'I know his passing is a great loss to your tribe.'

Bryna's expression hardened. 'He feasts now with our ancestors, hailed as a champion, as indeed he is. I am told he slew one of the hated *námhaid*, a feat unrivalled by our kind. He is forever part of the story of our tribe.'

Elowen noticed how Bryna avoided referring to her own feelings. 'You will miss him, I think.'

'His death saddens me,' said Bryna. After a long silence, she added, 'I do not believe my soul and Corcoran's soul were meant to be together. There was no love between us. If it had been so, the pain I feel would be worse. You understand, I think.'

'Yes, I do.'

Bryna stretched out her arms and crunched her knuckles. 'Come, it is cold and I am hungry. Let us find food and rest.'

The sudden and unexpected sound of trumpets stopped them in their tracks. Elowen said, 'Are we under attack?'

'It is not the sound of war,' said Bryna. 'Gnothi has arrived.'

And indeed, down the hills to the east, rode Gnothi, followed by a procession of Illuminati and Eldar. Elowen saw heralds carrying brightly coloured flags. Holy men and women of many different faiths carried sacred relics. A cacophony boomed out: handbells, bagpipes, trumpets and drums. Dryads laughed, a sound sweeter than any music. The tiny Kobolds and Woodwoses, leapt around in energetic dances. The Fauns carried Silenus on a litter stuffed with cushions, and the old Satyr quaffed from a wineskin and

426

hollered out slurred greetings to all he passed. The procession's arrival sparked the camp into life. Songs of rejoicing and triumph rang in the air.

The procession made for the heart of the camp. Cheering and laughing warriors surrounded Gnothi. Elowen and Bryna stood a little way from the joyful scenes.

'You should go to him,' said Bryna. 'You did more than anyone to defeat Prester John.'

Elowen hesitated. She wanted to stay in the background. 'I don't fancy pushing through the crowd.'

But no sooner had she spoken, she noticed dozens, then hundreds of hands pointing her out to Gnothi. He gestured eagerly for her to go to him.

'The *Protos* is summoning you, Elowen,' said Bryna. 'You must go.'

Blushing, Elowen reluctantly trudged forward. To her surprise and acute embarrassment, the warriors began as one to chant, 'El-o-wen! El-o-wen!' greeting her like a conquering general of antiquity. She kept her eyes trained on the ground until she came before Gnothi. The *Protos* greeted her with a kiss on each cheek. 'Bless you, Elowen. You've become the saviour we all prayed for. Since the raven brought us news of Prester John's defeat and fall, most of those who had remained at Omphalos determined to come here, to greet our victorious warriors and to begin building a new world, a better world. We travelled swiftly, directly and without fear, knowing that the power of Prester John has been swept away. A darkness has passed, Elowen, and you are the shining light of the new dawn.'

Uncomfortable with his praise, Elowen said, 'Thousands

427

of others played their part. I'd have scarcely got out of Trecadok without the help of others, let alone found the Tree of Life. Every step of the way I had help. Some lost their lives helping me. It should be them we remember.'

Gnothi said, 'We shall commemorate them all, but you must be honoured above all others. Your name will be sung and worshipped alongside the other prophets. We all look to you for guidance in the days to come.'

'I…don't want that,' said Elowen.

Not hearing her reply, or simply ignoring it, Gnothi said to the crowd, 'This is an historic day, a day of joy and thanksgiving. The crimes of Prester John scar this world. Healing may prove a slow and arduous task, one we must face with conviction and energy. Yet this mission can wait for one more day. For tonight, I propose festivities to celebrate our victory, and to give thanks for the gift of deliverance, the gift Elowen Aubyn, our saviour, has provided.'

The chants of 'El-o-wen!' sounded again, even louder than before. Gnothi bowed to Elowen. 'Our celebrations tonight shall be in your honour, you have my solemn word. And, as is proper, you shall be feted and given many gifts.'

As the chants continued, Elowen felt alone, and afraid. She did not fear for her life, it was more a fear of what her life might become, what she might be used for. Wanting to be alone, needing time to think, she slipped through the crowd. Her mind raced with rapidly firing thoughts. The power she felt, the *strength* she felt, troubled her, perhaps because she enjoyed the sensation. Was this how her mother had felt? Seduced by the praise and worship of others? Powerful, almost invulnerable?

428

Elowen worried where such feelings would lead her. Would they infect like her a sickness, guiding her towards evil and corruption? She could not ignore the thoughts and images that flashed in her mind in moments of weakness. She could rule, lead armies. She would be worshipped. Such things seemed possible, tangible. They tempted her. Others wanted her to have them too, she sensed that. Perhaps they would insist, beg her. They wanted someone to rule over them, to make them feel safe, not caring if others suffered for it. She only had to reach out…

Burilgi Maa. Burilgi Maa.

No. She shook her head, disgusted with herself. She did not want to be like her mother. She had seen how easily power warped and twisted people: Rubens, Bishop Serapion, even petty officials like Cornelius Cronack. Anything was preferable to that.

At last she knew what she had to do.

*

Elowen perched on a sand dune, away from the main camp. She glanced out to sea. The grey waves rolled in, crashing onto the beach in foamy explosions. The sounds of the celebrations waxed and waned on the impetuous wind. Elowen heard singing, music and laughter. Although she did not want to be part of the festivities, she did not begrudge or resent the revelry. Many of those celebrating had suffered during the rule of Prester John; they deserved this night of joy, this moment of optimism, of hope for a brighter future.

Sheltered from the wind, Elowen waited for her friends to

429

arrive. Diggory came first, followed soon after by Bo. Black Francis turned up after ferrying the crew of the *Husker Du* onto shore. Arigh Nasan and Batu arrived, and last of all came Bryna.

'This is all very mysterious, lass,' said Black Francis.

'Aye, there's to be a ceremony of thanksgiving in your honour,' said Diggory. 'If you wait around here too long you're going to miss it.'

'I know,' said Elowen, struggling to make eye contact. She worried how they would react to what she was about to tell them. 'I'm sorry to have called you here in this fashion. It has to be this way, I'm afraid.'

'What's wrong?' said Black Francis.

'I'm going away.'

Diggory looked alarmed. 'Going…what do you mean?'

Arigh Nasan said, 'After all you have achieved, you must take a part in rebuilding this world, indeed you should lead the efforts to do so. You are so important.'

'That's exactly what I'm afraid of,' said Elowen. 'I keep being told how I am important, how people will follow me, worship me. It's…dangerous.'

'Why is it dangerous?' said Black Francis.

'There is no sense in removing Prester John only to replace him with another oppressor. My control of the Earthsoul is greater than ever before. Of course, I would try to do good, I know that. But how long would it take for my good intentions to weaken? How long until I want to use the Earthsoul not to help people but for my own purposes? That power is too much for one person and…it tempts me. Part of me wants it, just as my mother did.'

430

'You're being too harsh on yourself, and not for the first time, I might add,' said Black Francis. 'If you end up being worshipped, then I can't think of anyone who deserves it more.'

'I don't want to be *worshipped*. Remember the Saviour. He came to protect the world, to guide people away from evil, to inspire love, peace and tolerance. Yet think of the evil acts carried out in his name. His words, his *message* sullied by the cruel, selfish deeds of others. I do not want temples or churches dedicated to me. I do not want people hunted down and slaughtered because they hold beliefs different from mine. Some have called me a Messenger. If I am, my message is simply this: don't blindly follow anyone's words and deeds without questioning, without thinking. Decide for yourself what is right and wrong.'

Bryna said, 'Elowen, your words are hard for all to hear, for all in their different ways have grown to love you. But I believe what you are saying is correct. Few have the character to turn down such power, and those that do are better for it. The *bládh* should never be used to destroy or conquer; a true *bana-buidhseach* works only for harmony and peace.'

Elowen nodded. 'I am grateful to all of you. Without your help, I would not be alive today.'

Black Francis looked at her, a sad expression on his face. 'So, when do you mean to leave? And where do you plan to go?'

Elowen swallowed hard. 'To my home, to Trecadok.'

'Trecadok!' said Diggory, half-laughing. 'We've survived countless terrors and you want to return to the Orphanage!'

431

'Something draws me back to Trecadok,' said Elowen. 'Back there I'll just be Elowen Aubyn; I doubt any tales of my adventures will have reached that far. As for when I go, I wish to go as soon as possible, immediately if I can.'

'How will you get there?' said Bo, who looked crestfallen. 'It is far away and even with Prester John dead and the Redeemers destroyed, there are still many dangers.'

'It might be a hard road but I'm not afraid,' said Elowen.

'Even so, Bo is right,' said Black Francis. 'If you mean to return to your homeland, the sea is the safer and swifter way. I'll carry you on the *Husker Du*.'

'I can't ask you to do that,' said Elowen. 'You've done so much for me already.'

'Ah, say nothing of it,' said Black Francis, holding up his hands. He turned to Bo and added, 'And from Helagan, I'll sail north again, this time for Prevennis.'

Elowen shook her head. 'It feels wrong for me to ask you to do this.'

'I'll do it gladly, lass,' said Black Francis.

'Thank you, with all my heart,' said Elowen.

Black Francis looked at her and winked. 'It'll be a pleasure to journey with you for a while longer, for our final parting will be painful and I'm glad to put it off. I'll soon have us under sail, though you'll have little time for farewells.'

Elowen gestured to all present. 'You are the people I want to say farewell to.'

'I'm mad for saying it, but I'll come with you,' said Diggory. 'I can't say I've missed Trecadok but perhaps I should go back, if only to keep you out of mischief.'

'I'd welcome it,' said Elowen, pleased and much relieved.

432

'I'll round up the crew and get them back on the ship,' said Black Francis. 'Elowen, I'll come for you later. The rest of you I'll see before we embark. Diggory lad, you can come and help me. You'll have time for your farewells later.'

Diggory's shoulders sagged but he did as Black Francis requested. Scratching his beard, the Captain trudged away, with Diggory close behind.

Arigh Nasan said, 'So, Elowen, this truly is farewell. We Oroks owe you so much, I owe you so much, there are no adequate words of thanks, nor a reward suffice.'

Elowen said, 'To have visited your lands, to have experienced the culture and bravery of your people, was more reward than I could ever have asked.'

Arigh Nasan bowed low. 'I hold you in the highest honour, Elowen Aubyn. Our lands are far apart, too far apart I suppose to have much hope that we may ever meet again. But the memory of your courage shall live with me, and act as an inspiration through many struggles.'

Elowen turned next to Batu. 'I don't know what to say. You saved me, so many times.'

'Yes, but you saved us all,' said Batu. To Elowen's surprise, he embraced her.

'I wish you peace,' said Elowen. 'And I hope that you get everything you want. Your land. Your wife. Children. You are worthy of such blessings.'

Batu, his face usually inscrutable, wiped tears from his eyes. From his belt he pulled out Chinua's knife and handed it to Elowen. 'This is a poor gift, but to me it feels somehow appropriate.'

433

Elowen held the knife, running her fingers over the warped and twisted blade. 'I'm grateful. It's a reminder of the Oroks' courage.'

'Your words are kind,' said Batu. 'Think of us sometimes, Elowen, and think of us with fondness. A better world it would be if more showed your compassion. The pain is bitter when friends part, but memories can salve the wounds, and as such, friends remain with us forever. So you shall dwell in my heart.'

With that, the Oroks turned and walked back to the camp. Bryna sighed. 'There is a part of me that wishes to go with you, Elowen. But I must return to the Dachaigh, to my tribe. Grievous are our losses in this war, and hard times may be ahead, but with Prester John gone, we Khiltoi have a little hope at least.'

'And so you should, with hearts as strong as yours within their ranks,' said Elowen. 'You'll become *taghta*, a magnificent one, I'm sure of it.'

Bryna smiled and brushed tears from her cheeks. 'You were a blessing to our tribe. If ever you wander close to our lands, visit us, you'll always be welcome, *bana-buidhseach*.'

'Maybe, one day,' said Elowen quietly.

'Please honour me by accepting this modest gift,' said Bryna. She took off her necklace of glass and amber beads and passed it to Elowen. 'I once swore to be your friend, until the sky falls upon us, or the earth opens up to swallow us, or the sea arises to overwhelm us. To that I hold true, today and until I part this world. We have a bond no distance can break. I hope my little gift is something for you to remember me by.'

434

Fighting back tears, Elowen said, 'I shall cherish it always, and I won't forget you, Bryna, I promise.'

The Khiltoi glanced skywards and laughed. 'Look, the new star has vanished. Perhaps it meant nothing after all.'

'We shape our own destinies, I believe,' said Elowen.

Bryna left, her head bowed. Elowen sat in silence, with Bo. He opened his mouth a couple of times as though he intended to speak but lost his nerve. Finally he said, 'I owe you my life. I do not know if I shall ever understand what happened, how you saved me. You have performed so many miracles. Now, this is a bitter parting and it wounds me. I had hoped...'

'Yes?'

He fidgeted. 'I had hoped that you would come north, to Prevennis.'

Surprised, Elowen blurted, 'With you?'

He nodded.

'I...I have to go home,' she said, a little flustered.

'Of course, I understand,' he said. 'Through all of this, I have always wished to get to know you better, but circumstances, duty even, always contrived to pull us apart. I sensed that there is...a bond between us. Did I imagine this?'

Elowen shook her head. 'No, I don't think so.'

He smiled shyly. 'That is...good. Duty pulls us apart again, and we seem powerless to resist it. But perhaps there will come a time when you wish to travel again. If you were to do so, I would be delighted to see you in Prevennis. I shall...wait for you.'

He stood, looking awkward.

'Bo,' said Elowen.

'Yes?'

'You will make a fine king.'

'I hope so, truly I do,' he said with a laugh. Then, to Elowen's astonishment, he leant down and kissed her. 'Until we meet again.'

- CHAPTER TWENTY -

Return

The canoe's keel ground onto the pebbly beach. Black Francis laid his paddle down with a sigh. 'Well, my young friends, you're finally back in Helagan.'

Elowen climbed out of the canoe, closely followed by Diggory, and looked around. They stood in a horseshoe-shaped cove, hemmed in by towering cliffs. Elowen spied a narrow path that climbed up the cliffs, the only way out of the cove by land.

'This is as far as I can take you,' said Black Francis above the waves wash and drag. He lumbered out of the canoe. 'If my maps are accurate, it's less than a day's walk from here to your home town.'

Gulping in the salty air, Elowen looked back out to sea and to the anchored *Husker Du*, which bobbed like a cork in the unruly seas. She and Diggory had said their sad farewells to the crew that had risked so much for them. And now Elowen knew she faced perhaps the hardest parting of all.

'I suppose, at last, this is goodbye,' said Black Francis, rubbing his beard. He took a deep breath. 'My, we've come a long way since first we met in the Black Boar in Dinas

Hein. It feels like an age has passed, though it's been less than a year.'

'It feels like a lifetime,' said Diggory with a laugh.

'Like a different life altogether,' said Elowen. Tears welling in her eyes, she said to Black Francis. 'I should say thank you, but the words don't feel enough somehow.'

'They are plenty, lass,' said Black Francis, wiping his misty eyes. 'But you have nothing to thank me for. I was drowning, lost, Elowen, until I met you. You saved me. You changed my life, as you've changed and saved countless others. You helped me into better waters, so to speak. I've not always done the right thing in my life. I've made more mistakes than any man should ever make. But I'm honoured to have known you, to have travelled and fought alongside you. There's no doubt about it, lass, you're special, in more ways than I can begin to guess.'

'Thank you, and good luck in Prevennis,' said Elowen. 'Bo could not have chosen a better man to rebuild his navy.'

Diggory laughed, 'Admiral of the fleet! Who'd have ever thought it?'

Black Francis roared with laughter. 'Aye, God must have a sense of humour. But I'm ready for the challenge. I'm no longer a smuggler or a pirate. It's time to prove myself.'

'You will,' said Elowen. They embraced, Elowen lost in his bear-like frame. 'I hope we'll see each other again, one day.'

'Who knows, lass, but I hope so too,' he said. He slapped his palm against his forehead. 'Ah, curses. I all but forgot. The bags.'

From a jumbled mound of sacks and old clothes in the

438

canoe, Black Francis pulled out the two bags of gold and jewels, each tied together with string. He gave the larger bag to Elowen, and the other to Diggory. 'Guard these carefully. Prester John and the Redeemers may be no more but I'll wager there are still common robbers and bandits around.'

'We've learnt how to look after ourselves,' said Elowen, with a smile.

'There's no doubting that,' said Black Francis. 'Good luck, young friends. I hope you find peaceful waters.'

Singing a sea shanty, the sailor shoved the dinghy back into the water, clambered in, waved once and began to row, heading back to the *Husker Du*.

'It's just you and me again,' said Diggory.

'Yes,' said Elowen. 'It's time to go home.'

'What will we find when we get there? And what will folk there say when they see us?'

'Let's find out,' said Elowen.

They scrambled over the bank of pebbles at the top of the beach, hurried up the path that ascended the cliffs and headed inland.

Unlike the warmer lands to the south, Helagan still buckled beneath the heavy dead hand of winter: trees shorn of leaves recoiled from the frigid wind, grey skies, cold winds, the only sign of life a pair of magpies squabbling in the bare branches. Spring remained a distant promise. By early afternoon, Elowen and Diggory had crossed a ford in the Gwindgack River, and they saw, for the first time since they had left, the town of Trecadok.

'By God, it looks more depressing than ever,' said Diggory, moving on, with Elowen trudging behind him. She found it disorientating to see the town again. For years, the crumbling, moss-smothered walls contained her whole life. Now, Trecadok seemed so small, a tiny bubble in an endless sea. She spotted the smoke-smudged remains of the Old Tower, rising from the walls like a rotten tooth.

The town gate hung wide open; Elowen felt no fear as she approached it. She was not the startled orphan who had fled in fear of her life. She did not come back to seek revenge for past ills. She did not want to hurt anyone, but she did want to return with her head held high.

A guard, gaunt, bored, stood by the open gate and picked at his scabby chin. He waved Elowen and Diggory through with barely a sideways glance. Once inside the town, a cheerless scene greeted them. Many houses stood empty; their shutters flapped open and closed by the wind. The townsfolk shuffled around, heads lowered, faces sad. They all looked thin and pale.

'I can see that nothing has improved here,' said Diggory.

'No, it's worse, much worse,' said Elowen.

They reached the Shambles, where only a few stalls, poorly provisioned with rotten vegetables and mouldy black bread, shivered in the wind. The townsfolk wandered around the stalls and picked at the meagre offerings. Elowen and Diggory started to draw attention. People pointed at them and whispered, frowning as though trying to remember who they were. A crowd grew around them: inquisitive, suspicious faces. Elowen felt a little threatened and steeled herself for a fight. Someone bundled through the onlookers. Elowen recognised him as Horatio Morvel, the town Magistrate. His black gown showed signs of wear and hung limply over his body. His face looked haggard, as though many years had fallen upon him in just a few months.

'Who are you?' he said. He sneered as he looked at their clothes. 'You don't look like folk from these parts. By God, why do we pay that incompetent guard? He'd let the devil through the gates. State your names, strangers, and your purpose for coming to our town.'

'You are mistaken,' said Elowen. 'We are natives of this town. I am Elowen Aubyn, and this is Diggory Bulhorn.'

'I know those names,' said Morvel, blinking as he tried to recall them.

'We both had the pleasure of being raised in the Orphanage, under the ceaseless attention of Cornelius Cronack,' said Elowen. 'And of course, I remember you, Horatio Morvel, and your family, especially your sweet-natured wife and daughter.'

The man's eyes narrowed as he gazed at her. 'I...I know your face. Elowen Aubyn. Yes, but you fled the town. And then the Redeemers came...yes, it is you.'

'It was after *she* ran away that all our troubles began,' said a woman, receiving many shouts of 'aye' and 'too true' in response.

Another voice in the crowd shouted out, 'They said she was a witch!'

'Keep your mouth shut, or I'll close it for you,' said Diggory.

'Throw these vagabonds in gaol!'

A sudden rage took Elowen. She wanted to lash out and perhaps, in the past, she would have done. But she knew how to control herself. She channelled her fury into her

441

voice and spoke with a strident tone. 'Whatever troubles have befallen Trecadok are not of my doing, and anyone who believes differently is a fool. Even with the oppression of the Null broken, are you still frightened to think for yourselves?'

The authority of her voice awed the crowd and they fell into a sullen silence.

Elowen continued. 'We are not the weak, defenceless orphans who left this town so many months ago. We've returned to help you, if you're wise enough to trust us. I am an Adept. Yes, you know the word, though Prester John made you frightened of it.'

Morvel looked horrified, and took a step backwards. 'Bishop Gorlas always preached that Adepts are necromancers in league with the devil.'

'The lies of Prester John poisoned you,' said Elowen. 'Before his coming, the Adepts acted as teachers, guides and healers. I want to help you, in every way I can. But first, tell me what happened here.'

Morvel rubbed his temples. 'Since the Redeemers came to take the orphans and the Old Tower was destroyed, everything has gone wrong. Many of our young men went off to war, summoned by the Mother Church. Some returned to us, many have not. Foul weather plagued us. Storms that must have been brewed by the devil himself. Crops failed. The Mother Church taxed us to pay for their armies and ships, left us with barely a penny. The price of bread has risen sharply. The burghers tried to buy in corn from Porth and other towns but the prices were beyond us. Many animals and poultry sickened too, stricken by all manner of pestilence, leaving us short of meat, milk and eggs. Even the greybeards, those that have survived, cannot remember a worse time. The mortality book filled as fast as the clerks could write.'

He looked round at the crowd, receiving many sorrowful nods and mutterings of agreement. Morvel pointed to his forehead and went on to say, 'And since this has…changed, folk have been frightened and confused. You return in dark times, Elowen. Perhaps you might have been wiser to stay in foreign parts.'

'I'm beginning to think that too,' said Diggory.

'No, I am exactly where I need to be,' said Elowen. She thought of the money and of what Ifueko had said to her. *I believe you will use this wealth for good, to help others, and not spend rashly or hoard greedily.* It is an important responsibility. She plucked out a handful of gold from her bag. 'Tell me—will this buy corn for the town?'

Morvel looked at the gold in wide-eyed astonishment. 'Aye, and plenty of it.'

'Then make the arrangements and buy fresh corn. Livestock too.'

'You give this gold…willingly?' said Morvel.

'Yes, and I'll give more,' said Elowen. 'I want to see Trecadok thriving, but there are conditions.'

'Name them,' said Morvel.

'There must be an end to any persecution of the Eldar.'

Morvel frowned. 'Eldar?'

'In ignorance they are called *tainted ones*. This land belongs to them as much as to us, perhaps more so. They must not be harmed.'

443

'I'll speak with the burghers,' said Morvel. 'It is a strange request, though.'

'A necessary one,' said Elowen. 'And the Orphanage, what has become of it?'

Morvel shrugged. 'It exists still. None of the children taken by the Redeemers returned, but others dwell there now, orphaned by war or disease.'

'And Cornelius Cronack?'

'He vanished some months ago,' said Morvel. 'The Redeemers came for him. I doubt he lives still.'

'Then that is my other condition: the Orphanage is mine to run.'

*

Gusts whipped off the grey waves and dashed across the Hammersund Palace; the flags on the defiant walls and soaring towers shuddered and billowed. Beyond the Hammersund, the roofs of the pavilions and tents positioned around the hill of Thingvollur rippled in the wind. Yet despite the blustery weather, the air carried the scents of spring. The snow on the mountain peaks had started to recede. Flowers sprinkled the lowlands. The rivers ran free of ice. The long, dark, iron-hard Preven winter faded, and spring approached.

Bo stood upon the natural platform formed by the *Logberg*, the Law Rock, looking out over the congregation. Hundreds of people from Prevennis and other realms stood before him: lords, bishops, farmers, labourers and, as he had insisted, representatives from the Barbeg tribe. He stood before them all as the newly crowned King of Prevennis. He had been the *Althing's* unanimous choice, and his coronation on the *Logberg's* rocky outcrop had been arranged in accordance with tradition, a reflection of the eagerness to bring stability to the kingdom so soon after the fall of Prester John.

Bo looked behind, where amongst a line of seated dignitaries on the summit of the *Logberg*, were Valbrand, resplendent in his newly fashioned Kingsguard armour, Black Francis, still in his greasy sea-faring clothes, and Albruna, Chief of the Barbegs. Princess Moriko sat there also, having travelled north to represent the Kojin, with whom Bo had formed such a bond. Bo knew he owed them all so much. He wanted to repay their faith. He wanted to be the man and the King they believed he could be.

He heard a gentle whisper, 'King Asbjorn, it is time.'

Father Ladislaus stood beside him. At Bo's invitation, the priest had journeyed with Princess Moriko from the Beauteous Isle. Bo said, 'This is worse than going into battle.'

Ladislaus smiled and winked. 'If you survived battle, then I judge you are strong enough to come through this ordeal unscathed. Good luck, Your Majesty.'

Bo faced the crowd, which stretched out like a forest of faces. He drew a deep breath. 'My friends, you have honoured me today, here at the *Logberg*, the hill used for the coronation of Preven monarchs since the beginnings of our history. That I speak to you now as King of Prevennis is down to the efforts, courage and sacrifice of many others, and not all of them lived to see this day. We are at the dawn of a new era, and many challenges, many hardships face us.

445

I do not stand before you as a prophet, nor as a ruler blessed by divine providence. I do not have all the answers. I am young, and will seek counsel from those older and wiser than me. I am resolved to rule with justice, equanimity and compassion.'

Bo flicked a quick glance at Ladislaus, who smiled encouragingly. Bo opened his mouth to say more, but a sudden gust of wind silenced him. He composed himself and continued. 'There is much to do to heal our kingdom. We must work together to rebuild villages ruined, sow crops and nurture those left without family. That is our duty, our responsibility. And I decree the northern lands shall be the domain of the Barbegs, and that they shall be free to rule their lands as they see fit, and in peace.'

He glanced at Albruna, who bowed her head to him.

Looking back at the crowd, he gestured towards Ladislaus. 'We are also blessed that Father Ladislaus has been ordained as our Archbishop, a man worthy of leading the Church in Prevennis through difficult times. His task is to return the Church to its true mission: charity, peace, learning and tolerance.'

Many onlookers clapped at this.

Bo went on. 'I do not demand your obedience, but I endeavour to earn it by sound rule rather than enforce it by the point of a sword. I am your King, but I am also your servant and protector of your laws, and that I shall never forget.'

With the crown feeling heavy and uncomfortable, he held aloft his sword, the Preven sword of kings. Cheers met his gesture, and chants of 'All Hail King Asbjorn!'

'I think you have won them over, Your Majesty,' said Ladislaus as the ceremony ended. 'As I knew you would.'

'Aye, you spoke like a true King, lad,' said Black Francis. 'Or should I say: *Your Majesty.*'

Bo smiled. 'It will take a while to get used to *that.*'

Albruna stood and took Bo's hand. 'I told you once that you could not live forever in the shadows, and so it has proven.'

'And I vow to protect the lands that are rightfully yours,' said Bo. 'I hope too that Father Ladislaus can do much to build friendship between our two peoples.'

'Yes,' said Ladislaus, bubbling with excitement. 'I would be delighted, if I may make such a bold suggestion, to visit the Gladsheim, for I have heard many marvellous things about the home of the Barbeg tribe.'

Albruna smiled. 'Your visit would honour us. It eases many burdens on my heart that wiser souls now govern these lands. It bodes well for all our futures.'

'In all my travels, I have met none wiser than Ladislaus,' said Bo. 'I trust that the Kojin Queen forgives me for stealing him from her.'

Ladislaus laughed. 'It is fortunate she holds you in such esteem, King Asbjorn. And I am glad to report her Majesty rules a happier land than the one you visited. Life improves daily in the Beauteous Isle. The ills suffered there won't be cured swiftly, but they shall be cured.'

'Well, we've heard some fine speeches today but surely it is time for feasting,' said Valbrand, banging his hand playfully against his armour to strengthen his words. 'I want a hot fire to warm my blood, and ale to fill my belly.'

447

'Aye, that's the spirit,' said Black Francis.

As everyone began to make their way back to the palace, Bo lingered. He wanted to be alone, just for a few moments; he sensed he would have precious little time alone in the years to come.

He looked towards the Hammersund Palace. No longer would he skulk in the vaults. He was King of Prevennis, and he knew he carried a heavy burden of responsibility. He knew this would be no golden age. There would be adversities to overcome. He knew how much faith his friends had in him, and he was determined not to fail them. He knew how much pain and loss had led to this moment, and how close he had come to losing his own life. But he had survived the obstacles; he had fought through the despair. He thought, as he often did, of Elowen. She had saved his life. He remembered her face. He remembered their kiss. He wanted to see her again, and believed one day he would. King Asbjorn smiled, tapped the hilt of his sword and strode towards the Hammersund Palace.

*

Elowen sat with her window open. Laughter and joyful shouting echoed in the Orphanage yard below. She looked down. Warmed by the generous summer sunshine, the children, all dressed in good clothes, ran, skipped and climbed. Happy faces, healthy faces. Diggory shepherded them like a sergeant, his manner firm but always friendly. Elowen smiled at the sight of him marching around to keep the excitable children in order. They adored him and never tired of hearing his tales of adventure, tales that grew with each telling. Not that Elowen begrudged him that. She knew that of all the blessings she enjoyed, the friendship of Diggory remained the most important and rewarding, and to see him happy pleased her more than anything.

The knife of Chinua hung on the wall; for Elowen the warped blade formed a constant physical memento of her struggles, and of the sacrifices of others. The necklace given to her by Bryna now hung from her neck, beside her mother's pendant; the first a reminder of a loyal friend, the second a warning of what could happen if she allowed herself to use the power within her for selfish reasons. Precarious piles of books covered her desk and the many shelves. Indeed, there were so many books in the Orphanage that townsfolk joked the walls were made from them. Elowen loved to read, but she also found immeasurable joy in writing too. She wrote down memories of her journey, of the places and people she had seen. Elowen also loved to *Link* with animals and birds, and recorded in detail those experiences in her books. She wondered if others might one day read and learn from her observations.

The clanging of the church bells nudged Elowen's memory. It was time to see an old friend. She put down her quill, closed her book and hurried outside. Months of hard work had transformed the Orphanage. A garland of flowers softened the strict lines of the main door, which itself had been painted green. The windows, cleaned of decades' worth of grime, gleamed in the bright light.

The children smiled and waved as Elowen strolled past. Diggory turned and said, 'So, you're going to see him then?'

449

'Yes, if I can find him.'

'You will, I'm sure of it,' said Diggory. Then with a laugh he added, 'Give him my regards, though I reckon he'll have forgotten all about *me*.'

'I doubt that,' said Elowen. 'After what we put him through on the Mengoon, he'll never forget either of us.'

'Strange, it's like Black Francis said, it already seems a long time ago, the whole journey, I mean.'

Elowen nodded. 'It feels like a dream.'

'Or a *nightmare*.'

'Yes, at times it was, and a nightmare I would never have woken from had it not been for you.'

He dug his hands into his pockets and shrugged. 'You befriended me when you had no reason to do so, even after I treated you so badly. I owe you everything, Elowen.'

She was about to reply when another voice interrupted her.

'Diggory? It's dinner time.'

Elowen looked up to see Rozenwyn, the pink-faced Orphanage cook. She and Diggory enjoyed a coy relationship that tiptoed further towards love with every passing day. And little gave Elowen greater pleasure than to think of her best friend happy.

'I'm now coming,' said Diggory, blushing. He winked at Elowen, knowing exactly what she was thinking. 'You be careful in that forest. You might be an Adept and you might've beaten old Lord Lucien but you should still watch your step.'

Elowen laughed. 'Don't worry about me.'

As Diggory and Rozenwyn herded the excitable children

450

into the Orphanage for dinner, Elowen headed for the town gate, enjoying the warmth of the day. Many a passer-by greeted her with a hearty, 'Good day, mistress Elowen', or 'Bless you'. Far from being a lowly, hated orphan, Elowen found herself liked and respected.

Her gold had helped to breathe fresh vigour into Trecadok and wash away the greyness and misery. The Shambles bustled with life, with stalls squeezed into every conceivable space. Elowen had funded the guilds, which had sprung up for tanners, barbers, furriers, butchers, bakers and many other occupations. They looked after their members and developed trade with other towns. More importantly for Elowen, the guilds helped the elderly, widows and the sick. They raised money for the Orphanage, the school and the church, and contributed to the upkeep of the town walls.

Elowen knew there was more work to do, there would always be more work to do, enough to keep her occupied for the rest of her life. However, she sensed that one day and perhaps one day soon, she would have the urge to travel again, to venture to lands far away. She thought often of Bo, the memory of his kiss lingered in her mind like the memory of summer, a glimpse of all that is good in life. She remembered the look in his eyes, the words unexpressed. She wondered if he ever thought of her, or even remembered her. She hoped to see him again.

Elowen passed through the town gates. The Witchwood stretched out in front of her. Encouraged by the sunshine, the forest displayed varied shades of green. Elowen stood still, absorbing details hidden to a cursory glance: insects plundering the soil, subtle dances of leaves, delicate wispy

451

shadows. Foxgloves bobbed in the breeze. Overworked bees hustled and bustled. Elowen heard the soft cooing of wood pigeons and the sweet songs of blackbirds. Oak trees creaked and groaned. With each step, she felt the Earthsoul's energy, pulsing from the forest in huge waves. The golden threads danced around her, forming intricate shapes and patterns. Her whole body tingled.

Deep within the forest, she knew Bucca Gwidden waited for her. She had so much to tell him, so much to share. Since they had first met, the world had changed and for the better. But despite the fall of Prester John, she knew the Eldar remained wary of any dealings with Men. She did not blame them for their reticence and scepticism, but she hoped to persuade them better days were ahead.

For although the Earthsoul was strong again, replenished by the Tree of Life, Elowen knew that it would only reach its peak when the bonds between races overcame hatred and suspicion, when Men truly respected and cared for the land they shared with so many other living creatures. Elowen wanted to do everything she could to achieve such an aim. It would be a mighty challenge, one without adventure or glory, and with no clear end, no declaration of victory and triumph. That thought did not daunt her.

Elowen closed her eyes. She breathed in the forest's earthy air. The Earthsoul warmed her every muscle, vein and bone. She felt no separation between the golden threads and her body. She opened her eyes and smiled. Then, with her heart trembling with anticipation, she stepped into the forest and vanished from sight amongst the ancient trees.